**CRITICS** ~~RA~~ ~~G~~
**AU** ~~T~~

~~CRIMSON CITY~~

"Shocking revelations, danger, and intense heat are ever present in *Crimson City*. For a fast-paced rollercoaster ride to hell and back, run—don't walk—to your nearest bookstore and snatch up a copy."

—Romance Reviews Today

"Maverick provides an intense tale with complex characters to kick off a new series set in an original, dark and fascinating world."

—*RT Book Reviews*

"Liz Maverick's *Crimson City* is everything you could expect in a paranormal thriller. There's action, adventure, steamy romance, chills and thrills, and thwarted love. The action will keep you on the edge of every page and the romance is as hot as any summer day in L.A. . . . This is paranormal romance at its best!"

—Roundtable Reviews

### CRIMSON ROGUE

"This is the powerhouse conclusion to the exceptionally creative Crimson City series, launched by the versatile Maverick. . . . With nail-biting suspense and fast-paced action, this novel is a spectacular finale!"

—*RT Book Reviews*, 4 1/2 stars, Top Pick!

"This is a terrific conclusion to a stunning excellent romantic fantasy saga."

—*Midwest Book Review*

RECEIVED

FEB 0 4 2010

NORTHWEST RENO LIBRARY
Reno, Nevada

### IRREVERSIBLE

"Maverick weaves a romantic tale where time can be manipulated in the blink of an eye."

—Darque Reviews

"As good if not better than the superb *Wired*, *Irreversible* is a great romantic science fiction thriller . . . Liz Maverick provides a strong romantic cyber sci-fi novel."

—*Midwest Book Review*

"Maverick returns to her mind-bendingly complex world where time and reality can be altered or manipulated . . . Maverick's mind works in wonderfully twisted ways."

—*RT Book Reviews*

### WIRED

"Maverick's fast-paced, genre-bounding novel . . . grabs readers from page one, throwing together romance, science fiction and cyberpunk. . . . This excellent piece of genre fiction shows much promise . . ."

—*Publishers Weekly*

"The intricacy of a plot that could easily have devolved into a confused mess instead highlights the craft of an author at the top of her game, earning the tale the coveted RRT Perfect 10. . . . An edgy, high-octane plot with anime-inspired characters and circumstances, check out *Wired* if you're looking for something a little unconventional."

—Romance Reviews Today

"This book kept me so captivated. . . . Ms. Maverick's imagination is superb."

—*USA Today*

# Temptation

She shook her head, eyes wide. Her face was streaked by mascara, and strands of her velvet brown hair were plastered to her neck, skin wet with tears where the collar of her crisp white shirt fell open. Marius ran his fingers across that damp expanse, closing his eyes against the dark desire to bury his fangs in her throat. How he'd longed to taste her blood.

Her lips trembled. "I heard that . . ." She couldn't finish the sentence.

"I have to marry her, Jillian. I can see nothing else that will accomplish so much good for so many."

She pressed her face into his coat. "I . . . I didn't bring you here to ask you not to marry her. I've given up on that." She went still and silent, and then her face slowly turned up toward his. "Give us one night. I know you won't give me more, and I won't ask for more, I promise. But, Marius, give us one night before you say your vows. I feel your presence everywhere, all the time, and I know you feel mine even stronger. Just give us both one night before you cross the line forever. Before it's truly impossible."

Other *Love Spell* books by Liz Maverick:

*IRREVERSIBLE*
*WIRED*
*SHARDS OF CRIMSON* (Anthology)
*CRIMSON ROGUE*
*CRIMSON CITY*
*THE SHADOW RUNNERS*

# LIZ MAVERICK

# CRIMSON & STEAM

LOVE SPELL

NEW YORK CITY

LOVE SPELL®

January 2010

Published by

Dorchester Publishing Co., Inc.
200 Madison Avenue
New York, NY 10016

Copyright © 2010 by Elizabeth A. Edelstein

All rights reserved. No part of this book may be reproduced or transmitted in any form or by any electronic or mechanical means, including photocopying, recording or by any information storage and retrieval system, without the written permission of the publisher, except where permitted by law.

ISBN 10: 0-505-52779-0
ISBN 13: 978-0-505-52779-0
E-ISBN: 978-1-4285-0794-4

The name "Love Spell" and its logo are trademarks of Dorchester Publishing Co., Inc.

Printed in the United States of America.

10 9 8 7 6 5 4 3 2 1

If you purchased this book without a cover you should be aware that this book is stolen property. It was reported as "unsold and destroyed" to the publisher and neither the author nor the publisher has received any payment for this "stripped book."

Visit us online at www.dorchesterpub.com.

# CRIMSON
# & STEAM

# CHAPTER ONE

The four leaders of Crimson City's glittering vampire world looked rather out of place, dressed half in battle armor and crowded into a ramshackle safe house located on the border between the vampire and human strata. The windowless room barely had space for chairs and the table that held two bottles of red wine, a water pitcher, a tray of glasses and a rather unremarkable bowl of mixed nuts.

"Well, certainly no one will think to look for us here," Kata Marakova sniffed. She abandoned the idea of removing the elbow-length gloves she wore under her gauntlets; there was too much dirt around. "Really, St. Giles. Lovely of you to step up and find us a place with some privacy, but is this your idea of a joke?" She puffed away at an exotic cigarillo, ignoring the bits of ash floating off the end into the dusty air.

Next to her, Rafe Giannini slumped in his chair and poked through the bowl of nuts now resting on his chest. Elegantly rumpled, he looked as though he'd rather be playing lawn tennis and quaffing cocktails than worrying about affairs of state. But if he sometimes appeared disengaged, he was always listening. After a moment, he selected a macadamia nut and devoured it.

On Marius's right sat Dominick St. Giles. Neat, precise, and perfectly attired in one of his bespoke European suits, the patrician vampire just barely concealed the fire inside that always kept him near the boiling point. He was holding court with the other two, pushing his agenda: the likelihood of a full-scale war breaking out in Crimson City, this time between the humans and the werewolves.

*So far, so good*, Marius thought. At least he'd managed to force the heads of the three other vampire houses here to powwow, rather than being forced to discuss things in a public forum where paranoia and fear would make sure nothing ever got done.

Marius Dumont was the leader of the Vampire Assembly—his cousin Fleur had stepped out of the spotlight due to her health—and consequently he was the ranking member of this meeting. As head of state he had the power to negotiate with the leaderships of the humans, werewolves and mechs that also populated the city. He had a mind to use that power before it was too late. In the past, an uneasy peace between Crimson City's denizens was the most any vampire leader had managed to achieve. Marius knew his people could do better. *He* could do better. For them.

Kata turned away from her debate with St. Giles. "Are you sure looking out of town is the answer, Marius? Should we take another look at Crimson City's werewolves? Where do you personally stand with the Maddox clan?"

"The Maddox werewolves have always been our—"
*Marius, it's me.*

Marius paused midsentence, blinking against the smoke that clogged the cramped meeting room air. Jillian? Oh, god—let her be safe.

"What?" St. Giles narrowed his eyes at Marius across the table. "What is it?"

"Nothing," Marius replied.

*Marius?*

Kata frowned. "It would be helpful, darling, if you could try to pay attention at your own meeting."

Marius shook his head as if it might clear away Jillian's voice. Three pairs of eyes glittered curiously at him from around the table. "It's nothing. I thought I . . . heard something."

"I made sure the room was secure," St. Giles snapped.

Marius gave a curt nod. Jillian was fine. He needed to focus. If he didn't get the three other houses to fall into line, any alliance with werewolves would never survive. "As I was saying, the Maddox werewolves here in Crimson City have always been our best allies."

"Then why aren't you marrying one of them?" St. Giles asked. "Why House Royale? Their interests are in New York, not Crimson City. I guarantee trouble if you set your sights on one of those Asprey bitches."

Kata leaned over, wicked humor flashing in her eyes. "You know how it is. All of Crimson City's *good* bitches are probably taken. But perhaps Marius is on to something—Tajo Maddox also ran off with an Asprey." Her lush mouth curled into a smile, white fangs exposed and gleaming hungrily. "I saw Maddox without a shirt once, and for a werewolf he was quite—"

St. Giles glared her into silence even as Rafe started laughing. "At least they were both werewolves," the former grumbled.

"If you think about it," Rafe suggested, still chuckling, "if Marius marries this Asprey dog, their alliance will make the Crimson City vampires and werewolves practically family."

St. Giles looked ill.

"Let's not bait him," Marius said.

"Too late," growled St. Giles. "Let me remind you, Marius, that not all of us view rogue males like Tajo as friends—nor the females as possible lovers. Some of us take our responsibility as house leader more seriously."

"Easy, now, boys," Kata murmured as Marius poured himself a glass of wine, working desperately to keep his fingers from throttling St. Giles. There was no mistaking the dig: Jillian Cooper was a rogue human, and St. Giles's insinuation was a direct attack.

Rogues—this was the name given to those renouncing dedicated allegiance to their own species. Some of those rogues had formed a mixed-species alliance called the Rogues Club. Marius considered the loose union of vampires, werewolves and humans complementary to the House of Dumont's goal of achieving peace among all species. The other vampire houses were less enthusiastic.

*Marius, can you hear me out there? It's Jill.*

Marius tensed. He could not remember a time she'd called to him so blatantly. He'd always just known when she needed him and had gone to her. He should have felt her fear if she were truly in danger, not just heard her voice in his head.

Across the table, Rafe lifted his legs and set them on an empty chair, crossing them at the ankles. He admitted, "I've got to go with St. Giles on the rogue issue. I don't know why being a traitor to your own kind makes you more trustworthy."

St. Giles's face hardened, his eyes burning as he leaned over the table and addressed Marius. "Do you trust the lover who has cheated on someone else to be faithful to you thereafter?"

"Be very careful, Dominick," Marius growled. "You know not of what you speak."

Kata and Rafe glanced uneasily across the table at each other.

"We should have called a meeting of the Primary Assembly," St. Giles declared, his voice rising. "That's the point of the Assembly: that every vampire in Crimson City gets a say."

Marius gritted his teeth. "That's not what *this* is about." He slowly stood.

"Here we go again," Rafe muttered, rubbing his thumb over a dirt smear on his black leather shoe.

Marius took a deep breath and put his hands on the table, and leaned down to speak in St. Giles's ear. With deadly calm, he said, "Your constant complaints about who runs the Assembly are getting tiresome. I'm aware that you'd like to have the House of St. Giles in control, but that's not what this meeting—"

St. Giles leapt up, standing toe-to-toe with Marius as he batted away his chair and it crashed to the ground. He clenched his fists. "I can get the votes I need to run the whole show whenever I want. You run things now because you Dumonts look strong, but don't assume you'll have power forever."

"Do you really think this is the time for internal squabbles?" Marius asked.

St. Giles smiled. "I'd just be careful not to show any sign of weakness."

"Is that a threat?" Marius bared his fangs.

"I'm putting you on notice, is all."

Rafe interrupted in a drawl, tossing a nut in the air and catching it in his mouth. "You've been putting him on notice for years." Still chewing, he added, "If you want control of the vampire Primary Assembly, put it to a vote already."

Kata took a drag of her cigarillo and exhaled a perfect set of rings into the air. The three other vampires fixated on the dissipating smoke, and she said, "It's quite a risk for you, Marius, this marriage business. I think you're mad to do it, even for the sake of peace. We all know how close the vote was when the House of Dumont was first elected to lead us. Old Lucien got the votes he needed because yours is the oldest house, and therefore the purest. Now you want to muddy your genes with a dog?"

"The House of Dumont is interested in peace. I would be a hypocrite not to enter into an alliance with a werewolf because I wanted to preserve 'vampire purity,'" Marius said. "The concept is ludicrous and counterproductive, no matter what our people believe."

St. Giles just shook his head and smirked.

*Why do you not come?* From somewhere across the city, Jillian's summons interrupted once more. Her heartbeat pounded a rhythm into Marius's head.

He forced himself not to let his agitation show, instead anchoring himself in the meeting, where he really needed to keep his attention. He could see the schemes already being birthed in St. Giles's mind. "Yes, Dominick. You should welcome this risk. Support me in this marriage alliance, and we'll have a longtime peace . . . or my failure could put the House of St. Giles in control."

"When do you need to give the Asprey werewolves an answer?" Rafe asked.

"Tonight." Marius looked around the table. "I need to give them a response tonight."

Kata smirked. "They say marriage really isn't something one should rush into."

"Don't you take anything seriously?" St. Giles snapped, shaking his head.

"I'm trying to lighten the mood," she retorted. "And if *you* want to be taken seriously, St. Giles, stop always saying there's going to be some war or another. Stop, shall we say . . . crying wolf?"

Rafe laughed so hard he choked on the wine he'd been swilling.

"He's right, though. There is always danger," Marius admitted, wearier than he could ever remember feeling. "That is what I'm trying to end."

*I need you!*

*No!* Marius thought back, finally snapping, wincing and pressing his palm against his temple. He could not go to Jillian now. If she were truly in danger, it would be one thing, but not now. It was so confusing: he sensed her distress yet not the nature of what she faced. He had a duty to his people, and he needed to maintain the control that had kept him so long from his heart's desire—what would keep him from her for his entire existence. No matter what, he could not go to her until this matter was decided.

"Marius?" Kata asked suspiciously. "Are you—?"

"God *damn* it!" He slammed his fist down on the table, and Kata lurched back in her chair. "There is no time for any of this." He stared around the table. "Will you support my marriage or not?" he thundered. "I need an answer."

As if she had all the time in the world, Kata swiveled in her chair and jammed the spent end of her cigarillo into a piece of broken body armor she was using as an ashtray. "I would appreciate it, Dumont, if you would not raise your voice at me."

After a pause, she continued. "It isn't like you, Marius. You're so edgy, it's making *me* nervous. Now, as for your question . . . I don't mind letting you try once more to salvage peace in this city. We don't have much to lose. Maybe your marrying an Asprey werewolf is the answer. I'm willing to find out. At the very least, we won't have to worry about the dogs teaming up with the humans any-more."

She was crying; Marius suddenly sensed it. Jillian was crying. He looked desperately around the table, wanting to finish this meeting, wanting to get to her. "This is an opportunity to show the humans that nobody is teaming up against anybody," he said.

"Yeah?" St. Giles asked. "How does this wedding do that?"

Marius cleared his throat and moved his hands under the table, balling them into fists. Crying was not the same as being in danger, he told himself. *You've* made her cry before, god knows. Many times. Jillian was never in dan-ger then.

Calmly he answered, "We do the wedding openly, Dominick, in a positive spirit. Everybody will be invited—vampires, werewolves, humans, mechs. And not just the humans who've helped us in the past. We'll invite mem-bers of their current government. We include everybody. It has to start somewhere."

"Bullshit," St. Giles sneered. "The humans will see this wedding as an act of aggression, not as some sort of 'Kumbaya' moment, even if they're included. They've been looking for an excuse to invoke Total Recall. We can't give it to them."

"Total Recall?" Rafe spoke up. "That old plan? For one thing, that would mean a lead-up to all-out war. For another, do you really think they could get anyone to sign a loyalty oath these days? There's more interspecies toler-ance than ever in this city . . . even if that's still not quite enough."

"If the human government is smart, they will see this wedding gives them an opportunity for unity," Marius argued.

"The human government has never been smart," Kata said. Then she cocked her head toward Marius and winked. "But I do love a good wedding."

Marius turned back to the glowering St. Giles. "The message this marriage alliance will send is 'All species united'—but I promise you that the subtext will make it clear we vampires are not doing this through weakness."

Rafe leaned forward with an outstretched hand and shrugged. "Well, the wedding's your funeral. I'm con—"

"Not so fast," St. Giles interrupted. He pressed the other vampire's hand down onto the table before Marius could shake it. "Is no one going to address the elephant in the room?" He stepped back and crossed his arms on his chest, glaring at Kata and Rafe with disgust. Marakova's smile gave nothing away. Giannini swirled and sniffed his wine with an air of overblown insouciance.

St. Giles slammed his fist down on the table. "Oh, come on, people! We all read the papers."

Marius felt red-hot anger building inside him. He hid it. "The gossip pages should hardly be counted as fact."

"In politics," St. Giles replied, "nothing is irrelevant, least of all gossip. Let's break this down. So, you've convinced a werewolf to marry you. What happens to your vaunted alliance when that werewolf discovers your taste for humans is focused on one particularly juicy piece of ass?"

Rafe laughed, hiding it as a cough.

"There's no need to be vulgar, Dominick," Kata spoke up, though the corner of her mouth twitched in a half smile.

St. Giles looked around the table and held out his palms. "Seriously, what happens to peace when our werewolf princess finds out about Jillian Cooper?"

"She has nothing to do with this," Marius growled.

"Oh, really? I'm not going out on a limb to ally with a bunch of crazy mutts only to have them turn on me because you can't keep your junk up the right skirt. Our status with the dogs is currently stable. This move could turn them all against us."

Underneath the table, Marius clenched his fists so hard his knuckles cracked. "Jillian Cooper is not an issue. That gossip column has created an affair where none exists, and I can assure you that not only is it a media fantasy, but also that the Asprey werewolves are aware of the truth."

Kata sat forward. "You must be more careful, darling. For all you know, Ms. Cooper has been feeding the paper with your private affairs. She is a reporter, is she not? I know the papers lie—I'm in them all the time. But St. Giles has a point. I believe I speak for everybody when I say that if you want us to champion your alliance, you're going to have to stop sleeping with that human girl."

Marius shook his head. "We need to end this discussion," he growled. "I am not sleeping with Jillian Cooper. I have never slept with Jillian Cooper. I never *will* sleep with Jillian Cooper. It is a gossip-column fabrication, and I'm certain she has told them nothing."

"Oh, come now," Kata said. "I'd be less shocked if you told me you were actually a mech. I'd believe *they* could be so cold. All that metal . . ." She shuddered delicately. "I don't give a damn what you do with whom behind closed doors," she continued, "but I do care about your honesty. I will not be lied to."

Marius grabbed a wine bottle and flung it across the room. It struck the far wall and smashed; glass and wine sprayed everywhere. He uttered a sharp bark of laughter, running his hands up the back of his neck and into his hair. "So, whether or not you support this marriage alliance comes down to whether or not I lie and tell you I slept with Jillian Cooper." He shook his head in disbelief.

The three other vampire leaders stared at him in shocked silence. Then St. Giles actually grinned. "You never had sex with her," he realized. "Seriously." He clearly enjoyed his adversary's discomfort.

"Seriously," Marius admitted. His heart broke a little as he explained. "I've hardly touched her at all. Those rumors are ancient. A kiss, yes. Long ago. And I've been called to her side many times, but always to rescue her from danger. It never went beyond that. I consider myself a friend and her protector. That's all." And his words held a truth that cut Marius as deep as any wound he'd ever experienced.

"I think we've heard enough," Kata said. With a softness in her voice that suggested she understood more than her words expressed, she added, "Look, if you're volunteering to marry a dog, be my guest. As long as *I* don't have to do it. Dirty beasts. As I said before, Marius . . . I'm with you."

"As am I," Rafe said.

Everyone looked at St. Giles, who finally gave in. "I'll back you on this, Dumont. But you owe me one."

"Thank you," Marius replied, standing and sketching a formal bow. "Thank you all. I will not forget that you have put your trust in me. I . . ."

He felt it then: Jillian's true fear. If danger had not been present before, it was now. Marius clutched at his heart through his clothes, then quickly dropped his hand, forcing himself to relax. His peers were watching, and this was the very relationship he'd just disavowed. He dashed from the table.

Kata raised an eyebrow. "Can't we at least enjoy the afterglow?" she called, lighting a fresh cigarillo.

Marius had already slung his gun belt around his waist and donned his battle gear. A moment later he was out the door, and in a swirl of black he stepped off the side of the safe-house platform and plunged out of sight.

# CHAPTER TWO

Marius flew swiftly down the vertical run of Crimson City, leaving behind the buildings of the vampire strata, thrust up like sword blades into the sky. Maneuvering deftly between the garish digital consoles of the news and advert drones winking against the darkness, he plowed straight through the smog layer, slowing only when he neared the city's midsection.

Jillian's heart was beating too fast. He could feel that through their almost otherworldly connection—a connection he'd never been able to explain, beyond that innate pull of protector vampires to the one special person with whom they were bonded. Soul mates, Jillian called the two of them. Marius did his best not to think of it that way.

Anxious to land, Marius closed his eyes and used his mind to home in on her position, quickly adjusting course to land in the three-species DMZ known as the Triangle. He chose an empty alley, alighting softly on the concrete, and immediately backed into the shadows. His long black coat fluttered around his legs. Staring unseeing at his leather boots, he probed the night with his senses.

Here at ground level, human scent dominated, and traces of others also began to build. Marius could almost feel the massive underground labyrinth seething with werewolf life beneath his feet. Perhaps the impending alliance between the werewolves and vampires would finally bring the dogs up in greater numbers. Most had been loath to travel to the vampire strata—not without some dark purpose, anyway.

Moving the placket of his coat aside, he slowly pulled his gun from the holster slung at his hip, and from the opening of the alley checked the street beyond.

*Marius?*

Jillian's thought was panicked, truly panicked. Marius burst into a sprint and ran like a wild animal through the streets, following her scent, following the turmoil that called out to him from her very soul. He'd had to finish that meeting, but god damn it if he'd waited too long and she was—

He found her on a stretch of Santa Monica Boulevard, just inside an alcove. Tempted to run straight for her, his mind registered the return of those infernal UV lampposts the human government was constantly installing and uninstalling, depending on the perceived threat from above. These installations were more than just a simple deterrent: while vampires could wear special cosmetics and drink chemicals to ward off daytime UV, the halos of light emitted by these fixtures were deadly.

Carefully bypassing the nearest lamppost, Marius steeled himself for the worst. Raising his weapon, he slipped into the alcove where he knew he would find her. She stood frozen, silent, her face obscured by shadow.

She swayed slightly, and Marius ran forward. "What is it?" He grabbed her by the shoulders and spun her toward some dull light oozing from a nearby store's half-broken bulb. "Did somebody hurt you?"

She shook her head, eyes wide. Her face was streaked by mascara, and strands of her velvet brown hair were plastered to her neck, her skin wet with tears where the collar of her crisp white shirt fell open. Marius ran his fingers across that damp expanse, closing his eyes against the dark desire to bury his fangs in her throat. How he'd longed to taste her blood.

"You're not in danger, then?" he whispered. "I felt you calling. It was . . . strong. Strange and dark."

"I called for you," she admitted, covering his hand with her own. Her pulse leapt, seeming to match his own.

Marius looked behind her into the darkness. "I don't understand. Did somebody try to hurt you?"

She didn't speak for a moment. "No. I just . . . I *needed* you."

There was no ambient danger. Suddenly Marius understood that while her sorrow was genuine, the rest had been faked. She had lured him here. There was no real peril. Such a situation had never happened. She had never before lied to him.

He braced himself and took in her expression. Her face was composed, but tears slipped uncontrollably from her eyes. Which showed he was not being fair: though the physical danger was a lie, her panic was not entirely fabricated.

He slowly brought his fingertips to the curve of her face, and teardrops ran over them. Jill's lips trembled.

"I heard . . . ," she began, unable to finish the sentence.

The words Marius needed to speak were just as difficult. He pulled her close and wrapped his arms around her body, squeezing tight. "I have to marry her, Jillian. I can see nothing else that will accomplish so much good for so many."

She pressed her face into his coat. "I—I didn't bring you here to ask you not to marry her. I've given up on that." She went still and silent, and then her face slowly turned toward his. "Give us one night. That's all I ask. I know you won't give me more, and I won't ask it, I promise. But, Marius . . . give us one night before you say your vows. I feel your presence everywhere, all the time, and I know you feel mine even stronger. Just give us both one night before you cross the line forever. Before it's truly impossible."

Her hair tangled in his fingers, and her tears ran down his wrists. Marius stared into Jillian's eyes, and his lips moved so close to hers that they breathed the same air. Warm, sweet air.

"You know I can't."

She flinched, pulling sharply away. "Can't? One night? It can't be because I'm human. Your cousin Fleur married Dain. *He's* human. She shattered that code of conduct, so—"

"It's more than that. And you're worth so much more."

"But I *want*—"

Marius shook his head, cutting her off. Summoning whatever fire remained in his soul, he spoke with the coldest conviction he could muster. This was his destiny, and he would accept it. "I must join the vampire and werewolf houses in this alliance. My life is not my own to give. I *will* marry Tatiana Asprey. I will never have you. There is no more to be said."

They stood in silence. Marius held himself back from basking in the warmth that radiated from her body, from indulging the craving that called out to every part of him. "I never meant to hurt you. Please . . . please find someone else," he whispered.

She pressed the back of her shaking hand to her lips, blinking rapidly. "There will n-never be anybody else," she choked out. "Not really. I've tried to forget you so many times. But you won't take me, and you won't let me go."

"I *am* letting you go."

"On paper. Through words. But everything else will be the same, and you know it. We were meant to be together, no matter what you do. This is our last chance. Why won't you admit that?"

With Jill sobbing, Marius did not trust himself to speak.

"I know you would never betray your wife," she went on. "When you marry her, this is over. We will never know what could have been. Never! And we've never even—"

Marius grabbed her roughly by the waist. "You don't understand. One night with you and I could never marry her. And you know I must. I *must*."

Jill was silent for a long time. At last, a strange look came over her face and she shoved him back with all her strength. "All these years, what the hell have you been doing? Why did you leave flowers on my doorstep?"

"Jillian, I—"

"Is this just a game to you? You know that everybody talks. You know what they say about me."

He'd never made any promises. When Jill took up with another, he'd never once complained. He'd never let himself. Just as he'd never let himself find physical solace anywhere else. Jill's misery and his own had been his fault, his alone.

"It's never been a game. I . . ." Marius reached inside his coat and retrieved something. He saw Jill's face soften. She took the dried flower gently in her hands. The bud had once been pure white, a blossom from one of the unmarked bouquets he'd taken to leaving at her door. He'd known it was misleading, given their situation, and yet he'd wanted her to know someone was watching over her, someone who cared. The white roses seemed a symbol of their bond: unmarked, pure, timeless.

"I kept one," he murmured. "They will always make

me think of you, and when you see them, they should remind you what is always in my heart. I won't pretend that this bond between us means nothing, but it cannot mean more."

He reached out to retrieve his precious token, but she dropped it to the street, grinding it into the pavement with her shoe. "Symbols, tokens, unspoken understandings . . . Show me how you feel just *once* with your mouth and with your body. This is our last chance," she begged.

He stared at her, silent.

Her expression hardened. "Coward," she spat. "Do I have to make it really easy for you, so you can't refuse? Should I just rip my clothes off and beg?" She pulled the tie holding together her wrap blouse, and the fabric cascaded away. "Screw me here in this alley, Marius. Please."

"Jillian, don't!" Marius's blood raced. Exposed neck, pale shoulders, pink-tipped breasts—all delicate flesh and the black lace of her transparent bra. He'd never seen Jill this way. He'd only dreamed of it.

"I will. I'll beg," she continued. "I'll do whatever you need to make this okay. I'm not afraid of what we have. Why the hell are you?"

She pulled the hem of her skirt up and leaned back against the brick wall. Marius tried to wrench her skirt down, but she was pulling out all the stops and rudely pressed her palm against his groin. "Don't try to tell me no," she murmured. "I know what you want. I know what I feel."

"Stop, Jillian. Stop!" Marius begged. He forced himself to ignore the pulsing of his erection in her hand and grabbed the ends of her shirt, tying them together as best he could. Without thought, he closed his eyes and pressed his mouth to the crown of her head. "Please," he whispered. "I never meant to hurt you, and—"

"'Hurt me . . . ,'" Jillian echoed.

She reached into her pocket and pulled out a switchblade. Flicking it expertly open she said, "Hayden gave this to me. Hayden, your worst enemy. At the time I thought it was a really shitty birthday present, but it always seems to come in handy." Transfixing Marius with her stare, she held the knife to her own neck. "Could you resist me if I made myself bleed for you? I know what it's like when you smell blood. That means *my* blood will make you insane, if you feel half of what I think you do for me. You won't be able to stop yourself, and it won't be your fault." She swallowed hard. "I'm not afraid."

"Enough!" Marius roared, baring his fangs. The switchblade clattered to the pavement. "Enough." He took her face in his hands. "This isn't you. This is not who you are."

Jillian slowly pulled free and backed up, collecting her weapon.

"Do you think this helps?" Marius continued, unable to contain himself any longer. "Do you think I feel no pain? I watch you run around with Hayden Wilks, and you think it doesn't kill me? He gets to have you in every way that I cannot. It makes no difference that I understand why you're with him, that you don't love him. It doesn't matter, because . . . *yes*." His hands dug into Jill's shoulders as he struggled to stay in control. "I can feel you. Do you understand? I can sense you. I know when he's with you, when he's touching you, when . . ." He had to look away. "Knowing I could make you feel so much more, that my feelings for you go so much deeper, that you've given yourself to someone who doesn't deserve you because I'm not allowed to have the life I want to live . . . It makes me feel like dying sometimes. You *must* understand how much I care about you. But—"

"But not enough," she interrupted. Then, with a hitch

in her voice she added, "Soul mates aren't supposed to end like this."

Marius dropped his hands. "I'm sorry."

Jill swallowed. "Well, that's it, then," she said, her voice suddenly too calm. "If your damn honor, your obsession with duty, all the excuses you've always used to keep us apart . . . if you can't see what you're giving up, it ends here."

Marius could not bring himself to speak. Part of him was dying. It was best that that part should die.

Jill lifted her chin and clasped trembling hands behind her back. "It ends here. Don't ever use our link again. Don't go 'probing with your senses' for me, or whatever you want to call it. Go probe your new bride instead. Stop listening for me, stop watching for me, stop coming to my rescue. Stop leaving me flowers." She stomped on his dried rose one last time. It was no longer white. "You got it, Marius? You don't get to be my knight anymore. You've lost the right."

Marius maintained his silence, barely. Just like his composure.

Her shoulder slammed against his arm as she strode past him toward the street. At the last moment, she turned. "I hope your big damn sacrifice is worth it," she said, walking backward while swiping at her tears with her sleeve. "Someday I won't cry for you anymore. I'm not as weak as you think."

"I've never thought you weak," Marius murmured, digging his knuckles mercilessly into the brick wall behind him to stop him from reaching out to her.

"When we meet again, you won't be able to tell I ever cared, no matter what our stupid bond wants." Jill stumbled awkwardly on the uneven pavement, then turned suddenly on her heel. After a few quick steps, she sucked in a breath and broke into a run.

Marius stared at his bloodied knuckles, then moved to the mouth of the alcove, where he leaned against a wall to watch the distance between them expand. In the foggy street, Jillian was illuminated in violet-tinged fits and starts as she passed beneath the deadly UV lampposts.

*Call out to me, Marius,* he heard her think. *No matter what I said, call out to me and I'll swallow my pride and turn around.*

It took every ounce of Marius's strength to fail her.

# CHAPTER THREE

*Three weeks later*

It was difficult, given that she was a world away from the werewolf life she'd always known—a vampire world away, at that—but the Dumonts had taken great pains to make Tatiana Asprey feel welcome, to keep things as familiar as possible. Her private rooms in Dumont Towers were carefully and ornately appointed. Her soon-to-be family had acquired many antique pieces of furniture, shipped in sconces from her rooms back home, linens, objets d'art. Whatever she'd wanted, they'd provided.

She'd wanted quite a lot of things to remind her of home. Silly, some of them: a musical ballerina figurine, an oddly shaped pillow, a settee of no particular aesthetic merit. The vampires certainly had the money to afford her the life she was used to, but the people here just needed a bit more . . . discipline.

Her family, the aristocratic House Royale werewolves of New York City, was the finest example of propriety among her kind, and she meant to set the same example in Crimson City. Tatiana knew she could thrive here, if she set her mind to it. Throughout history, princesses had given themselves in marriage to strengthen alliances, often with barbarian hordes. She doubted her service here would be as difficult, if there were similarities. And it was not as if she was entirely alone: her people back home and the werewolves here were the same in fundamental ways. She believed in according loyalty first by species.

Tatiana studied her reflection in the dressing-table mirror, where her younger sister was working with delicate fingers to secure a lock of her hair in place with a hairpin. She shifted her gaze to Folie's face. This alliance would assure safety and security for her family and friends. What more could she hope for? What better purpose?

The sisters' eyes met in the mirror. "Have you decided yet?" Folie asked.

Tatiana looked down at the table, where a massive glittering diamond comb lay next to a simple curve of fresh orange blossoms. "I want to wear the rings Mama gave me, and if these diamonds don't work with them, we'll weave in the flowers."

Her younger sister nodded, still fretting over the disobedient lock of hair. She made a final adjustment, smoothed her hand over Tatiana's intricate arrangement of pin-tucked curls and waves, then turned to rummage through the lace and satin, feathers and velvets, spilling out of the trunks open on the canopy bed.

"I watched them pack it . . . ," the young girl muttered. Then a cry of discovery burst from her lips and Folie produced a worn red leather train case from the depths of the first trunk. She set it carefully on top of a pillow.

Tatiana plucked the lid off one of the silver toilette canisters lined up along the bottom of the three-part mirror in front of her. She gently tapped all excess powder from the puff before dusting a crystalline trail across the rise of her breasts.

"Ready?" Folie asked.

Pushing away from the dressing table and adjusting her corset, Tatiana carefully stood, turned around and stepped into the open center of her satin skirt, which was pooled on the carpet. Folie lifted the heavy, cream-colored satin, and Tatiana inhaled as her sister fastened the waist. The girls fluffed and smoothed the fabric in order to best display the gold-thread embellishments.

Folie retrieved the matching bodice from the bed and held it up. Tatiana slipped her arms through, watched her skin vanish behind another layer of tight satin, choking only slightly as her sister connected the buttons up the nape of her neck. She tried to suppress a cough but failed, and a strangled sound slipped from her lips.

Folie quickly undid the last button.

"No, it's as it should be," Tatiana chided. "Put it back."

"I'll do it just before you go out . . . and let me loosen your corset laces, Tati. Please. You'll faint!"

"I won't faint," Tatiana argued, raising her chin even as she gripped Folie's arm for balance. She slipped her feet into a waiting pair of Louis heels with her initials embroidered on the toes, and then examined her appearance from every angle.

Behind her, smiling into the mirror, Folie clasped her hands in delight. "You are Her Royal Highness, Princess Tatiana Asprey—a true princess. You look *so* beautiful."

Tatiana tipped her head and surveyed herself with dispassionate approval. "Yes. I think they will be pleased." She grabbed both of her sister's hands in her own. "Thank you, Folie." She gestured to her hair but meant the whole of it: being here, leaving the safety and comfort of House Royale so that Tatiana wouldn't be entirely alone amongst strangers.

Wheezing a little as she tried to take a bigger breath, Tatiana gestured to the train case. Folie brought it to the dressing table and unlocked the latch. Both girls leaned forward. The leather smelled faintly spicy, and the lining inside was worn to white where decorative jewels and the corners of the smaller boxes had rubbed against the velvet.

Folie fumbled here and there in excitement. She lifted a soft cloth from the lower tray of the train case and removed the lid from a box holding Tatiana's wedding jewelry. "Oh!" she said, pulling back her hands. She wrinkled her nose. "Those two rings, they're so . . . ugly! The stones don't even match on that one. And the other is so black. When mama wore them round her neck, they seemed prettier somehow."

Tatiana stared down. One ring was a simple band featuring a row of mismatched colored solitaires. The other was made from black enamel and braid.

They looked more appropriate for a funeral than a wedding, she admitted. She jammed both rings onto the fourth finger of her right hand. "Such small hands they used to have! Well, it's tradition. They've been passed down through the family forever. After the wedding, I can put them on a chain and wear them as mama did." She looked up at Folie, suddenly stricken. "Oh, how I wish she were here!"

Folie's eyes filled with tears, and her hands fluttered nervously at her sides. She looked so tiny and frail, the pale blue of her bridesmaid dress bringing out the color of her wide eyes. Tatiana reminded herself that Mama and Papa were both gone, and that her sister Gianna and Gianna's husband Tajo Maddox were busy taking care of House Royale back in New York. That meant Tatiana had to be strong. It was her duty to Folie.

"Tatiana, are you sure?"

"Sure? What do you mean?"

"Are you sure you want to go through with this wedding?" her sister asked in a halting voice. "Do you at least love him a little? You haven't known him very long."

Tatiana thought how best to explain. Folie was still so

young, so sheltered. "All I ask is that Marius pay me due respect for my sacrifice, as I will to him for his. We will have a very happy marriage based on mutual respect, loyalty and duty. He said those very words himself during the negotiations."

Folie frowned. "Respect, loyalty and duty. Is that enough?"

"Of course it's enough," Tatiana snapped.

"I—I think it might be better to marry for love. Don't you think it would be better to marry for love?" Folie asked.

"No, I do *not*."

"And you don't care that he loves someone else?" Folie continued. "Gia says—"

"'Gia says, Gia says . . . ' There's a reason why you're here with me and not with our sister, Folie," Tatiana growled. "She is such a bad influence on you. I don't think she *ever* successfully managed to get through the Change without becoming a beast."

"I don't think she tried very hard," Folie replied.

"Well, there you go. She's hardly the model of ladylike behavior, and I won't have you fashioning yourself in her image.

"My earrings, please," Tatiana demanded, struggling to remain composed.

Folie remained silent. She picked up a set of chandelier earrings from the case and handed them over.

Tatiana watched her sister's face in the mirror. As she slipped the posts through her ears, she couldn't help but ask, "How do you know that he loves someone else?"

"Everybody knows. It's always in the gossip pages. People think . . . " Folie clasped her hands, shifting her weight from one foot to the other.

Tatiana's eyes narrowed. "People think what?"

Folie looked at the ground. "They think it's very romantic," she whispered. "Like Romeo and Juliet. But with vampires and humans."

"Everybody knows that those gossip rags make their stories up. They're vapid creations designed to entertain the common people, idiots with nothing better to do than waste their mundane lives reading tripe!"

"I'm sorry! I—"

"Never mind," Tatiana said, stepping back and surveying her appearance. "All of that means nothing compared to what Marius and I can accomplish together. Consider history. All through history, royalty has married for reasons other than love. This is a privilege. It is my *privilege* to do my duty and create an alliance that will strengthen the position of our species. House Royale stands together with the werewolves of this place, but now, because of my marriage to Marius Dumont, we will also have the strength of Crimson City's vampires to stand alongside us."

Folie nodded, though she remained a bit bewildered.

Tatiana went on. "Marius understands all this. He understands about duty and sacrifice. We will be partners, and eventually a kind of love will grow between us. I'm sure of it. It will be all right, Folie." She pressed her palm against her coiffure. "We should go down. I'm ready."

Her sister picked up the wreath of orange blossoms carefully, with both hands.

"The diamonds please, Folie," Tatiana corrected firmly. "The rings are sentimental enough, and rather dull after all. I want the Dumonts to have stars in their eyes when they look at me."

Folie traded the flowers for the comb. She tucked the diamond-encrusted ivory into the back of Tatiana's hair, adding a few pins for security. Then she stepped up next to her sister, and the two clasped hands and looked into the mirror.

"If this doesn't make Marius forget that girl . . . ," Folie began. She trailed off as two red spots burst brightly across Tatiana's cheeks. "I meant—"

"Do button me up now," Tatiana interrupted. Her voice seemed almost disconnected from her body.

Folie reached behind Tatiana's neck and slipped the loop over the last button. Tatiana nearly retched at the pressure.

"Tati?" Folie asked, her voice tremulous.

Tatiana turned and gave her sister a serene smile. She gave assurance. "I will not faint. Nobody will even be able to tell it chokes."

Folie turned to fetch the bridal bouquet, a gorgeous cluster of Asprey roses. Tatiana grabbed her sister's shoulders so suddenly and so hard that the young girl nearly jumped out of her skin, sending a few errant blossoms cascading to the floor.

"Just promise me something," Tatiana hissed. "Will you promise me?"

"I—"

"Promise me. Promise me *you'll* marry for love, as our sister did. Marry anyone you like."

"Tati, you're hurting me!" Folie whispered, tugging desperately at her hand. "I promise! I promise!"

Tatiana took a deep breath and exhaled. Trading her sister's hand for the bouquet, she pulled her shoulders back and gestured for Folie to take up the train of her skirts. Then the two werewolf princesses moved slowly out into the candlelit halls of Dumont Towers.

# CHAPTER FOUR

Gregory Bell felt very strange indeed. His entire body tingled with the pain of what felt like thousands of pins pricking his skin. He couldn't place his whereabouts in Dumont Towers. He'd simply found himself midway up a staircase without remembering where he was going or how many flights up he'd come.

*The ballroom. They will all be gathered in the ballroom.*

Grasping the banister with both hands, he turned and looked down the center of the spiral staircase. It seemed to go on for miles. A wave of nausea struck him as he leaned over. His top hat slipped from his grip and he watched mesmerized as it tumbled in free fall out of sight, end over end.

He pulled himself quickly upright and closed his eyes to quell his panic and focus on other senses. He'd thought he was following the buzz of the wedding attendees, yet now he couldn't hear them at all. He couldn't hear anything. For all he knew, he could easily have been walking up and down the same stretch of steps, covering the same ground for the last thirty minutes. He wasn't even clear how long it had been since this latest setback began. And while this certainly wasn't the first time he'd blacked out, it hadn't happened in a while. He'd thought he had more time to get the cure. He'd fallen to his knees in gratitude when the bastards told him he would be fine as long as he did what they asked. Now, if he could just remember where he'd stashed—

A giggle floated down the hallway. Figures turned a corner into view and proceeded across the corridor at the far end. Bell gasped for breath in the stairwell. He blinked, wondering if he imagined the gauzy figure of a young girl in a light blue gown carrying an armful of cloth and another girl dressed in white. A bride. The bride!

Once more Bell tried to speak, to make his presence known, but his lips seemed paralyzed and the words wouldn't come. He reached out, staggering forward up the last steps to catch them before they turned the far corner and disappeared from sight, but he was too late. An errant swath of fabric fell from the younger girl's hands and dragged on the Persian runner before vanishing around the corner.

Bell lurched down the deserted corridor, meaning to follow the pair to the gathering where he was sure to find Marius Dumont. But after stepping through a series of doors and navigating what seemed like an endless labyrinth of halls, he found himself disoriented once more. Dumont Towers was massive, and there was nobody around to ask for help, much less for direction. Everyone was already at the wedding. The bride and her attendant were long gone; he couldn't even detect their scent trails.

He should find the elevator bank and go to the lobby, that's what he should do. Bell looked desperately at the row of doors lining the walls of the room he'd stumbled into. He gripped one doorknob after the other, each dead-end closet or adjoining room making him that much more desperate to escape.

The final door led to a library of sorts, with leather club chairs and a small table covered by crystal decanters and barware. There would be water, at least. Alongside the crystal was a simple silver candlestick. A flame bobbed from the center of the crimson candle like a guiding light.

He was so tired. The pain throbbing deep in his bones seemed to grow, and each step he took toward the table amplified the sensation. It was happening again! Bell's forehead began to itch. He felt his skin pulling, as if it no longer fit his face. He moved his hand to his mouth, desperate for something to drink, and a terrible pain shot through his jaw. He pressed his fingertips to his cheeks. Losing his balance, he veered away from the bar and slammed into the wall with his shoulder. Excruciating pain seared through his head, pooling in his mouth along with the taste of his own blood.

Dropping to his knees, Bell took his hands from his face and stared down at his palms. They were smeared with blood. His blood. He screamed. No sound erupted, but the physical action seemed to rip at his raw nerves. Bell's body was somehow losing all calibration. He'd lost the ability to modulate his five senses, which each now veered wildly from one extreme to the other.

He'd thought he was improving! Just yesterday he'd experienced a kind of euphoria, a superior strength of body and mind that ran contrary to the downward spiral he'd been experiencing over the last weeks. He'd thought he was getting better. He understood now that he would never get better.

But those humans said—*Oh, please, no.*

Crawling forward on his hands and knees, unable to break through the pain to issue a cry for help, Bell paused to rip the cravat from his neck. It fluttered to the ground. He tore at the buttons of his shirt, seeking some kind of relief. The pleated front ripped at the seams and fell likewise to the carpet. The muscles in his arms gave out, and he fell forward, his face buried in the shirt linen. A low keening was the only sound he could make.

He marshaled his remaining strength to place his forearms up on the bar table and raise his upper body off the floor, but he misjudged. His head struck the side. The candlelight flickered. Smoke from the unsettled flame blurred his vision.

No, it wasn't smoke. The world was fading again. His eyes were losing focus. He reached out for the decanter, but his hand would not make contact.

*Water. Please . . .*

Bell's skin burned, his body suffused by heat so fierce that he could feel it spread through his veins like molten iron. The back of his hand finally made contact with the decanter, knocking it hard. The crystal smashed against the marble tabletop, sending shards of glass twinkling everywhere, onto his black tuxedo pants and across the floor. The water followed. Bell stared desperately as it saturated the carpet, lost to him forever.

Still without being able to utter a coherent sound, his face now feeling cleaved in two, Bell reached out in a last-ditch effort to find some nonexistent savior. At last he gave up, falling backward to the carpet, lying sprawled on the floor. His teeth shifted, scraping bone against flesh and nerves. He thrust his head back as pain blindsided him, his jaws bursting open wide. Blood streamed from the corners of his mouth.

Eyes bulging from their sockets, his mouth open preternaturally wide, the vampire Gregory Bell convulsed a final time and then went still forever.

# CHAPTER FIVE

Marius stood before his wedding guests at the front of the room. Ian and Warrick flanked him, and a delicate sonata floated off the strings of a nearby quartet. He was well aware he and his brothers formed an impressive front. All of them, with their jet hair and black-blue eyes, decked out in formal wear, undoubtedly looked every inch the dark, dangerous heroes of some theatrical spectacle.

*Heroes.*

He'd always had a code he lived by, always considered the consequences of his actions before settling on them. He'd lived his life for others, acted as protector to kin and allies. But doing the "right" thing used to feel more . . . right. Marius Dumont found it very odd that he should feel so conflicted now, at a time when all his plans were coming to fruition. Shouldn't he be ecstatic? Wasn't he becoming the very man he'd always aspired to be? Wasn't he living the life of a hero? Or was he a pantomime of his younger self, a shadow of his old ideals? Perhaps too much had happened in Crimson City over the years, and it had changed him more than he realized. Perhaps he'd become more selfish as he'd aged. . . .

Or perhaps he was simply expecting too much of himself, expecting to go through with this wedding with a smile when he was so painfully aware of Jillian's presence.

"You look a bit grim, brother," Ian whispered. "Remember, they're all watching you."

Marius adjusted his expression and forced himself to avoid seeing the back of the room, where members of the media were making a valiant effort to stay quiet while jostling for position. He didn't need to look; he knew exactly where she was. Yet as long as the two of them left things as they'd agreed—at an end—they would get through the night.

Nothing had been left to happenstance. From the ceremonial decor to his tuxedo, from the historical "re-creation" chosen for entertainment out in the ballroom to the almost disgusting excess of exquisite food and drink offered in the reception hall just outside, everything about this wedding was designed to convey a specific message. Just as he'd told the other houses, the implication to a breathless city through witness and later tabloid page was "All species united," but the subtext remained that the vampires had no intention of ceding control. And Marius was showcasing the House of Dumont's power, too—he had no intention of ceding *anything* to Dominick St. Giles.

The surroundings boasted heavily gilded ceilings and ornate mirrored arches modeled on those at Versailles. The lighting, purposely dim, relied entirely on a line of spectacular chandeliers that bisected the ceiling, laden with crimson-hued wax candles whose flames flickered and smoked, billowing from the movements of the trussed and coiffed spectators waiting restlessly and shoulder to shoulder just below. Servants stood posted along the wall at perfectly determined points, their militaristic parade-rest stances the only hint that there might be weapons holstered under their uniforms: there was always the chance of interlopers.

The Aspreys had not been consulted about the wedding details. Tatiana had not had a say in anything but her own appearance. To be fair, she had not asked about anything, which Marius liked to believe reflected her mature understanding of what this union was all about. Their interaction had been limited.

He clasped his hands behind his back and forced his shoulders to relax. "You can get the bitterest of enemies to sit next to each other if there's free booze involved," he murmured in Ian's ear. When his brother began chuckling, he followed suit in the hope of appearing more at ease.

Warrick leaned over and added his own observation. "You can cut the tension in this room with a knife . . . but considering you used to need a chainsaw, I'd say this is progress."

The Dumonts had purposely not provided seating assignments for the ceremony. They were now keenly watching where people sat, interested in how past alliances would manifest in this rare moment when all kinds could sit together in peace, as one.

*We require so many distinctions*, Marius thought. Crimson City had it all: humans, vampires, werewolves, mechs—and in particularly unlucky and unstable recent times, demons. And those were just the species. Never mind the disparate political bases.

"She'd better show," Warrick mumbled.

Marius raised an eyebrow. "Who?"

"The bride," his brother gritted out.

Ian shushed him. "Don't consider that it's even a question," he chided. He drew his body back into line and then, after a moment, leaned slightly toward Marius and whispered, "She'd damn well *better* show."

If Tatiana didn't appear, she'd be disappointing a lot of

people, Marius admitted, resisting the urge to tug at his cravat where the stickpin was digging into his throat. Himself included?

The Dumont and the St. Giles vampires sat up front on one side, the Marakovas and Gianninis together with Crimson City's full complement of werewolf clans on the other. For dogs to enjoy such an indulgence—a visible display of numbers and power on vampire turf, encouraged and permitted—was an extraordinary moment in the city's history. The wolves all appeared on their best behavior, apparently saving their own internal power struggles for their return to strata -1.

Odd, that there weren't more humans.

Marius was sorry to see that no mechs had dared attend, not even his trusted friend Finn and Finn's wife, Cyd. He didn't blame them; mech soldier escapees were still very much targets of bounty hunters. The human government wanted their bioengineered marvels back, as they still hadn't accepted that it was impossible to surgically remove the soul from a man's body.

The members of the Rogues Club had all chosen to sit together in the back gallery, even though there were still seats available midway up the aisle. No surprise, Marius decided. These individuals, who'd each turned his back on the idea of blind allegiance to his species, weren't always sure how they'd be received by others.

The light string music faded, and a larger group of musicians joined the quartet. Some of these were brass, and they initiated the House Royale trumpet hail. A grey-haired officiant stepped into place at Marius's side. Ian and Warrick stepped away.

At the signaling fanfare, the uniformed footmen at the opposite end of the room ceremoniously opened the carved double doors. Tatiana Asprey stood framed just outside, her sister visible a step behind. A wave of emotion struck Marius from the far end of the room as Jillian reacted. He forced himself to block her out, to focus on the one who would become his wife.

As previously arranged, the werewolf princess deigned to accept both ladies-in-waiting and a male proxy to escort her down the aisle. She walked the long stretch with her head held high, each step deliberate and controlled. She'd chosen not to cover her face with a veil, and her pale features harmonized with the white dress, even to the point that she seemed to radiate a ghostly nimbus as she moved toward Marius.

She looked straight into his eyes, and he felt a twinge of hope penetrate his stoic heart. *I will try to make you happy, Tatiana*, he communicated silently. She gave no sign of understanding, or that she'd intuited his communication.

*Jillian would have—Enough, man! You gave her up.*

Tatiana's beautiful face remained serene, though a tension at the corners of her mouth suggested the expression was not natural. A sudden wave of despair swept through Marius. Oblivious, the werewolf princess took her place at his side and turned her angelic countenance downward, watched her sister arrange her white satin train over the red-carpeted dais.

"Mr. Dumont?" the officiant whispered.

Marius looked up and blinked. Tatiana was staring at him, the rigidity of her smile even more obvious now as she held out her hand.

"Please take her hand in yours, sir."

Marius did so. The hand was surprisingly soft and warm.

"From above, middle and below, all species join together," the officiant began. "We have been through much. We have vanquished the demons from another realm that sought to bring down this great city. We have overcome attempts that the short-sighted few have made to divide us. We have struggled mightily to maintain peace with our neighbors. Let this moment, this joining together of two people, reflect a greater union. Let this celebration herald a new era, a new world! We have entered this room in factions. Let us leave it *together.* . . ."

As the officiant continued, Marius nodded and smiled and did his best to listen and believe in what he himself had set in motion, all while holding Tatiana Asprey's soft, warm hand. Her other hand held—

Only then did he see her bouquet of flowers. White roses. Of course. They were nearly identical to the ones he'd left for Jillian, identical save for a thin streak of red down the center of each petal. Marius flinched and touched his fingers to his temple, feeling Jillian's anguish as if it were his own. Clearly, she had noticed, too.

A noise sounded beside him. It was soft, but he looked up and saw Tatiana staring into his eyes. A corresponding flicker of doubt crossed her face.

*No. This cannot fail.*

Marius blanked his mind, silenced his heart, and forced a brilliant smile to his lips. Then, when the officiant finished talking, and after no individual in the room— that massive room filled with old and new alliances, filled with friend and foe alike—could find a reason why he and Tatiana should not be joined, he kissed the bride.

Watching Marius embrace his new wife through the long zoom lens made the moment a little less raw—not to mention that holding the camera equipment in front of her face saved Jill from both the curious and pitying stares of other guests and also the brazen attempts by other reporters at capturing a reaction shot. The last thing Jill needed was a teary photo of herself against this particular backdrop.

She steadied her camera at eye level and continued to shoot a nonstop stream of pictures. *A meticulous, frame-by-frame account of the death of a dream*, she thought dramatically.

*God, that werewolf princess is so photogenic. Blonde, tiny . . . Ugh. Couldn't she at least be one of those people who blinks compulsively or has a lazy eye? Nice that I still have a sense of humor. Good girl.*

She'd forced herself to come here, truthfully telling everyone that it was for the money, that the tabloids would always pay her extra for Dumont stories and pictures because of the rumors that she had "special access." But that wasn't the real reason. She'd forced herself to come here to watch, to see for herself so that there would be no mistake in her mind about the possibility of a future with Marius Dumont, to confirm that there was no hope. It was a moment long overdue. She'd wanted one of two things from the moment she first laid eyes on Marius Dumont in an alley in Crimson City: his love, or relief from the ties that bound them.

Through the lens, she zoomed in on Marius and Tatiana's clasped hands as the couple turned together to the cheering assembly and started down the aisle toward the back of the room—toward the place where Jill stood with her peers in the photographer pen. As a shower of white rose petals filled the air, Jill felt her resolve slip. Her heart pounded. She continued to snap away, though her hands were shaking so much she'd never be able to use the pictures. She closed her eyes and waited for Marius to pass.

*Don't look at me. Just pass. Show me the line's gone dead between us.*

The photographers pressed in closer, jostling Jill between them. Squeezing her eyes shut, and with her fingers sweaty on the heavy camera, Jill stopped shooting.

She couldn't even pretend. It was all she could do to stand there without bursting into tears.

*Cut the line, Marius. Do it now.*

But as the photographers yelled and rose petals clogged the air with fragrance, as the guests pressed in on all sides to shake hands and congratulate the newlyweds, the thread that seemed to connect Jill's soul to Marius's never wavered. The relief she'd counted on did not come.

Almost numb, she let her hand holding the camera move slowly to her side. She opened her eyes. Marius was close enough to reach out and touch. He stood with his profile to her, smiling and shaking the hand of another photographer.

*Can't you just set me free?* she begged.

His response was a tangled mess of emotion that had no beginning or end. It took Jill's breath away in its intensity. He caught her gaze with his own for a split second . . . and then the newlyweds passed through the back of the press corps and out the door toward the reception hall. She fought back rage.

He would have freed her if it had been a simple matter of flipping some sort of switch. Jill knew that. Her bond with Marius was inscrutable, and special. But that it was something ethereal and beautiful and not of this world did not make her feel better. In fact, it made everything worse.

In a daze, she filed out of the ceremony chamber with the remaining press. A riot of color and sensation greeted all the guests who passed into the adjoining event rooms. Table after table supported a wedding feast. Huge bowls of sugared fruits glistened in the candlelight. Entire tables dedicated to all manner of cakes and sweets tempted from one direction, while the aroma of savory cheeses and meats beckoned from the other. Ice sculpture supported a caviar bar, and what seemed like miles of carving stations offered up further options.

Jill lackadaisically lifted her camera and snapped a few shots of the culinary splendor before following the sound of music to the adjacent ballroom. There, an infamous Dumont vampire "re-creation" was already in full swing. She snapped another series of photos: glamorous ball gowns and entertainment stylized with the aesthetic details of much earlier historical eras. The tabloid readers would eat this stuff up, and press rarely got an invite. This would pay her rent for months, she admitted gloomily, wondering how many more seconds would pass before she could leave. She didn't need anybody realizing one extra moment at Marius's wedding just might kill her.

A hand suddenly snaked through the crook of her elbow, and Jill was more than happy to find it belonged to her friend, Rogues Club manager Bridget Hathaway Rothschild. Bridget's tastes were as tony as her name. She winked, wasting no time steering Jill back into the reception area and beelining them directly to a long banquet table piled with a champagne pyramid. She gaily plucked two glasses from the champagne and crystal scaffolding, handing one over, oblivious to the sloshing of the expensive bubbly over the sides of the glasses.

She held up her flute. "To you, Jill. I'm glad you showed. Took serious balls."

"Everybody's staring," Jill replied numbly.

"Let 'em." As long as they had everybody's attention, Bridget postured a little to present her best side to full advantage. The girl liked attention, and though she was human and had worked for their government at one time, was happy to accept it from any species. She was dressed in bright yellow silk.

Conversely, Jill had worn a matte, chocolate brown evening dress. She would have preferred black, to blend even farther into the shadows, but her pride had warned people might take the color as a sign of mourning. She wished now that she'd risked it.

"The women are on your side, anyway," Bridget assured her with a sympathetic pat on the shoulder.

Rationalizing that her friend had managed to spill at least a quarter of the glass's contents, Jill downed her champagne. She placed the empty on a silver tray maneuvered by a passing servant with an uncanny sense for an impending discard, and was tempted to take another glass, but the last thing she wanted was to read a story in the morning tabloids about herself getting wrecked at the Dumont wedding. Instead, she sucked in a deep breath and told herself to keep it together. Neither smile too much nor too little. Neither clasp your hands together so that they won't tremble, nor let anyone see them do so. Don't look down when you should look up, don't let your face show what you're feeling when you do. Don't swallow too hard or blink too much. Don't show too much emotion or seem too obviously blank.

*Oh, god.*

No, she *could* keep it together. The gossip and the rumors and the pitying looks mixed with suspicion—there was no place for that anymore. Jill had moved beyond it, and everyone else would have to as well. A little dancing with her friends, just a smidge more liquor and as much dessert as she wanted would get her through the night. . . .

And indeed, some hours later, when a Dumont servant bearing a tray of full champagne flutes caught up with her on the dance floor with the other Rogues, Jill had almost managed to forget her troubles.

"Oh, come on. This could be the last party for us

for a while," Bridget pushed, proffering a fresh glass of bubbly.

"Why do you say that?" Jill asked.

"Didn't you hear? The human government invoked Total Recall. It's all hush-hush, of course, but—"

"Are you serious?" Jill tossed back her drink and towed Bridget off the dance floor. "When?"

"Pretty much as of the *I do*'s. Seems they're 'calling the vampires' bluff.' They want all humans back in the fold. I heard about it from an intel fencer on my way over here, that cogs are starting to turn. I was sort of hoping this wedding would make species feel all warm and friendly toward each other. It would have been a great opportunity for our species to make nice and take tensions down a notch." Bridget frowned. "But our kind never seems to take those opportunities, do we?"

"I was wondering why members of the Rogues Club were practically the only humans at the wedding. What a nightmare! That's the last thing Mar—That's the last thing the vampires intended." Jill moistened her lips and scanned the room. "Do you think we should be scared?" If Total Recall was meant to cajole, force or threaten humans back into line, the Rogues Club, with its open charter welcoming all species, would be full of prime targets.

Bridget's silence was unexpected. When Jill looked back at her, she just shrugged and grabbed another glass of champagne.

Bridget's gaze suddenly shifted beyond Jill's ear, and a throat cleared. "Miss Cooper?"

Jill turned to find a manservant wringing his white-gloved hands.

"Miss Cooper, I was wondering if you would be so kind . . ." The servant ushered her away from the dance floor to a quiet corner of the room, and Jill tried to ignore Bridget's raised eyebrows.

"Hayden Wilks seems to be . . ." The pained expression on the servant's face indicated that there was no polite way to say Jill's on-and-off boyfriend had made an unwelcome appearance at the wedding, and that he was probably causing a scene somewhere—or was about to. At best, Hayden was behaving like an inappropriate ass. At worst, he might be intending to do real harm to one of the Dumonts.

"Yes, of course," Jill said, relieved, really, for an excuse to leave. She waved to Bridget, collected her purse and camera and followed the manservant out of the ballroom and down the hall toward the elevator bank. "Where is he?"

"At last sighting he was 'investigating' the ladies' powder room on the eighty-third floor," the servant said with a wince. "We thought perhaps you might assist us in keeping him . . . contained, given that he is your—"

"I'll take it from here," Jill agreed.

The servant escorted her into the open elevator. "Thank you very much for your help with this matter, Miss Cooper. This is an important evening for the Dumonts. Anything you can do to"—he cleared his throat—"defuse any potential . . . situation would be most welcome."

"Sure," Jill said with a tight smile. "I apologize on his behalf for any inconvenience."

The look on the servant's face as the elevator doors closed left no doubt he knew the truth: Hayden Wilks would never apologize to the Dumonts for anything.

# CHAPTER SIX

Hayden Wilks wandered across the landing, uncorking the champagne he'd pilfered from the kitchen. It was time to make a little trouble, have a little fun and watch the House of Dumont squirm—the last most of all. He liked to remind them that someone was always watching, waiting for a weakness to exploit. And one of these days? Payback. The kind of payback that would restore the peace this family had taken from him.

Absently swigging from the bottle as he stalked the corridors, he trailed the fingers of his left hand along the walls, meaning to permanently mark them with his presence. But someone else's presence was recently marked, and the familiar scent stopped him dead in his tracks.

A sharp intake of breath sounded behind him. Hayden gripped his champagne bottle so hard it might shatter, and then he turned to find her standing in a doorway. They looked at each other, the delicacy of his onetime lover's pale features a contrast to the boiling enmity within those familiar blue eyes.

"The party is downstairs," Fleur Dumont said coldly. "Although I don't remember you being on the guest list."

"Don't worry, I'll blend right in," he replied.

Fleur cocked her head. "As time passes, I don't feel quite so guilty anymore," she remarked. "Perhaps if you hadn't turned into such a bastard—"

"Perhaps if you hadn't turned me into a vampire," Hayden interrupted, growling, "I wouldn't be such a bastard."

She swallowed so hard that the emerald choker around her neck undulated with the movement, and her knuckles showed white as she gripped the door. Hayden could almost imagine the wheels turning in her brain as she tried to decide how to handle him, but there was something uncharacteristically nervous in her features. Interesting.

He fixed his kohl-rimmed eyes on her face. She looked pale, puffy, a bit unwell, and as he surveyed her person, he saw that her dark green dress was rumpled as if she'd been lying down. "Missing your cousin's wedding?" he sneered.

Fleur's hand followed his gaze, stopping protectively at her voluminous skirts. It took Hayden a moment to process that swell of fabric, that it concealed a late-stage pregnancy. The familiar chill of a most hideous bitterness made Hayden literally shiver.

"So, that's why you and Dain are hiding," he whispered. He glanced over her shoulder. "Except he's not here right now. You're all alone."

Fleur's free arm reached for something out of view. Hayden caught a glint of steel as she slipped her hand behind her back. But Hayden couldn't stop looking at her stomach. His mouth shaped words, but he could make no further sound.

"Get away from me," Fleur commanded, one hand gripping her skirts.

"Unfair, Fleur. Unfair," Hayden murmured. "You moved on so easily." He slowly raised his head and looked into the eyes of the bitch who had turned him vampire while knowing it would ruin him, all because she'd been unable to control herself and her passions. The hate he saw there made it seem impossible she had ever loved him at all. When she looked into his eyes, she probably saw the same thing.

They stared at each other in silence for a moment, and then Fleur slowly pulled a gun from behind her back and switched to the UV setting. She pointed it at Hayden. "If you keep this up, you only give us more reason to hate you. You've turned yourself into an enemy of this house, and one of these days we will lose patience. When all my guilt has gone, the House of Dumont will have no reason to let you live. More than one of my cousins wishes he'd killed you long ago." Then, very deliberately, Fleur took a step back, blending into the unlit room beyond the threshold, and she slammed the door in Hayden's face. He flinched as the lock turned.

Unseeing, he stared at the wood grain of the door. So his ex, Fleur Dumont, and her human husband Dain were going to have a kid. How fucking charming was that? How perfect. How brilliant for her and the whole Dumont gang. Everything always worked out for them. What else was new? Hayden tipped the champagne bottle up and drank the balance without tasting it.

Turning his back on the door, he moved swiftly to the staircase and walked blindly up the spiral until Fleur's scent faded. When it finally disappeared, he heaved himself onto the nearest landing, sweating and wired by a combination of alcohol and emotion. A sob burst from his throat before he could control it, so he took the empty champagne bottle and threw it as hard as he could against the wall.

The destruction was satisfying, but it didn't last long enough. Nothing took the pain away, not really. Pressing his hands against the wall, Hayden gently touched his forehead to the plaster, trying not to heave up the liquor roiling in his stomach. Fleur had turned him into a vampire and then left him alone to rot. She'd taken his humanity when she knew better, and now he had nothing that held any meaning, and she had everything.

A trickle of sweat rolled down between his shoulder blades. He'd spent years trying to teach these Dumonts a lesson. He'd haunted Fleur, shadowed Ian and Warrick, used Jill to make Marius crazy with jealousy. . . . But he couldn't break them. No matter how hard he tried, he couldn't break any of them. His past was one of failure and lies.

A chime sounded, followed by the sound of an elevator door opening.

"Hayden, are you up here?"

Hayden wiped the sweat off his face with his coat sleeve and swaggered back toward the central landing. Jill appeared through the alley of the elevator banks.

"Hey, beautiful," he called. And leaping casually onto the banister of the massive spiral staircase, he landed back on the line between caring too much and not at all.

The hell-raiser looked like a drunken parrot about to fall off his perch. Jill stared at Hayden and fought back annoyance, explaining, "I've been looking for you everywhere. I've been to at least five different floors!"

He raised his arms and gave a lopsided smile. "Here I am. What do you think? Suitable for a royal wedding, no? Wouldn't want to disappoint." He stood up on the banister and bowed, showing off his blue velvet coat, white satin double-breasted vest and striped cravat. He did cut a dashing figure, although the sprinkling of glass on his sleeve was not likely part of the fashion statement.

"Your looks have never been your problem," Jill muttered, taking in the strong smell of champagne.

Her sometimes boyfriend grinned. "Oh, don't be so grim. Let's get this party started!"

"The party started a long time ago. People are already leaving." She studied Hayden's face carefully. "You said you weren't coming."

The rogue vampire leapt gracefully to the floor, alighting in front of her. "Guess I changed my mind. I'm here now."

Jill crossed her arms over her chest. "They've sent me after you," she grumbled. "I . . ." Her voice trailed off as she studied Hayden's face. He appeared rattled, as if he was working hard to muster his usual bravado.

"I didn't break any windows this time," he reported.

Jill looked pointedly at the remnants of a champagne bottle shattered against the far wall.

Hayden suddenly noticed her camera. "Hey, take a picture! I'll bet my feud with the Dumonts still sells papers!" He gave her a big showy smile.

"I'm not taking your picture," Jill snapped, wondering how she'd ever thought having a long-term relationship with this man could be a good idea. Well . . . of course she knew what she'd been thinking at the time: Make Marius jealous. He'll come to you, then. He'll realize what he's about to lose.

It hadn't worked. She was embarrassed she'd gotten mixed up in it, even if she and Hayden had always shared an understanding.

"Damn. You really mean it," he realized. "Okay, no pictures. Then, let's go drink more of that really nice free champagne."

He slung an arm around her waist—already sloppy, she realized. He'd apparently been drinking "really nice free champagne" for some time. Hayden seemed to think showing up at Dumont Towers whenever and however he wanted was his right. In spite of their overblown sense of morality, one of these days a Dumont was going to get around to putting a UV bullet through his head.

The sad thing was, he seemed to want them to get on with it.

"I'm sorry, I just don't want to," Jill said.

"Of *course* you want to. You're an even bigger masochist than I am," Hayden crowed.

Jill pulled gently away. She felt strange and miserable and alone. They hadn't outgrown their respective demons at the same pace. For a while, Hayden had gotten her through some really bad nights, and she'd always be grateful to him for that. But she'd never love him in the way he wanted or needed, and vice versa. It was time to move on. Past time, maybe. Hayden's brand of caring was toxic, and the idea of staying with him made her want to throw up.

"We've always been a strange combination," she murmured, unsure how much to say to him in his present condition.

"Come *on*," Hayden continued, ignoring her. "The Dumonts screwed us both. The least we should do is drink their liquor." He spread his arms wide and gave her a come-hither look, then resorted to actually pulling at her hand. "You're at the wedding of the man whose very soul is supposedly bound to yours, watching him marry someone else. I mean, seriously, kid, this is what could reasonably be called the worst day of your life! Come with me, Jill. Let's go make a scene. It'll be fun. We'll piss the Dumonts off, make 'em toss us . . ."

Jill pulled back and rested her head against the wall. "Not this time, Hayden. This time we both let go. We have to let it all *go*. We have to move forward, move on to something else. Some*one* else. I want to make a fresh start."

"I can do fresh," Hayden suggested, taking her in his arms. He pressed his lips to hers. They were wet and tasted like ash.

Jill turned away. "You're so drunk it's ridiculous."

"I *want* you."

"Oh, Hayden," she said, pushing at his chest.

"You can't have him," Hayden hissed. "We might as well have each other. You know how good it can be."

Jill flinched.

Hayden didn't seem to notice. His hands roamed down her hips. He slid one palm up inside her skirt and headed north. "Come on, Jill," he whispered. "You know we're good together. I know just how you like it."

"No," she said, trying to squirm out of his arms. "Hayden . . . We need to talk."

He shook his head and rested his mouth on her neck. She felt his fangs, though they didn't penetrate her skin. She'd never let him do that, and he'd never asked. "What's there to talk about that hasn't been said? You want Marius? Close your eyes and fuck me. 'Cause that's as close to fucking *him* as you'll ever get."

She shoved him off her, as hard as she could. "You have no right to be such a bastard. Not to me."

He stumbled, nearly falling to the ground. Steadying himself, he just gave her that stare—the one that made him look as if he was about to burst into laughter. For some reason, when he laughed, he scared her more than ever.

"Are you going to do something crazy?" she asked when the silence became too much.

"No," he said, with an infuriating air of nonchalance. "Are you?"

"I'm not going to do anything. Ever again." A lump rose in her throat. She stared at Hayden's handsome features, at that face that hid a maelstrom of anger and unhappiness, and she couldn't bring herself to tell him—not then. "You and I . . . We're just a big, dangerous mess."

He blinked and then laughed very suddenly. "Last

call!" he shrieked. Raising both arms, he started walking backward toward the stairs. "Fine champagne . . . caviar . . . a massive silver platter full of desserts . . ." He placed one hand on his heart and took an exaggerated bow. "And *me*. You'll be missing out, Jill."

He needed to know what was going on in her head. She clutched her camera. "We have to talk. Let's just go back to the apartment."

"You women always need to talk," he sneered, if amiably. "Tomorrow, okay? Tonight, we celebrate!"

Then he realized she wasn't coming with him to the party. "Fine," he said, turning abruptly. The smile on his face was gone. "I'll meet you at home."

Jill watched him, nervous. She had to ask again, "Are you . . . are you going to do something?"

Hayden stopped and looked over his shoulder at her. His eyes were guarded, his lip curled. "Whatever do you mean?"

"You know what I mean," Jill said.

"*Do* something? Well . . . not until I'm done eating and drinking." Then he leaned on the banister and raised his hand in a kind of salute. Lifting his other hand, he rose and then descended, sliding gracefully out of view. His long blue velvet coattails rose up like wings.

Jill ran to the stairway. "Hayden!"

He paused in the middle of the massive spiral staircase and looked up, then continued downward. A moment later he'd vanished from view.

It was nearly silent on the landing, the hum of activity below nothing more than a slight vibration through the thick Persian carpet. Jill bowed her head and closed her eyes for a moment, admitting that maybe Bridget had proposed the right idea. Drinking herself into oblivion didn't seem like such a bad option, especially not now.

The emotions she'd managed to control all night were suddenly winning the war.

She looked around for a quiet room where she could be alone for just a moment, if for no other reason than to not have to worry about her expression. Down a corridor she headed, trying out a couple of doors that seemed as if they could lead to lounges, but they didn't. At last she turned a corner and stopped so quickly she almost dropped her camera. On the wall, underneath a serene pastoral painting, was a stark red smear followed a little farther on by a number of crimson droplets. *Blood* was spattered across the inlaid wood floor.

Jill froze, hitched her camera strap more securely on her shoulder and pulled her switchblade from her purse. Then, taking short, deliberate steps, she followed the trail around the corner to the threshold of a small library. The red vanished inside that room, out of her line of sight.

Gripping her blade tightly in her hand, she leaned forward and craned her neck around the doorway. A man lay on the ground, motionless, his eyes bulging out of a horribly contorted face. His mouth, throat, cravat and tuxedo shirt were completely soaked in gore. She felt the stench of blood wash over her.

Jill's calm professionalism and ability to accept the day's events with any sort of grace were finally tapped out. Nauseated and overwhelmed, she screamed at the top of her lungs.

# Chapter Seven

*Derbyshire, England*
*September, 1850*

"Who is that strange girl?" came one whisper.

"I believe she's related to the *gardener*."

"She can't mean to join us, can she?"

"Oh, dear. I do hope not."

Charlotte Paxton was the strange girl, and she did mean to join them in the greenhouse. Well, not so much join the gentlewomen as not be deterred by their stares.

This was all rather awkward. She walked around the enormous water tank to the opposite side. Her cousin Joseph Paxton, the celebrated gardener and architect, had invited her to witness the *Victoria regia* lily bloom at the Duke of Devonshire's Chatsworth estate, but now urgent business with the development of a structure for Prince Albert's Great Exhibition prevented him from joining her—and from looking out for her.

Well, she'd traveled all the way from London and refused to be prevented from making the most of her trip by the rude looks of the society ladies attending this garden party.

"It's so large!" one of the ladies remarked, peering through the rail.

"*Quite* large!" said another.

"Yes, it's *very* large," agreed the first, with overblown authority.

Charlotte suppressed the urge to roll her eyes.

"Is it going to change color soon?" the third lady asked after a moment.

The one who seemed to be in charge turned her head slightly, and Charlotte recognized from the servants' talk the well-dressed society chit as one Lucy Vaughan.

Miss Vaughan replied, "I don't know. Well, seeing it was very interesting, wasn't it? Now, shall we go change for dinner?"

With no small amount of relief, Charlotte watched the women file out of the greenhouse. Left alone, she was able to study the plant at her leisure, and she would do so for much longer than the others. The *Victoria regia* was an extraordinary botanical discovery in the world of horticulture, and it had only just recently been coaxed into bloom.

As the society women had at least noticed, it was very large. Some of the leaves looked to be nearly three meters in diameter! Joseph had written to Charlotte about perching his young daughter Annie dressed as a fairy upon one of these very lily pads. Remarkable, that a plant could withstand the weight of a person. In fact, Charlotte herself was of slight build. Perhaps if she went slowly . . .

She lifted the hem of her skirts and slowly extended her leg, pressing down on the enormous lily pad with the toe of her boot. It responded with only slight give. She leaned forward and put more weight on the massive pad. The water undulated dangerously below. Charlotte swayed.

A pair of hands encircled her waist. "I find myself at a loss."

Charlotte started, nearly losing her balance. The hands gripped her tighter, and she looked down to find one of the gentlemen who was attending the garden party. He had very dark hair—almost black, it was—and very blue eyes, and he was not even trying to conceal his admiration for her exposed ankles. He held her waist in a most familiar way.

Though she could not force words from her mouth, Charlotte at least managed to drop her hem.

The man smiled. "You see, I cannot find anyone to introduce us, and if you must risk your life in this manner, I feel compelled to at least know your name before I am obliged to pull you from the water."

Charlotte smiled. "I'm Charlotte Paxton."

"Put your hands on my shoulders, then, Miss Paxton," he entreated. He did not let go of her waist, and Charlotte had no choice but to let him help her down.

As he lifted her away from the pool, she fell against him. They stepped away from each other in a flutter of activity that did not quite mask a shared and pleased awareness of such close contact.

"I am Edward Vaughan. And if you are Charlotte Paxton . . . you must be related to Joseph Paxton!"

"Indeed," she admitted with a curtsey. "It is his generosity that has allowed me to make this visit. Unfortunately, business in London keeps him away."

Edward Vaughan nodded with great enthusiasm. "He must be working on his plans regarding a hall for the Great Exhibition. I understand that the engineering of the Crystal Palace is based on the load-bearing capacity of this leaf."

Charlotte smiled. "That is exactly what I was testing."

A look of wonder bloomed across Edward's face. Then he stared at her intensely. "You are interested in such matters?"

Charlotte blushed. "Oh, I should not like to misrepresent the extent of my knowledge. I have a small gardening project, is all. . . ." She waved away its significance.

"What sort of project?" Edward pressed.

"Oh." She found herself unsettled. No one other than her famous cousin had ever expressed any interest in her hobby. "I am trying to grow a new species of rose that I read about in a fairytale once but have never seen."

"Enchanting," the man replied, but his gaze made it unclear whether he meant the idea of the rose or her.

"What is *your* project, sir?" Charlotte asked hurriedly, to cover her awkwardness. Her heart was beating quickly, and her hands felt damp and warm.

"I belong to the London Inventors Club. I am an amateur. A dilettante, really, as far as my own work is concerned. I like to take things apart and put them back together." He shrugged. "My friend Lord Gilliam, who is also here for the garden party, is one of the club's foremost members. He is the one who displays a genuine talent for invention. I daresay he'll have something to show at the Great Exhibition."

"How marvelous!"

Charlotte and Edward stood in silence for a moment before Edward blurted, "May I escort you to dinner?"

Cousin Joseph had meant for her to see the lily, that was all. She was quartered with the servants, and she doubted very much he had had any intention of his poor relative taking a seat at the duke's table. "I don't think there are enough places," she demurred delicately.

Edward frowned. "Your cousin is not here to see that you are taken care of. Therefore I shall arrange it." He strode away before she could make further protest, and did exactly what he claimed.

Unfortunately, his generous nature was not shared by the whole of his party. Lucy Vaughan did not bother to hide her shock.

As a personal friend of the absent Duke of Devonshire and an heir to a dukedom in his own right, Lord Gilliam set the tone for the gathering: he managed a polite smile. His sister, Maxine Gilliam, made a most valiant effort with polite conversation during the beginning of the meal, then last year's London social calendar was given a very detailed rundown and a kind of post mortem, and at last the talk turned to the remarkable gardens at Chatsworth.

"Is it true that you are related to this estate's infamous Joseph Paxton?" Lucy spoke up, once all present had again agreed the *Victoria regia* lily was "very large."

Charlotte nodded. "Joseph is a distant cousin, Miss Vaughan. He has always been very kind to me."

"Where is your family, then?"

"In London. I have a sister."

There came a slight murmur from the ladies. "Just a sister?" Lucy pressed. "Whose protection are you under?"

"It is just my sister Maggie and myself," Charlotte admitted. "We . . ."

She lifted her chin. It was no use. Her clothes already revealed the truth of their difficult circumstances, even though she'd bartered fabric with a dressmaker for some better things. Compared to the other ladies at the table, she might as well be wearing rags. Besides, Lucy and Maxine's ill-concealed derisive glances and backhanded comments made it clear that they understood the truth: while her connections to Joseph Paxton might be improving her gardening, they were not improving her prospects.

"We have a draper's shop." A horribly debt-ridden draper's shop.

"How extraordinary," Lucy said. Then she turned her

back on Charlotte and began a private conversation with Lord Gilliam.

Maxine blinked rapidly, clearly unsure how to respond. She decided to focus on the raspberry ice being placed in front of her.

Edward Vaughan looked at Charlotte a little helplessly down the length of the table; they'd drawn an awkward seating arrangement. Lacking him to converse with, and having no willing partner on either side, Charlotte tried to concentrate on the food. Oh, if only she could have shared some of these lovely comestibles with Maggs.

"I don't understand what the fuss is all about. Do you, Miss Paxton?" Maxine asked when Charlotte was half-way through her ice. "This Great Exhibition your cousin is building a palace for . . . I don't understand what they shall put inside." Before waiting for an answer, she turned to her brother and added, "Will it not be just another party like the ones at your Inventors Club, Alastair? Just a collection of machines, half of which seem to stop before you can even get them started. That was such a strange business with the leeches. The idea that those disgusting creatures could predict the weather . . . Why, I still have nightmares! I don't think I shall ever go back to that club." She turned to the others. "Not even if Alastair does something extraordinary."

"I think you are referring to the tempest prognostica-tor," Lord Gilliam informed the table with a frown. "Merryweather will have it working for the exhibition. We spoke of it just after we received word about the event. Discovery and invention take time and patience, Maxie. Without trial and error, we would never have many of the things you now take for granted."

"I do not like it," Maxine complained. "I cannot help but imagine you gentlemen all down there creating some sort of Frankenstein's monster." She shuddered, and Charlotte had to suppress a smile. The girl looked quite serious.

Lucy Vaughan burst out laughing. "Oh, I do wish Rupert were here to hear that. My fiancé accuses me of having a wild imagination." Leaning forward, she flashed Lord Gilliam a smile as she said to his sister, "You look so aggrieved, darling Maxie! You must not blame Lord Gilliam, when it is your own imagination that gives you nightmares." She looked around the table, an amused smirk on her lips. "Maxine has been reading too much gothic fiction. I try to tell her there are no such monsters in our midst, that the idea of a man turning into some sort of animal is absolutely impossible, but she gobbles those horrid books up and then worries and frets."

"Oh, *do* change the subject!" Maxine cried, wringing her hands.

"You should not worry," Edward spoke up. "The Great Exhibition will display articles from all over the world. Silver and tapestries . . . porcelain and jewels . . . It will be like a museum, I should think. The exhibits of machinery and inventions will be just one part. And if there are animals there, I'm certain there will be nothing monstrous about them—and certainly none like the circus sideshow you must be imagining. There will be many beautiful things, I'm sure, many more things wondrous than horrible."

At his words, Maxine smiled gratefully.

"Oh, yes," Charlotte enthused. "I agree with Mr. Vaughan. It will be wonderful. A collection of marvels from all over the world, brought together to be seen by everyone, all in one place."

Lucy's glance flicked disapprovingly over Charlotte's attire. "Not everyone will be able to attend, I should think. I suppose it will be quite expensive." Charlotte suddenly wished she had borrowed a few small pieces of jewelry, if only to give the others one less thing to titter about after dinner.

"Prince Albert means it to be affordable for all," Edward inserted. "And perhaps Miss Paxton will be one of the exhibitors. She is a gardener like her cousin, and is engineering an entirely new species of rose."

The ladies were clearly shocked by his words.

"Really, Edward," Lord Gilliam murmured.

Charlotte felt her face flame. "Please, Mr. Vaughan. There is no need—"

Lord Gilliam interrupted. "I think it's time for the gentlemen to retire to the library, don't you, Vaughan?"

Edward inclined his head in agreement, though a frown still pulled at his mouth. "If you will excuse us, ladies."

Lucy and Maxine looked at each other, and then at Charlotte. They looked about to say something.

Charlotte cut them off, remarking, "I'm afraid I will be unable to join you. I have a rather bad headache, and should take some air before I retire. I'm leaving quite early in the morning. It was a pleasure to meet you all."

Her words were accepted with no contradiction. However, as the gathering dissolved and as Edward followed his friend from the room, he took the time to whisper in Charlotte's ear, "There was every need to defend you, Miss Paxton. I would not have them mauling you like a pack of wolves."

Charlotte smiled. Wait until Maggie heard about this! A man had stood up for her—and a *gentle*man, at that.

The gentleman in question settled into a chair in one of his absent host's finely turned-out libraries. Across from him, Alastair Gilliam wasted little time making himself at home.

"Turned out to be a rather small party," Lord Gilliam remarked, examining the hue of the claret he was pouring into a glass.

Edward nodded. "Something tells me the rest stayed behind in London to keep the duke—and his wallet—company."

Gilliam shrugged. "He plays a good host, even from afar. I think that cut of meat was the finest I've ever sampled. Divine." He leaned back upon a velvet settee and exhaled a contented sigh. "By the way, what on earth were you thinking?"

"What do you mean?" Edward asked.

Alastair Gilliam's eyebrow arched.

Edward groaned. "I should not have invited her, I realize that now. It was a sudden decision. I should have known it would make things uncomfortable for everyone."

Lord Gilliam gave him a dubious look, tossed back his glass of wine and poured himself another.

"In my defense, old boy," Edward said with a grin, "if you'd had the opportunity to see her fine ankles, you might have done the same."

"That hair! Curls practically springing out in every direction like that. Made her look rather wild," Gilliam said with unbridled distaste.

"Hardly," Edward said, laughing. And what if it did?

Gilliam shook his head. "You have always had such *odd* tastes."

The penultimate word had almost sounded . . . vicious. Edward winced. When his friend burst into laughter, he demanded, "What is so funny?"

"Where shall I even begin?" Lord Gilliam asked. "Shall I begin with 'She is in trade' and end with the fact that you will probably have to tolerate her mooning over you for the duration? You are embarrassing yourself over this girl, and embarrassing your family."

Edward picked unhappily at a tufted throw pillow. "I'm merely adhering to the principles of the Inventors Club. Or do you still not subscribe to the egalitarian values of the very institution you helped found?"

"Of course I subscribe to them. I pay my dues," Gilliam said with wink. "But I didn't vote to let in the riff-raff. Unfortunately, I was outvoted by the likes of you."

"Perhaps so far above the riffraff, one cannot imagine what such a situation would be like," Edward suggested.

"Oh, don't tell me *your* situation is as bad as all that."

"No, it's not," Edward agreed awkwardly, rubbing at a red scar on his hand where he'd burned himself at the club. He'd been lucky. More so than Gilliam, who had mutilated himself so badly that he never removed his gloves in the company of others. Edward knew he would do well to remember that Alastair had his own share of difficulties.

"I think the days of catering to one's boyhood fancies are coming to an end—for both of us," Lord Gilliam said seriously. "What happened to that lovely American heiress you spoke so highly of in the spring?"

Edward stared over Gilliam's shoulder through the window . . . and saw Charlotte Paxton poking about the rosebushes in the fading light of dusk.

"Vaughan!" Lord Gilliam snapped his fingers. "The heiress. Jane St. Giles. She seemed rather taken with you. But perhaps she did not realize that all English gentlemen have the same 'delightful accent.'"

Edward could not help but laugh. "She's a lovely girl, if a bit stiff. She'd do, of course."

"She'd *do*? She's got all the money you require. You're not going to inherit anything worth speaking of, so what is there to consider? So she's stiff. You can always take a mistress." Gilliam's eyes followed Edward's off into the rosebushes, and he added, "Nobody really cares where a mistress comes from."

Edward stood up.

"You are not really going out there, are you?" Gilliam demanded. "I wouldn't, my boy. She'll try to trap you in the hedgerow—although I dare say I'd be happy to deny I saw any wrongdoing, whatever comes off."

Edward cast a look of disgust upon his friend. "Excuse me, Alastair. I must apologize to Miss Paxton for our rudeness at dinner, and I must do it before she leaves for London."

He pushed open the double doors and strode into the garden, conscious of the possibility of being watched by any number of fellow guests from inside the great house. For that reason, he kept a wide berth as he approached Charlotte Paxton in the dimming light.

She looked up from the rosebushes and smiled. "Ah, I have been caught."

"You do *not* have a headache, Miss Paxton," Edward accused with mock displeasure.

Charlotte smiled. "No. I do not."

Edward sighed. "They behaved abominably. You must accept my apologies."

"You were kind to invite me, Mr. Vaughan. You need not apologize for being more of a gentleman than anybody else. I must really be going inside, however. That I leave early in the morning was not part of my fabrication." And without another glance, Charlotte set off in the direction of the servants' quarters.

"Miss Paxton!" Edward blurted.

She looked over her shoulder, surprised, and he caught up with her. "Must you go?" he asked lamely, finding himself unsure what he wanted to say, just knowing he did not want her to leave.

She blushed. "I abandoned my sister in London with the work of two. It hardly seems fair."

Edward nodded. "Of course. Well, then . . . I expect to see quite a lot of the Great Exhibition. In fact, I will make it a point to be there at the opening." He paused, unsure if he was saying far too much . . . or not enough. "I do hope we meet again."

"I hope for the same, Mr. Vaughan."

Edward hesitated for a moment, and then he took Charlotte's hand. He held it for too long, pressed his lips to its back too fervently. He smoothed his thumb along her palm when he should have let go.

She trembled beneath his touch, and when Edward straightened after a bow, neither of them spoke, not even to exchange a simple good-bye. Perhaps because they both understood that they would see each other again.

# CHAPTER EIGHT

Marius stood outside the door of Tatiana's private bed-chamber with a bottle of champagne and two flutes, reminding himself that a wedding of this kind was an empire-building strategy that had been repeated many times throughout history. There was no shame in taking someone as a wife without loving her. Nonetheless, he did feel an obligation to convey that he gave Tatiana all due respect.

The door suddenly opened a crack, and a wide blue eye slid into view. "Hello," his new bride said, her voice muffled by the heavy oak.

Marius smiled. "Hello." As the crack widened, he saw his wife shiver and awkwardly fold her arms across the lace bodice of her underclothes. "May I come in?" he asked.

She nodded, and moved away from the door.

Marius stepped over the threshold and shut them both in. He went to her dressing table, put down the champagne flutes and turned, removing the foil from the bottle. "You were a vision in that dress," he remarked.

She blushed but did not reply.

"And you are a vision out of it."

"Thank you," she said. She dropped her hands from her body.

He wasn't lying. Tatiana Asprey was extraordinarily

beautiful. Any man would be more than happy to share her bed. He himself should be. But in Marius's mind, Jillian arched her back against that alley wall. In his mind, she bared her shoulders and neck to him and begged him to take her. In his mind, she took her hand and—

Marius blinked and focused his attention on popping the cork from the champagne. He filled the two flutes in silence and then held one out to her. "To . . . the future," he said.

"To the future," she echoed. "And to happiness."

Her hand shook as they toasted. The crystal collided, and the harsh chime sent a faint shiver down Marius's spine. He downed the contents of his glass, struggling not to reveal the suffocating edge of desperation that seemed to accompany the alcohol through his blood-stream.

Tatiana also drank greedily, then pressed the back of her hand to her mouth and smiled.

*Do it, man. Just do it now.* The physical act, the reality of Tatiana in his arms . . . Perhaps after making love to her, Jillian would no longer haunt his dreams.

He took the flute out of his new wife's hand, placed it on the bureau and then cupped her face in his hands. She sucked in a breath.

"Don't be frightened," Marius murmured, pressing his mouth to the side of her face and trailing a careful line of kisses along her cheekbone. Her fingers gripped the lapels of his tuxedo, and she sighed. It should not be unpleasant in any way to make her his wife. She responded to his caresses, did not try to hide what she was feeling. Marius only wished he could give her the same courtesy.

He moved his mouth to hers, and tried to enjoy the sensuality of tasting the champagne on her lips. But it was too silent in the room. He was too aware of who she was—and who she wasn't.

His tongue pressed into the damp warmth of her mouth. Tatiana gasped . . . and Marius felt his heart break. Unshed tears stung the corners of his eyes, and he told himself one final time, *I did the right thing letting Jillian go.*

Anxious to do Tatiana the courtesy of giving her his full attention, he worked to stay in the moment. There was much to enjoy. He grazed the side of her breast with his fingers, and the combination of smooth silk and rough lace that covered her delicate, supple body, the soft sounds of her experiencing something exciting and new . . .

If only he could block out everything else.

From the corner of his eye, Marius registered the petals from Tatiana's wedding bouquet fluttering on the side table. The image conjured Jillian, cradling the memento of his single white flower in her hands. He watched the curve of Tatiana's bare neck reveal itself, but was swamped by the emotion of watching Jillian nearly cut hers in front of him. He followed Tatiana's fingertips moving lightly across his chest, but felt Jillian's hand pressing roughly against his groin. And through it all, a female voice sounded in his mind:

*Marius . . .*

He ignored it. Untying Tatiana's laces, he pressed his lips against her naked flesh, wanting to believe he was only imagining Jillian's voice in his head along with the other memories. But . . .

*Marius!*

He would not give in this time. He could not give Jillian what she wanted, and he would not torture them by making further excuses.

His new bride sighed, reacting with pleasure as Marius slid his mouth down her breast and touched his tongue to her delicate nipple. He tried to lose himself in mindless physical pleasure. But something dark and harsh reached out through his soul, and an alert tore through the weak defenses of his mind.

*Marius*, Jillian called again.

With greater urgency, he lifted his bride in his arms and carried her to the bed, moving atop her with a ferocity he knew was too much, too soon.

*Marius!*

Suddenly, he was certain that Jillian was not purposely calling out to him, that it was not consciously done. This was like the times before that she had called, desperate times in her past. She needed him with every part of her being, but she was not actually crying out. It made the pain of the summons all the more excruciating. Yes, Jillian had asked for freedom, and Marius would do anything to give it to her, but his very being was still tracking hers. He could not be rid of the sense that something terrible was confronting her, and in his own house.

Marius took Tatiana's mouth, bruising her with his intensity. His inexperienced bride was clearly startled. He tried to let lust overtake his reason, but it was not just danger that he felt in Jillian's heart. It was the specter of death.

*You cannot deny her. You could not before, and you never will.*

Marius abruptly pushed himself away. He touched his forehead to Tatiana's, wishing to imbue her with some kind of understanding but knowing she would neither hear nor feel his silent plea.

*Forgive me, Tatiana. I believed it would change, but her heart still beats in tune with mine, and I know she's in danger. She has no one else, no one else to go to her aid. I will be true to you, I swear . . . but I must go. Now.*

"Is something wrong?" the princess asked in bewilderment.

"Tatiana," Marius murmured into her ear. "I will come

back. But I sense danger and death in my house, and I cannot ignore it. Please understand." He looked into her eyes and saw that she did not, but he had no more time to spare. Slipping his coat on even as he opened the door, he promised, "I'll be back."

"You told me that was done," Tatiana blurted.

Marius froze. He slowly turned.

His wife's cheeks blazed red. She held a sheet up to cover her nakedness. "Are you going to Jillian Cooper's bed? You told me those rumors amounted to nothing. 'We will have a very happy marriage based on mutual respect, loyalty and duty'—that's what you said during the marriage negotiations."

"I meant that," Marius swore. "And the rumors are just rumors. I will never go to Miss Cooper's bed."

The firm guarantee seemed to please his wife, for Tatiana's demeanor softened. She still looked puzzled, however.

"Please understand. I *will* make this right," Marius promised. He moved to the bed and pressed a cursory kiss to her bee-stung lips, then dashed away over the threshold.

Once out of his wife's room, Marius leapt into the center of the spiral staircase and soared quickly upward, Jillian's distress roaring in his bones. This time there was no question. No undertones of self-serving, desperate purpose muddied the call. Her distress was pure fear.

He alighted on the landing where he most felt her presence. Odd, that he would trace her up here, to the more private area of the Towers, away from the rooms used for entertaining outside guests. She should be at the party, or not here at all. Yet if someone had lured her away, if they'd hurt her, he would never forgive himself.

The hall was clogged with a human scent, with *her* scent. With her fear. He saw blood on the floor, on the wall, and tore down the hallway calling her name, praying that whatever he saw in the room beyond, it wouldn't be too late.

A body lay on the ground inside the room, limbs at awkward, stiff angles, posed as if all life had left the victim swiftly in the midst of his agony. A white bar towel covered the man's face, one half still clean but soaking slowly with blood.

"Jillian," Marius murmured to himself, relieved that this wasn't her, though he'd have felt if she were dead.

He stepped over the threshold, crouched down and carefully lifted the corner of the towel. Was all the blood from the victim's mouth? His hand reached out to turn the face, but when he had, he drew back in surprise. The man looked like the vampire Gregory Bell. Except the scent was all wrong.

Marius pressed his fingers to the corpse's neck. When he could find no pulse, he followed Jillian's perfume into the adjoining room.

She was sitting stick straight in a large library chair, facing away from him. He could see the fabric of her skirt through the chair legs. A camera sat upended on a side table next to an open bottle of liquor. Jillian's hand reached out, that slim feminine hand with its tiny wrist, and her fingers gripped a glass so hard he thought it would break.

She was shaking as she took a sip; ice clattered violently against crystal. "He's dead," she said dully, her face still hidden from view.

"You are all right, then. Nothing has happened to you?" Marius whispered, feeling slightly drugged. He didn't move. Jillian's scent was everywhere, enveloping his senses. It made him feel giddy and unbalanced.

She popped suddenly out of the chair and whipped nervously around. Her eyes were enormous. Her chest heaved. She stood stiffly, not quite meeting his eyes. "I'm fine." She pulled at her bloodstained dress. "All his. Listen, I don't know what happened, but I swear I had nothing to do with it. I just found him like that."

Marius raised a palm. "I believe you."

"Congratulations!" she blurted. Then, ducking her head, she hurried toward him and took his outstretched hand in hers, staring straight into his chest. "Congratulations, Marius. You really did it. You're married." Their fingers entwined, then Marius drew his hand back as though he touched flame. Jillian's fingers slowly curled inwards, into a fist, and she dropped her hand, and her shoulders drooped slightly. "Okay, so much for pleasantries."

"You found the body," Marius said, working hard to affect nonchalance in her presence.

"Yes," she whispered. "I walked up here looking for . . . a place to be alone for a second, and I saw the blood and followed it. He—he was there, just the way you see him. Apart from the towel. I took his pulse, that's all." She looked miserably at her feet.

"Has anyone else been here?"

"No," she replied.

"Did you take pictures of the body with that camera?" Marius asked.

"Yes. I took the same pictures the police would."

"May I have the camera, please?"

"No."

"I must have the camera," Marius demanded. "No one else can see this. On the night of my wedding, this murder . . . ? It would look very bad for our House. St. Giles would have a field day. I need to keep it from the public eye until I know what's going on. If this is some sort of plot . . ."

Jillian's face slowly tipped upward. She looked into his

eyes, finally, her beauty nearly slaying him, and the cloudy nervous haze seemed to clear. As if she'd decided on something. Her lips became a firm line.

"It's my camera. Your press office issued me a pass to cover your wedding. You'll just have to trust me with the photos. And since you're here now, I can go."

She turned away, but he grabbed her by the arm and saw a smear down the side of her neck. He yanked her closer before logic had time to set in. "Jillian," he breathed more than said. "Blood." Horror sparked through him.

"Let go!" She stumbled back, wrenching her arm away. "What's the matter with you? I'm sure it's his, not mine. When I took his pulse . . ." She shuddered and then licked her thumb and rubbed away the gore.

Marius forced himself to think straight. "I . . . need to ask you a few more questions before you go. Do you know who that man is?"

"I have no idea. I figured *you* would. There weren't many humans who bothered to show up here, were there?"

Marius cocked his head. "Humans?"

Jill gave him an odd look. "Yeah. Isn't he human? I didn't notice any fangs. Is he a werewolf?"

Marius moved quickly back to the body. Carefully avoiding the blood on the ground, he bent down and studied the victim. "The scent is wrong. At first sight, I would have sworn it was a vampire I know from Giannini's jurisdiction—one Gregory Bell. But . . . this scent clearly reads human, not vampire."

Jill followed him reluctantly, leaning over his shoulder. Then, as if the truth dawned on her at the same time it struck him, they looked at each other in horror.

Marius yanked another bar towel from the cart and wrapped it around his hand. He removed the first from the dead man's face, and just over his shoulder Jill sucked in a quick breath. Marius then wiped blood off the corpse's front teeth. Instead of sharp, pointed vampire incisors, or normal human ones, what he saw were misshapen ivory stubs.

He looked up at Jillian. "My god, this *is* Gregory Bell."

Jillian went pale. "He's not a vampire anymore. What could do something like this? The man obviously died in agony. If the demon portal weren't locked down again, I'd guess it was dark magic."

"No," Marius said, "I sense none of that here. Which leaves . . . dark science?"

It took him a moment to process what that even meant. Dark science? What could affect the biology that made Gregory Bell a vampire? Those incisors had collapsed into themselves!

Jillian caught his eye. "Is this some sort of . . . contagion?" she asked. "A kind of disease, the beginning of a—?"

He did not wait for her to utter the word "plague." He leapt up from the body and moved quickly to the bar. Wrenching an antique tapestry off the wall, he revealed a comms panel labeled EMERGENCY and a doorway marked with the same word.

Marius entered a code into the panel, lifting the comms receiver. "Please find Ian or Warrick and patch them in," he commanded. "This is an emergency."

"Yes, Mr. Dumont," said a voice on the other end.

"And initiate our contamination protocol, centering on the eighty-eighth floor. Wing out to the C-level coordinates."

"Yes, sir, Mr. Dumont," said the operator. "Here is Ian."

As Marius explained to his brother what was going on, he watched Jillian surveying the room like a police inspector at a crime scene. She'd recovered from her initial shock, and her press training was kicking in. She no longer looked squeamish at all. He couldn't help but admire her resilience.

"I'll get Fleur into quarantine immediately, just to be safe," Ian was saying on the other end of the red line. His voice was grim. "And the mechs at Lab West—you're going to have to go to them. You know the protocol we set up with them; they have the best tech around. Keep yourself out of contact with anyone, and . . . Well, when you get a clean bill of health from them, for god's sake let us know."

"As soon as I know," Marius repeated.

"And be sure to—"

His brother's voice was cut off as Jillian blurted, "God, I hope Hayden didn't have anything to do with this."

Ian's tone was cold. "Who's with you?"

"Give me a second." Marius covered the phone, and he stared at Jillian. "You think *Hayden*—"

"No! I mean, I don't know. . . . He was up here. Listen, you know how he is. A lot of talk."

"I know him well enough to give him credit for the fact that he's *not* just talk," Marius snapped. "And you think he had something to do with this?"

Jillian shook her head. "No. Not exactly. All I'm saying is, he was around."

Marius uncovered the comms receiver, which was humming with the sound of Ian trying to get his attention. "We should keep an eye on the possibility that Hayden Wilks might somehow be involved."

Ian released a harsh breath on the other end of the line. "Who was that? Who else knows about this?"

Marius sighed. "Jillian. She found the body."

"You might have mentioned that detail up front," Ian said, sounding rather testy. "I don't have to ask you to keep her quiet, but I do have to remind you that we just allied ourselves with a high-profile werewolf house, and that Jillian Cooper has the potential to be a major embarrassment if you don't keep your head on straight."

"It was coincidence, Ian," Marius promised. "So let's focus on making sure we don't have a bigger problem. If you could see what has become of Gregory Bell's fangs, you wouldn't waste a second worrying about Jillian being here."

"Sorry, brother," Ian allowed. "Of course. Just make sure to stay safe."

Marius hung up, and turned back to find Jillian on her knees. Bell's blood was now more than just a smear on her arms and clothes. She'd replaced the cloth on the dead vampire's face and was staring through the library door as the contamination protocol went into effect. Metal plates scraped against each other as barriers moved into place. The elevator whirred as it sent all cars to the ground floor. A startling suction sounded as the floor's center staircase was plugged from above and below.

"What now?" Jill asked.

Marius knelt down next to her, alongside Gregory Bell's rigid body. "I need to make sure you understand. Nobody else can know about this, about any part of this night. We can't afford the panic, and we can't afford the political instability. We could damage everything my marriage is meant to—"

"I get it," Jill interrupted. "But what now?"

"Now we go find some answers."

Jillian regarded him through narrowed eyes. "Define we. My part in all this ends here, right? You reminded me not to tell, I said I wouldn't and that's that. I'm out of here." She rose, stepped over Bell, grabbed her camera and purse and headed for the door.

He would have loved to let her go. The more distance

between them, the better. He would have been thrilled to let her walk out the doors of Dumont Towers without looking back, but that was impossible.

"Stop!"

She froze.

"There's no exit that way. I'm sorry."

Very slowly, Jillian turned. "You're kidding me, right? You're telling me I can't leave?"

"I can't allow it. I'm sorry. It's for the greater good of—"

"Yeah, yeah," she snarled, her eyebrow arched and a cynical sneer twisting her lips. "The greater good. *Again.*"

By way of an answer, Marius just inclined his head.

Jillian's expression softened a bit. She studied his face, looking almost dazed. "I think I really believed that there would be a last-minute reprieve, that one of you would step forward and call it off, that she'd hand her bouquet to me. Those flowers looked like the ones—"

"It was coincidence," Marius said. "I'm so sorry."

Jill nodded.

"Look, I know that the last place you want to be right now is with me, but you must stick with this a little longer. We've been exposed to something foreign, as you yourself pointed out. We know very little about what Bell contracted, other than that it is deadly to vampires and that it can physiologically change a vampire back into a human. Whatever it is and whoever's behind it, this is a nightmare waiting to happen. I've got to get this body to the contamination suite, and both of us must be tested."

Jillian blinked rapidly. "I really—"

"Help me roll him up in the carpet."

"What?"

"We're taking the body out of here. Would you please help me roll him up in the carpet?"

"I am really hating you right now," Jill muttered as she took a place next to him on the floor.

Marius positioned himself carefully on one knee, and together they managed to twist Bell up in the Persian rug upon which he lay, hoist it onto Marius's shoulder and balance the weight. Jill put her hand out for support, and Marius stood and walked carefully to the special exit near the emergency comms.

"Do—do you think this has something to do with Total Recall?" Jillian asked, her voice hesitant. She helped him steer the carpet through the doorway.

Marius glanced at her in surprise. Total Recall? Had he miscalculated the human government's reaction to his marriage? Were they really so stupid? It would explain why there were so few humans present, if the human government had begun such an initiative. But Ian and Warrick would have had warning. Had they wanted not to spoil his wedding?

"Bridget just warned me," Jill said. "The timing doesn't leave much to the imagination. Still, someone else could be using this as a convenient shield. Dominick St. Giles and his vampires seemed . . . ambivalent about the idea of your alliance three weeks ago. I was surprised they even showed up. And there are still plenty of werewolves out there who hate you guys more than anything."

Swearing under his breath, Marius gestured for Jill to hit the exit button. The door to the library closed behind them, triggering another churning sound as they were locked into a stone room leading downward through a tunnel that periodically veered left or right at odd angles. Eventually, the tunnel led to a plain white door. Marius leaned against the wall to take some of the weight off his shoulders and punched a code into an exit panel. The door unlocked with a whooshing sound and a change in air pressure. On the other side was a vehicle.

The car was devoid of any Dumont insignia. Jill walked around it. She opened the trunk and helped maneuver Bell into position. Marius then took the driver's seat. Jill spent an angry moment muttering to herself outside before she joined him. As she did, a plastic pod enveloped the entire vehicle.

"Pretend you're on an amusement-park ride," Marius suggested, pushing a button that raised up a pair of cushioned restraints inside the car. "It's designed to drop us straight down to the human level, car and all, and it moves pretty fast."

Jill shrugged and stared with fascination at the cloudy plastic shell. "So this keeps contaminants inside," she guessed. "And the next time it opens, we'll be far away from the vampire world—or at least its population center. I bet biosystems are cleaning everyplace we've been."

"That's the idea," Marius agreed.

He disengaged the brake, and the pod went into free fall. Jill's hands plunged to the armrests. Her fingers clawed at the foam. Marius sucked in a quick breath. A moment later a harder jolt sent them both crashing forward against their body restraints. The pod settled, and right after that it split open. Marius drove the vehicle out into the city streets.

At the first stop, Jillian surprised him—she opened the car door suddenly and stepped out. Grabbing her camera and purse off the seat, she bent down to look at him through the open door.

Marius shook his head. "Get in the car, Jillian. You can't just walk off and infect the city with some mystery bug."

She looked miserable. "I feel fine." Glancing over her shoulder into the night air, she shifted her weight from one foot to the other. "Besides, Hayden's going to wonder, if I don't come back." The way she said his name was pointed.

Marius suppressed the urge to comment that Hayden was unlikely to worry about anybody but himself. "Get in the car, Jillian. I know you just want to get away from me, I understand what you must be feeling, but—"

"You understand zero, Marius. Don't *even*." But she didn't turn and walk away, just clutched her belongings against her chest like a breastplate.

"Please get in the car," he said. "Please?"

Jillian turned her head. He thought she must be blinking back tears, but when she got back in the car and he next caught a glimpse of her face, it was completely dry.

# CHAPTER NINE

In her beautiful lacy white nightdress, Tatiana lay on the bed in her silent room and felt the edges of her heart harden as the seconds drained out of her wedding night. There was no danger. Her werewolf senses were every bit as attuned to such things as Marius's vampire ones. If there were truly any imminent peril in the Towers, she would have sensed it.

Actually, she did. But the danger of which Marius spoke, Tatiana knew by a woman's name. It was not "done." It was not "past." And her husband had lied when he told her that the rumors of this other woman amounted to nothing.

He'd *lied*. She'd accepted this marriage because she believed that at the very least they could be honest with each other. The House of Dumont had revealed up front the uncomfortable gossip about the human girl. House Royale had explained the uncomfortable facts about their requirements for being excused from all matters of state during the full moon, when Tatiana would be going through the Change. All things had seemed fair and equal. But, no.

He was out of his mind to go to Jillian Cooper on his wedding night! If he came back smelling like her, Tatiana would . . . She would . . .

She blinked back tears. *If he insists, I will do whatever I must, of course. This alliance extends the power of Asprey werewolf royalty across the entire nation, and I will not be the cause of failure in this regard.* She would not disgrace her family or her bloodline.

A thump sounded from the hall. Tatiana didn't move. She lay paralyzed in bed with her eyes wide. But when the floorboards outside her door groaned, she sat up, her heart racing.

"Marius!" she blurted in a whisper.

He either didn't hear or didn't bother acknowledging. Or perhaps it wasn't Marius. Tatiana lay down again and pulled the covers close, suddenly feeling colder than ever before. She clutched at the rings hanging from the chain around her neck, wishing with all her might that she were home with her family when she and her sisters were all still young and had never heard of the House of Dumont.

# CHAPTER TEN

"Oh, my goodness, what a gray June it is," Charlotte Paxton remarked, rushing into the shop and closing the door firmly behind her. "Did my other gloves pop up anywhere? These are too thin for such a chill." She stuck her basket of embellishments on the table and looked under a stack of fabric for a warmer pair.

"I'm afraid they haven't turned up yet," Maggie answered, looking away from the careful row of stitches she was embroidering into a hem. She leaned her head over and poked around in the contents of the basket, her mop of curly hair falling into her eyes. "That silver thread is lovely. It will be perfect. Thank you for fetching that."

"Where *are* my other gloves? I shall be late!"

Maggie cut a length of ribbon with small bird-shaped scissors and wrinkled her brow. "Charlie . . ."

"Hmm?"

Her sister stared fixedly down at her work. "Jenny at the milliner's shop told me that the girls are talking about how often you and Edward Vaughan have been seen at the exhibition together."

"You know Cousin Joseph waived the three guineas

necessary for procuring a season ticket. I may go whenever I choose, at no cost to either of us!"

"I'm not talking about the exhibition fee. It is Mr. Vaughan. It's beginning to seem odd to people. So many times . . . You said you were going over there this afternoon," Maggie pointed out. "Perhaps you should rethink your plans."

Charlotte could not hide the hot flush that covered her face. "I want to have a closer look at those remarkable elm trees they built the palace around."

"You *know* you will see him," Maggie said. "You always see him." She pushed her sewing aside. "He is a gentleman. You are in trade. You forget yourself. It's been a month of this. Do you not think he would have said something if he had anything to say? I wish you would stop going. If it were just to see the exhibits—"

"You know how much I love the exhibits!"

"Yes, but it is not just to see them, is it? You put yourself in his path, Charlotte. And he puts himself in yours."

"He explains the mechanical inventions to me, and I explain the flora and fauna, and it is quite—"

"You must stop this! If you and Mr. Vaughan do not have an understanding, you must stop! You are only hurting yourself."

The sharpness of her sister's tone caused Charlotte to wince. Maggie gently took her hand and pulled her around. "I must speak plainly. We are in debt. If I thought for one moment that a wealthy gentleman like Edward Vaughan would marry you, I wouldn't say a thing; I could not afford to. And you know how much I want you to be happy. So when I ask you to stop seeing him, you must believe that it is for a good reason. People say—"

"People say this, people say that." Charlotte waved her

hand in the air as if to disperse all ill feeling. "People will always talk."

"People will always say something when there is the appearance of wrongdoing."

Charlotte scoffed. "Mr. Vaughan is an acquaintance who shares a fondness for the event. I've done nothing wrong! Nor has he. I visit the exhibition weekly to look at the things that intrigue me. He does the same. We discuss what we have seen. It passes the afternoon, and we part. It is all quite innocent, I assure you," Charlotte added too cheerfully, the red spots burning in her cheeks speaking more honestly than her tongue.

"I do not believe it is so innocent," Maggie said. "Not on his end. He might trick you and make you think he means one thing, when he means something else entirely. For him to—"

Charlotte cut her off. "What on earth are you talking about?"

"Why does a man want to be in a woman's company so very often if he will not make her his wife?"

Charlotte flinched. She pulled away from her sister, retrieved her exhibition program and flounced toward the door. "I'm late."

"Stop!" Maggie cried. "Charlie, I must beg you to stop. I don't want you to see him anymore. I am afraid for you, afraid that he will compromise you in some way. Who will have you if your reputation is in ruins? You have no fortune, and no family other than me, save for a single connection who has done as much as he is going to do." She leapt up from her chair, sending the ribbons on her lap cascading to the floor, and clutched at Charlotte's arm. "Don't let him touch you. If he has nothing to promise, you mustn't let him touch you. Don't let what happened to me happen to you!"

Maggie never spoke of her own disappointments in life. Ashamed that she'd forced her sister to bring up such painful memories, Charlotte said, "I promise, Maggs. He wouldn't try, and I certainly wouldn't let him succeed."

Her sister took a deep breath and then nodded.

Charlotte grabbed the ribbons off the floor and playfully looped one under Maggie's chin, where she tied a beautiful bow. "Let neither of us be angry," she proposed.

Her sibling managed a smile. "I'm not angry. I just worry." She paused, and then with a sigh added, "I fixed the hole on the sleeve of your green coat. It looks quite smart again."

Charlotte exchanged her brown jacket for the moss green one, looking down at her sister's handiwork. "What a lovely job! When I return, I'll see what I can do with the finances for the coming week." Then she settled for her old gloves, affixed her bonnet and gave Maggie a wave.

"It's a bad business," Maggie muttered too loudly, addressing the clump of ribbons in her lap as her sister opened the door and slipped out. "A bad business, indeed."

Charlotte hurried toward Hyde Park, holding her collar closer against her throat to ward off the unseasonable chill. A fog had draped low over the city and would not seem to let go, but the weather was all but forgotten as the Crystal Palace came into view. Cousin Joseph had indeed taken inspiration from the *Victoria regia* lily pad, and his massive glass and iron structure, which now housed Prince Albert's Great Exhibition, never failed to give Charlotte a thrill when she approached.

The day's rendezvous spot was the West Indies nave. She knew this because on that day in May when the exhibition first opened its doors to the public, Edward

Vaughan had approached her from across the room. Their first meeting in Chatsworth had felt like yesterday, and they'd toured a small number of exhibits in deep conversation.

"I was thinking, Miss Paxton," Edward had remarked, "that one way to tackle such a large exhibition might be to make a habit out of looking at one small thing each week, always at the same time. One might simply follow the order suggested by the program." He'd looked straight at her. "What do you think about that?"

"I think it's a fine idea," she'd replied shyly, afraid to misunderstand his seeming implication: that he wanted to experience the whole of the exhibition with her. Every month, every week . . . He wanted to see her again!

As hard as Charlotte's heart had pounded in that moment, it did the same thing every week when she stood in the appointed nave and waited to see if Edward would come.

He did not disappoint. "Good afternoon, Miss Paxton."

Charlotte smiled as she turned. She bowed her head and curtseyed. "Good afternoon, Mr. Vaughan."

"May I join you?"

"That would be lovely."

They strolled down the center of the exhibition hall toward the West Indies exhibit, their noses buried in their programs. Edward remarked, "This one apparently has some rather fine living specimens."

"Oh, I'm glad! There are fewer animals at the exhibition than I expected, somehow," Charlotte admitted. "I'm not sure why I should be so surprised. It is, after all, an exhibition primarily dedicated to our empire's preeminence in industry."

Jammed in the back of the nave, rather like an afterthought, was a very tall cage. Charlotte moved to it. "This is rather odd," she said, peering into the darkness. "I don't think there's anything in here." She wrinkled her nose at the dank, sour smell and stepped back.

Edward Vaughan moved close. "Something living is in there." He glanced down at the description placard. "*Desmodus rotundus*. Vampire bat. From the West Indies, it says."

Charlotte turned to the cage with renewed interest. "Really?" Her heart fluttered. "Do you see them?"

Edward Vaughan squinted into the shadows. "No. But something's in there. . . ."

Charlotte went to wrap her gloved hand around one of the bars and mistakenly placed hers on Edward's. "I beg your pardon, Mr. Vaughan," she murmured, her heart pounding.

Shifting to another bar, she could feel his gaze upon the side of her face. It was all so overwhelming. All these people were making it so hot inside. Gripping the bars, she slowly looked up to meet Edward Vaughan's gaze, but the cacophony inside the exhibition, the smell, the way he was looking at her—it all made Charlotte feel rather faint. To have so many emotions, to have so many words you wanted to say, and to express none of it . . .

Edward Vaughan dropped one hand. The other gripped the cage with an intensity matched only by the look in his eyes.

Charlotte sucked in a breath, stepping quickly away. The movement knocked her head against the bars, and her hair ornament struck the metal with a loud ringing sound. This summoned terrifying shrieks, which echoed through the cage like a hundred hell-bound voices, and a flapping of wings.

Edward Vaughan's face went white. Charlotte screamed,

clutching at him in terror as a swarm of small, birdlike creatures swirled chaotically through the confines of the cage. Outside the bars, in the whole West Indies nave, ladies and gentlemen viewing the exhibition did the same, mimicking the panicked behavior of the animals.

The moment passed at last. The cage went silent, the terrified spectators slowed and all was still. In that moment, a tiny winged body dropped from the top of the cage, landing in the dirt and rock at the bottom. Charlotte stared at it in disgust.

"Oh, it's repulsive! Such a horrid little face!" she cried. The smell was too strong, and she felt a swell of nausea overtake her. She stumbled back from the cage. Edward took out his handkerchief and handed it to her, and Charlotte pressed it against her mouth.

*That's what you get for being too modern,* she told herself, suddenly unable to maintain her cool, collected facade under Edward's close gaze. She staggered a bit, quite undone.

"Come," he entreated. "Take my arm, Miss Paxton." He clearly felt none of her discomposure. Instead, he simply waved away a faint red-orange mist that was collecting in the exhibition hall, likely from some invention or another that was malfunctioning, took her arm and half-dragged her outside to the refreshment area.

"Mr. Vaughan, I mustn't—"

"Nonsense," he interrupted. "You are unwell. I'll find you a more suitable chaperon once you are settled."

"Really, I'm quite all right. I just think I should be getting back. I don't care for a lemonade just now."

"Edward, is that you?"

Charlotte drooped, but Edward took a deep breath and turned around. "Alastair," he said. "Excellent timing."

Charlotte wanted to collapse into herself. Lord Gilliam stood before them, escorting two other gentlemen of his set. He demanded, "What on earth are you doing with that poor, bedraggled girl?"

"I'm afraid the young lady has had a rather bad shock."

"Oh?"

Charlotte needed no acting skills to convince anyone of the revulsion that welled up inside of her regarding those awful little creatures. If these were what the outer reaches of the empire had to show for themselves, they could be kept to their foreign lands. No need to share such a thing, not as far as she was concerned.

The room began to swim again. She could make out the faces of tedious people peering at her again, as if she were the bat fallen to the bottom of the cage.

"My sister has our carriage, Alastair. May I ask the favor of borrowing yours?" Edward asked.

"Oh, no. That's much too much trouble," Charlotte spoke up, wanting only to get away from them all. But as she stepped back, Edward would not let her go. He procured the carriage and steered her toward the main exit.

Alas, their simultaneous departure did not go unnoticed, neither as they made their way across the exhibition floor nor as they waited for Gilliam's carriage to arrive. Edward managed the business quite well, with prodigious uses of "Joseph Paxton's cousin is quite ill" and "Lord Gilliam has commanded that the lady be escorted to his carriage." But Charlotte was horrified nonetheless.

"Won't people talk?" she asked fretfully, looking over her shoulder and nearly missing the step as she climbed into Gilliam's equipage.

"A duke's heir commanded it," Edward remarked dryly as they set off. He had given the correct direction to the coachman. "If someone of importance says something is not a scandal, it is not scandal. Very convenient, for those in his good graces."

They both went silent as they realized he'd said too much. The horses' hooves clip-clopped outside.

"You look flushed," Edward observed awkwardly.

"It is a bit warm," Charlotte agreed.

Edward swallowed hard and then he slipped his hand behind her neck. Charlotte took a startled breath as his fingers worked on the most confining buttons.

"Please don't," she whispered.

He paused for a moment. "You'll breathe easier," he promised, and unbuttoned a third clasp, then pulled the fabric so that it did not sit so tight against her throat.

Every time his bare skin touched hers, Charlotte's breathing hitched. Her reaction seemed to fuel his. Edward's eyes met hers as he dragged his index finger down the side of her jaw, down against her throat into the neck of her dress.

*Tell him to stop, Charlotte. You must tell him to stop! You promised Maggie you would not let him touch you— you know where this leads.* But Charlotte did not tell him to stop, instead indulging for a fraction of a moment longer.

At last she moved out of Edward's reach. "Do you think it is a scandal, talking to me at the exhibition?" she blurted.

Edward blinked, trying to collect himself. "A simple conversation between two acquaintances," he prevaricated.

"Once would be a simple conversation. Week after week . . . perhaps it is not so simple."

Edward didn't say anything. He didn't say *anything*! They both fell silent again, and the truth of the matter— that which Maggie had tried so desperately to explain—

was roaring loud in Charlotte's ear. He would never speak, because they could never be an acceptable match. He might enjoy her company, but he could never speak. Oh, Maggie had been right.

The carriage lurched to a stop in front of the draper's shop, and Charlotte fumbled with the door.

"Miss Paxton, do wait for the footman," Edward said in alarm. He reached over to stop her from leaping out without use of the footplate.

In a confused panic, Charlotte pulled at the handle. "I have to get out. I have to get out!"

"You must stop!" he argued.

Charlotte bent her head over into her lap, desperate to hold back her tears until she was inside with her sister. Glancing up, she could see Maggie at the window, peering curiously out at such a fine carriage in front of their establishment. Edward continued to hold the door closed until the footman came around and opened it.

"Please excuse me, Mr. Vaughan. I am not well," Charlotte hurried to say, placing her glove in the footman's hand and stepping out of the carriage. Then she rushed into the draper's shop and closed the door firmly behind her with her back.

She shut her eyes. When she opened them, Maggie stood there in the middle of the shop, the ribbons she'd been working with curled gaily round her feet.

"What's he doing?" Charlotte asked in spite of herself.

Maggie moved to the side of the window and peeked through. "He's pacing, saying something to the driver. . . . He's coming toward the shop! No, he's stopped, now. Oh. He doesn't seem to know what he wants. Now he's gone back to the carriage."

Charlotte squeezed her eyes shut again and waited until the fading sound of the horses' hooves told her the carriage had moved on. A sob welled up in her throat, and it was all she could do to make it across the room into her sister's arms. There, she burst into tears. "I don't know what I was thinking. Oh, Maggie, all this time, what have I been thinking?"

# CHAPTER ELEVEN

Jill stared forward through the windshield as Marius piloted their vehicle along a dark stretch running below the raised bustle of the 405 Freeway.

She sat stiffly in the passenger seat, her camera and purse in her lap, trying to take up as little space as possible so their bodies wouldn't touch. That Marius wasn't using a driver, that they were in a car devoid of Dumont markings, that they were alone on a dark road while lights and life swirled around them . . . everything made this silent voyage too intimate—too intimate for the relationship they were stuck with now, anyway. On Marius's wedding night, for god's sake.

She stole a glance at Marius's face. He still trusted her, even now. She could tell. Even after she'd essentially used Hayden Wilks to repeatedly slap him in the face. She could sleep with the enemy, take sides with the Rogues and accept gray-area jobs for any species with the cash, and he'd still trust her on the deepest, innermost level.

Well, what of it? Turnabout was fair play. He could keep her at arm's length and marry somebody else, and he'd still matter to her, no matter what she tried to do about it. And not just *matter*, either.

With a sigh, Jill clutched her camera with its memory card containing hundreds of pictures of Marius and Tatiana's wedding, and looked out the window. "Do you really think it's contagious?" she asked.

"We can't afford to assume it isn't. We definitely need to understand what killed Bell and whether we're likely to contract it or act as carriers." Marius frowned. "I hope Ian's convinced Dain and Fleur to get out of the Towers by now. Just in case there are others infected."

Jill gripped the armrest as he eased their vehicle down an almost vertical stretch of ramp, but she relaxed a little as it ended with a swoop onto a platform just below ground level. They were on her turf, now. Human turf. Strata 0.

"We'd probably know," she suggested, forcing an optimistic tone into her voice despite her completely unfounded statement. "If we were sick, I mean."

"I don't want you to be sick," Marius said, unconsciously curling one hand into a fist. "And it's unlikely. Bell was a natural-born vampire. You're not. There's no particular reason to believe a natural-born human would fall ill. Our physiologies are different. We drink blood, for god's sake—*your* blood. Or at least we were made to do that, even if most of us try to give that a pass."

"Haven't you ever heard of mad cow disease?" Jill joked. "Sometimes both sides of the food chain gotta worry."

Marius looked over at her, anguished, and they both looked awkwardly away.

"But this turns vampires into humans." Jill tried to recover from her failed attempt at humor. "Meaning that I agree it's not me likely to be at risk. It's you." She sighed and shook her head. "So, where are we going?"

"Dumont protocol for a biological emergency. We have an arrangement," Marius said. "We go directly to the best . . . and the best scientists these days aren't human, werewolf or vampire."

"The mechs?" Jill sat up straighter in her seat. "The best scientists? Aren't they all pretty much computers in a partially human shell? Cutting-edge science requires a degree of creativity, it seems to me. Not robots."

Marius managed a slight smile. "How many do you know?"

He turned the vehicle very suddenly, and Jill gasped as it seemed they'd drive straight into a brick wall. The optical illusion morphed into a narrow driveway, however, and Marius eased the car through a narrow passage and stopped in an alley she'd never seen. For a fraction of a second, red light flashed everywhere. Marius didn't move, letting the engine idle.

The rusty flip lid on the mail slot of a nearby door, one that appeared to have fallen into disuse, suddenly rose to reveal a camera mounted on the end of a remote-controlled tube. Marius looked into the lens, and a red laser skimmed the surface of his face. He spoke into the microphone.

"We may be contaminated," he said, calmly and clearly. "One vampire and one human, living. One vampire, dead."

"Voice recognition complete. Park in the isolation quadrant. Use door four," a voice squawked from the slot. "Follow the instructions listed on the wall, and use the supplied equipment. Leave the body in the unlocked vehicle. See you shortly, Mr. Dumont."

Marius eased the vehicle around a corner and into a brilliantly camouflaged parking area. There, he turned off the engine. He pressed a button, and the vehicle doors winged upward.

Jill looked around as she got out, but saw no one. She and Marius stepped away from the vehicle, and a glass slab lowered from the ceiling to meet four similar slabs rising up from the base of the parking unit, sealing in the car. Jill watched the car lower into the ground, and then she turned away, wrapping her arms around her chest against a chill.

Marius put his coat over her. She tried to reject it, but he clamped his hands down on her shoulders and kept the garment in place while he guided her through a winding alley alongside a building with at least ten numbered doors. With all the myriad knobs and hatches and levers, she would not have been able to identify which was door four, but Marius had clearly been here before.

Beyond the door, inside a hatch, the light was harsh and artificial. A set of biohazard suits and accessories were carefully lined up on hooks and shelves across from a wall of lockers. Marius helped Jill find a set that fit, then set about dressing himself over his tuxedo. They stood there, staring at each other through close-fit visors, until a distant buzzer sounded and the noise of a pressure lock's releasing accompanied the popped latch on the inner door.

"This is scaring me more than the corpse," Jill muttered, following Marius down a narrow stairwell that was nearly pitch-black.

He tried to take her hand to lend support, but she pulled her arm away. He said nothing as they reached the lower level and stopped at a door, and they both waited in silence once more.

A man stepped through. He held a small white toolbox in one hand and wore a protective metal mask over part of his face. No, Jill suddenly realized, the mask wasn't protection—the metal was actually part of the man's face. He was a mech.

He focused on her for a moment and then flicked his gaze back to Marius. "Mr. Dumont," he said. "What can we do for you?"

"Call me Marius, please, Leyton. And this is Jillian."

"Miss Cooper," the mech said, giving a formal nod.

Jill managed a smile even as she died a little inside. Everyone knew who she was, and she'd bet that was because of her relationship to Marius. Or rather, she'd bet it was because of the relationship everyone *supposed* she had with Marius. Jill would have given a lot to be a fly on the wall when Marius tried to explain the tabloids to Tatiana.

He was currently giving a different explanation: what they'd found at Dumont Towers. Jill watched Leyton's face as Marius talked. The mech showed little emotion. She wondered what he was feeling inside, and where his loyalties lay. She'd only met one mech before now, but she knew that most mechs who had escaped from their human creators and started the process of adapting to freedom in Crimson City tended to extremes: some turned their backs on all technology, some avoided interactions with other species. Almost all had trouble acclimating to their human feelings.

Leyton turned to Jill and caught her staring. "I'll take samples now." He opened his toolbox and took out a multineedle, a small partitioned disc with three small heads that would extract and compartmentalize biological specimens.

Jill wrinkled her nose as the mech unfastened a round patch on the shoulder of her suit, aligned the disc perfectly and pressed down hard. She sucked in a quick breath as the needles penetrated her skin.

"What are you working on here?" she asked to distract herself, speaking quickly to keep her voice from quavering. "I mean, in general. Not on me."

The mech's eyes flicked up to her, and she wondered if he was suspicious. "Primarily how to replace our mechanical apparatuses with real organic material, how to regenerate nerves and grow new organs. What you and Mr. Dumont might be carrying should be of great interest." With all the bedside manner of a rock, he retracted the multineedle, laid it carefully in a round bed in his toolbox and then jammed a cotton ball against her shoulder. He moved to Marius, removed a new multineedle and followed the same procedure.

Pressing the cotton ball against her arm and making a point not to watch what Leyton was doing, Jill cut to the chase. "How can you help?"

The mech looked up at her in surprise, removed the disc from Marius's arm and closed it in the toolbox. "We'll see. We're interested in anything that makes something not wholly human. Give me a little time with the body. I'll be back."

Jill tugged the accordion folds of the neck of her hazmat suit as he took the box and retreated. She was beginning to feel seriously claustrophobic. She concentrated on taking slow, deep breaths, trying to moderate her racing heartbeat. *Keep it together*, she told herself.

"This will all be over soon," Marius murmured.

His hand moved toward her as if to give comfort, but stopped. Jill looked away, and the double doors before them suddenly swung open. They would have knocked her clean unconscious if she'd been a little closer.

Leyton reappeared. He pressed the pads of his fingers against his temple. Part of his metal faceplate shifted upward, making chaos out of his hair and exposing a thin thread of silver wiring running across his scalp. "It's like having blinders sometimes," he muttered. He pulled a small tablet computer from his lab coat pocket and raised it in the air. "We've seen this bug before. Does the stiff have a name?"

Marius advanced. "Gregory Bell. He was born a vampire, but by the time we found his body, he'd changed to human form. You've seen *that* before?"

"Yeah, we've seen it. You're looking at a pathogen that

I have reason to believe could mutate in the future and eventually be transmitted through airborne or casual contact."

Marius's eyebrows arched. "Eventually. So, Dumont Towers is safe."

"Well, I'm not saying that exactly," Leyton said. "I mean, there are other ways for this to spread. But this current incarnation doesn't seem excessively contagious."

Marius exhaled slowly, his shoulders slumping. "Any thoughts on how Bell ended up with it?"

Leyton already looked deep in thought. "Gregory Bell," he said. "That name doesn't mean anything to me, but . . ." The mech suddenly cocked his head and stared blankly into space. Jill looked at Marius, but then she realized the mech was likely accessing a database. Leyton finally announced, "Gregory Bell is—make that *was*—a waterman. It seems the specimen collector has become the specimen."

"I'd enjoy both the slang and the irony of his end, if it weren't all so gross," Jill said. "Watermen pulled bodies from London's waterways in the Victorian age. They'd scavenge or sell them to anyone in the market for a corpse."

The mech looked at her in surprise.

"Victorian history in college. It was the longest semester of my life, but I'm great at cocktail parties . . . and autopsies, apparently."

"Okay, there's no Thames in Crimson City," Marius said. "Where are his bodies coming from? And who the hell has he been selling them to?"

Leyton frowned. "Let me make it clear that we don't live-harvest. And we don't buy murders. All right?" He glanced nervously at Marius and then with an air of resignation said, "We have need of human tissue before it has degraded." He cleared his throat, again shooting a glance at Marius. "It's used to regenerate flesh, nerves, bone, cells . . ."

The mech shook his head and rolled up the left sleeve of his lab coat, revealing a forearm that was all metal and wire. He rolled up the right sleeve next, revealing a normal, human-looking arm sporting tan skin delicately lined with a faint white grid of scars. "It gives my kind back what was taken from us. That's the focus of what we do here—what we research, what we work on." He added hastily, "We make a lot of adjunct discoveries and develop many technologies in the process, which is what you are here to take advantage of, but changing out mechanical parts for flesh and organs is essentially what we attempt. And the organic material we need doesn't come out of thin air. Someone's got to find this stuff and bring it in."

"Someone like Gregory Bell," Marius said. "So this lab did business with him."

"Actually, no," Leyton said quickly. "Our database just shows his name, vendor description and an NSC mark. Meaning no security clearance. He would not have been able to do business with us."

"Is it that he never tried, or he tried and you rejected his application?" Marius asked.

"We rejected his vendor application . . . but not a lot of research was done. There's no reason specified." The mech shrugged. "We might block someone for the smallest reason. Our assumption is that a vendor's materials are not pure enough to satisfy us until he proves otherwise. He never did so. Which means, you'll have to go to the Market if you want to know more about Bell's business."

"Market?" Marius repeated.

"The one where watermen like Bell . . . trade their wares."

"Corpses," Jill said.

Leyton frowned. "I was trying to be subtle. Working on my idioms. I didn't think I should say that." He shrugged.

"We'll need to go as soon as possible," Marius said.

The mech grabbed a notepad from a worktable and wrote down a set of coordinates alongside the opening and closing times, then handed it to Marius. Jill looked over his shoulder and memorized the numbers.

"Don't get there too early or too late," the mech warned. "Wear a bag over your head, if that's all you've got, but don't show your face or anything else that's going to give you away. Protocol is zero identity for everyone."

"Can you take us there?" Marius asked.

The mech shook his head. "I don't go."

"Why not?"

Leyton hesitated for a moment and then said, "It's really not my thing. Number one, it smells like hell. Number two, everyone has his place."

Marius narrowed his eyes. "What do you mean?"

"I do very specific things, and I do them very well. Re-animation of the body for those who were made mechs against their will—that's my business, and it requires a certain amount of delicacy." The mech looked pointedly at the vampire. "A slippery slope is right outside my door. I keep things as clear and clean as possible. I play fair. I don't mix with people who do things I don't want to know about. I do what I can to make sure that what comes in here is legitimate. For that reason, I don't get involved in situations where I'm not necessary." The mech fell silent as he stared Jill up and down.

"What?" she asked.

Leyton answered Marius instead. "I wouldn't take her there if I were you. She's got an excellent body, is in really good shape. There's a dearth of human female corpses in that condition. Someone might tag her."

Jill couldn't help but smile, macabre remark though it was.

"But all mechs are male," Marius said.

"The internal organs work just fine. They don't know the difference," the mech replied. "But that's not the issue. We're not the only ones in the market."

"Her body is off-limits, dead or alive. I'll keep it that way," Marius growled.

Under less ghoulish circumstances, Jill might have been thrilled by Marius's words of ownership over her body parts. "Um, guys. Could we stay relevant?" she said.

"Okay," Leyton agreed. "Your test results should be logged by now." He punched something into his tablet computer. "You're fine," he said bluntly.

Jill beamed, overcome with relief from a fear she'd been denying. "We're not infected."

The mech looked up. "I mean *you're* fine," he said. "You're totally out of the picture, actually. One hundred percent human. Thus, not going to get it. Not this strain." Then he looked at Marius. "You might be totally fucked." His brow wrinkled. "I think that's the right idiom. Anyway, the good news is that you're clean now. But your biologicals match Gregory Bell's initial stats, so you're definitely susceptible. That means you could present symptoms in the future if this bug figures out how to get around."

"Is there a cure?" Marius asked—rather calmly, Jill thought, given that they were talking about a potential vampire-killing plague.

"I don't know. We don't have one. We looked into it when we first came across the bug, but we didn't follow through."

"You found a vampire plague and didn't follow through?" Jill asked.

The mech leveled her with a stare. "Why should we? Anything that comes through these doors gets a full battery of tests. Meat like what we just pulled from your trunk has come through these doors twice before, presenting the same pathogens we found in Mr. Bell. But we don't use anything that's not one hundred percent human, even at the testing level, because we can't trust our physiology not to reject it. Thus, the only reason to spend time and resources on something like this would be if we want to cure a plague that has nothing to do with us—or to give us the ability to infect and cure other species for political purposes." He looked at Marius. "We're not so concerned with world domination. We'd just like everybody to leave us the hell alone."

"Do you have any sense of how hard it would be to find a cure?" Marius asked.

The mech studied him for a moment and then shifted his gaze to Jill. Finally, he picked up his tablet and set off at a brisk pace. "Follow me."

In her heavy, awkward suit, Jill struggled to keep up with the two men as they wound through a maze of corridors and finally through a set of metal swinging doors. It was quite chilly at their destination, what with its floor-to-ceiling wall of refrigerators labeled with the names of organs and body parts. Jars were filled with odd bits of tissue, and prosthetic limbs were carefully stacked on wide tables.

The place was already quiet, most mechs not being natural talkers, but an even heavier silence fell across the occupants as Marius and Jill were led through the massive laboratory.

"We'd have to go deeper into the biology of this disease to know if it's something we can fix, but I can tell you a few things," Leyton said, his voice soft but nonetheless echoing through the room. The mech stepped aside, revealing a long operating table upon which was laid Bell's corpse.

Jill gasped at the sight of what remained of the erstwhile vampire. Her memory of discovering his corpse was almost cartoonish: the vast amounts of blood, the horrible expression. She'd reported on murders and other deaths for her work many times, but somehow, seeing this body splayed open and plugged into a network of tubes, the enormous machines crunching numbers and spitting out glowing streams of information across multiple screens, it all created a horror transcending mere fear of the grotesque. Her dread was of what all this portended.

Leyton stood by Bell's mutilated head and began to describe the underlying science of the vampire's death. He did it as if he were giving a museum tour. "This virus seems to unpack itself in the body over an extended period of time, something like a downloaded executable file. It's a genetic aggressor attacking species-specific DNA." He looked at Jill. "Which is why, as a human, you don't have to worry. This baby seems to regard human genetics as holy, instead seeking out any mutations to that form. Whenever it finds the cells it is looking for, it attacks. As it succeeds, it begins the process of mutating its conquests back. The process works . . . but apparently kills the host." Leyton paused and wrinkled his brow. "So, I guess in *that* sense, it doesn't really work."

Jill swayed, light-headed and sweaty. The sight of the dissected vampire slowly disintegrating on the table was just too much. What if Marius caught this horrible disease? What if *he* were the body falling to pieces on a slab of metal in this sterile lab? She backed away from the table and leaned against the lab wall. *Breathe. Take deep breaths.*

"Where do you think this came from?" Marius asked. "I've never heard of such a thing."

The mech looked up, a defiant glint in his eyes. "Who do you think I'm going to blame? The human government, of course." He clearly struggled with emotion for a moment before pulling himself together. "But I have no evidence, and therefore the appropriate answer is, I don't know."

Marius put his hand on the mech's shoulder. "I need you to find a cure for this, Leyton. It's important."

The mech's eyes were blank. "Not to us. Relatively speaking, of course."

It's important to *me*, Jill thought, feeling as if the walls were beginning to close in. She had never really contemplated Marius's dying. He had always seemed invincible. Biting back a sob, she put a steadying hand out to the wall and looked away.

"I'd like you to *make* it important to you," Marius replied.

Leyton cocked his head. "Make me an offer, Mr. Dumont. And no offense, but don't tell me you'll be friends for life. We're not interested in political alliances. We're only part of your contamination protocol as a courtesy."

Marius smiled and interrupted. "I'm sure you're part of our contamination protocol because you worry about contamination. Today, it's vampire flesh that's in jeopardy. What happens when it's your turn—something that dissolves metal, something that eats human flesh?"

Jill tried not to heave. Her fear and disgust were triggers; she felt herself shift into a kind of automatic pilot. At the same time, her mind reached silently out to Marius, as it had done so many times before.

*Stop, Jill. Stop!* she told herself. *You can't go there anymore.*

The mech blinked. "Our primary concern here is the human body manipulated in conjunction with mech upgrades. We don't put our resources into werewolf or vampire matters. We can't. I'm sure you understand."

"Money is no object," Marius pointed out. "That goes without saying."

Leyton brightened. "No. It doesn't, actually. That's good to know."

*For god's sake, just make a deal.* Jill retreated to the far wall and leaned against the cool metal.

"We'll foot the entire bill, Leyton, and then double that price. That should pay for a great deal of whatever work you want to do on your own. Put your best men on this bug now, and when you find the answer, you'll never have to wonder how you're going to keep funding this place." Marius held out his hand.

Leyton looked down at the thick contamination glove, then gave him his palm. "It's a deal. A pleasure doing business, Mr. Dumont."

Business. But what could the mechs really do against this sort of bug? And were they trustworthy? Was anyone in this godforsaken city? The scene began to fade from Jill's sight. Everything was going black. She told herself not to pass out, but her heart beat faster. Panic began to overtake her, and a sob slipped from her throat.

On the other side of the room, Marius had his back to her while he shook Leyton's hand. His head lifted very suddenly. Jill could feel him linked to her, and she watched his hand move to his chest. He slowly turned and caught her eye. She lost track of time. She lost inhibition. She made no pretense of not caring, of disinterest, of being okay. Her eyes welled up and a tear slipped down her cheek. Marius pressed his palm against his heart, took a deep breath . . . and calmed her. It was as if he'd literally given her oxygen. Jill stared in shock as her blood pressure eased and her panic faded.

"I think we've seen enough," Marius said to the mech.

Leyton ushered them back through the labyrinthine corridors into the room they'd first entered. Marius turned to the mech, who unlocked the main door. "I understand that this doesn't make me your friend," he said, "but it makes you mine."

A look of surprise, then wonder, blossomed on Leyton's face as he processed that statement. Finally, the young mech nodded and raised a metal hand to his temple in a parting salute. "Perhaps you mean what you say, Mr. Dumont." After a pause he added, "There are clean clothes in the lockers. Please take what you need." He vanished back from whence he'd come.

Alone in the empty room, Jill felt Marius watching as they stripped off their suits, stuffed them in marked bins and waited in silence for the light above the main door to turn green. There was a whoosh of air as the door unsealed and the light changed, and it masked Jill's own sigh of relief.

Jill's brown dress camouflaged bloodstains well enough, but Marius looked something of a mess. He'd lost his boutonniere and tie, and the front of his tuxedo shirt was soaked with so much blood that only the wing-tip collar still showed white. In silence, Jill grabbed a shirt from the lockers, ripped away the wrapping and tossed it to him.

He wiped off the blood, scrubbed at his skin with antibac wipes, changed into the shirt, and they exited the lab into the dark alley. Their vehicle was there, and it was spotless.

Jill stopped suddenly at the back of the vehicle as she made her way around it, and she impulsively popped the trunk, half-expecting to see the carpet in which they had brought Bell's corpse likewise pristine, without a trace of blood. But some things you can't make disappear, she thought, closing the trunk and joining Marius inside the car.

The drive back from the lab again nearly drowned them in weighted silence. At last, Marius drew the vehicle to a stop. He rested his wrists on the steering wheel as the engine idled and looked at Jill. "I shouldn't let you leave with those pictures," he said softly. "Anything you've got of Gregory Bell is dangerous to the House of Dumont. We can't run the risk of looking weak or unprepared. If this virus was manufactured, that might even be the creator's intent."

"I'm not leaving without my camera," Jill vowed, staring forward. "I've got to file my story on the wedding. It's a lot of money and it's a legit story." She turned and stared at him, managing a half smile. "Some of us need to pay our bills."

Marius hesitated, but a moment later met her smile with one of his own. He reached into the backseat and produced Jill's camera. Handing it over, he said, "I will trust you. I've seen your press credentials, after all. Just make sure I get everything related to Bell—and be sure to wipe the card when you're done."

Jill took the camera, pulled her purse from the floor of the car and got out. She slammed the door but didn't let go of the handle. *Just walk away and let him figure out the rest of this mess on his own*, she told herself. *It's a problem for the House of Dumont. It doesn't have to have anything to do with you.* But who was she kidding? A vampire plague existed that could kill Marius just as it had Gregory Bell. She wasn't walking away. Marius didn't have it now, but that didn't mean he wouldn't, and she could never live with herself if she did nothing and that happened.

Silently cursing, Jill knocked on the passenger-side window. Marius lowered the glass and leaned out.

Jill rested one hand on the roof of the car and crouched down. "I'll see you at the Market, Monday morning at ten thirty," she said, keeping her voice even. "The northwest corner, near the entrance. I saw the address." Then, turning on her heel, she headed to her apartment.

Marius called her name, undoubtedly intending to talk her out of future involvement, but Jill didn't look back. Well, there it was. She didn't have any weird bug in her system, and she wasn't going to die. Just as the mech said, she was going to be *fine*. Even if it still felt as though Marius himself was the very breath that allowed her to exist.

# CHAPTER TWELVE

Camera and purse clutched against her chest, shoulder aching from the mech's multineedle, head spinning over the possibility of a virus set upon the city, Jill found her relief at being home even shorter-lived than she'd hoped. As soon as she shut her apartment door, the light flipped on. Hayden stood in the bedroom doorway, wearing only a pair of boxer briefs, his hair disheveled and one thick lock falling over one eye. A giant purple mass of swollen flesh obscured the other.

"Where the hell have you been?" he asked.

Jill stared at his battered face. "I thought you said you weren't going to do anything crazy."

A slow grin blossomed. "What's your definition? There's still time."

Jill went cold, remembering again her early fears about Hayden's involvement. "What were you doing up there?" she said in a near whisper.

He stared at her. "What? Where?"

"At Dumont Towers. Before I saw you . . ." She moistened her lips, afraid to ask. "Did you do something you didn't tell me?"

His eyes searched her face. "Nice of you to show so much concern for my well-being. Yes, I'm fine. No, it doesn't hurt much anymore. Thanks for asking," he joked.

"I *am* glad you're all right," Jill said. She shifted her gaze to Hayden's hands, searching his skin with a practiced eye and trying to match his injuries to any he might have suffered while subduing an opponent. Maybe Bell? But he would have had to infect Bell long before tonight. Of course, this was Hayden, and Hayden was just the type of guy who might pick a fight with a man he'd already saddled with a death sentence.

*Please don't let Hayden have anything to do with this awful disease,* Jill thought. *He's running out of chances.*

"Jill." He drawled her name. "I'm not loving the way you're looking at me. Don't you trust me? What exactly is it that you think I've done?"

"I'm tired," she whispered, heading for the bedroom. *I'm tired, and Marius will never be mine, and I don't want to argue tonight.*

Hayden blocked the door.

"Not funny," Jill said.

"I wasn't trying to make you laugh," came his reply. "You said we were a dangerous mess. You said it as if you thought I wouldn't care. You used to trust me. You used to have my back. Remember all you told me? It was us against them. Tell me you still trust me. That's all I want to hear."

Jill couldn't prop Hayden up, and she didn't want his brand of support. Not anymore. She tried to walk past him. He continued to block her path.

"Tell me you trust me. It's easy."

Her lips trembled so hard that she had to bite down on them. "I've been holding everything in. Just holding it in and holding it in. Can you cut me some slack tonight? Please?"

"Tell me . . . tell me you love me."

She stared at Hayden in shock. "I thought we had an understanding. Love was never . . ." The hurt in his eyes was hard to look at. So hard. She understood, but she couldn't tolerate it anymore. He didn't want her, he wanted *someone*. And they both needed to face facts.

"I need someone—"

"That's right. You just need *someone*. You don't need me."

"Jill?" Hayden said, his voice small. "It's us against them."

*I make him feel it's justified to want the Dumonts to come to harm. I don't want them to come to harm. I never did. I just wanted someone to share my pain.* "I can't do this anymore," she whispered. "This relationship. I'm sorry. I'm not the same person as when we met." *Not at all.*

"What's that supposed to mean?" Hayden snapped.

"I don't want to hurt you," Jill explained, reaching forward.

He stepped out of reach. Jill watched as coldness seemed to sweep over him. He knew she was no longer on his side, that he couldn't trust her, and he was shutting her out, shutting down like a machine.

"You *women* . . . You always leave me." He tipped his head back and stared up at the ceiling, shaking his head. "Marius doesn't want you. He doesn't love you. He just married someone else. Didn't you notice?" He looked her straight in the eye. "You'll *never* have him," he reminded her. "You're such an idiot. Don't you get it? He married someone else!"

"I know," she replied.

They studied each other in silence. "You never loved me," Hayden finally whispered.

"Oh, Hayden, you never loved me either. It's over. For both our sakes. It's *over*. All of it. You were with me to get back at the Dumonts because Fleur turned you vampire. I was with you to make Marius jealous. But that's finished now. We're all moving on. You need to move on."

Hayden struck his chest with his fist, knocking out a sound more like a sob than a breath. "If you really love, there's no moving on. Believe me, the pain only gets worse." He struck again. "It never goes away. It's his fault. Marius. All the Dumonts ever do is cause other people pain. They deserve to pay!"

The look in his eyes scared Jill. She clutched her camera bag, holding it against her body like a shield. "You *did* do something crazy, didn't you? Did you kill that man?" she blurted. She backed toward the front door.

Hayden's jaw clenched. "'Did you kill that man,'" he mocked. "What man? What exactly do you think I've done?" His voice was clogged with emotion. "You wouldn't have stayed with me this long if you really thought I was that bad, would you?"

Would she? "I know. I'm sorry. I—"

"Yeah, I can be a real bastard. I own that." He bared his fangs. "And I'm not sorry for making sure the Dumonts will never forget the evil they've done. Some people have a real hard time remembering the past. Some people just don't want to. But I've never killed anyone who didn't deserve it. I doubt *that* family could say the same."

"I'm not saying you're bad, Hay. You've done some good things, too. I know that. And I do remember. I remember how you put your life on the line for Tajo Maddox and Tatiana's sister Gia, as a matter of fact. It wasn't that long ago. It's just that sometimes . . . sometimes your need for revenge just takes over. It's as if the darkness will see no light."

The very darkness she meant seemed to pool in Hayden's eyes. "That's all you got? That's what you think of me?" he asked with a sneer. "I left that stupid wedding and went to a bar in Dogtown, Jill. Someone said shit about you and Marius, so I took him into the street for a little dance. We threw down, worked things out. Then I came home and waited for you." He shook his head sadly. "The only dead man I know tonight is me. And that's old news."

Jill opened her mouth to apologize once more, but Hayden raised his palm, warding off all words. He took a step backward, moving under the ray of moonlight coming through the window. Jill saw the damage done to his beautiful skin—some old, some new. The cuts and bruises were from fighting to protect her. "Hayden!" she cried, suddenly afraid he'd try to hurt himself.

"I'm not your problem anymore," he said, then gave a desperate-sounding laugh. "I'm not a 'dangerous mess,' Jill. I'm just a vampire who never wanted to be one. Too bad we can't trade places, you and I. Do me a favor and be gone tomorrow while I get my stuff. I'll move back to the Rogues Club."

"We're still going to see each other." She put her hand on his arm. "Let's not do this badly."

He pulled away, moving abruptly from the light. Hastily drawing on the clothes he'd scattered across the floor, he slung his battered figure into his leather jacket and slammed the door as he left. Hating herself for feeling as much relief as remorse, Jill tossed herself into the chair by the window, pulled a blanket around her and fell asleep staring at the lights of Dumont Towers.

# CHAPTER THIRTEEN

Marius waited in the car until he saw Jillian safely enter her apartment building, then slowly eased back into the driver's seat and looked into the rearview mirror. There were quite a few people in the street, walking alone or stopped in groups of two or three. He imagined many of them were walking home from nuptial festivities, and was surprised by the dark mood.

The night of such a momentous occasion should have felt different, and it hit Marius rather hard that no sense of hope or joy from his marriage had impacted the general populace. He'd hoped it would. His interspecies alliance was supposed to put them all on the path to peace. Instead, he sensed an increase of fear. And if what he'd heard was true, the human government had misinterpreted everything. Or perhaps St. Giles was right and the darker elements had just been waiting for an excuse, had taken advantage of his wedding as a justification to invoke Total Recall.

Though he couldn't see it, he felt in his soul the TR initiative clamping around the city like an iron fist. Ironically, this time around it would be worst for the humans— at least, for those who wanted to stay independent. The werewolves and vampires had more power than ever, and a lot more weapons. It wouldn't be the same as the first Recall, when even up on strata +1 you could smell the smoke from giant bonfires built in the intersections below, burning vampire and werewolf possessions by the truckload.

Marius rolled down the window and looked out. His instincts told him someone was watching the car. They'd probably latched on when Jillian got out. He should have dropped her off a couple of blocks back, but after what she'd been through tonight it seemed better to give her the full escort.

Something thumped hard against the side of his vehicle. The street had suddenly become much more crowded, and he presumed that as word of Total Recall silently spread, the humans who hadn't attended his wedding were coming outside, joining the revelers, taking stock of things and trying to calculate what the human government's intent would be. The crowd was a river around him.

Marius raised the window and pushed the ignition, but before he could pull away from the curb, his back tires collapsed and the rear of the vehicle hit the pavement. He accelerated slightly, avoiding pedestrians, but metal scraped hard against the ground. Not exactly a seamless getaway. And what exactly had popped his tires? He couldn't see anyone in the crowd focused on his car.

He swore, instinctively pressing his palm against the pistol he kept concealed beneath his coat. One thing was certain: this vehicle was no longer drivable. He'd have to ditch it and get it picked up in the morning—whatever wasn't scavenged overnight, anyway. Once away from the crowd, he'd go airborne. As long as no one jumped him.

Marius opened the door and stepped out, one hand on his pistol, the other mussing up his hair to conceal more of his face. *Damn humans*, he thought again, glancing over his shoulder as he sought to blend into the heart of the crowd. *They can't just relax. They can't just wait and see.*

*Always have to take steps before they have all the information, before they understand our intentions.*

"Looking for poppers, man?" a bug-eyed teen asked, separating from the crowd. His face came too close, and he put his hands on Marius's arm.

Whatever the kid intended, pushing drugs or something more sinister, Marius wasn't interested. He flung him away. Ducking his head, he tried to take advantage of an overweight reveler creating a nice, wide path through the mob, but the corpulent fellow stopped to chat with some friends and the opening closed. The masses flooded in like confused participants in a dark street carnival.

It suddenly seemed as though there were too many people touching Marius, too many people in his personal space. Hands grabbed, people shoved, their bodies and faces digging into his back and his shoulders. Marius gritted his teeth and plowed forward. The mob seemed to surge around him. There were vampires, werewolves, humans and mechs in the crowd. The scent of mixed-species tension was sharp and unmistakable.

As he fought his way toward Dumont Towers, Marius felt a whisper undulate through the crowd. He'd caught someone's attention, but he wasn't sure whose. He tried to move faster. Shoving harder through the bottleneck, he looked ahead for some space to take to the sky. But just as he found what he was looking for, a wide-open expanse, a bright cold shock of fresh air swept in from a less crowded side street. He had time only to glance over before being rammed in the side by an oncoming group of riled up teenagers, intent on violence, though he couldn't discern to what purpose.

*Take to the air. Take to the air and get out of here.* Every synapse in his brain was signaling emergency. His body seemed suddenly on fire as a rain of blows struck him. They must have dislodged something or hit a nerve, for he was swept by a wave of exhaustion. Pain seared his left arm. Marius stumbled toward a nearby wall, disoriented. No way could he take to the air now. He backed into a doorway, pressing his body into the shadows of the tight space as the mob flowed onward. The teenagers were shouting.

Marius closed his eyes against a swoon and realized he was sweating, hard. He had the sudden urge to claw the clothes off his body, but instead he shrank himself as small as he could and let his heavy head drop to his chest while waiting for the tail of the crowd to pass.

He wasn't sure if he stayed conscious the entire time; he just knew the street was suddenly quiet. He braced his body against the doorway and stood up, flinching in surprise that he should still be in so much pain. There was no possibility of flying. It was as if all his strength had drained from his body. Nonetheless, he could now reach his destination. Marius half-stumbled and half-walked to the street-level entrance of Dumont Towers.

# CHAPTER FOURTEEN

*London, England*
*June, 1851*

In her room above her shop, Charlotte poked at the soil in the pots lining the windowsill and frowned. It was said that one's mood could affect that of a plant. Maybe that explained why she was not getting the results she wanted. She'd been out of sorts since acting the fool in front of Edward Vaughan last week, and it must have rubbed off on her roses, the poor things. She'd thought she was on to something, that she'd managed to graft together two different species to create an entirely new one: a hybrid white rose with red striping, just like a flower she'd once read about. But this bud was pink all over. A failure.

She pushed the tray away and sat back, discontented. Everyone around her seemed to be doing such extraordinary things. Inventions and discoveries filled the Crystal Palace. Everybody said cousin Joseph would be knighted after the success of the Great Exhibition.

*And what have you done, Charlie? Nothing.*

She sighed and stared at the *Rw*'s and *Rr*'s scrawled across the page on her little plant-fertilization chart. What was she doing wrong? Joseph would know. So she folded the parchment into a little envelope, unceremoniously clipped the pink rosebud off the stem to show her cousin, put on her bonnet and coat and headed outside.

As she walked, Charlotte tried to focus on the lovely green grass and the blooming summer flowers peppering the park grounds. But in her heart and her mind she was wondering about Edward. Would he acknowledge her socially after her revolting outburst and the ensuing scene?

Rather than approaching the main office to ask after her cousin, Charlie entered the front of the palace with the rest of the public. Then, though she'd told herself she was here regarding her rose project, Charlotte reviewed her exhibition program and determined that Edward would be in the Machinery wing if he'd chosen to continue their meeting routine. She was both fearful and dubious, but Charlotte could not help herself. She did not *want* to help herself. She went to the Machinery wing.

A number of men and women clustered around a pedestal, upon which sat a very large apparatus that seemed to be oozing a trickle of red-orange smoke. All of the male onlookers found this remarkably interesting. A loud honk emanated from a brass bell-shaped device atop the machine, and the spectators erupted in peals of laughter. Then the horn-shaped proboscis belched a great cloud of the red-orange smoke. Everyone jumped back, startled, and applauded.

"I say, Vaughan! Is *that* the sort of thing you spend your time doing at that hobbyist club of yours?" a male voice asked.

Charlotte craned her neck between two onlookers and recognized the face of Lucy Vaughan. The man next to her was likely her fiancé, Rupert Murray. He waggled his walking stick and said, "A machine that makes vulgar noises and belches smoke. Ingenious!"

Charlotte shifted enough to catch a glimpse of Edward's annoyed face as he responded. "If you read the card, Murray, you will note that it does a great deal more. Lord Gilliam is a brilliant mind, and I daresay—"

"Well, then." Lucy's fiancé leaned over the machine, blocking the information card with his prodigious girth, and adjusted his monocle. "No . . . I still don't quite see its purpose. Still, at least it spews an infernal quantity of rusty miasma and makes a rude noise!"

"Do explain your invention to Rupert, Lord Gilliam," Lucy said.

The bystanders around them moved closer. Alastair Gilliam puffed himself up. "Oh, yes. You see, I purchased a mixed supply of herbs and berries from an adventurer recently returned to London from abroad. Samples of things that we do not have here in Great Britain. Well, Vaughan can tell you that the materials were rather unpredictable, and though at one point I did set fire to the both of us—Edward, have I told you lately that you are a stand-up chap for not holding it against me?" The assembled crowd laughed. "But I discovered that one of the berries had unique properties the likes of which I had never before seen. I began to combine the juice of the berries with other chemicals in my stock, and the results were quite interesting. So interesting in one case that I built the invention you see here today."

He turned to the contraption.

"It has a small device inside that informs the device to perform on the hour. You see, it would take more fuel to start the machine up again from rest than it does to keep it running around the clock." A pained expression came over his face. "I do not know when—and if—I will be able to get more berries. They come from a place in South East Asia called Cam-bo-dia."

"*Cambodia*," a young woman breathed, eyeing Lord Gilliam like a piece of candy.

"When a vapor created inside the machine from the mash of the berry combines with the chemical expulsed from this second tube, a special microcosmic weather system is formed and a cloud of fog is created of a density depending on existing atmospheric conditions. The machine records all data and produces a kind of report, which is what these lines are over here . . . which will be useful in not only predicting weather, but in solving some of the problems associated with the worst kinds. So you see, if we can determine how fog is created, we can certainly, by employing the logic in reverse, figure out how to rid our London skies of it!"

The bystanders broke into applause.

At that moment, Lucy looked around and saw Charlotte. "Why, it's Miss Paxton!" she said. "What a marvelous coincidence." It did not escape Charlotte that, in spite of Lucy's smile, Edward's sister found her presence neither marvelous nor a coincidence.

The young woman examined Charlotte from head to toe. "I heard you weren't well, Miss Paxton," she continued. "How lucky you were to have my brother to escort you home in Lord Gilliam's carriage. That must have been a nice change for you. The fabric on the seats alone must have cost a fortune. I'm sure that you, being in the trade, must have been quite delighted to see such fine examples. Perhaps it gave you some ideas for your shop."

Charlotte bristled inwardly at the overt slight. "I'm sure it was lovely, Miss Vaughan, but unfortunately I was too unwell to consider the upholstery. I hardly even remember that it was your brother who was kind enough to escort me home."

"Good day, Miss Paxton," Edward greeted her in a carefully modulated voice from behind his sister. "I am so pleased to see you looking so well. I wasn't sure if you would come," he added, flicking a careful glance at Lucy as he stepped forward. "I imagine your experience in the West Indies nave was rather . . . trying."

"Yes, it was, Mr. Vaughan," Charlotte murmured, blushing.

Edward made several introductions. Charlotte gave the appropriate bobs and curtseys and proffered hands, trying not to feel undone by the horrible sensation of being the least entitled of the assembly. She recognized several of them from their disapproving glances sent from the far end of the table at the garden party in September; others were complete strangers. She tugged self-consciously at the hem of her sleeve in the company of the ladies' inevitable finery.

"My brother tells me Joseph Paxton has made it possible for you to come for free to the exhibition as often as you like, seeing as he is your cousin. How lovely for you," Lucy remarked. "And how often you come."

From the corner of her eye, Charlotte saw Edward wince. She managed a smile, but was saved from the difficulty of a reasonable reply by Lucy herself, who had not yet run out of things to say. The chatterbox waved a languid hand in the air. "Oh, the crush can be so tiresome! But there are so many things to see, I suppose," she continued vaguely, waving away some red-orange smoke that had wafted in her direction from the machine. Behind her, Edward looked impatiently into the distance.

Lucy's stream of words continued. It seemed to blur the air between Edward and Charlotte, and as the young woman talked, Charlotte looked over and saw that Edward was maintaining a carefully blank expression. Charlotte gripped her program and tried not to hate herself for pretending she was here to see one man, when the truth in her heart was that she had hopes of seeing another. *You're in trade, Charlotte. You have no money, no position* . . . And being a vague relation of a man du jour wasn't enough. She wasn't good enough for Edward Vaughan, and perhaps he'd realized it. He was kind not to trifle with her further.

"I should leave you to enjoy the exhibition," she blurted to the group. "To be honest, I've come to ask my cousin for gardening advice."

Lucy tucked her arm around Charlotte's with iron purpose. "Oh, do tell us something of Mr. Paxton. You must be so proud of him. After all, he was just a common garden boy. To achieve success from such meager beginnings is positively inspiring! The duke himself taking him in like that . . . I personally have never met a garden boy who could put two meaningful sentences together."

Charlotte doubted Lucy Vaughan had ever spoken to a garden boy.

"Quite remarkable, what he has done," Lucy rambled on, giving glances at the rest of the assembled spectators. She took a deep breath. "Do you have a similar green thumb, Miss Paxton? I recall some talk of it at our dinner."

Charlotte relaxed, eager to take advantage of a question she actually could answer with some confidence. "Though I don't pretend to own the talents exhibited by my cousin, I do have some modest projects of my own. I'm very fond of gardening, and have taken a particular interest in roses. They—"

"Yes, roses are very pretty," Lucy interrupted absently, craning her neck to look over Charlotte's head. "Come, let's have a lemonade. It's so warm in here with all of these people.

"You'll excuse us," she remarked to the others.

Charlotte struggled to keep up as Lucy dragged her off. The girl seemed to have no curiosity about the myriad inventions left in their wake, propelling her single-mindedly toward the refreshment area. Charlotte looked behind, but Edward and Lucy's fiancé had been swallowed by the crowd. "How . . . how will we find the others again?"

"My dear Charlotte," Lucy replied, piercing her with sharp eyes. "Leave the men to their machines. Each to his or her own."

Charlotte blushed.

Edward's sister found a table in a deep corner against the wrought-iron enclosure of the refreshment area and managed to signal a passing waiter for two lemonade ices. Charlotte arranged her skirts and tried to feel solicitous toward the fern fronds poking through the railing that were tickling her neck, but it would have been impossible to feel less comfortable, sitting there with Lucy Vaughan, who had made a point of seating them so that Charlotte faced away from the crowd.

There was a pause, and then Lucy likewise looked in the direction of the men they'd left behind. "Are you acquainted with Edward's fiancée?" she asked bluntly.

Charlotte was lucky she happened to be looking over her shoulder and through the iron railing, so Lucy did not catch the first flash of unguarded shock that surely flared across her face. She squeezed her eyes shut for a second, took a deep breath and turned to smile, fully composed. "I'm afraid I have not yet had the pleasure," she said carefully.

Lucy's eyelashes lowered, and she pursed her lips in a show of faux delicacy. "Well, he is not yet engaged, but we are quite sure that any day now . . . She is *extremely* rich. She will be a good match for our Edward, better than any other that anyone might have dared dream. One Miss Jane St. Giles."

Charlotte wasn't sure which was more offensive, Miss Vaughan's vulgarity in discussing the heiress's wealth or the thinly veiled attempt to make it clear that Charlotte was making a fool of herself by aspiring above her station.

"American," Lucy admitted, patting Charlotte's hand. "But it can't be helped. As I said, she's very rich."

Charlotte forced herself not to react to the grotesque emphasis Lucy placed on money, satisfying herself instead by internally telling Lucy Vaughan that she was the most unpleasant woman in the world.

"Oh, you must forgive me!" Lucy suddenly cried, leaping up from the table. "I'm terribly late for an appointment I just remembered. I shall have to leave you."

Charlotte could not find any words to reply, but as Lucy had suddenly dispensed with all etiquette, she felt no compulsion to overcompensate. She simply watched Edward's sister push her way off through the crowd. When she could see her nemesis no more, Charlie fished her drooping rosebud out of her reticule and tried to figure out what had gone so terribly wrong.

# CHAPTER FIFTEEN

Tatiana Asprey held her skirts delicately above her ankles as she stepped across the grass at the far end of the wide terrace that jutted out from the side of Dumont Towers. She'd given her bodyguards a stern setdown, making it clear in no uncertain terms that she did not wish to always be in their company.

Her cheeks burned at the humiliation of it all. The one person she wanted around her had gone on some disgusting bender—on their wedding night! If she were honest with herself, he had probably gone to his mistress. He'd slept ever since coming home. He was probably sleeping even now. Yet everyone else, everyone she'd prefer to avoid, would not leave her alone. Not until she'd practically thrown a fit and insisted on privacy.

She shielded her eyes with her hand and looked around. At least the sunshine had managed to burn through the nasty gray that clogged the upper strata in this godforsaken city. It *was* rather pleasant out: a lovely day to be outdoors, if an odd way to spend a honeymoon. Tatiana had expected to spend more time with her husband—and she certainly planned to take up some of his interests so that they might be more companionable, just as she'd been raised by House Royale to believe a wife should act—but Marius had not even joined her in bed, let alone talked about daily routines. Tatiana didn't know what he expected or wanted from her. So, choosing a nice patch of sun for her intended work, Tatiana laid out her shoulder wrap as protection from the grass and settled down to sketch plans into her journal for a landscaped garden here.

Sighing, she watched a darling yellow dandelion bob in a trim square of grass just ahead. Once this grass was replaced with flowers, it would be a marvelous place for escape. And that sleek glass footpath and stark marble slab with water running down it that was supposed to be some sort of fountain? Tatiana raised her chin and wrinkled her nose at such modern affectation. They would have to go. That's where she would plant an entire wall of Asprey rosebushes.

"Hey, Princess," a voice called out from behind her.

Tatiana slammed her journal shut and shoved it under the hem of her voluminous silks. She looked over her shoulder. Half-blinded by the sun, she turned. At first she could just barely make out the figure of a man, but he came into focus quickly and she studied him in utter fascination. He wore a maroon brocade smoking jacket over an untucked white linen shirt. A black necktie hung loose around his neck. His hair was a deliberate scramble of unruly locks. She must be half-drowned in Dumont scent to not have noticed another vampire approach.

A frisson of guilty excitement sliced through Tatiana's senses when she recognized his face. Hayden Wilks. She had seen the rogue before in pictures, when her family and that of Marius had made disclosures before agreeing to their marriage alliance. The House of Dumont had produced a photo of Hayden and his alleged girlfriend Jillian Cooper—the woman in love with Marius. They'd explained that while Hayden was a member of the Rogues Club, a group supposedly allied with their house, the vampire himself was an enemy. The Dumonts had turned him vampire accidentally, and peace had never been made.

Tatiana looked across the terrace, but her guards had taken her at her word, long ago retreating indoors to give her the privacy she'd demanded. As Hayden approached, Tatiana's pulse began to race. No one was going to stop him. A dangerous enemy of her husband was moving closer, perhaps close enough to touch! Turning her back to him, she lifted her nose in the air and said, "You are not supposed to be here."

He leaned over her shoulder and seemed to think nothing of his cheek nearly touching hers. "Aw, you put it away," he said.

Tatiana's heart pounded as he walked around and knelt down on the grass in front of her. His raw musky scent sank deep into her soul. Hayden's dishabille and lack of reverence for her position, her person and her sensibilities was truly astonishing. Then the infamous creature actually slid her journal out from under her dress, as if he had every right! On the journey, his fingertips grazed her ankle. Tatiana gasped. Hayden flashed her a grin.

She turned up her nose again. If there was some intent in the action . . . Well, no man had ever dared so much without leave—not even her new husband, the werewolf princess was forced to admit. She glanced around to see if any of the security she'd refused was looking to help her, saw there were no guards and reminded herself to show her enemy no sign of fear. The Dumonts would be livid once they discovered this rogue had dared approach her so boldly. She should have screamed for help or quit his company immediately.

But . . . she didn't want to. She *should* have wanted to, and she knew she would have to think about her behavior later.

"I think Marius might actually go mad if he had any idea who you were with right now," Hayden suggested as he sprawled out on the corner of her shawl, his elbow pinning part of her dress to the ground. Tatiana simply stared down at him. He winked, stuck a piece of grass in his mouth and stared up at the clouds. "Of course, maybe he doesn't really give a damn."

Tatiana narrowed her eyes as his gaze met hers. She could see he was trying to get a rise out of her, and he wasn't going to get one. "I know all about you, Mr. Wilks. You're that bad man who goes around with that Cooper girl." Her tone was even, cautious, and she kept her eyes steady and clear. *Well done,* she thought. *If he's looking for me to show hate for Jillian Cooper, he's out of luck. I'm a better actress than that.*

"Ah. Jill," Hayden said. "She and I aren't together anymore. We were just trying to screw with Marius," he explained. He seemed to wait for a reaction.

"So, you're here to see if I'd play a similar game," Tatiana guessed. "What an outrageous suggestion! Ours is an arranged marriage. Marius and I aren't pretending it's anything else, and I don't see the point in complicating things. Not with anyone, and certainly not with my husband's enemy."

"I'm starting to agree with some of those sentiments," he replied, an inscrutable note in his voice. But he rose up on an elbow and leaned close, putting his hand on her knee, a fiery touch even through her dress. "Complications . . . pretending . . ."

Tatiana stared half in horror at his hand. Only her husband should be granted such license. Why did she not tell him to stop?

"Pretending is so—"

"Exhausting," Tatiana blurted, watching his hand

graze along her calf through her dress. She bit down on
her lip so hard that she tasted blood, and then watched in
fascination as Hayden shivered.

"Exhausting," he repeated, appearing to have a difficult time focusing on anything but his bloodlust, on her
mouth, as she licked at her lip, "Well, just so you know,
the last thing old Marius would ever do is cheat on you. If
that's the kind of pretending or complication you're worried about."

"I'm not worried," Tatiana said, lifting her chin in the
air as she struggled to relax her body beside him. She
needed to stay nonchalant. "Why should I be worried?"

"In case you were wondering," he replied.

Tatiana just narrowed her eyes.

"What? I'm saying a *nice* thing. That Marius won't
trade your bed for Jill's. If he weren't so damn torqued up
about right and wrong in the first place, he would have
married her instead of you. He's a goody-goody. A duty
whore. He gave her up and—"

"He hasn't given her up," Tatiana blurted, giving voice
to the dark suspicion she'd been struggling to disbelieve
all day. "I believe he was with her last night."

"But last night was your . . . Whoa," Hayden said, his
voice a mix of incredulity and sympathy, and Tatiana felt
the blood drain from her face as she realized she'd revealed too much. "Marius hasn't even touched you yet."

Tatiana swung her head away. "I don't know what
you're talking about."

"I know you don't. That's my point."

She didn't look at him, and they sat in silence for a moment.

"I don't want to give you a big head or anything, Princess, but you're the most beautiful woman I've ever seen.
If Marius is able to resist you, then his bond with Jill must

be on some otherworldly level, something you and I couldn't possibly comprehend."

Fingertips lightly touched Tatiana's shoulder and slowly raked down her naked arm. She inhaled sharply and turned to look at Hayden. In his eyes, she thought she detected a reflection of her own feelings, that everything was broken and spoilt.

*Oh, don't be a fool, Tatiana*, she chided. *It's simply that we've been disappointed in a similar way. It isn't romantic.* But when her eyes searched his, if nothing else she was wise enough to understand the glimmer of desire there.

Hayden changed position, rising above her, arms strategically placed at her sides. A smile curled the corners of his mouth, which hovered over her lips. She could feel his hot, rushed breath. "Marius doesn't know what he's missing," he whispered. His eyes were like onyx.

Tatiana glanced around for the guards she'd dismissed and saw no one. She swallowed hard, all previous fanciful notions giving way to fear. It would be so easy for Hayden to hurt her, to take her here, to ruin everything for Marius. . . . But the rogue seemed to soften as he looked at her. He moved his face slightly so that their lips aligned but did not touch, and he breathed in her scent as if it were a wonderful perfume. She was sure he was going to kiss her.

*I should push him away. I should slap him. I should tell him how disgusting he is.*

She did none of those things. Tatiana simply waited, allowing a much too lengthy chance for Hayden's mouth to act according to his reputation.

He pulled away. Standing, a bit unsteady at first, Hayden sketched a formal bow. Then, without another word, Tatiana's husband's worst enemy disappeared behind the fountain and was gone.

Tatiana stared after him for some time, awash in a tumult of emotion. At last, recovering some composure, she went to record her feelings in her journal, but it seemed to be missing. She shifted, sweeping back her skirts, but the journal was gone. Hayden had stolen it!

She leapt to her feet with a cry, shaking out her dress, and her journal fell to the ground. Staring down at it, she knew it would have been horrible: Hayden Wilks reading her personal thoughts and examining her drawings. Well, it *should* have been horrible. Somehow, it wasn't. The idea was titillating. She couldn't help but feel a pang of disappointment.

The afternoon ruined, Tatiana picked up her things and went inside. Handing her wrap to the porter, she asked, "Will Mr. Dumont be down for supper?"

"He is already downstairs, Mrs. Dumont."

Tatiana started at the new form of address, but she had little chance to reflect. Voices leaked from the dining hall, and Folie laughed. Tatiana was sure she heard Marius himself. He was speaking her name.

"I'll just go change," she said, her spirits lifting. Perhaps he *was* thinking about her, and all her fears were unfounded.

She took pains with her appearance and moved as quickly as she could, but the scene was not what she expected when she finally returned. Yes, Folie was laughing, but it was Ian and Warrick who smiled and joked with her.

Marius was there in the dining hall. He greeted Tatiana politely and pulled out her chair, but each action seemed strained. From the moment the meal started he was listless and distant, hardly saying a word, hardly eating a thing.

"Did you have a good day?" he finally asked her in a low voice.

Tatiana smiled nervously, not quite sure how to broach the subject of Hayden. "It was lovely. I took my journal to the park and sketched plans for a garden I intend to build. There was something—"

But her husband seemed to have already lost interest. His focus slipped from her face, and he grimaced and pressed his hand against his jaw.

"Marius, are you quite all right?" Warrick asked, leaning close to clamp his hand on his brother's shoulder.

Marius flinched. He swallowed hard and then reached for the third goblet of water he'd downed since they'd sat. "Not quite myself," he muttered.

When he looked up at Tatiana, she smiled, but not without effort. He did not smile back. Tatiana lifted her chin in defiance, but then realized that was counterproductive.

Before she could try again to break the ice, Marius stood. "Tatiana," he said. "I—I'm terribly sorry. I've a rather bad . . ." He didn't seem able to finish the sentence.

Ian moved to his brother's side, and he and Warrick looked at each other. "Let's get you upstairs, Marius," he said quietly. "Ladies—Miss Tatiana, especially—please excuse us."

Tatiana rested her chin on her hand. Through narrowed eyes she watched her husband stumble off through the doorway.

*A headache*, she thought with disgust. *Do I look like a fool?*

# CHAPTER SIXTEEN

Monday mornings were never pleasant. A Monday morning involving time with Marius at a body-parts market was certainly not going to be the exception, particularly given that within five minutes of leaving her apartment, Jill realized someone was following her. Someone who either wasn't trying to pretend otherwise or was the worst tail she'd ever had to shake.

Except, he wouldn't shake, not even after Jill added several extra blocks to her route in the course of trying.

She tried to outrun him. Unfortunately, there was no way to do so while loaded down with her bag of body armor, and the cavalier manner with which the guy gave chase was even more disturbing. It suggested he wasn't focused on concealing his identity. For that reason, Jill eased her knife into her hand and flicked up the blade. She turned a corner and ducked into a deep doorway, lowered her bag and waited.

Nothing happened. No one approached. Jill adjusted the handle of the switchblade in her sweaty hand and pushed her fringed scarf away from her face for better visibility.

"I'd rather not get my shoes dirty," a man's voice called pleasantly. "I'd appreciate it if you would just come back out to the sidewalk."

Jill hesitated a moment, then hoisted her bag so that it

shielded most of her upper body. She couldn't hide here all day, so she eased back onto the sidewalk.

Her pursuer walked toward her. He was a man with a friendly smile, and he extended his arm for a handshake. "Max Horschaw, Internal Operations."

Jill inwardly groaned. In some ways, she'd rather have a gun pointed at her. You knew what you were getting there. The weapons wielded by agents on the streets weren't half as scary as their smiles. I-Ops strategy was often to mess with your mind.

She supposed this meant Total Recall was no joke. She hadn't heard anything further, and so she'd taken to hoping. But the human government was clearly nervous, which meant it would put its two Fed-run defensive divisions on offense: Battlefield Operations and Internal Operations. There was a traditional police department responsible for keeping the peace, but the charters for B-Ops and I-Ops went far beyond. B-Ops marshaled teams of combat-trained field agents, spies and military personnel. I-Ops ran information teams. They were analysts, researchers and policy wonks, and also a shadowy group referred to only as "general management." With his sharp navy suit and pomaded hair, Max Horschaw was one of the last.

Jill managed a bright smile. "I'm sorry, do I know you?"

Horschaw didn't drop his hand. "Come on, Jill, unless you're antihuman, give us a shake."

Two seconds in and the manipulation was in full-swing. Jill frowned, but shook hands. "I'm actually a little behind schedule this morning. What can I do for you?" she pressed.

Horschaw straightened a little, a big grin on his face. "I don't get that question very often. Usually it's the other way around." He chuckled, and the sound made Jill's skin crawl. "So you're behind schedule. We'll make this quick. You used to be pretty loyal to the human government. At least, until you started making eyes at the vampire boys."

Making a concerted effort to stop her body language from giving away her true feelings, Jill evened her voice and said, "Does this pertain to Total Recall?"

"See, I knew I'd like working with you. You're a newspaperwoman. You keep up on things, you know about things—you're up on the Recall. You don't pussyfoot around." Horschaw reached over and slapped her on the back.

Jill flinched. "I'm neither disloyal nor blindly loyal. I'm not against my own kind, let's get that straight. But I don't like the official agenda. I don't like what we do to those poor mechs. And I won't give single-minded loyalty to any human government as long as we maintain an 'us or them' mentality. I'm one of the Rogues. We aren't against humans. We're for everybody."

Horschaw let the silence between them string out until it became uncomfortable. At last he said, "Yes, that's a nice thought, isn't it? Anyway, the thing is, we'd like you to work with us again."

"Again?" she replied. "I'm not sure what you mean."

"Oh, don't," he said. A muscle in his face twitched. "I thought we weren't going to do that 'ignorance' thing. Don't do that. Just listen. Your profile fits our needs."

"What's my profile?" Jill asked.

"Not too many humans go rogue, and even fewer so successfully. We like your access, we like your contacts. We like *you*. You've even had some decent training."

"I've never been formally trained in anything," Jill argued. "Check my file. I did a little investigative reporting on staff for the city paper a couple years ago, and I've been working freelance ever since. I'm great with a camera and filing a story, but that's about it."

Horschaw just tipped his head and stroked his chin.

"Can I go now?" Jill asked.

"Are you done trying to make yourself sound less appealing? You're as close to the Dumont family as a human can get without being married to one. You're a member of the Rogues Club, which means you interact with every species on a regular basis and are welcome in most—if not all—parts of every community. If you're not the picture of a sleeper agent, I'd like to know who is."

Jill blanched. "You can't be a sleeper agent if you never sign up."

"If that's your last objection, we've got nothing to worry about. I'm here to sign you up. And I've got the perfect mission."

She raised her palm, frantic. "Don't tell me! You're going to tell me something and then say that I know too much to not get involved."

"You'd like to give a commitment without knowing what it is?" He chuckled. "Well, I suppose it doesn't matter. You'll do what we want in the end."

"You're twisting my words," Jill said, horrified. "I don't want to do it. Whatever it is, I don't want in. I'm not political. I don't want to do anything for anyone, no matter what it is. I'm really sorry. I'm just not interested. I just want to live my life."

Horschaw leaned forward and adjusted her scarf—paternal, like a dad dropping off his kid at school on a winter day. Except there was the sensation he might give a single forceful yank and strangle her to death. "You'll want to do this, because you're going to want something I can give you in return. Something more than anything you've ever wanted in your whole life. Trust me."

The fabric pulled against her throat. Horschaw was staring at her, and Jill cried out a silent plea: *Marius, I need you.* But, oh god, she'd told him not to listen for her, not to answer her anymore. Would this be the time he didn't answer? *This is all you, Jill. This is all your problem*, she reminded herself. Fear coursed through her.

"What do you think I want?" she asked, pulling her scarf in the opposite direction.

"An antidote," Horschaw said, letting go.

Jill's stomach flipped over. "What for?"

The man had the audacity to laugh. "Not for you. We don't kill our own kind unless it's absolutely justified."

"Who *is* it for?" She swallowed hard, and then released a breath of anger. A different thought had occurred to her. "Does this have something to do with Hayden Wilks? Because we're not together anymore."

Horschaw's eyes searched her face. "Don't be stupid," he said. "And please listen, will you? It's chilly out here, and I'm dying for a cup of coffee. I said you would want this more than anything you've ever wanted in your life, so you'll do it," he promised. "Let's just move forward."

Jill felt the blood drain from her face. He was talking about Marius.

She opened her mouth to answer, but Horschaw suddenly struck her, hard. Jill staggered. Her right arm flew back from the impact, smashing her knuckles across the red brick wall behind her. She gasped, raising her other hand to her stinging cheek. She couldn't speak for a moment, just looked at her assailant in shock. He was shaking out his hand, not bothering to hide the fact that he was likewise in a bit of pain.

"You had that look on your face," he explained. "Like you were going to ask, 'What if I say no?' That question really irks me."

Blinking watering eyes and trying desperately not to cry, Jill put one foot behind the other and backed away. She still wasn't ready to concede.

"My friends are the Rogues," she reminded Horschaw, "and I plan to stay loyal to them. It's not as if we're anti-human. In fact, I think we're an important reminder to the other species. We're proof that not all humans want to kill them. There are others like me in the Rogues Club—"

"Yes," Horschaw agreed with a dismissive wave. "And we'll be in touch with all of them."

Jill swallowed hard against the desperation blooming inside her and tried another tack. "Listen, I get people who tell me things like this all the time. I never negotiate without knowing all the facts, and whatever you think I might want . . . Well, my life is about business. It's not personal. I'm a reporter first and foremost. If you want to make a deal of some kind, I suggest—"

The man reached out and took her hand, cradling it as a lover might while examining her bloody knuckles. Jill swallowed, but couldn't stop her body from shaking.

"No, Jill. It *is* personal. But I'll give you a break. Still, you're not going to get a lot of time to think about this, so you better go and ask all the people you care about how they've been feeling. That will help you decide whether you're going to come home willingly or . . ."

"Everybody feels fine, thanks," Jill said, trying to pull away. "So we can just—"

Horschaw pulled back, squeezing his hand around hers and crushing down until she cried out. "Please, don't," she whispered, her knees buckling. He lowered her gently to the ground, and she knelt at his feet.

"Gregory Bell is not feeling so fine, I think." Horschaw hunched over, his damp lips suddenly against her ear. "And maybe you should ask your better friends how they're feeling. Friends like . . . Marius Dumont."

Jill cringed. "I just saw Marius the other night. He's fine."

"Someone *I* know saw him after you. He wasn't so fine then."

"You're bluffing," she whispered.

Horschaw let go of her hand, then pulled her to her feet using the collar of her coat. He buttoned up the neck. "Like I said, it's a bit cold out here. Time you came back inside, don't you think? Playing fetch with the dogs and having tea parties with the fangs . . . It's just not natural. Think about it, get comfortable with the change, do what you need to do, but don't wait too long. Come have a drink at Bosco's, on us. But do it soon, 'cause we'll be waiting for you. We'll get you all squared away."

He reached into his coat pocket and pulled out what looked like a receipt. She blinked numbly at it, so he stuffed it into the breast pocket of her coat. "You've just been recalled, Jillian Cooper. Welcome back to the human race."

Horschaw walked away. As he did, Jill plucked his paper from her pocket. It was a piece of propaganda from I-Ops, a kind of welcome-back certificate in the form of a loyalty oath, written in faux script on flimsy, translucent recycled paper. Jill's body shook so badly she couldn't stand, so she leaned back against the brick wall behind her and let herself slide down again to the dirty cement.

Marius hadn't come.

*So this is what it's like when nobody comes to the rescue.*

# CHAPTER SEVENTEEN

*London, England*
*July, 1851*

Edward Vaughan stepped into the warm confines of his club, turned over his hat and gloves to an attendant and then slipped out of his coat.

"Mr. Gilliam asked me to send you directly to his workroom, sir."

"Thank you, Brighton," Edward replied. Then, hurrying past the library and sitting rooms toward the staircase at the back of the property, he headed down the steps with great anticipation.

The first row of rooms he passed were all occupied, holding a wide variety of men of disparate backgrounds, all coming together in the name of invention. Edward bypassed these and headed directly to Lord Gilliam's private space, dodging errant sparks and plowing resolutely past puffs of acrid steam coming from a malfunctioning generator.

"Edward! You must see this!" The boyish delight in his friend's face indicated that the time and money the young heir had expended on what his disappointed father referred to as "all that mad tinkering" had not been wasted.

Edward eagerly approached Gilliam's workbench, upon which lay a metal facsimile of a human arm, connected by tubing to a steam generator. The arm featured several small crankshafts that led to a palm, fingers and thumb of a mechanical hand.

Gilliam smiled in greeting, selected a small apple from a basket and placed it on the table, turned on the generator and used a series of knobs and levers to turn each of the crankshafts until the fingers slowly unfurled and then curled again around the fruit. "What do you think?" he asked.

"I think it's brilliant," Edward replied. "May I?"

Gilliam stepped aside, and Edward moved to the controls. Gingerly, he manipulated the equipment, opening and closing the fingers as his friend had done, but this time a squeal of angry metal sounded. A gear slipped; the fingers snapped closed. The apple was smashed into bits. The two inventors stood in funereal silence.

"Oh, dear," Gilliam said at last. But he quickly returned to his former state of animated happiness, waving his hand in the air as he proclaimed, "It does want to do that now and again. Not to worry. Not to worry."

"Still very impressive," Edward encouraged.

Gilliam turned off the generator and after the gears shifted down said, "The important thing is not to give up. I have the most extraordinary plan."

Edward picked up the metal hand and gently flexed the fingers. Brushing away bits of apple, he stared at the striated strips of curved metal held together by a series of screws. Indeed, he'd never seen the like.

"I'm going to make the whole body," Gilliam remarked, already having lost concern for the failure. He peered down at a large sheet of scored metal. "A series of connecting body parts. I've seen some of the mechanical men at the exhibit, and I think I can do better. Why, they just give the poor fellows a barrel for a body and call it a day! My 'mech' shall have a wholly articulated skeleton."

Edward glanced over at a pile of discarded inventions in the corner, all forward-thinking but half-perfected creations in which his friend had nonetheless lost interest. He gave a wry smile. "Fantastic, Gilliam. Really fantastic. Now, dare I ask . . . How are the repairs coming?"

Gilliam scowled, his face turning bright red. He turned and tried to cover his emotions by grabbing another apple from the basket and slicing it up with a work knife. "I was to bring it back to the exhibition this afternoon, but I am considering pulling the thing entirely. I'd rather retract my submission than be asked to remove it again." He picked up one of the apple slices, removed a smear of grease from the flesh and popped it into his mouth. "I must confess, I rather regret pulling the strings I did to get the placement. The internal clock is malfunctioning and some of the chemicals . . ." He swallowed and trailed off, glancing over his shoulder to confirm the door was closed. "Well, they're a bit unstable."

Edward raised his eyebrows. "Well, it's all just . . . *fog*, isn't it? They're not going to hurt anyone, are they?"

Gilliam looked at him in surprise. "Well, not if you don't drink them. Do you think I need a sign?" He raised his arms and swooped out the shape of a billboard. "'Do not drink the toxic chemicals, if you please.' Of course, most of the riffraff they let in can't even read. It's really quite extraordinary, you know, this business of letting the basest, most degraded members of society mingle with the ton."

"Reminiscent of our Inventors Club."

Gilliam's hands stilled on his machine. He looked up. "Oh, fine. You've got a point there. I suppose the exhibition is nothing more than a global version of our Inventors Club. But with one exception."

"What's that?" Edward asked.

"Inventors Club membership requires a brain." Gilliam leaned against the worktable and folded his arms across his chest. "I can't pretend it doesn't bother me to sit for refreshment at a table next to the stablehand's half-soused father or, say, a draper's girl. Or worse!"

Edward blanched. He wondered how much Gilliam knew about his continued friendship with Charlotte Paxton, if his borrowing of the man's carriage the other month had not incited his friend's remark. Too, Lucy might not be exaggerating about the rumors going round. Of course, Gilliam was an eccentric and an artist, forgetful at times, absentminded and dismissive. It was quite possible he had spoken without recollection of Charlotte, of the fact that she was indeed one of the very people he eschewed.

"What would you say if I told you I was madly in love with the 'draper's girl'?" Edward asked, not quite looking at his friend.

"I'd cut you, of course," Gilliam said, slapping Edward on the back. "We'd be finished socially. I'd certainly miss you."

The words shocked Edward into silence. At last he said, "That would be your right, of course. You have everything you need in life. You were born into wealth and privilege—and I suppose some familial obligation. But I don't hold it against you," he added, trying to give his friend a warm smile. "Such a lucky inheritance couldn't have fallen to a nicer fellow."

"Oh, were it not for the weight of familial obligation . . . ," Gilliam replied, waving his tools melodramatically in the air. After a pause, he lowered them and became morose. "I must give up everything when I inherit." He looked at Edward and quietly added, "Such conjecture means nothing to you but everything to me. You see, I must also give up the draper's girl."

Edward was about to reply, but Gilliam's machine for the exhibition suddenly roared to life. It belched red-orange smoke in a billowing cloud. The two men set to work for the next hour trying to shut the infernal contraption off.

# CHAPTER EIGHTEEN

The Market was nearing its peak hour when Marius arrived, and he wanted it that way, with the crowd of buyers and sellers pressed so close you couldn't get distance enough to steal a detailed look at anyone. There was something almost medieval about the place. Hooded robes and coats were worn atop body armor and masks, all to better obscure one's identity. Gauntlets and helmets concealed the likely telltale metal components built into the hands and faces of mechs.

The buyers and sellers milled casually as they clogged the square, as if attending a Sunday farmers market, but the wares for sale here wouldn't fill the typical picnic basket. From his vantage point in an alcove just off to one side, Marius could see body parts displayed in icy packaging, each labeled with a list of stats, including time and nature of death, blood type and a column of genetic markers.

He was surprised the stench wasn't stronger, given Leyton's comment about the place, but he still caught acrid undertones of chemical preservative and the unmistakable tang in the air of human and animal flesh. It was insane: bloodscent was intense enough here to send even the most subdued vampire into a swoon—so much so that Marius thought he should have been more affected. Certainly he felt a twinge of bloodlust, but it was manageable. Thanking his lucky stars, he focused on the Market as a source of information and kept his eyes on the display tables where steam from dry ice wafted up into the sky.

Checking time and coordinates, Marius saw Jillian was a no-show. That was unexpected. He should have felt relief at the situation, because if something had been wrong he would have sensed it. So perhaps she'd just decided not to get involved. It was what he'd wanted, really, no matter how useful in this mess she might be, as a human. It was just . . . surprising. Surprising and disconcerting, considering she'd set the meeting time herself, throwing her terms through the window at him and then just walking away. But she was over ten minutes late.

Marius walked along the rows of sellers, tossing out the description of Gregory Bell's disguise he'd managed to dredge up with a call to the House of Giannini. The dark green body armor and robe definitely was familiar to some, and once a few bills were exchanged Marius was directed to a seller waiting under a small freestanding tent with a stack of coolers, beside whom was an empty stall with a single folding chair. On top of the chair was perched a ratty "for rent" card.

Marius approached and looked down at a set of fingers poking over the side of an improperly sealed IceePak. "You're buying?" asked the corpsemonger.

"You're thawing," Marius replied.

The vendor looked down and hastily stuffed the digits back into the container, securing the latch properly. "Thanks."

"Are you the one renting out space?" Marius asked, pointing to the card.

"Sublet. I'll take cash or product."

"What happened to the last tenant?"

Behind the seller's mask, the eyes narrowed. "If you're

not interested in renting and you don't need a new hand or a liver or something, then we got no business." The seller turned away and began hawking his wares again.

Marius reached beneath his robes and pulled a few leaves from a wad of cash. He put the money on the table, keeping his leather-clad fingers pressed down on the bills.

"Okay, maybe we got business," the man allowed with a half smile, searching the blackness of Marius's garb to find something he could recognize.

"You don't know me, so don't bother," Marius laughed, adopting a more informal speech pattern. Confident in the anonymity provided by his own armor and robes, he kept his body relaxed and lifted his hand.

The money exposed, the seller's enormous black gauntlet–clad hand swept it away like an eclipse of the sun. He whispered something into the ear of the seller on his right side and tapped the lid of his top icebox before stepping backward under the dark eaves of the dilapidated storefront behind him. He gestured for Marius to follow him into the building.

"Tell me about a certain man," Marius said when they were over the threshold and away from listening ears. He described Gregory Bell's Market-wear and then waited to see what he might learn.

"Greg Bell," replied the vendor. "Rumor says he turned up dead at Dumont Towers."

"Know why?"

"No."

Marius crossed his arms. "Why don't we brainstorm a little. By all means, you first."

The hulkish corpsemonger shifted his weight from one foot to the other. "He was just another waterman, you know? That's what I thought. He used to come in with a pair of feet or a set of high-quality fingers . . . normal booty. But then one week he shows up with a lot of product all at once. A lot, and real fresh. I couldn't figure out where he got it. Shows up the next week, same thing. He had a line running end-to-end here in the Market." He shrugged. "It wasn't kosher, I figured. And the guy sublet from me, you know? Stood right next to me every day. I got nervous. He attracted too much attention."

"So what did you do?" Marius asked.

"Do? Nothing. I didn't have a chance to talk to him about it. He turned up dead."

Marius sighed. "Tell me about his . . . product."

The corpsemonger looked around, scratched behind his neck and looked longingly at the exit over Marius's shoulder. "I don't like to get too specific."

"I just paid you to get specific."

"Pay me to get *more* specific."

Marius took his time deciding. Finally, he peeled off a couple more bills and handed them over.

"Beautiful fresh human body parts and organs," the man said. "Perfect stuff. The guys who sell to the mechs bought him out the first week, but they didn't come back the next week. Per instructions, I'm guessing. Most of the mechs still have that thing—some weird code of honor, you know? Guess they figured it was too beautiful, too fresh, if you know what I mean."

"And then what?"

"Then? I guess he died."

Marius got right in his informant's face and though he spoke softly, infused his voice with all the danger he could. "I'm not paying you any more, leech. Give me proper value or I'll raze this place. I know you're used to a rough crowd here, but trust me, I'm worse. I'm not someone to mess with, so tell me, how did Gregory Bell die?"

"Okay, bud, okay." Clearly the corpsemonger was cowed. "The human government probably killed him.

When you piss those guys off, they either do bad stuff to you or get you to do bad stuff to other people. My bet: he stepped over some line."

"What exactly did he do?"

"At the very least I think he was creating his own product—killing humans just for parts to sell here. I'll bet that's what drew attention. It certainly drew mine."

Marius waited, knowing there was more.

His informant rubbed his nose. "Those Ops guys like to try things. They like to invent things. They like to *experiment*. Well, I heard . . ." The informant leaned in close. "I heard a rumor from someone who saw Bell a couple of days ago that he couldn't fly anymore and was in a lot of pain. They said more, too. They'd seen his condition before on a fang who died, and this wasn't like when fangs get that surgery to chop their teeth and pass as human. This was something chemical. Something done to him against his will. I think it was payback for whatever he did to get that product." With a shrug the corpsemonger added, "Last time I saw him, he wasn't feeling too good. Now he's dead."

"Where'd you get this intelligence?" Marius asked.

His informant cocked his head. "Around. But lemme just say I trust my source, even if it's crazy stuff."

"And you think it was humans."

Leaning back, the informant folded his meaty arms across his chest. "Our government, yeah. It's always us, isn't it?" he grumbled. "Not that us grunts have much say about what they do."

It occurred to Marius that he hadn't registered this man as human. Why would the guy be using a pheromone blocker in this place? It was an expensive method of disguise when, as Leyton said, this place held a constant flux of species. A bag over the head was more than enough.

The man craned his neck to look over Marius's shoulder. "I got a customer," he pointed out. Turning back he asked, "We good? 'Cause that's all I got. I swear."

Marius nodded and left the vendor to barter his goods. Hurrying back past the rendezvous point, it was with no small amount of surprise and relief that he sighted Jillian. Though she wore a full face mask, there was no mistaking her identity—she was encased in body armor, but he recognized her stance. As she turned toward Marius, Leyton's warning rang in his head: the Market's no place for a human body as sweet as hers.

"Sorry I missed the meet time," Jill said, raising her visor.

Marius shoved it back down. "You shouldn't have come," he said gruffly, taking her by the elbow and steering her toward the exit. "I want you out of this place as soon as possible. I learned what I needed to. The bottom line is, Bell may have killed humans for parts to sell, and the human government retaliated by infecting him."

"I feel like an idiot. I missed the whole thing. Who was your source? What was his name?"

"He wasn't going to give it, and I didn't ask."

Jill shook her head. "What species was he? Did he have an ulterior motive?"

Marius shrugged. "Did he have an ulterior motive? Maybe. Who doesn't? And he suggested he was human, but he didn't have a scent. He must have been using blockers. I had no idea that tech went mainstream. It's prohibitively expensive."

"He probably swapped 'prohibitively expensive' body parts for it," Jill replied.

The crowd closed in, threatening to separate them. Marius grabbed her injured hand, and she yelped as the casing of her heavy gauntlet pressed against her scraped knuckles. He stopped short, and she ran into his back. He turned around and raised her visor again, and then raised

his own visor. His eyes narrowed. He took her other hand
and then snarled. Before Jill knew what he was about, he
was half-pulling, half-dragging her out of the Market,
running her through the backstreets of the city.

When it was clear they weren't being followed, he
dragged her into a deserted alley and pulled her helmet
completely off her head. Upon seeing the bruising on her
cheek, a bright red pulse of anger flashed through his
eyes. Without ceremony Marius threw off his own gauntlets and began stripping the battle armor off her body.

"I knew I should have made you stay out of this!"

"It wasn't your fault," Jill gasped.

"What else did they do?" he growled.

"Nothing."

"What else did they do!" he shouted. He was practically tearing her clothes off. Jill grabbed both his hands,
forcing him to look her in the eyes. "Nothing, Marius!
And it wasn't 'them.' It was one guy. And I'm fine. It looks
worse than it is."

The two of them stood together in a kind of daze. His
hands and fingers moved faster and faster over her body,
over her skin, stripping off the metal and leather and bal-
listic nylon. Jill suddenly stood in her undershirt, the top
of her cargo pants unbuttoned and the waistband sliding
precariously down her hips.

Marius shook his head, stepped back and stared at her.
His hands were balled into fists. "One man? Tell me who
it was. He will answer for this. He will *pay*."

Jill couldn't reply. She was undone by his hands all over
her body and by the evil possibility Horschaw had planted
in her brain—that Marius was sick. If he confronted
Horschaw and the vampire plague was indeed connected . . .

*I can learn to live without you in my life, Marius, but don't
ask me to live without you on this earth.* Before she could

stop it, a sob slipped from her throat. Marius likely thought it was from her beating.

"Who *was* it?" he asked. When Jill didn't answer, he pressed the issue. "What did he want? Tell me everything."

Jill swallowed hard, trying to decide how much to reveal. "It was some guy from I-Ops. Max Horschaw. I was probably getting the same pitch every other human is going to get this week. They're going to be . . . persuasive."

She pulled the loyalty oath from her pocket and handed it over. Marius glanced at the paper then crushed it in his fist. Jill regarded him miserably.

"It's not as if it's a surprise they're interested in me," she said. "But don't worry, I'm not going to give them any dirt on the Dumonts. TR initiative or no, you can trust me."

"I know," Marius replied, looking away. "But they don't realize that. We could cook up a story to feed the beast. I'll talk with Ian and Warrick."

"I—I didn't get the impression it was that simple," Jill said. "I think they want something more."

"Such as?"

Jill hesitated. "I didn't say I'd do anything, and he didn't describe what my assignment would be if I . . ." She trailed off, and once more she searched Marius's face with her eyes. "Are you feeling sick?"

"There's nothing wrong with me," Marius said, dismissing the question with a wave of his hand. Gently he probed the bruises on her face. "I don't feel anything broken." He examined her hand, which was swelling.

"It looks much worse than it is, I promise."

Marius sighed. "Well, what did you tell him?"

"Obviously, I said I wasn't interested in anything he was offering. As you'd expect, he suggested it would be smart to *get* interested. He implied he knew something about Gregory Bell's death. . . . Marius, are you *sure* you are feeling all right?"

"Jillian! You're the one who got jumped." Marius shook his head. "My god."

His hands continued to caress her cuts and bruises, and Jill had to push him gently away for fear of losing her mind. "I'm fine," she repeated, trying her best to be convincing.

He backed off a moment and allowed her to collect herself. He took her wrist, removed a clean tissue from his bag and pressed it over her torn knuckles. Holding it, he stared down at her hand.

"There's something else," she admitted. "I mean, I think he was bluffing to force me to work with him—I hope he was bluffing—so maybe it's nothing. I almost didn't want to tell you because it's so alarmist and he *must* be bluffing, but . . ."

Marius arched an eyebrow.

She raised her lashes and looked in his eyes. "He implied that you might be sick. Infected. With something that needs an antidote, and I assume—"

Marius looked surprised for a moment, then an expression crossed his face Jill had never before seen: fear. A moment later he was back to normal. "Clearly he *was* bluffing. I'm fine."

Jill pressed gingerly against the tissue on her hand, looked downward to hide her unhappiness. "That's what I said, but . . . did anything happen to you on the way home from the lab?"

Marius stilled for a fraction of a second, but then shook his head. "No. Nothing."

"Why did you hesitate?"

Marius put his finger under her chin and gently raised her face. "Don't worry before there's something to worry about. I was just thinking. But nothing happened. Just to be safe I'll go back to the mech lab and get retested. Then we'll know if Horschaw's *really* bluffing or not, and then we can decide what to do about it, yes? We need to investigate the human government's connection in all of this, anyway."

"Okay," Jill agreed in a clogged voice. She blinked back tears, removed the sodden tissue on her hand and then stood in silence while Marius finished administering a modest bit of first aid.

But he didn't let go of her hand when he was done, and then his gentle fingers again found her bruised face. Jill looked up in alarm, and found him staring at her with a stricken look. There was no question what he was thinking.

"Hey, look at the bright side," she said, trying to defuse the moment. At one time she'd lived for these moments, when Marius's true feelings broke free of his well-known restraint. But those few grudging moments weren't something you could build a life on, and she wasn't going back to being that person. She couldn't go back to that.

Against her every desire, she pulled away and, carefully modulating her voice, said, "Stop looking at me like that. I'm fine."

Marius's face was paler than she'd ever seen it. "No. You don't understand. I just realized something. The reason I didn't come when he did this to you . . ." He couldn't seem to find the words at first, but then in a hushed voice explained. "I didn't *hear* you."

"I was blocks away . . ." Jill trailed off as Marius pressed his palm over his heart.

"I didn't *hear* you," he said, by way of further explanation.

They looked at each other in silence. "Oh," Jill said at last, trying to sound normal but overcompensating with a chirpy tone. "Well, that's good. No, I mean . . . Well, you know. It's better that way. I suppose the marriage to Tatiana—" She turned so that he couldn't see her blink back a sudden swell of tears.

Marius swallowed. "'Better that way,'" he repeated. His voice was completely devoid of feeling. The two of them stood awkwardly in the alley, listening to the intermittent pings of water dripping from a cracked pipe.

"Soooo," Jill at last mumbled nervously, looking down at her boots and straightening her clothes. "Where do we go from here?"

Marius ran a hand through his hair, staring up almost angrily at the sky. "Well, we've got a disease that kills vampires. With what you've told me this Horschaw said, plus what I've learned about Bell, it seems obvious that the human government is responsible, and they don't seem to be particular about who knows. They might be bluffing about their control of the disease, but either way they've got a fear campaign started. That, along with the invocation of Total Recall, seems as though they're gearing up for a new war between the species."

"That's big-picture stuff, Marius. Call your brothers. Let someone else handle it. They were suggesting that *you've* been infected! If that's true, we need to get you a cure—now," Jill blurted, angered all over again by Marius's focus on helping the masses.

He cupped her cheek in his palm. "There's not much I can do, Jillian. Maybe the humans have a cure, but if they don't, our only chance is the mechs. Assuming I'm infected, which is by no means certain."

Jill nodded, realizing there was something she could do. "I'll see what else I can find out about Horschaw and the government's plans. I'll—"

Marius's expression went dark. "No! You stay away from I-Ops. Don't do anything. Don't go find them, don't let them find you. And stay away from me. Got that? Don't give them more reason to come after you. They don't play fair, Jillian. You know that. This is a vampire problem, and if there's a way to solve it without your getting involved, without your getting into trouble on my behalf, that's the only way it's going to happen. You stay out of it."

Jill gave him a noncommittal smile, the best she could do without lying. Then she stuffed her armor and face mask back in her bag, hyperaware that while Marius was standing in front of her, staring right at her, on some level they were more disconnected than they'd ever been. It was surely strange for him, too, losing their bond like this.

She tried to laugh. "I guess . . . we'll be in touch."

"Be careful," he whispered.

"I will," Jill replied, slinging her bag across her back and heading toward the street.

She waved down a transport, got inside and took solace in the fact that the rearview mirror showed Marius standing on the sidewalk, watching to be sure she got safely into the cab. But over and over on the drive to her apartment, she repeated to herself, "Better that way." It was better that Marius could no longer hear her emotions. They'd never been in worse disarray. Her cheek throbbed and her hand was a mess.

When she finally got home and closed the door, it seemed almost fitting that the apartment should reflect her inner turmoil. Hayden had decided to toss the place while gathering his things. It felt incredibly empty without him, too. He had a big personality, and now, more alone than ever, it was easy to remember how grateful she'd been for their relationship on those really bad nights.

Her phone rang as she dumped her bag on the ground

and slumped onto her couch. Jill glanced at the number. Bridget. She sighed and took the call.

"Man, you are hard to get hold of. I heard you and Hayden are over. Are you okay? Everybody at the Rogues Club is asking about you," her friend said by way of a greeting.

"Yeah, we broke up. Have you seen him?"

"No. He's probably doing what you are: moping. Come out with me tonight. I'm meeting some of Tajo Maddox's old buddies. Dogtown's much safer than strata zero right now and you know how those werewolf guys are about human girls; it's better than being from a foreign country. They'll pay for *everything*."

Jill couldn't help but smile. "Thanks, but I just need to be alone for a bit." She stood up, walked over to a cabinet above the kitchen sink and pulled down a bottle of red wine.

She heard Bridget heave a sigh. "Ice cream or wine?"

Jill scrounged for a corkscrew but didn't find one. "If I choose to be a living, breathing cliché, it's entirely my business."

Her friend laughed. "You know, if I weren't going to see you at the club tomorrow, I'd come over and drag you out. You need to get out of that apartment."

"What?" Jill asked. "Tomorrow . . . ?"

"Didn't you get the alert?" Bridget sounded surprised.

"No. It's probably sitting with the rest of my messages. I've been ignoring them," Jill admitted.

"It's a shitty time to be ignoring your messages. Check your comm. It's about Total Recall. The Rogues Club members are all supposed to come compare notes. We're going to try to figure out what, if anything, we want to do about it."

Jill sat up straight, suddenly wondering: "Did I-Ops tag you?"

"This morning. They've been making the rounds. They made it kind of personal, if you know what I mean, which makes me think the next couple of years are going to be a riot. I'm gonna have some fun while I still have the chance. You sure you won't come out tonight?"

Jill sighed. "I'm sure. But you have a great time, okay? I'll see you at the meeting."

"'Kay. Later." Bridget hung up.

Jill tossed her comm onto the kitchen counter, scrounged some more and finally found a corkscrew. Picking it up, she popped the cork with a little more aggression than usual.

"I was supposed to want this," she reminded herself. "I was supposed to want Marius to leave me alone and stay out of my head. But it's not better," she admitted as she poured herself a glass and took a long draft. "Not better after all."

# CHAPTER NINETEEN

The greatest factor in Marius's having himself tested again was the sudden disconnect of Jillian's emotions from his own. For her to be in danger—struck, even!—and for him to be oblivious was unacceptable. She had attributed the change to his marriage with Tatiana, but for some reason he doubted that was the case. Also, though he didn't want Jillian to know it, he felt like hell.

He sat in the waiting room at the mech lab, allowing himself to slump against the wall. He didn't waste the energy to right himself; the ride over had practically done him in. A fine sheen of sweat covered his face, and he felt his body temperature spiking.

The door opened, and without fanfare Leyton walked over and sat down. "Just curious—did you find a needle?" he asked.

Marius shook his head, confused.

"Well, you would have if you looked early enough. Too late now."

Marius swallowed hard. "A needle? Is this part of your diagnosis?"

The mech paused. "Well, it needs longer study, but . . ."

Marius felt as though all the blood were draining from his body. "You're saying I *have* been infected. By someone who stuck a needle in me."

The mech nodded. Then he seemed to process Marius's response. "Oh. Yes. Sorry. I suppose I could have broken that to you differently." He frowned. "Sorry. But . . . yeah, you're infected with the same thing that killed Gregory Bell."

"You're saying I'm dying?" Marius clarified.

The mech opened his mouth, clearly trying to calculate an appropriate response. What he finally settled on was "Yes."

Marius cleared his throat. "How long do I have?"

"I can't give you an accurate picture. Every system is different, and every iteration of the virus. Months, weeks, days? I wouldn't say more than two months, tops. Do you feel ill? The way this virus eats cells, I should think you're in a hell of a lot of pain."

Marius laughed to himself, bested by the dark humor of it all. *God love these bastards' inability to process emotion. I'm dying. I could be dead in days, maybe hours. And right after my wedding, which was intended to unify the species.* Glancing down at his ring, he couldn't help but wonder, *Who's going to watch over Jillian?*

"Yes, it hurts," he admitted. Then, looking up at the mech, he shrugged off his fear. "Is it contagious yet? Can it go airborne?"

"No," Leyton said. "It's not like a cold. It still needs to find its way into the bloodstream—which is why I assumed you'd found a needle. Of course, the virus could still mutate. . . ." He blinked a couple of times. "That would be a whole different ball game."

Marius pinched the bridge of his nose, trying to focus. "Where do things stand with your lab team? Have you started any work on this? Is this something you can cure? I'd like to think that whoever created the virus, created an antidote, but I can't count on getting it. What are the chances that you can reverse-engineer this bug? Everything I said before still goes, double."

Leyton ran his finger down a skinny strip of metal traversing the underside of his jaw. "Well, Mr. Dumont, I love a challenge—and that money would really help us here—but let's be honest. We're missing a main component. For a bug like this, it would really help to have a sample of perfect genetic material. Otherwise, we've got a long road ahead. Too long for you, I'd wager."

"Perfect genetic material?" Marius repeated.

"The original stuff. The first of its kind. As I've said, we're looking at a kind of evolutionary virus. From what I'm seeing so far under the microscope, and from examination of Gregory Bell's body, we were right: the virus kills the host during the act of morphing them back to human form. If you can come up with first-generation genetic material from the first humans turned vampire, when that DNA was at its purest, we've got a shortcut. We can reverse-engineer and counteract the virus much more quickly."

"With this original genetic material, how quickly?"

Leyton studied Marius's face and smiled proudly. "I like you, Mr. Dumont. You've always been a decent fellow. A fair guy. For that reason I'll admit that whatever advances in science you and your brothers imagine are practiced here, those are in fact a mere fraction of the whole."

"How quickly?" Marius repeated fiercely. "Leyton. It *has* to be quickly enough. Do you understand? Or your human creators will win."

"I understand," Leyton said.

"So," Marius asked with a halfhearted smile, "genetic material from the beginning of our evolution—where might I pick up some of that? The local 7-Eleven?"

The mech gave an odd smile. "It's funny that none of you ever before asked the question, 'Where did they all come from?'"

Marius blinked. "Who?"

"You vampires and werewolves, in Crimson City and before." Leyton wrote something down on a prescription pad, tore off the top sheet and handed it over. He pointed at the piece of paper, the metal thread in his hands gleaming under the harsh lab lights. "Ask *him*. Ask him about the Blood-Taint."

"Blood-Taint? I haven't heard that term in ages," Marius mused.

Leyton didn't reply. Instead, he wandered over to the door and glanced out through its small porthole. "Where's the woman?"

"Going forward, I'm trying to keep her out of this."

"I don't recommend that," Leyton replied.

"Why?"

The mech looked down at the vials in front of him. "If this really is the beginning of a full-blown plague, you'll want someone else in this town who knows what you know. A nonvampire, who knows to come to us. Someone who isn't dying."

"That's true," Marius realized.

"Not many humans you can trust," the mech pointed out. Then, punching in a clearance code, he stepped out of the way as the exit slid open. "Have a nice day. You probably haven't got many left."

The heaviness in Marius's body was foreign and unsettling. Dumont Towers seemed quiet, and it felt in many ways as if he were returning home after a long trip abroad.

He hesitated. Ian and Warrick were his first priority, and then he must see Tatiana—there was no avoiding it. Though only a couple of days had passed since the wedding, he'd slept half of that time and been absent the rest. To his new bride—a near stranger, he reminded himself—his absence must have dragged on for an eternity. It was unacceptable and unfair.

He headed for the library, cognizant that he likely had Jillian's scent all over his body, even if he could no longer smell her himself. Well, his brothers already knew she was involved.

He found them in the library, and as he crossed the threshold, they broke from a close, intense discussion. "We need an update, Marius," Warrick said. "Fleur is out of range and ready to pop. Warrick and I have been running the ship, and we're all set with an agenda for the next Assembly. It's not a problem to cover your absence—so far, anyway—but you were chosen to lead, and—"

"We're worried about you," Ian interjected, pouring out a drink. "We want to know if you're okay. Oh, and if we can take the eighty-eighth floor off quarantine. Also, we're running out of excuses to give your wife."

Warrick's nose twitched, and he asked, "Is Jillian Cooper in this picture? I'm not sure House Royale—"

"She was in it from the beginning." Marius rubbed tired eyes, wishing his brother could read his mind. "We don't want to tell anybody else what's going on yet, and as a human she could end up being useful. A liaison. The mechs recommended it. Also . . . she was contacted by I-Ops today. She'll be full of useful information."

"So, the humans are definitely at the bottom of this," Warrick mused.

Marius shrugged. He explained everything Leyton had told him at the mech lab, and everything he'd learned at the Market. He skipped informing his brothers that he, himself, was infected. It was irrelevant, and would only cause worry and distract from the bigger picture.

"Is it contagious?" Ian asked.

"No. You can't just catch it from standing next to someone or anything like that. It needs to hit the bloodstream. You have to be specifically infected," Marius said. "Someone specifically infected Gregory Bell." *And me.* "We should find a way to quietly increase our people's awareness. Luckily, a warning won't seem out of place with Total Recall in play."

"This means war," Warrick snarled. "If we have solid evidence that the humans have essentially declared biological war, we attack. We can have that regime out of power so fast—"

"We don't have it yet," Marius said quietly. "But, soon. One step at a time. First we need to learn what the disease really is . . . and then, how to counter it. We don't want to make a move until we have a position of power."

"I agree," said Ian. "The most important thing is to counter the contagion and find a cure. Then we'll make those murdering bastards pay." He squeezed Marius's shoulder. "We were afraid we'd lose you."

Marius gave his brothers a smile he didn't feel. "It doesn't infect like that. Not yet."

Warrick narrowed his eyes. "Are you *sure* you're okay, Marius?

"I'm fine. Just tired." He looked between his siblings. "But I do need to speak to my wife, to spend some time with her." Downing the rest of his drink, misjudging the distance to the bar cart and slamming down his empty glass, he added, "Believe me, I know that I've been remiss."

Ian and Warrick looked at each other uneasily. Then Ian said, "You're too late."

Marius wheeled around. "What do you mean?"

"She's in seclusion. With Folie. They insist on being left alone for that Change business. Remember?"

Ian glanced at Warrick, who muttered, "Pride." The two brothers appeared to be fighting back a laugh.

"What are you talking about?" Marius asked.

"It's a full moon tonight. Tatiana and Folie have shut themselves in for the duration. You know, so no one sees them . . . being unladylike—fetching sticks and chewing on socks and stuff like that," Warrick joked. "Look, Tatiana's waited this long for you, she can wait a little longer."

"And you look like hell," Ian added. "Get some sleep."

Marius nodded, struggling against his weariness, feeling as though his legs might give out beneath him. He made it to the doorway, turned at the last moment and looked over his shoulder. "You two make a good team, running the ship. Keep it up."

He barely made it to his chamber before his legs really did give out. Pulling himself onto the bed, he rolled over to stare at the ceiling. His body might be falling to pieces, but his mind was working overtime.

He'd always considered his connection to Jillian both a blessing and a curse. For her, he'd felt it was a curse. That was why he'd intended to suppress it after the wedding, even though he himself welcomed the ability to instinctively sense her relative state of mind, her safety, no matter the pain it brought. But now it was gone. Really gone. Marius could sense nothing. And he hadn't given the talent up; it had been taken from him. Some thug had beaten her up in an alley mere blocks away, and he had felt and done nothing. For some reason, this terrified him more than dying.

He couldn't remember life before Jillian, before he'd experienced their connection. And yet, his world now seemed so still and silent. Happy, sad, in danger, in safety, under the loving touch of his enemy—before, he'd sensed everything. Now there was nothing. The line had gone dead. The story of her life on the walls of his soul was stalled out in midchapter. And there was nothing he could do about it.

A new remorse struck him: he should have accepted Jillian's love when he'd had the chance, but instead he had turned his back on her more times than he could count. His wedding had done none of the things he'd hoped, and now he was going to die. He was going to face his consequences, would lie in the bed that he'd made.

His legs pinned to the mattress by their own weight, Marius gripped handfuls of sheet in his fists and stared up at the cherubs and angels frolicking on the ceiling mural. Something wet slipped from the corner of his eye and slowly traced its way down his temple and sunk deep into the pillowcase, but he told himself it wasn't a tear. Dumonts didn't cry.

# CHAPTER TWENTY

Tatiana sat listlessly in the seat of an enormous upholstered chair with a round of embroidery she'd been picking up and putting down for the better part of an hour. It was not distracting her at all as she'd hoped, and she was tempted to call for a servant to leave some other form of entertainment by the door.

*We should have pressed harder to postpone the wedding until after the full moon*, she thought crossly. Clearly, these stupid fangs hadn't really understood what she meant when she'd explained the Change during their marriage negotiations. They hadn't had proper isolation quarters ready!

It was so different here than in New York. Crimson City's werewolves lived mostly underground, a de facto isolation that made it unlikely for other species to witness their struggle against the dark pull of nature turning them from human to beast. This morning, when she'd tried to explain with proper delicacy that she wanted to "go away for a bit," they'd thought she was talking about a honeymoon. She had rather enjoyed their discomfort, seeing as how Marius had vanished and nobody could explain where he was. Well, he'd have to ask about her when he returned. Maybe her absence would make him think twice about continuing his affair. They'd have to talk when she came out of quarantine.

Also, as soon as she and Folie felt comfortable rejoining the others, she'd have them fit out proper rooms for her monthly sequestering. Tatiana had temporarily convinced Marius's brothers to assign her a servant and give her a set of keys to the guest rooms in the most remote part of the Towers, but these weren't ideal. The rooms were more modest than some others on the same floor, and she'd only picked them because this particular chamber had a rather large picture window looking down on the city—a nice feature, especially when one felt like the walls were closing in.

Though Tatiana preferred to curl up in a ball with her eyes closed, Folie insisted on chattering away, lolling on one of the two enormous canopy beds, squirming and restless. "Did you know Gia doesn't quarantine herself anymore? She said Tajo likes it. She said *she* likes it. She says it's like nothing else in the world, being completely free. Maybe Marius would like it, too," Folie suggested a little breathlessly. She struggled to unbutton her high collar, which was clearly choking her. "Maybe he would finally take you to bed."

Tatiana slammed her basket of thread down on the side table and glared at her younger sister. "You know I love Gianna as much as you do, but do not choose her as a model. We both know she's rather odd."

Folie clambered off her bed and went to the window. She cracked it open to let more cool air inside, then rested her forehead on the pane and stared at the drizzle outside. "She's not a good role model? She always gets what she wants—and you *never* do."

"I don't know what you mean," Tatiana replied. "I wanted to marry Marius Dumont. It was the right thing to do, and I wanted to forge an alliance that would last for generations." Yet, even as she spoke, Tatiana tugged at the rings on the chain around her neck. She went back to stalking the meager length of the small room.

"Let it be, Folie," she added, when she saw her sister fretting with the lace at her neck.

"It's scratchy. It's like it's burning my skin!" The younger girl folded her arms across her chest and announced, "I want to take off my corset."

"Not during the full moon. It reminds us who we want to be."

"Maybe I *want to experience the change*. Maybe I want to see what it's really like to be a werewolf. Maybe I want to quit pretending to be something I'm not."

Tatiana whirled around and raised her hand. Folie stared with wide eyes.

Tatiana lowered her hand, her face burning. "You see how precarious it is," she murmured. "I'm so sorry." She dropped onto the bed. "It's hard enough to maintain *emotional* control. I understand how you feel. I can scarcely breathe, and it feels as though my skin is crawling." Indeed, her fingers tingled, desperate to change into claws. Her mouth ached and her teeth hurt as if they were shifting against the nerves at their roots. "We will overcome this," she muttered, pouring herself a glass of water.

A tremendous crash from outside sent both girls shrieking to the far side of the room. When someone knocked on the window, Folie and Tatiana clutched at each other.

"Good god!" Tatiana cried, feeling quite stupid. Obviously, vampires could fly, though she had never seen them doing so until she arrived in Crimson City. Where the curtain did not quite cover the window, a shock of white pressed against the glass. "That's one of my roses!" she realized. "They haven't even been transplanted from the pots to the ground yet. I didn't think Marius knew they'd arrived."

"Oh, my goodness," Folie said. "How romantic! Marius has finally come, and he brought you a rose."

"Now? He's come now?" A flurry of feelings swamped Tatiana, and the knocking persisted. "He can't want me *now*. I'll have to send him away."

"You can't send your husband away."

"He only thinks he understands, Folie, and I'm certainly not about to explain. Not in this state. Not while unable to control myself. Look at me! Quick, fix the back of my gown!" At her command, Folie fumbled at the buttons up her sister's back while Tatiana attended to her hair and ran a handkerchief over the damp sheen covering her skin.

"Open the damn window already!" a voice bellowed. "It's raining out here."

Folie and Tatiana both froze. Tatiana gestured for Folie to stop, smoothed her hair with her hand and then stood up from the dressing table. Walking slowly to the window, she took a deep breath and swept the curtain aside. Hayden Wilks stood on the ledge with an Asprey rose in his hand, the rain-swept backdrop of Crimson City behind him.

"Are you going to open it?" Folie whispered.

"Of course not," Tatiana said.

Hayden reached out, produced a blade, stuck it in the window latch and jiggled. The window unlocked. He stuck his dripping hand through the gap and presented Tatiana with the rose. She didn't take it.

"May I enter?" he asked. Not waiting for an answer, he leapt off the sill into the room, then turned around and shut the window.

Folie sucked in a loud breath. Hayden sketched her a dramatic bow. "How's Dumont Prison treating you? Can I get you anything? Chocolate bars? A change of underwear?"

The girl shook her head, eyes like saucers.

Hayden turned back to Tatiana. "Heard you were

locked in for the Change. I can totally relate to your self-loathing, so I thought I'd stop by for support. And maybe to see you chase your own ass."

"You . . . disgusting man!" she accused, raising her nose in the air. She hated herself for not being sorry it was Hayden instead of Marius.

"So I'm told." He stood, water dripping from his black leather jacket onto the plush Aubusson carpet. His hair was plastered to the sides of his face, and a shockingly dark swath of stubble contrasted with his pallid jaw.

Tatiana looked down at the red and white flower he'd brought. "You stupid boy," she murmured. "You never pick the first bloom so early." When she looked up, Hayden was still staring at her.

"Better early than never. I wasn't sure how long you'd be stuck up here."

"How did you even know I was here?"

"I know everything that happens in Dumont Towers. Fleur can tell you as much." His gaze faltered, and his lashes swept down as he glanced away.

Tatiana bit her lower lip, unsure what to say, then blushed as his gaze moved to her mouth.

"Come outside with me," Hayden suggested. "See the city. Not the official tour, of course. I'll show you things off the beaten path. In other words, *real life*."

"Oh!" Folie exclaimed. Unthinking, she took an eager step forward.

Her sister dragged her back. "Certainly not," Tatiana said. She turned. "Folie, remember yourself."

"Mr. Hayden Wilks," Folie proclaimed, her hands on her hips and her chin raised, attempting to look imperious. "We are in the midst of the Change, and it is most . . . most . . . It is most *unseemly* for you to be here. You must leave at once!"

A smile twitched at the corner of Hayden's mouth. "Why?"

"No one is to see us."

"Why not?"

Folie faltered, glancing at Tatiana for instruction, but Tatiana was staring again at the rose in Hayden's hand. "Because we're princesses, and people will think we're disgusting animals."

Tatiana's head snapped up. "Oh, Folie. You can't say everything you think out loud."

"Why not?" Hayden repeated, smiling. "What does it matter? Why are you worried what people think of you, especially if you're royalty?"

Tatiana found herself blathering. "It matters *more* because we're royalty. Of course it matters! We have a position and a name and responsibilities. . . . Even you would think—"

"What does it matter what I think?" Hayden asked.

Tatiana was taken aback. "It matters what everyone thinks. That's just the way it is."

Hayden walked to a floor mirror standing in the corner, picked at the gilt while watching Tatiana in the reflection. "So, you don't care what I think, in particular."

"Of course not."

"No, of course not," he agreed, turning. "Well, for what it's worth, you look good to me. Better than good. Gorgeous. I don't care that you're a dog."

Folie gasped, and Tatiana snarled. Such terminology was never used in New York—at least, not by anyone whom her family allowed to live. *Control yourself. Control!*

Hayden stepped forward and brushed rose petals under her chin, his gaze intense. He looked at her as if he was really seeing her, whereas Marius always seemed somewhere else. Tatiana moved back, rather undone.

"You're not supposed to touch me," she muttered.

"Why?"

She wheeled. "Why do you always ask *why*?"

Hayden moved so fast, Folie flattened herself against the wall to avoid his rush. He took Tatiana in his arms and whispered, "Maybe the question is, why don't you?" The rain on his lips was wet on her ear.

"Because I have responsibilities," she whispered. "Duties."

The full moon was roiling within Tatiana. Hayden slowly moved his mouth down her jawline. *Pull away. Fight him.* Hayden's blatant sexuality contrasted sharply with Marius's indifference. Tatiana let lust pool unfamiliarly between her thighs, and she gasped, nearly giving in to the animal instinct pulsing so strongly within her. Were it not for Folie plastered against the wall, her eyes shining like the moon itself, Tatiana might have let his lips slide across hers.

With all her strength, she pushed away from the vampire and stared mutely into her sister's eyes. "This is what happens . . . ," she began. "This is what happens if we are not vigilant." She made a show of smoothing her hair and straightening her dress.

Hayden studied both girls with a curious smile, then released a shaky breath. "Well. All right then. I'd better go before you two get down on all fours and start barking. Of course, that could still be fun. . . ."

Folie's jaw dropped. Tatiana felt much the same. Hayden opened the window and stepped back through, standing on the sill in the pouring rain. He leapt to the balustrade and raised his arms straight out at his sides. Then he broke into a wide smile and fell backward.

A flash of light split the sky. Folie screamed. The two sisters rushed forward and looked out, and Tatiana saw Hayden hovering a few stories below, his dark clothes sodden by rain and plastered by wind against a lean and powerful body. He gave a jaunty salute and then disappeared into the dark.

Tatiana and Folie stepped back, both dazed. A smile began to curve Folie's lips.

"Preposterous behavior," Tatiana muttered, not liking her sister's expression. She collected herself, closed the window and grabbed a throw from the bed. Then, with her heart nearly pounding out of her chest, she cleaned up the leftover water from Hayden's visit.

Her sister gave a small whimper, which seemed half of pleasure, half of pain. Tatiana recognized it as Folie about to change. But at the same moment, the clock chimed. Tatiana looked up and noted the time, and she managed a small but triumphant smile.

"Look how long we've lasted, Folie. We've done well. Very well! Maybe someday we'll learn to suppress the entire process."

Her sister's voice was tremulous. "But we'd be able to do it when we wanted, wouldn't we?"

Tatiana gave Folie a sharp look before she was stymied by a wave of nausea—her own change coming on. She spun and caught a glimpse of herself in the mirror, saw the initial deformations of her body. All she could hope was that Marius would not come. No matter what Hayden claimed, she felt certain her husband would not find her werewolf form "gorgeous," no more than he would find attractive a complete and wanton lack of self-control.

# CHAPTER TWENTY-ONE

*London, England.*
*August, 1851*

Halfway across the greens of Hyde Park, Lucy Vaughan's alarming soprano caught up to Charlotte on a particularly forceful gust of wind. "Miss Paxton!"

Charlotte gritted her teeth, took a deep breath, fixed a smile on her face and turned. "Miss Vaughan. How lovely to see you again."

"Likewise, Miss Paxton. And may I introduce my dear friend, Miss Jane St. Giles, all the way from New York! I believe I have mentioned her before."

The three ladies smiled at each other in pregnant silence. After a pause, Charlotte noted pointedly, "You take a rather keen interest in the exhibition all of a sudden, Miss Vaughan. You have caught the fever for invention and industry?"

"Yes, Miss Paxton," Lucy replied. "I *do* take a keen interest in what goes on here. A very keen interest. I wouldn't be at all surprised if I were to visit this place every week. There is so much to see, as my brother seems to have discovered before me. He has promised to escort Miss St. Giles and me around whenever we ask."

"How lovely," Charlotte managed.

"Quite." Lucy gave her an amused smile. "We were just going to a rather exciting auxiliary exhibition. Have you heard about Mr. Gould's hummingbirds? They say they can fit in the palm of one's hand and have skins like rainbows. You must come with us. We can't have you scampering about all alone and unescorted. So, shall we?" She tucked one arm through the crook of Miss St. Giles's and the other through Charlotte's, and began leading them both toward the Crystal Palace.

To Charlotte's dismay, Lucy's scheme took them to a carriage destined three miles hence, to the auxiliary hummingbird exhibit at Regent Park. Like a schoolmarm wrangling her charges, Lucy marched the trio into the special exhibition hall, paying the necessary fees with such brisk efficiency Charlotte couldn't help but feel the entire trip had been planned. It was unsurprising, really. If Lucy was intentionally trying to keep Charlotte from Edward, as Charlotte assumed, she'd been a wild success; the two had seen little of each other in any meaningful way for the past few weeks.

The crowd was thick, and each narrow, glass-encased exhibit was surrounded. Inside the displays, birds were posed in shockingly lifelike scenarios. Lifelike, however, was not the same as alive. The specimens were only stuffed in a way that gave them shape and suggested movement, for they had clearly expired some time ago.

"Oh, I thought they would be . . . alive," Charlotte murmured, not at all sure she liked this science they called taxidermy. This was the first such display she'd seen, and frankly Charlotte wasn't even sure it should be called a science.

"You silly girl," Lucy replied. Glancing over at Miss St. Giles, she reported, "He brought an entire flock from America. Isn't that what you told me, Jane?"

The heiress lowered dark eyes. "Indeed, but they all died. Every single one. Apparently they were stored at a gentleman's club of some sort prior to the exhibition."

"The Inventors Club," Lucy said officiously.

Jane shrugged. "Yes. Well, I'm told the conditions were all wrong. Terribly disappointing that they should all die, but it's much better this way, don't you think? We can admire them so much more easily."

"Quite," Charlotte agreed, biting back the satirical urge to execrate the hummingbirds for their inconvenient partiality to moving and breathing. She backed away from a display case, but as she did, she backed into one of the exhibit's guards. "Please excuse me! I was not paying attention," she gasped.

The guard smiled kindly. "Terrible sorry to be in the way, miss."

"Could you tell me . . . How did the birds die?"

The guard stood taller, seemingly pleased to be of service. "Some say it were the temperature, it were, miss. Some others say it were the infernal machines—them little birds breathing all that smoke. I'd not like to breathe the smoke all day, and these little things so delicate and all . . . Even the hardier creatures is having a time of it in there, I understand. They . . ." He trailed off.

"Did something happen?" Charlotte pressed.

The guard leaned forward, eyes wide with excitement. Charlotte wondered just how secret and possibly sordid the tale was. "Accident at the exhibition, miss. My friend wot guards the West Indies nave says they're too close to the inventions. Breathing in the smoke, that's wot it is. And after that last big eruption of Lord Gilliam's machine . . ."

Charlotte shivered, thinking of the dead bat she'd seen. "Are the animals in the West Indies nave all dead then?" she asked. "The . . . bats?"

"No, miss. But they moved the sick away from the viewing naves and brought in some new. He reinstalled it, but I won't be s'prised if they take Gilliam's exhibit away afore the end. The critters left there aren't quite right in the head—if you knows wot I mean."

Charlotte pressed her gloved hand to her chest. "That's horrible," she breathed.

"A friend of yours, Miss Paxton?" Lucy Vaughan asked, coming up and dismissing the guard with a look. He managed a twisted smile that showed he understood, and quietly stepped back into anonymity.

"My, you *are* an interesting girl," Lucy continued in flat tones. "Such equity in your connections. However, we're off to tea. We shall drop you at the exhibition, pick up my brother, and the entire thing will be quite convenient for everybody."

"How kind of you," Charlotte replied, even more certain that the encounter had been orchestrated. It was therefore with no small amount of satisfaction that Charlotte regarded the displeasure on Lucy's face when Edward met them at the main fountains of the Crystal Palace, giving a start at seeing them all in company together. Her satisfaction was increased as Charlotte watched Jane St. Giles and Edward and could detect no intimacy between them.

*Is it true?* she wondered, glancing at Edward's face. *Is there an understanding between you and Miss St. Giles?*

He stared at her, his expression one of helplessness. "Miss Paxton, delightful to see you again."

"Likewise, Mr. Vaughan. However briefly." Charlotte turned back to the other two ladies. "Thank you so much for your kind invitation to see the hummingbirds. Now, I suppose I must be going."

"Oh, you mustn't," Lucy announced, a wicked look appearing in her eyes. "I have just had an idea. Tea must wait. Now that we have seen one set of winged creatures, we must compare." She turned to the others. "Let us go see the winged beasts that had poor Charlotte in such a faint the other day!"

Seeing Charlotte's alarm, Edward remarked quietly, "I don't think that a good idea."

"I would like to see them," Jane spoke up, stepping forward. She looked Charlotte up and down. "And perhaps Miss Paxton would like a second chance."

Hating to be so humiliated, Charlotte found herself agreeing.

"You needn't go, Miss Paxton," Edward pressed with a frown, clearly trying to communicate with his eyes. "You have nothing to prove to any of us."

Charlotte gave him a beseeching look, begging to let the issue drop, then followed behind as Edward and Jane crossed the floor of the palace, locked in the crooks of Lucy's arms.

At the West Indies nave, where the bats had indeed frightened her, there was a sign saying the exhibit piece was temporarily incomplete. A colorful drape of exotic paisley had been flung across the area, bisecting the nave so that one who did not wish to see the bats could still enjoy the remainder of the exhibit. Charlotte froze, staring at the drape behind which she could hear an inhuman rustling and murmuring.

Lucy and Jane moved up to the bat cage. Charlotte and Edward stood back.

"Are you afraid, Miss Paxton?" Lucy called. She flounced up to the cages with Jane and began banging on the metal bars with her parasol. The animals flapped and fussed and made louder noises. "Oh, I think that one has had too much to drink!" Lucy cried, dissolving into peals of laughter.

"They want to get out," Charlotte murmured, not sure

where to look but unwilling to move closer. "The smoke has made them ill."

Lucy put an arm around Jane's shoulder, forcing her would-be sister-in-law to stay with her at the cages. With her other she continued to beat on the metal bars with her parasol, stirring the animals into a frenzy.

"Lucy, stop. You're frightening them. They may lunge at you," Edward said. He attempted to draw back both her and Miss St. Giles.

Lucy turned, face sweating, hair disheveled, and she sneered, "*I* am not afraid."

"Neither am I," Jane chimed in. She gave Charlotte a pointed look, though she appeared faintly unsettled and green.

A sob slipped from Charlotte's lips, and she feared making a spectacle of herself a second time. Edward saw, and took her hand to drag her behind the drape. There, though hidden from view, Charlotte could still hear everything: the banging, Lucy mocking the animals, their cries. Edward stood with his hat in his hand, the rise and fall of his chest visible. It was very warm in the nave. Charlotte's heart beat too fast.

"Charlie," Edward said.

Charlotte looked up, struck by the sound of his pet name for her. The look on his face was stormy. Edward held out his hand, and Charlotte stared at it for a moment before slowly taking it with her own. He sucked in a quick breath as their fingers met.

"They just want to get out," she whispered. "They just want to be left alone."

Edward exhaled very suddenly, then pulled her back against his body. Charlotte could feel his heat. His jaw pressed against her temple; she could feel his quickened pulse. Then he reached around her body and began to roughly remove her glove.

Naked skin—Charlotte watched as Edward's fingers uncovered her hand and stroked it. The heat of the entire nave was charged with a kind of electricity, and she felt as caged as those otherworldly creatures, similarly unable to act upon desires and needs. At the mercy of others . . . she was always at the mercy of others.

She closed her eyes as he caressed the delicate flesh of her arm, her heart pounding. A strange desire began to pool between her legs, and where his groin pressed up against her back she felt him turn hard beneath his trousers. With her eyes closed, Charlotte pressed her head back against his chest.

A fluttering sounded, followed by a dull thud and then a pair of screams. The paisley drape lurched. Edward dropped Charlotte's arm just as Jane and Lucy burst into view, squealing in delighted horror and amusement. Charlotte and Edward had already turned away from one another, but Lucy surveyed the close quarters behind the drape with fading triumph. She realized she had made a grave miscalculation.

# CHAPTER TWENTY-TWO

"Hey, stranger. Nice to see you. I was hoping you'd get here early," Bridget said. She pulled herself off the chaise in the entry of the Rogues Club where she'd sprawled and walked across the polished parquet floor.

Jill took one look at the mischievous smile on her friend's face and inwardly groaned. That look usually meant a new bit of gossip was making the rounds. "What's the latest on TR?" she asked quickly.

"Every human in the club has been tapped," Bridget replied, heading for the security desk.

"Where's everybody meeting?"

"Back lounge." Bridget studied her intently. "So, on the continuum of emotional stability, is your needle pointing anywhere near fragile?"

Jill managed a smile. "I'm fine."

"Good, because this came for you from Dumont Towers." Bridget reached behind the desk and pulled out an envelope. Jill recognized Marius's personal stationery. Her face went hot.

Bridget raised a palm. "I'm not here to judge. Why do you think I kept it out of the mail slots before everyone and his mother saw it?" She leaned close and lowered her voice. "I kinda figured the whole thing would fade when he was married. Hardly seems like him, with all that misplaced honor and crap that made him marry that bitch in the first place."

"This isn't what it looks like," Jill replied in a mutter.

Neither woman spoke for a moment, Bridget standing expectantly in Jill's way. Jill pointedly raised the envelope. "We'll talk later, okay?"

"Right. You want to sniff the paper in private. Oh, hey, don't look at me like that! You brought your business to the club. You're just lucky you're friends with management. I won't tell anybody," she laughed, pointing to the envelope. "And if there's counterintelligence you want me to spread, I'm happy to do it, but you've got to give me the backstory."

"Counterintelligence?" Jill laughed as well, even though Bridget's way of speaking was nothing new. Her friend didn't see a difference between real life and the scheming that so often went along with trying to earn a living—or even survive—in this town. But Bridget's explanations weren't going to stop any of the nasty innuendo undoubtedly crossing Crimson City. Jill almost felt sorry for Tatiana Asprey. Almost.

"Thanks but no thanks," she replied, adding ruefully, "Now, get out of my way and let me sniff the paper in private."

Bridget smiled and stepped aside. Jill headed down the hall to the lounge, opening the envelope on her way. There was written a set of GPS coordinates and a time, and a hastily scrawled note.

*Please come.*
*Marius*

Jill slowed and stared down at the script. In spite of everything, the message was a thrill. He was actually asking for her. She could ignore it, make the point that he was on his own now, that they'd handled Gregory Bell's murder to the limits of her ability and she would report back when and if she discovered anything new . . . but he wouldn't be calling her back into an active role if it weren't important. She wondered what exactly had changed.

*He calls, I come. He says jump, and whether he can hear me or feel me anymore, I still somehow believe he'll catch me if I fall. I'm a fool . . . and he's married.*

Jill crumpled the paper in her fist and pressed it to her chest, then crammed it back into the envelope and retraced her steps. In the lobby, Bridget looked up in surprise.

"I can't help it," Jill mumbled. "I have to go."

"Try harder," Bridget said sharply. Then her face softened and she said, "I'll take notes for you."

She could have taken any of several possible routes to get to Marius, but Jill couldn't help thinking about Horschaw's parting salvo. "Come have a drink at Bosco's," he'd said. They'd be waiting. She wanted to pass by and check things out.

On any given day, Bosco's was where you could find the balance of the city's outsiders. The Rogues Club was a private affair; this establishment was public. If you had issues with authority and a penchant for working the black markets of the city, either offering labor or goods, this was both your watering hole and your temp agency. Bosco himself worked the bar, either welcoming visitors or making it clear via a gun barrel that a visitor had better hit the street. Normally, even mechs were willing to show their faces there, because there was no way an official known to be working for the human government could get through the door.

The disconnect hit Jill hard as she turned onto the

street leading to the bar and followed the noise. The idea of Horschaw getting past Bosco reminded her of tanks smashing across a border to occupy a neutral country, and she wondered what threats had been made—or deal brokered. The human government was holding nothing back, sending the message that strata 0, the swath of Crimson City between the vampires above and the werewolves below, had been wholly reclaimed.

The bar was teeming. Jill wished she had time to go inside and sit, really take the pulse of the city and get the latest word on the street. Well, she could already tell that the city's pulse was racing. There were so many people present, they spilled out of the bar and were gathered in small groups on the sidewalk, probably sharing Recall stories and making grandiose statements about how they'd never sell out. That was how it once would have been, at least. Horschaw might have changed things.

If the I-Ops "manager" really was lurking inside, waiting for his turncoats to collect on their drinks, she didn't want to see him. Ducking her head, Jill swerved and used a side street to escape. After a short walk, she reached the coordinates written on Marius's note: an intersection in a dilapidated part of town. He had already arrived. He was sitting in front of an abandoned and half-crumbled church, on a cracked curbside, with his head in his hands.

Jill stopped in her tracks, unnerved by the unusual frailty of his body language. And when he looked up and she saw his eyes, what she'd thought was despondency looked more like . . . pain?

"Thank you for coming," he said, standing.

She cleared her throat and affected an air of nonchalance. "Sure. So, what's this all about? Why am I here?"

"I learned something fairly intense from the mechs

yesterday," Marius explained. "They believe they can complete an antidote for what killed Bell if they have original genetic material from the very beginning of our vampire evolutionary stream. They want to reverse-engineer a cure using DNA from someone infected at the time when humans were first turned vampire and werewolf."

"But that goes all the way back to the London Blood-Taint. Is that what you're talking about?" Jill asked in surprise.

Marius nodded.

"That's fantastic. I mean, in theory it's fantastic. But I thought every scrap of official vampire history was destroyed during the first Recall, when humans started freaking out about turning monster by standing too close to somebody else's sneeze, or whatever. Do you even have anything left from that far back? Isn't all your stuff just re-creations and models?"

Marius nodded. "Unfortunately, yes. And it's the same for the werewolves. They were caught up in the same purge."

"I guess if there's anything left in Crimson City from the DNA of original vampire and werewolf families, the government has it under lock and key in some hermetically sealed box." Jill looked at him in surprise. "Is that why you wanted me to come? To go sneaking—"

"No!" Marius looked ill at her suggestion. "No. That's not at all what I was thinking."

"Okaaay." She watched Marius curiously. His agitation was palpable.

"That's not at *all* what I meant to suggest, Jillian," he repeated. "You are *not* to contact the human government. Do you understand me?"

Jill followed his gaze to the doorway of the church behind him, and then looked back. "If you don't want me to make contact with the government, why am I here?"

"I . . ."

"Yeah?"

Marius searched her face so intently it made Jill blush. "What?"

Marius glanced away and seemed to be struggling with something. Finally, he cleared his throat. "I thought . . ."

Jill raised an eyebrow.

"I thought you'd find the information useful."

"You thought I'd find the information *useful*?" she asked. He must be going mad. One minute he wanted her to stay out of the whole affair, the next minute he was calling for a rendezvous to drag her back in. Something wasn't kosher, and it killed her that she had absolutely no sense of what he was thinking or feeling anymore. They stood staring at each other, and that new and disconcerting blankness between them passed through Jill like an ice-cold breeze.

"Well, it's all great fodder for a news story," she said, mostly to gauge his reaction. "Maybe we can spin it so that the Dumonts seem in complete control."

"Fine," Marius said. "I know you'll use discretion."

Jill narrowed her eyes, surprised by his distracted acquiescence, but he didn't remark further on the topic.

"Let's go inside," he suggested, offering his arm to help her over some rubble. She rejected it, trying not to laugh when it seemed as if he could have used her help more than she needed his.

Before they could knock, a metal screen at the top of the huge wooden door pulled away from its moorings, and a set of bright green eyes peered out. They glanced side to side and up and down several times, then the right one glowed neon and emitted a spray of light beams that surrounded them in a grid, and Jill realized the eyes belonged to a mech. They were being scanned for information.

Marius didn't seem concerned, and at last the door opened.

"You are Marius Dumont and Jillian Cooper," said the mech behind it. "Leyton and I were in the same barracks. Escaped together. I'm not looking to go back. He must trust you." He cocked his head and eyed them, head to toe. "You take nothing with you and you tell no one I am here."

"If it's our word of honor you want," Marius said, offering the mech his hand, "you have it. No one will hear of this place through us, and what is here, stays here."

The mech looked past them into the street and then turned and studied Jill for a long moment before offering Marius his hand. "They call me the Librarian," he said as the two men shook on the arrangement, and he ushered them inside.

The church was not large, and the air was clogged with a combination of dust and the odor of preservation fluid. Brightening the mood were beams shot through several panes of stained glass, splashing the walls with colorful light.

"I should have taken your hand as well," the mech suddenly said. Jill turned to find him staring at her, and she smiled and made to shake. The mech shyly took her hand in both of his, and turned her palm over, apparently examining her skin. "I don't know any women," he said.

Marius cleared his throat. "If you've spoken to Leyton about us, I'm sure you understand our urgency."

The Librarian let go of Jill and nodded. "He said you are trying to find genetic material from the onset of the Blood-Taint. I may be able to help you."

He led them through the narthex and nave to the back

of the church, where a metal door had been built into the wall. He raised his hand, and an oddly shaped metal pick slid out from under the nail of his left index finger. He unlocked the door with the tool.

Jill gasped. The revealed quarters were beautiful, a riot of rich color. Clearly the mech had taken great pains to make a home for himself that was different from his early life in the stark I-Ops barracks where the human government kept such soldiers captive. Here the walls were covered with framed engravings and pages salvaged from illuminated manuscripts. Bookshelves took up half the space. Papers and tomes were meticulously organized and labeled, and placed in perfectly aligned stacks. In a corner was a small table where he'd been repairing and polishing leather bindings, and in another was a work sink with the sides piled high with chemical bottles. He'd clearly been interrupted in the course of applying fresh gold leaf to restore one small illustration.

The Librarian pointed to a long workbench at the back of the room, where research materials were laid out in small stacks. "It's organized by preservation priority, but if you tell me what you're looking for, I'll be able to get what you need, no problem."

Jill looked around the room for something besides documents. "This is great, but do you have any *things*? I don't mean to be disrespectful, but it seems that we need DNA. We'd do better with a lab—a jar of preserved body parts or something." She turned to Marius, thinking he was uncharacteristically quiet. "Is this going to help?"

Marius looked unconvinced.

The Librarian frowned. "These books contain stories of those who lived around the time of the Blood-Taint. They might well lead to what you are looking for. They are the best I have, and Leyton obviously believed they might help."

"Maybe he can lift DNA from the paper," Jill muttered.

"Everything here is chemically treated as soon as it comes in," the Librarian remarked, giving a shake of his head. "No useful DNA would survive."

"If no biological material, do you have any physical items from the past? Any relics from the period?" Marius asked, clearly disappointed.

"This is a library, not a museum," the mech replied, leaning between Jill and Marius and touching his fingertips gently to a leather cover holding a sheaf of letters. "Although it would please me to find relics for preservation."

Jill turned to Marius. "Now what?"

He tapped his fingers on the table for a moment. "Now, I suppose, we trace a genealogy to someone who lives in Crimson City. We'll look for the earliest mention of someone being turned and see if we can find a familiar name. That person, that family . . . that line will hopefully have some forgotten artifact with some form of DNA that we can use."

"The earliest mention . . ." The Librarian nodded and disappeared into the shelves.

"Hello, haystack, have you seen our needle?" Jill asked. "I'm not trying to be funny!" she said when Marius smiled.

"Something tells me you did not get an A in that Victorian history class of yours. Perhaps it still rankles?" he teased.

Jill glowered at him. "B-plus is still good," she muttered.

The mech returned with two enormous binders. "I've

pulled the oldest collection I have. These are the papers of Charlotte Paxton. They span the time of the Blood-Taint." The desk groaned as he set the volumes on the table and then disappeared back into his workroom.

"I guess we just dive in." Jill opened the closest binder and paged through sheaves of letters, journal entries and clippings dating back to London's Victorian age in the 1850s. She frowned as she saw the papers and letters were completely out of order. "I suppose if you have RAM in your brain, it's not a big deal to sort stuff on the fly."

Marius flipped through the beginning of his binder. "Look. Here she is writing about some sort of disease. It's dated 1853. If we can just get all of this in order, starting from the very first mention, we'll look for names and perhaps—"

The Librarian returned from a back room and lowered a third volume. "That's all of it."

Jill looked at Marius in dismay. "You're kidding me!" She stared down at the mass of paperwork. "It'll take days to get through all this, and we don't know what it may hold."

Giving a sigh, she removed her jacket and hung it on her chair. The mech suddenly raised his head and moved his face close to Jill's. Marius leapt up, sandwiching her but clearly meaning to offer protection. Jill wasn't exactly sure what either man intended.

She stared at the mech. "Er, is something wrong?"

"No," the Librarian replied. "You smell nice. You smell as I imagine Asprey roses smell."

Jill glared at him. "Are you trying to be a jerk?" she blurted. "Maybe tweak that sensitivity chip, bud."

"He's helping us," Marius murmured into her ear, clearly relieved. He sat down again. "He doesn't know any better."

Jill clenched her teeth so hard she could feel a vein in her jaw throb.

The mech could not have looked more confused. "It was a compliment. 'You smell nice.' Nice. *Nice* is a positive." He looked between her and Marius for a moment, and then the nonmetal portions of his face paled. "Dammit," he said with complete frustration, smacking himself in the forehead. "I must have missed something." He moved to the reference wall and took down an enormous dictionary.

"He's never been so close to a beautiful woman," Marius said.

"Don't flatter me," Jill retorted.

Marius sighed. "I'm sorry. I—"

"Forgot who you were with?" Jill finished.

Further comment was cut off by a strangled cry—Marius's. It was as if he tried to both suppress pain and prevent her from seeing his sudden suffering. Before she could say a word, he blinked rapidly and stood, his hand like a claw on the back of his chair.

"Need to get some water," he mumbled, staggering toward the sink at the far corner of the room. He leaned over it, supporting himself with his arms.

Jill leapt up. "Marius?"

He splashed some water onto his face, turned and faced her with a smile, though his skin was paler than normal. "I'm fine. I don't know what that was. Just a . . . migraine." He tried to walk back to his seat, but she stood in his way, searching his expression in the dim light and trying to discern what he was feeling.

Marius tried to back up, but he had nowhere to go. Instead, he raised his palms in a defensive gesture. Jill's heart sank. Such a vulnerable motion was not like him at all. She had to clasp her hands together to quell her instinctive desire to embrace him.

"I'm *fine*," he repeated, trying to keep his tone light.

"You're not."

He brushed past her and sat down in his chair, bent his head over the Paxton papers and pretended to read, but Jill saw that he was too distraught to process anything.

"I said, you're not, are you?" Jill said a little too loudly.

A long moment of silence passed between them. At last Marius looked up, and what Jill saw in his eyes made her own well with tears. She knew what he was going to say, and though she'd pushed for the truth, she wasn't sure she could bear it.

"No, I'm not fine," he finally admitted. "Whatever killed Gregory Bell is in me now."

Jill bit down on her lower lip to stop it from trembling. She could not speak.

"If the mechs don't get me the antidote, I'm going to die."

Jill stared up at Marius's face, a kind of numb horror sweeping her. A terrible gasp burst from her lips, but she didn't weep. If she did, that would mean she accepted what he said, that she accepted the reality of such a nightmare.

She gestured to the papers covering the desk. "Why are we wasting our time on *this*?"

"If I can get some original DNA to Leyton—"

"No," Jill snarled.

Marius looked confused.

"I said no. This . . . You're not thinking straight." She looked at the stack of ancient papers in horror. So much paper. "This isn't going to work. We're not going to find any DNA here. Not in time." She gestured dismissively to the volumes. "When we were just thinking about this theoretically, it was one thing, but now it's totally different. These are books and papers, dusty documents from a world far less advanced than today. We don't even know if we can find what we need! It's not like this girl's diaries will mention some ultrasecret DNA blob she left hidden in a time machine. Marius, we need another plan."

"These documents may tell us something, somewhere else we should look, someone we should talk to. Look, it's not what I was hoping for either." He ruffled his hair in exasperation. "I thought we'd get something tangible. But . . . Leyton understands the situation. He wouldn't send us here if he didn't think we'd find a clue."

Jill felt tears press against her eyes. "A clue? We need more than a clue. You just told me you're dying!" Her self-control crumbled. "Unless this Charlotte Paxton had a goddamn antidote recipe in her reticule, this is wasted time."

She leapt up so fast her chair pitched to the ground. The Librarian appeared at the door, staring curiously inward from the shadows of the church nave, but he said nothing and kept his distance.

"Don't leave. Please, Jillian," Marius begged. "Not like this."

She retrieved her jacket and stuffed her arms through its sleeves. "I came here because, for once, you asked for me. So I came," she hissed, her voice shaking. She paused and clutched at her heart. "But it's the same damn thing. This plan you have is idiotic. You never could see the forest for the trees. It's the same old story. I mean, what else is new? The part about you dying? Big deal. Just go ahead and die for all I care. Either way, you're choosing to leave me all alone—and you won't let me do anything about it." Jill turned and ran into the nave and toward the front door.

"Jillian!" Marius cried, taking a few steps after her. "Don't."

"I'd follow her if she were mine," the mech called out.

"I'm not his!" Jill screamed in response. Then she turned and shoved the heavy main door of the church with all her might. It flung wide, and she took off running. "I never was."

# CHAPTER TWENTY-THREE

*London, England*
*September, 1851*

Edward had felt for some time that the world was becoming smaller and smaller around him. He spent long hours at the Inventors Club, as much to stay out of female company as to enjoy that of his male friends.

Charlotte had given up their assignations after he'd touched her hand so intimately and then failed to make any promise of intentions. Though Edward could not blame her for doing what he did not have the strength to do himself, he found that he could not forget her, and that her absence these past few weeks was a taste of what life would soon be like. Nothing could shake his desire for just one more afternoon with her before he was forced to sell his soul to society and engage himself to Miss St. Giles, so he still pored over his program to determine which exhibit to study next, and every week he went to the Crystal Palace.

He began to attend at off-hours—at *all* hours, really. He was stuffed with as much lemonade ice and information about farming techniques in the colonies as he could ever want. He found himself standing for long periods at Lord Gilliam's invention, letting the warm red-orange smoke wind around his body like a blanket.

Today, in the afternoon, he left the building, despondent once again over her absence, understanding that if he did not have the courage to say aloud what he felt in his heart, then he did not deserve Charlotte Paxton's company at all. He pressed his hand against the token in the small pocket of his waistcoat. He *wanted* to say something; he was ready to say something, if only he might have the right opportunity. . . .

He wandered the park for some time before his attention was grabbed by a peddler selling a rather ingenious home-tooled invention. Seeking to show solidarity, he purchased a couple of items from the man's tray.

It was when he turned for home that he saw her: Charlotte, just coming down from the palace steps. She was clutching a pink rose in her hand and looked quite put out, striding purposefully away from the exhibition hall. Edward had to smile. She was still working on her project, still bringing the results to her cousin for analysis. She would never give up. Edward found his heart beating too quickly, his hands trembling, as he watched her walk.

Despair consumed him. Then resolution. *I cannot stand here and do nothing. I must go to her.*

He moved quickly—as quickly as he could. He dared not call out her name, dared not actually run. But when he was close enough to reach out and grasp her shawl, she stopped short as if she knew he was there. He had not touched her.

She turned, eyes wide, chest heaving.

Edward bowed and breathlessly said, "It has been a long time. Too long. I am surprised I have not run into you lately, Miss Paxton."

"Mr. Vaughan," she replied, flustered enough to drop her rose on the ground. The delicate bloom broke apart at their feet. "I have decided to take a more spontaneous approach to viewing the exhibition. I have not been following the program."

"Oh, I see," he replied, feeling quite miserable. He looked back at the Crystal Palace and said, "Well, I'm sorry to have missed you. I visited the white wolves today. Their fur is extraordinary. Quite exotic, but docile as dogs. I think you would have liked them. . . ." He balled his gloves in his hands. "I seem to be having trouble. . . . Lucy, you see—she's doggedly interested in the exhibition these days, and she requires quite a lot of attention."

"Yes, I know," Charlotte said. They stared at each other for a moment before she adjusted her bonnet and said with a small smile, "Keeping you out of trouble, I should think, Mr. Vaughan."

"That seems to be the idea," he agreed. He looked around, tipping his hat to an acquaintance passing through the park, overly conscious of the impropriety of their standing here when Charlotte did not have a chaperone.

"I should go," she said.

"You're on your way home," he pointed out, hating himself for the inanity. He felt as though he were caught in some sort of script, as if he knew the lines that were required of him yet bitterly wished he could say something else.

"Yes, I am going home," Charlotte agreed, a rather pained expression on her face.

They stood a little longer, awkward, neither one wanting to part, yet neither having an excuse for further conversation. "Good day, Mr. Vaughan," Charlotte finally said. Then she bobbed a curtsey and began plowing through the park in a most unladylike manner. If she could have escaped him faster, Edward was quite sure she would have. Most likely it was only a tight corset stopping her from breaking into a run.

He followed slowly, watching with a kind of hollow despair, then saw her pass along a small grove of trees. Without thinking, he ran the short distance between them and pulled her into the copse alongside a white stone rotunda.

She stared at his hand around her arm in shock, and Edward quickly dropped his hands. "I purchased something outside the exhibition today, Charlie," he blurted, instead of any explanation. "I think you'll find it very interesting."

Charlotte glanced over her shoulder. The large tree trunks hid them from both sides. They could see to the street but, it seemed, if they stood in just the right spot, they could not be seen.

She peeked back at him. Edward held up his package. Charlotte appeared confused. "Edward?"

Alone. He'd never been so alone with her before. They both looked at each other for a moment, and Charlotte swallowed, hard.

"What is it?" she whispered.

"What is what?" he replied.

"What did you purchase?"

After a moment he realized what she meant. He cleared his throat and ripped the paper away to expose the contents. "A rather handy new invention a man was selling. He'd made a whole basket of them. The man claims that, if one places this crème on the skin first, this blade will glide easier. I believe it is intended for shaving."

"Really? Is it the crème or the blade that has unique properties?" Charlotte whispered.

"I don't know. Shall we see how well the blade can cut?"

He'd wanted a token of hers for so long—something

he could keep for himself that no one else could see, something he could touch. Charlotte blushed. She stared into his eyes and nodded, so, with his free hand, Edward slid his fingers into her hair, gently unwinding a strand from its mooring of pins.

Edward could hear Charlotte's tremulous breathing as the curl slipped free. He pressed his palm against her cheek and temple, felt her skin burn beneath his touch. His knife fell to the ground. It was as if the entire world simply slipped away, as if he and his beloved were alone with no one to say that this was wrong or he was wrong or anything at all was wrong. His other hand swept up and raised her face to his, and he crushed his lips down upon hers.

In all his life, Edward had never dreamed of such exquisite joy taking physical form. Charlotte melted into him, gasping in exultation, and Edward murmured her name against her mouth. And then he felt her hands begin to lose purchase on his arms.

He slowly lifted his mouth away from hers. With his head slightly tipped, he regarded her wordlessly, nearly too overcome to speak. He stepped back.

"Miss Paxton," he said hoarsely. "Miss Paxton, I . . . There is something I need to tell you." But footsteps and laughter filtered through the trees, people somewhere nearby. "If someone sees us together here, you will be compromised!" he blurted before he could think.

"Oh," Charlotte said, more of an exhalation than a word. He saw a range of expressions twist her face. Being compromised wouldn't matter, if his intentions were true. He saw she knew that.

"What are you doing, Edward?" she asked. "Why did you kiss me?"

Edward could not remember such a feeling of torture consuming his soul. "I have so many things I wish to say," he promised. "I feel as though you and I . . ." He glanced nervously over his shoulder and then back at her. "You and I, we . . ." He pressed his closed fist to his trembling mouth.

Another peal of laughter sounded, this time closer.

"Everyone expects me to marry Miss St. Giles," he blurted.

"Yes, I know," Charlotte replied.

"I don't love her," Edward added. He wanted to leap out of his skin. Charlotte's eyes were welling with tears.

"Yes, I know."

"Charlie, I'm not the heir. Everyone expects . . ."

"Everyone expects you to marry Miss St. Giles. Of course. She's very rich."

Charlotte reached out and took Edward's hand, giving a squeeze before trying to pull away. Edward could not let go. He reeled her in, very, very slowly, as if every bit of space that disappeared between them was both torture and a gift.

"The exhibition closes in a month," he whispered, his lips grazing her cheek. "I have a duty to . . . I don't even know what I'm saying! You are so dear to me, Charlie, but I—"

"Mr. Vaughan," Charlotte interrupted. Her voice was bleak. "Mr. Vaughan, let go of me at once. Sir!" Abruptly, she pulled away, making a show of searching for something in her reticule, the walls of the purse not thick enough to conceal the trembling of her hands. "It has been lovely having the opportunity to make your acquaintance, Mr. Vaughan. I look forward to seeing some of your own inventions at the next Great Exhibition. And, well, it was . . . quite . . . illuminating to spend such a quantity of time with your sister."

"Charlie, I—"

She continued, attempting a light, teasing tone. "I shall take great pleasure in calling you my friend." But when Charlotte glanced up, Edward saw how much he'd really hurt her. "A very good friend, Mr. Vaughan," she finished in a rush. "Truly."

Edward moved an errant strand of hair from Charlie's face. "Friend," he muttered.

Charlotte took a great step backward, which was almost comical, as if she were playing a children's game. They stared at each other. Edward moved forward.

Charlotte stepped back. "Don't," she said. "You are making a fool of me."

Edward went pale. "Please excuse me, Miss Paxton. I—I had no right."

Charlotte lifted her chin. "No, you had no right. You *have* no right. Please do not impose on me again," she added, extending her arm. "Good-bye, Mr. Vaughan."

Edward took her hand and slowly bent over to press a kiss on the back of her glove. He recalled touching the flesh beneath and was tortured by the memory. A moment later he released her. "Good-bye, Miss Paxton."

They turned simultaneously, immediately striding off in opposite directions. If they had had any company, the scene might have been mistaken for pacing before a duel. Indeed, walking away from Charlotte, Edward certainly felt as though he'd been shot. And that he deserved it.

# CHAPTER TWENTY-FOUR

*I'm not his. I never was.*

A bigger lie Jillian Cooper had never told, and Marius knew it. He sensed that in her heart and soul she never left his side. One did not need a sixth sense to understand such things. Honor, trust, loyalty—everything he had strived for in politics, Jillian offered him in a personal relationship. She embodied what he prized most, and he had let her slip through his fingers.

*You know where she's going, no matter what she says. Don't let the last thing you're aware of on this earth be Jillian falling into the hands of I-Ops because she tried to find answers you should find yourself.*

With a nod to the Librarian, Marius pulled himself upright and staggered to the door. He moved as fast as he could, though he was winded and felt fragile. His head throbbed with every step, yet he was afraid she would get too far ahead if he didn't run. He could no longer find her through their bond.

His balance was off, and outside he nearly fell to the sidewalk when he tried to fly—it was impossible. He regained his feet, and at the last moment caught sight of her weaving determinedly through crowds of people on the sidewalk. She never looked back.

He followed, giving chase on foot through several neighborhoods. The cold wind whipped at his skin, turning hot sweat to ice, and it was tough to keep her in sight. He managed nonetheless, and began to close the distance between them.

Jillian finally glanced behind her; he wasn't sure why. Realizing he'd followed, she suddenly stopped in her tracks. He forced his sluggish body to continue moving, shaking his head in a futile attempt to clear the veil of darkness settling over his eyes.

"Why did you ask me to come here?" she demanded when he approached. "Tell me the truth."

Marius swallowed and looked down at his boots. The world was spinning. He straightened and herded her into an empty alley. "Leyton suggested it would be wise to have someone else in the know. Just in case something happened to me."

"Ah." Jillian balled her fists and blinked back tears.

"Hear me out," Marius pleaded, raising his fingers to trace the side of her face. "Leyton was right. But that's not all of it. That's not *really* why I asked for you. You see, when you realize there's something you'd do with the one day left to you, you try and do it while you still can. I think I . . . I just wanted to see you again."

He ran his thumb across her mouth. Her lips felt like velvet. "I've never been one for that sort of indulgence. Not in the past. You know better than anyone. But now . . ." He embraced her with such force, it drove them both straight back against the wall. "Oh, Jillian. I regret so much. Because even if I am to live, I've made a mistake of such magnitude. . . ."

Her stoic facade cracked. "I didn't mean what I said," she murmured. She was sobbing into his shoulder. "I didn't mean what I said about letting you die back there. I just want you to live. I take it back. Say you believe me, I'm begging you. I take it all back."

"I believe you," Marius murmured. "I knew you never

meant it." And then suddenly he was crushing his mouth down on hers.

He had not even realized how much he'd been damaged by this cursed virus until she reminded him what it was to live. It was as if a light inside him switched back on. Though everything else in his being felt artificially dampened and dimmed, a pure electricity bloomed within Marius, as if life itself could not be stopped. *I'm still alive. You make me feel alive.* His tongue swept the wet warmth of Jillian's lush mouth and she gasped softly, answering the urgent caress of his fingers moving under her shirt on her naked back.

His lust for her swelled in his groin and pooled bright in his bones. His hands pulled her close, his lips moved against her ear. "Know this: If I live, I will make all of this right. Somehow I will. I vow it."

He had not understood before that he was a lesser man without her. If he lived, he would be hers. If she still wanted him, he would love her forever. He would undo what he had done for cold, political purpose, do his best to make things that he'd made so wrong by his marriage right for everybody. "To the future . . . and to happiness," he'd toasted on his wedding night. Those words were meant to be spoken in joy and love. If death could be forestalled, Marius *would* see that they were.

He was nearly blinded by a desire to take her without regard for anything but their want and need. He could feel a like desire in Jillian: the pounding of her heart, the jut of her nipples through her shirt, the way she responded to his kiss. She clung to him as he cupped her face in his hands, and he kissed her over and over. She moaned, the sound of one who has waited too long for something rightfully hers. He tipped her head back, pressing damp kisses against her neck, fangs grazing her delicate skin.

Jillian. She was in his soul and in his heart. She *was* his

soul and his heart. Try as the humans might to differenti-
ate their species, she had always been part of him. And
though he knew she could no longer hear his innermost
thoughts, he spoke to her nonetheless. *I am yours, Jillian. I
have always been yours. I always will be.*

She stared straight into him, her eyes wide, chest heaving with frenzied breaths. But he saw she could not hear
him.

"I know what to do, Marius," she whispered.

Dizzy with passion and also regret, Marius leaned
against the wall to steady himself. "Oh, Jillian." He
cupped her face in his palm, blinking rapidly. She'd gone
blurry around the edges. He blinked again, one hand
gripping his collar in a failed attempt to get a little more
air. "Not that. Don't sell your soul to them. Not for me. I
beg of you. You'll find yourself entangled in their schemes
for the rest of your life. I may not be here to protect you.
Just give me a little more time . . . a chance to make things
right. For everybody."

Suddenly, a spasm took him. His back arched, but he
forced himself to otherwise maintain his composure,
knowing that the more pain he revealed, the more Jillian
would be compelled to act on her own. He could see her
lips moving, and the expression on her face. She reached
out a hand, but all he could do was stare at it rippling in
and out of focus.

His jaw went rigid; a new and incredible bolt of agony
transfixed him. Marius stumbled as his knees went weak,
his hands gripping the sides of his face. It was as if his
very bones were shifting. He saw Jillian move away down
the alley, and felt a sick feeling in his stomach as he considered that he might never see her again. But she reached
the street and raised her hand to hail a transport, opened
the door when it came.

"Get in," she said, returning to help him toward it. Her

voice was thick in his ears. "Go home and save your strength."

"I can't do that," he said softly. "Not yet. There are answers with the Librarian, I'm sure of it. I will go home—soon, but not yet."

"I'm telling you to go home and rest," Jillian thundered.

Marius stepped backward. The cabbie turned and looked at him through the glass, gave a honk.

Jillian got inside the cab instead of shutting the door and sending it on its way. "Come with me," she begged. "Let me take you home."

"Jillian," Marius said, studying her face. "Leyton wouldn't have sent me if he didn't think the answers were in that church."

"Leyton's a mech. He can't process the idea of asking humans for anything." Her face was very pale as she slammed the door shut and lowered the window, and her resolve frightened him. Her voice was clogged with tears. "I'll do the right thing, Marius. Trust me to do the right thing for both of us."

Marius reached through the open window to grab her but wasn't fast enough. Jill moved to the far end of the seat and signaled for the cab to drive away. With her comm already up to her ear, she turned and gave a last, frightened look over her shoulder, and then the transport disappeared around a corner. Marius was left with his fingers curled around nothing but a fistful of air.

Slowly, very slowly, he made his way back to the Librarian's burrow. Gaining admittance, he walked to the back of the church and sat down with his binders. There he cursed violently and pressed the back of his hand to his trembling lips, and the words on the pages blurred before his tired eyes.

Was the true measure of honor committing oneself to

a great cause through every circumstance? If he faltered in the end, did that lessen the sacrifices he had already made? Was it possible to retract one's mistakes and still be respected? He didn't know anymore. But he did know this: he'd meant what he'd said about making things right. He had to find the answers before it was too late.

*You were there when it happened, Charlotte. What exactly can you tell me?*

Blinking to clear the fog from his mind, Marius pressed his fingertips down on several yellowing pages in the third binder. He turned them with a sinking heart, scanning their contents: letters to Charlotte's sister Maggie; handwritten records of a rose project, with combinations of alleles running like code down the page; sections clearly torn from different sets of diaries and memoirs from later years, all with ragged edges, as if the writer second-guessed the safety of even a private journal. He reviewed the rose project, flipping through the earlier pages of her experiments to the later ones, which took on a slightly different tone. The most recent pages leading up to her success with the final plant were much more carefully penned, her notes taking on an odd style as if she was trying to say something without actually coming out and saying it.

Well, she'd made reference in some of the letter fragments he'd already read where she was writing to her sister what she would not say to her husband. Marius winced, thinking of Tatiana, then forced himself to focus on finding a letter that would give him a better clue.

*Tell me something more, Charlotte Paxton. Tell me something I need to know.*

# Chapter Twenty-Five

*London, England*
*October, 1851*

Two weeks passed from when Edward Vaughan led Charlotte behind the trees in Hyde Park. Charlie spent her time talking with her sister, trying to make good on several debts at the draper's shop and puttering about the window boxes upstairs, tending to her roses. She'd gone a bit sour on her rose experiments actually. The red and white blooms seemed more appropriate for happier times.

At first, her resolution to remain separated from Edward remained strong. But as the exhibition moved into its final weeks, Charlotte realized that any opportunity for her to see him again would soon be gone forever. She had wondered for four weeks if the lack of news meant anything. No announcement of engagement to Jane St. Giles appeared in the newspapers, nor did any gossip.

On the second day of October, Charlotte looked mournfully down at the small bush upon which she'd successfully managed to grow a plant that would produce both red and white roses on the same plant: an impressive feat, if one actually meant to do it and could repeat the achievement. Unfortunately, she was still trying—and failing—to produce white rose petals with a streak of red.

She sat down on her bed and stared out the window over the plants, searching in the direction of Hyde Park, where visitors would be streaming in and out, eager to see this accumulation of the world's wonders before it was too late. Maggie was in the small kitchen behind the bedrooms, making a batch of jam. The smell of ripe strawberries nearly masked the stench of garbage coming from the back alley.

*Oh, Edward. When the glass plates of the palace are gone and the metal stays brought down, will you remember our time together? Do you ever think of me?*

"Go."

Charlotte started and stood up. Her sister hovered in the doorway. "Just go, Charlie."

Charlotte studied her sibling's face. "Just because there has been nothing in the papers about Jane St. Giles doesn't mean—"

"Go. I know very well what you're mooning about up here. Go to the exhibition and see him." Maggie crossed her arms over her chest. "You'll never know unless you do."

"But you've been saying all along—"

"He doesn't seem to have moved on, has he? From everything you've said, I wonder if any of my advice was correct. I thought he'd be spoken for by now, and I was wrong. So go, will you? It's better for me than knowing you're up here moping about. We'll save the jam for tomorrow's tea."

"I don't know, Maggs. I'll say something silly. He won't understand why I'm there, especially after what I said last time. It's already so late in the day."

"I think going late is better than living with the regret

of having said and done nothing," Maggie replied quietly. Then she turned and headed back toward the kitchen.

"I love you, Maggs," Charlotte called.

Her sister peeked back around the door. "I love you too, Charlie."

Charlotte went downstairs and slowly retrieved her shawl, bonnet and gloves, brushed away the fine red-orange dust stuck to her exhibition program. She slowly opened the pages and calculated where she and Edward would be by now if she'd attended each week. It wasn't hard; she'd been keeping track without realizing.

The trip to the exhibition was short. Once there, Charlotte stared at the frayed edges of a Persian carpet. After these many months of show, nothing was fresh anymore. It was quite obvious how things had changed. Softening chocolate sculptures, faded tapestries, welded metal scratched and burnished from being touched—all of the exhibits showed wear, the inevitable degradations that come with time. Something clutched at Charlotte's throat, a kind of terror, a kind of bitterness. So many wonderful things, and all were meeting their end.

If her time with Edward was over and he and she must part, she should not place any blame on him. She was not a victim. She'd looked for him here after that long-ago dinner party, she'd gloried in catching his eye, she'd stood too close. When given the opportunity, she'd behaved badly enough for people to wonder, for Maggie to worry and for Lucy to rally the troops. And if Edward had found her hard to resist, his actions were never any sort of promise. Charlotte maintained only the right to enjoy, not to expect.

Bonnet in her limp grasp, ribbons dragging behind, Charlotte wandered the halls of the exhibition, taking a last look. The West Indies nave was just up ahead. As she allowed herself the indulgent memory of Edward's hands touching hers, a shriek of a delight came from the side where several wolves on display contended with a small boy poking a souvenir through the bars. The normally docile beasts seemed unnerved.

Charlotte stared, somewhat apprehensive. There was a strange charge in the air, and she retreated to the opposite side of the hall. The young boy continued thrusting his toy, and the beasts kept circling.

She inched forward, meaning to tell the child to stop baiting them. The wolves paced and batted their paws against their muzzles every now and again, and then one swung his head around and looked right at her. A set of lashes blinked down over strange red-orange-colored eyes, and Charlotte gasped, clutching her reticule against her body.

A small group of conventioneers had gathered beside her to watch the wolves pace. Sweat broke out on Charlotte's palms as the first animal studied her through the bars. An odd popping noise erupted from an exhibit nearby, and a belch of red-orange smoke enveloped the entire nave.

Charlotte was mesmerized by the wolf's gaze. He stared at her, his tongue hanging out of his mouth in a pant. Then, without warning, he threw himself against the bars of the cage.

She couldn't move. Her bonnet slipped from her hand, was crushed under the feet of bystanders attempting to flee the area. The wolf's eyes wouldn't let her go; the beast seemed to physically have hold of her. She stood like a statue despite the engulfing panic of the others. The rest of the wolves joined the first, like white streaks at the side of her vision, over and over throwing themselves against the cages. The heavy metal chains and locks clanked violently against the bars.

"Charlotte!"

It was as if the wolf were saying her name. Charlotte stared in disbelief, then started to laugh. Her reticule, bonnet and shawl lay scattered, all three whisked off in the stampede. Charlotte stood paralyzed, unable to look away from the strange lupine eyes seducing her.

"Charlotte! Run!"

Edward? *Edward* was calling her name. Charlotte snapped out of her reverie and turned. At the same time, she heard the sound of the lock breaking off the cage, metal links shrieking and shattering, and the howl of victorious wolves.

Edward was suddenly beside her, taking her hand and pulling Charlotte along after the rest of the crowd. Cages were overturned on all sides, inventions jostled and destroyed, machines set into motion and chemical components spilled.

"Edward!" Charlotte screamed as they entered the stream of panicked spectators. His fingers slipped through hers. Engulfed by the crowd, she lost all sight of him.

The din that closed in around her was so loud that she could not hear his response, though when he reappeared in the next moment, his lips formed her name. Elbowing and shoving people, he reached out his hand, grasping and straining. Her gloved fingers swept his . . . but then the crowd once more tore their tentative grasp apart. His face again vanished into the stampede.

Charlotte was swept by the crush of spectators fleeing like rats off a doomed warship, hustled with the crowd outside and away from the Crystal Palace. A hideous barking and howling rose up, and she had a sense that the wolves were attacking. She heard screams, and people and animals alike scattered into Hyde Park.

Charlotte looked around for shelter. All seemed a whirl of fur and teeth and human fear, and then suddenly, as if he were standing beside her, giving her the instructions himself, Charlotte felt Edward draw her through the park. In the graying evening, Charlotte ran toward the copse where he'd kissed her, and stumbled into the center of the rotunda.

Edward had not come. Charlotte threw her arms around one of the columns to help support her trembling legs, and from her vantage point watched as wolves smashed through the glass wall of the exhibition palace. Jagged shards swirled like raindrops through the air, setting the wolves howling as their flesh was pierced. Frozen in horror, Charlotte clutched the pillar and prayed for Edward to find her.

A high-pitched whine curled through the air. Charlotte began to shake uncontrollably. She could tell something was close, something was watching her.

"If I can't see them, they can't see me," she murmured, intoning the old adage from childhood games. But even if that was true, they didn't have to see her. They smelled her.

Charlotte slowly opened her eyes and moved her face just slightly to peek. Nearby, two wolves pawed and stomped and tossed their heads in a strange twisting motion, something that wasn't entirely animal, something that frightened her all the more for its alien nature.

Screams and other chaotic sounds filled the park as people continued to stream away from the palace, and this distracted the wolves. One of them peeled off, attracted more to those running for their lives. But one remained. Charlotte imagined he was the first, the one who'd trapped her with his feral gaze.

The beast took two steps forward, and then one back. Three steps forward the next time. He shrank the distance until Charlotte could smell a strange sourness on his fur.

"H-hello, doggie," she mouthed more than said, terror

making it almost impossible to speak. Pawing at the ground, the wolf whined, again made its twisting motion and then lowered its head to bat at its muzzle with a paw.

Charlotte clutched the column as hard as she could, but her muscles were shaking; they seemed to have lost all strength. She closed her eyes and prayed for the beast to go away, knowing that she had little other option. Sinking to the bottom of the pillar, she pressed her forehead against it and closed her eyes, silent tears covering its porous stone.

The wolf howled and paced behind her. Charlotte reached out one trembling arm. "There, there. Hush, now. Hush . . ."

The beast cocked his head, eyes like red-orange flames.

"Hush, now . . ."

With an otherworldly snarl that sent terror straight through Charlotte's soul, the wolf sprang forward. She tried to protect herself, throwing up her arms, and felt a burning pain as the beast's teeth sank deep into her flesh.

Edward awoke to a strange crackling noise. A burning sensation tickled his nose. He blinked, and found himself lying facedown in the dust on the floor of the exhibit hall. Bodies and glass shards littered the floor alongside him, some of the bodies motionless, some with signs of life. A man pulled himself slowly to a sitting position and looked over. He and Edward stared blankly at each other for a moment, as if it took both gentlemen to give permission for such a breach of etiquette, then they removed their respective cravats and opened the necks of their shirts. Neither looked at the other again.

Able to breathe easier the filthy constricting air, Edward tried to settle his mind and develop a plan. Smoke was flowing everywhere, originating in the far end of the palace. And there were flames. Every few seconds an explosion rocked the building, followed by the tinkling sounds of broken glass.

*Charlie. God, what of Charlie?*

He pulled himself to his feet and looked around, holding his bunched cravat to his face against the heat, smoke and glass dust. Exotic woven carpets and silk textiles, burled woods and stubborn rubber: all of the objects that had so recently awed the world were now aflame. The faint sound of fire bells seemed a hopeless gesture in the face of such large-scale destruction, and Edward watched in awe as the metal frame of a massive chandelier melted and the crystals came crashing down, an opulent fatality, winking and glowing in the fire.

There were real fatalities, too. He flinched as his gaze shifted to a woman lying face up in the wreckage. A shard of ceiling glass protruded from her chest, and blood pooled under her lifeless body. She was fair skinned, like Charlotte.

The thought of Charlie in distress inspired Edward to throw off the shock that paralyzed his muscles and muddied his mind. He had to get out. He had to find Charlie, make sure she was all right. He looked wildly around. Where the fire had done its work, there was still a chance to escape. Broken glass and molten metal were everywhere, but the flame had moved on toward the largess of tinder provided by as yet unscathed exhibits.

He moved quickly, forcing his aching body to respond, running fast over the smoldering remains and nearly toppling into dangerous debris as the bottoms of his shoes softened in the heat. Edward ran until he felt the air change, until the fire was far enough behind him and the cold air of Hyde Park blew into his lungs. Glancing back over his shoulder, he saw what was left of the exhibition hall, now engulfed by a fireball clearly fed by the enormous elm trees that once so proudly rose as the center of the Crystal Palace's infrastructure. The last panels of glass warped and exploded.

Out of the gaping hole created in the collapsed roof, a group of winged creatures rose, colliding and tumbling through the air in an instinctive drive to escape danger. Their high-pitched shrieks bored into Edward's bones, and he watched them, backlit by a blazing orange fire, rise high into the darkness. In the air the creatures reorganized, recognizing their sudden freedom. His legs braced wide, his chest heaving in terror, Edward watched as they spread in a calculated swarm across the smoky sky. And then, as he stood frozen in place, he saw them dive one by one at terrified bystanders.

There was nowhere to run. Hyde Park was enormous, but as he had found with Charlotte, it contained so few places for concealment. And now, so few places for escape.

Edward turned and sprinted across the grass, his melted soles failing to offer much purchase on the damp terrain. He fell hard, his face hitting leaves and dirt. Wind blew across the back of his neck. Then came a strange fluttering sound and a painful high-pitched scream in his right ear. He'd heard those sounds before, when he'd stood with Charlotte in the West Indies nave: the vampire bats. Edward gasped in horror as something awful wrapped itself around his neck.

He reared up, unable to shake himself free, arching his back as pain shot through his body. Wings beat against his face and shoulder. At last, however, the intense pressure binding the animal to him eased, and with a delicate flutter along his cheek it set itself free and vanished into the night.

Edward moaned and gathered the strength to draw his trembling body to his knees. Warm, honeylike fluid tickled his neck and chest. He put his hand up to his throat and his fingers came away dripping blood. He unballed the dirty cravat clutched tightly in his hand and fumbled to retie it, this time as a simple bandage around the two small holes in his neck from which blood dripped.

A wave of nausea swept him, and he nearly lost himself to shock once more, but the thought of Charlotte pulled him back. He was struck by the sense that she needed him. That she was calling to him.

Edward stumbled through the dark, blinking against the swamping drowse that tried to pull him under. Bodies lay everywhere, and screams still punctured the air. Looking back, the glowing remains of the Crystal Palace seemed far away.

*Life is so short. We know this. We are told this, yet we never listen. And then we chastise ourselves for letting our chances pass us by. Charlie. Please be here. Be alive. I will make things right.*

# Chapter Twenty-six

As the cab delivered Jill to Bosco's, her lips still burned from Marius's kiss, the kind of promise she'd been waiting for as long as she could remember. Ever since she first met and fell in love with Marius, he had pulled away from her as hard as he could. He never made vows, never admitted to feelings he couldn't indulge. Until now. It would be too cruel to lose their love before they even were allowed to enjoy it, before he could even say the words.

Jill could not—would not—let that happen. And there was no cure in the Librarian's dusty pages of an era gone by that could save him. He was grasping, deluded. He didn't want her to get hurt, didn't want her to get embroiled in a deal with the human government that would haunt her for the rest of her life. But nothing would haunt Jill more than Marius's death, especially now. He had finally allowed himself to believe they were meant to be together. Nothing the humans could ever do would be worse than stealing that.

Bosco's usual roar of conversation was condensed into a low, thick murmur, punctuated now and then by a newscast squawking from the monitor above the bar. She'd called I-Ops from the cab before she could chicken out, and they'd asked her to describe what she was wearing so one of Horschaw's agents could find her.

She wandered the shadowy perimeter of the place until a couple of guys finished making a deal and vacated their table. She'd hardly settled in against the far wall before a female voice called, "Jill? Hi!"

Jill looked up and produced an equivalent smile. The girl wore a fitted black blazer over a black T-shirt and black jeans set off by tall, black leather boots. She carried a drink and a shopping bag. Her bouncy ponytail gave her a friendly air, if the knife in her boot qualified that assumption. She reeked of some nondescript floral perfume, which she undoubtedly used to foil the olfactory senses of any nonhumans who might be in the bar, but her open demeanor implied she was a friend to all. All in all, her disguise was well done. If Jill hadn't known she was looking at a government spook, she might have thought she'd found a new buddy.

"It's been forever," Jill extemporized, gesturing to the opposite chair.

The girl set down her drink, pulled a box wrapped in shiny blue paper from her shopping bag and stuck it on the tabletop before taking a seat. The tag said, *For Jill. Love, Emily.* "I know it's early, but since I won't be seeing you before your birthday . . ." She shoved it over. "But you know you can't open it until the big day."

"Thanks . . . Em."

The girl placed her comm on the tabletop and clicked a button, undoubtedly scrambling any close-quarters electronics in case anyone had a mike pointed at the table. She leaned in. "Took you long enough. I've been in and out of this shithole too many times in the past two days."

Jill wasn't about to apologize.

Emily cocked her head and studied Jill's face. "You seem on edge. Need a popper?"

It took Jill a fair amount of energy to hide her disgust.

The only people who ever offered you free drugs in this town were those who wanted to see you hooked.

"No? Okay." The girl sighed. "Well, now we can talk, anyway. The instructions are as follows. There are four kits in the box. There are two serums, one for each species. We're only interested in the fangs at the moment. Select a subject from each of the major vampire families. We need a representative cross-section," she explained briskly. "Stick them, wait a second or so, then take a strand of hair from each subject and put it in the empty syringe holder. The DNA in the strand will prove you did what you were supposed to."

"I'm not sure what you're asking," Jill said.

"I just explained it! There are four kits with syringes. You just stick 'em. It's fast."

"What do the serums do exactly?"

The girl huffed. "You're one of those, eh? You're gonna make me say it. I don't know why you people want me to say it."

Jill looked down at the gift box. "What do the serums do?"

"It's for the greater good, if you really think about it."

"I hate that expression," Jill muttered.

The girl leaned back in her chair. "We're in the middle of Total Recall," she said, clearly annoyed she had to give any details. "We want the fangs and the dogs to be . . . more human. I would have thought that was evident."

Jill's stomach roiled. "If this is what I think it is, I've heard this serum doesn't successfully revert vampires to human form. It *kills*. And if you aren't willing to speak the truth, you shouldn't be conducting these kinds of experiments. Every needle stick is like a death sentence. Which means you're asking me to kill four people."

"Humans are *people*. Vampires and werewolves are not *people*. And it's not a given that all of them will die. Honestly, we'd much rather they revert. It would solve the whole damn monster problem." She released an exaggerated sigh. "Look, save the morality for when you really have a choice. This is a test of loyalty: you infect someone, or else. Try to focus on 'or else.' It makes things so much simpler. Remember, you called us. You *need* us."

Jill shook her head to clear it. "Let me make sure I have this right. Horschaw promised me an antidote to the virus if I prove my loyalty to his government— to *humanity*, as he would say. The proof he's looking for is having me infect four new vampires with the same damn disease I'm looking to cure. Why should I make such a fucked-up deal? And how do I know you have or will even give me the antidote I need?"

"What choice have you got? If the rumors are true, you'll do anything for love. For Marius Dumont," Emily added with a cloying smile. "If you do what we're asking, we might be able to help you."

"It's the 'might' part I'm struggling with." Jill leaned slowly forward. "It might help if you can explain why Gregory Bell is dead."

The rhythmic tapping of the girl's fingertips against the table belied her blank expression. She was clearly trying to decide how much to impart.

Finally, the agent shifted in her chair and said, "Bell was the perfect example of why we need to rid this city of fangs and dogs. You went to that market. I'm sure you've figured out the score. Bell was murdering human beings for body parts and blood to sell to the mechs and god only knows who else. We gave him a chance to save himself. He failed."

"What do you mean?"

Emily narrowed her eyes. "Let Bell be a lesson to you. He waited too long to make good on our deal, and now he's dead. He was supposed to infect Marius at the wedding."

Jill wanted to scream. "You tried to kill Marius at his wedding, and now you're asking for my help? Are you kidding?" She narrowed her eyes, racking her brain to remember the order of things. "These experiments of yours trying to revert vampires to human form . . . You infected Bell first as payback for murdering humans. Knowing he'd have access to the wedding, you promised him an antidote if he would infect someone else—Marius. Done. Experiment in play. And now you're promising me an antidote for him if I infect someone else to continue the experiment."

"It's frustrating that he didn't get the job done," Emily admitted, wrinkling her brow. "I had to send someone else later that night."

"There's no way to stop this," Jill whispered.

Emily's wary gaze flicked about the bar in constant surveillance. Poking her drink's straw so aggressively into her cocktail napkin that the paper started to shred, she said, "We're trying to keep this all a controlled experiment. It's important that we know who is infected and under what circumstances, or the data isn't as useful. Plus, we have specific targets we think should be priorities. . . ."

Jill couldn't believe they were discussing Marius's impending doom like a high-school science project.

Emily took a swig of her drink, leaned forward and said in a low voice, "Look, you're totally in love with him. I get that. I mean, I'm not a total bitch. But . . . girlfriend, he's a *fang*. What are you thinking? Don't you remember how many of us they've killed? They're made to drink our blood, even if they're trying to stop." She straightened up and sighed. "Now, I don't mean to rush you, but if you don't do this, Marius is going to die. So you'll do this. Right? But you can take some comfort that it's *not* a never-ending cycle, because I can promise you aren't next."

Jill raised an eyebrow.

"Because you're human," the girl explained patiently. "We'd rather not have to keep reinventing the wheel, using pesky dogs and fangs. Sure there are plenty who are willing to turn traitor, but they keep dying unexpectedly. Human agents make a lot more sense—and you have access to high-level candidates. We have no incentive to harm you . . . as long as you help us."

That would have explained why the humans who belonged to the multispecies Rogues Club were at the top of the recall list, if Jill hadn't already guessed. "By 'candidates,' I believe you mean victims," she pointed out. "But by 'dying unexpectedly' . . . Are you saying the virus doesn't kill in predictable ways? Are you sure you know what you've got there?"

"I'm interested in science, not semantics," the girl said, collecting her possessions. "And this is the best chance we've got for making the world human again. I'm so pleased to have you on board. Air kiss for show?"

Jill's chest seized up. "Give me an antidote for Marius first. Then maybe I can—"

"Oh, please! If I give you an antidote, what's your incentive to help?"

"I can't," Jill whispered, wondering if she could. "I can't do what you want."

Emily reached over and patted her hand. "You can . . . and you'd better." She heaved an enormous sigh then said, "Let's try this: You infect a top fang—one of the other house leaders, say—so that we know you're good for the rest of the deal, and we'll give you an antidote for Marius. Just enough for him. Then you do the other three." A small smile creased the corners of her mouth.

"So there *is* an antidote?" Jill pressed.

Emily stood and looked expectantly down at her, clearly wanting her air kiss. Jill moved in to do her part, and the I-Ops spook held her close. "You give us that first data point, we give you our antidote," she whispered. "Then you give us the other three data points. If you don't see through your end of this bargain, he'll be dead and you'll wish you were. That's it. That's the only deal you're going to get." She pulled away, pressed her palm down on Jill's wrapped gift and said in a louder tone, "I hope you like it!"

"I'm sure I'll love it," Jill said with a fake smile. She grabbed the present with one hand and then stood, pushing past Emily and barreling through the crowded bar to the exit. She was terrified she was going to be sick.

Jill headed back to the Rogues Club in a surreal haze, racking her brain to think of the worst person in Crimson City she'd ever met. Well, the worst vampire. There had to be one worthless, murdering son of a bitch whom no one was going to miss.

"Oh, my god," she said, sliding haltingly onto a park bench. "What am I even talking about? This is real. This is a real situation." She wasn't the girl who went charging out into the world in black leather, weapons strapped to every part of her body, ready to take on evil and kill for good. She was just a journalist. She wrote articles. She took pictures. That's all she did. She didn't want to choose who lived and who died. How had it all come to this?

The cold stone bench sent shivers through her body. Jill tried to wrap her coat tighter around herself, but it didn't help. And while she could sit out here all night with her shiny blue box of death, Marius was running out of time.

# Chapter Twenty-seven

Up on the terrace of Dumont Towers, Tatiana worked in the sun, diligently turning the space into a botanical marvel. It was grand to be out of isolation, and her shovel plunged in a most satisfying way into the earth that workers had uncovered after ripping out the glass footpath during Tatiana's full-moon confinement.

The Dumonts had offered her the permanent assistance of a gardener, some poor working boy who would do everything she ordered, but she'd put her nose in the air and refused. In truth she was beginning to regret that a bit, if only because of the blister developing on her palm. Gardening was hard work, and she'd certainly underestimated the mess. But, ah, the smell of freshly tilled soil and flower petals was doing wonders for her mood.

The temperature was rather warm, even this late in the afternoon. The werewolf princess wiped her sleeve across her damp forehead and removed her gloves. Wrinkling her nose, she studied the blister marring her otherwise-perfect skin and decided to replant just one more rose bush before calling it a day. But then she heard a sound and knew it was *him*.

Hayden's musky scent hit Tatiana hard, a thrill chasing through her bloodstream as he neared. She whirled, taking care to assume a mask of arrogance.

"How did you get in here again? The household is more obsessed with security than ever."

"I told them you were expecting me, and then didn't wait around for them to check."

Tatiana narrowed her eyes. "I can't imagine they let you through without specific leave from me. They're probably on their way with reinforce—"

"Yup." Hayden raised his face to one of the newly mounted security cameras and waved, even as a furious-looking bodyguard in battle armor floated toward them from the double doors leading back into the Towers. "Tell them it's fine," he challenged.

Tatiana stared at Hayden with wide eyes, waited until the guard pulled a weapon from his holster, then thrust her chin in the air and called out, "Don't! He's my . . . guest."

The bodyguard stopped abruptly, clearly confused, and radioed something into his comm device. Backing off, he maintained watch from the far end of Tatiana's staked-out landscape design.

"Come out and see the city with me," Hayden said.

"I couldn't possibly," Tatiana replied.

"You can." The rogue vampire grinned. "It's just that you won't."

"The fact of the matter is that I really have no interest in the . . . in the . . . in the goings-on of that nasty city down there."

Hayden laughed. "Who talks like that? *Goings-on?*"

Tatiana suddenly found herself trying to suppress a giggle. She lifted her chin and bestowed upon him her most imperious expression, then, only half-fighting a smile, repeated, "Yes. *Goings-on.*" She held out her hand, expecting him to take her fingers and kiss their backs. "Thank you so much for calling on me, Mr. Wilks. Now, I really must go."

Hayden reached out and took her hand, but he flipped it over, running his fingers gently over her blister. Tatiana shivered, confused by her excitement. She tried to pull her hand away, but Hayden caught it fast and even as she pulled again, leaned over and kissed her palm.

Tatiana snatched her hand free as the security guard started toward them. "*Good day*, Mr. Wilks," she said in a stony voice. Turning her back, she flounced inside.

In the Towers, she hurried down a hall, pressing her hand against her beating heart. Her skin was covered in a fine sweat, her white dress was spattered with dirt. All thoughts of her appearance faded as she came face-to-face with Marius. Her husband stank of that damn human girl, and he'd taken the elevator rather than flying up the center staircase. Perhaps that was how he'd managed to avoid her so far—acting unlike all of his kin. Did he even realize that he'd left her alone for days? Such indifference was worse than any disgust he might suffer regarding her Change.

He seemed unsure what to say. "Tatiana," he began, before his voice gave out. He swallowed hard and looked away, trying to compose himself. He looked like hell, she thought unsympathetically.

They eyed each other in silence, Tatiana still awaiting an explanation. Any sort of explanation would do, about his excessive absences, about his neglect of her—about that scent, for god's sake!

His hair was ruffled. He seemed to realize that he was something of a mess and made a pathetic attempt to straighten himself out, and she looked him over, trying to hide her disappointment and growing disdain. There would be no chance at all for a "very happy marriage" or even a pleasant one if he did not change course.

In a questioning gesture she raised her hand—the hand that Hayden had kissed—and watched Marius curiously, hopeful, unsure if she wanted him to be angry but sure she wanted him jealous. *I know you can smell him on me.* But Marius made no comment.

He surely scented his nemesis upon her, which meant therefore . . . he simply did not care? Tatiana's heart hardened that much more. Not so long ago, the idea of their union was exciting. Visionary, really. It now disgusted her. Hayden was twice the man that Marius Dumont was. Hayden, at least, did not pretend to be anything he wasn't. From all the news clips she'd read, his demons were there for all to see. And while the notion of showing so much darkness frightened and bothered Tatiana, it thrilled her as well.

*I shall have you once, Marius, to make official this sham of an alliance, and then I shall never let you touch me again.*

"Come and have a drink with me, husband," she suggested. *I won't change out of my dirty clothes, and after we drink too much you can make love to me while I wear the scent of your enemy. If you don't care, neither shall I. I'm quite sure I can live with it.*

She swept down the hallway and into the library, a refuge she and Folie had found during their time here in Crimson City. Her sister was indeed present, with Marius's two brothers, and all three looked up from a card game. Folie's giggle cut short.

Tatiana moved to the bar and poured two large goblets of wine, gulping hers like a peasant before Marius had even taken his glass to his lips. She put down her half-empty goblet and glared at her sister, who opened her mouth, likely to comment on the amount of spirits she'd lately been consuming.

*Why shouldn't I get a little drunk? Nobody else seems to care for decorum or manners around here.* She took an obscenely large gulp and nearly choked.

"I believe I owe you some kind of explanation," Marius

said quietly, trying to stay out of the hearing of the others. To Tatiana's shock, he approached her and touched her cheek. Though it was a stranger's hand and so long since he'd touched her, she softened a little. *Maybe* . . .

"I have much to tell you. Much to . . . work out with you," he added.

Tatiana smiled. "I believe you do."

Marius searched her gaze. "Something very serious is happening here in Crimson City. Not many people know about it, and it needs to stay that way."

"Can you not tell me?"

He looked torn. "It's best if I don't. Not yet. There are . . . so many aspects. . . . I feel it's better for your personal security if I don't discuss them with you yet."

"It was always my understanding that a husband and wife share everything: their hopes, their dreams . . ." Her voice grew harder, and she worked to keep her emotions under control, to keep the others from hearing. "Their secrets and their bed. Your West Coast ways are rather difficult to understand."

Marius sighed. "You are right that we need some sort of resolution."

"Are you speaking about the matter of consummation, husband? Or about some other aspect of our sham of a marriage?"

Tatiana fought a combined wave of giddiness and vertigo. Her wine dripped over the side of her goblet, red drops spattering the white marble at her feet. She overcompensated in the opposite direction and Marius tried to catch her, but they both stumbled, off balance. She was surprised by his weakness. She was also surprised that his brothers didn't say anything.

Tatiana sneered, abandoning any attempt at discretion. "It seems you have a delicate constitution. Everyone was so careful to make sure that I was in form, fit enough to bear an heir. No one thought to ask about you!"

The room went silent. Folie stared up at her. Nervously she excused herself from her game and walked tentatively over. "Shall I go with you to your room, Tati?" she whispered.

"Darling, you're clearly having such a lovely time. Stay." Tatiana swigged the last gulp and dropped her wineglass on a side table. Missing completely, it plummeted toward the floor. Marius tried for it but missed. It shattered. Tatiana gave him a withering look of disdain.

Her husband winced. "Tatiana . . . ," he began. But he trailed off, and to her surprise he instead reached out again and touched her face. From the corner of her eye, she saw the others look discreetly away.

"I'll just go upstairs"—Tatiana swallowed hard—"and change out of this dirty dress." *Just once. Once to make the marriage real.* Her shame would otherwise be complete.

Hating herself and him, she headed to the doorway. There she turned and looked straight into Marius Dumont's eyes, so that there could be no mistake as to her expectations. Then she headed for the stairwell and her rooms.

She waited for over an hour. Marius did not come. Tatiana could imagine no acceptable reason, and the silence in her chambers was deafening. She had the unpleasant sensation of having made a scene and stomped out of a room only to find cold loneliness her only reward.

She sat down at her dressing table and opened one of the sterling canisters there, a wedding gift from family friends back home, and removed the rose Hayden gave to her the night he'd crashed her quarantine. What a thrill that was! It sparked something in her blood, and she kept the memento to remind her even now of what that felt like. How she wished Marius could evoke the same reaction. How she wished that he *wanted* to make her feel that way!

First Tatiana cradled the drying blossom in her hands, and then she impulsively placed it in her coat pocket. When she replaced the canister lid, she saw the entwined monogram which joined her and Marius Dumont's names. Perhaps Folie had been right to look to their sister Gianna as the ideal model. Gianna embraced the Change; she never suppressed her true nature in the name of "being a lady." That human slut Jillian wasn't a true lady. She wasn't any kind of ideal with which Tatiana was familiar . . . yet Tatiana's own husband could not or would not free himself from her snare.

"I do not want to be here," Tatiana whispered. "I do not want to be married to that man." She would ask for an annulment. It was as simple as that. They had not consummated the marriage. She could demand an annulment, peace in this godforsaken city be damned.

She dramatically removed the chain holding the ancestral rings she'd worn for the marriage ceremony from around her neck and tossed it on the bureau. Duty be dammed! *If I were a vampire,* she thought, *I would simply open my bedroom window and fly away.* Walking over to it, she stared through the glass into the darkening sky.

*If I were a demon, I would cast a spell on Marius. If I were a mech, I'd blow this place to bits and walk out of the rubble. But I'm a werewolf, and a wolf taught not to take advantage of any of the things that make us superior. So I'm as useless as a human. As useless as one of the humans we try so hard to be.*

*And yet . . . I'm not a prisoner here. I'm the lady of the house. I can come and go as I choose.*

*I choose to go.*

\* \* \*

It took a great deal of effort for Marius to stand, to breathe, to speak. He suddenly realized, as he tried to get a sense of what Tatiana had been doing and with whom she'd fraternized, that he had absolutely no sense of smell anymore. His vampire senses—his *instincts*—had completely slipped away. He was as powerless as a human.

She'd looked at his hands, and he'd known she thought guilt made them shake. He indeed had feelings of guilt, but they weren't the problem.

*I'm dying.* The thought was finally sinking in. He downed a glass of wine and let the truth slide off his tongue and down his throat: he could not taste the flavors, only a vague bitterness. His olfactory powers were almost nonexistent. His eyesight had lost its keenness, a gradual degradation along with his hearing. One by one, he was losing the characteristics that made him vampire. He was devolving to human form, and the virus was going to kill him just as it had Gregory Bell.

He had watched Tatiana walk to the stairs, watched the rumpled white fabric of her dress slip up the crimson stairs like a river of milk through blood. His wife had turned at the doorway and looked back, and Marius knew she expected him to give chase. He couldn't.

*I'm dying. I can't follow her. I can never follow her. It's no good. If I die, it will have been a disservice to take her virginity. And if I live . . . I will be with Jillian. I love her. As I always have, I always will.*

He had not found the strength to voice the truth to Tatiana, but it was only a matter of time. He had to explain that he would never go to her bed. It was not her fault, but his. He had made a terrible mistake, and that mistake was compounded by recent developments. This political alliance was good for no one. He had to release Tatiana from all of this. He had to explain.

Marius slowly pulled himself up the stairs using the banister. At the top, however, he realized he could not handle the explanation. Not now. So, turning wearily in the opposite direction from Tatiana's room, he smashed his shoulder against the hallway wall en route to the swaying doorway of his personal bedchamber.

Just a nap. Just a rest, and he'd be able to think with a clearer head. What was it Charlotte Paxton had been trying to say? If he found the rest of that last letter from 1854, would it be just another piece of information jumbling around his brain? Or would it trigger the answer at last? What was it?

> *Dear Maggie,*
> *I hope this letter finds you well in America. Though we now know the infections affect change at different rates, I think we would know by now if you were destined to be something other than human. I shall assume that your departure from England was in time, and I hope you are safe in New York.*
>
> *I am smiling here in London with such wonderful news! Joseph was kind enough to review my attempts at creating a hybrid rose. He has sent me a most glorious result, and tells me he has inquired about—*

Marius's head began to swim again. He lay down on the bed and closed his eyes. So many pieces, so many fragments. He knew the answer was in Charlotte Paxton's papers . . . if only he could *think. Charlotte* . . .

*Tatiana* . . .

*Jillian* . . .

*If I live till sunset, I'll make it up to them. I'll free Tatiana, and I'll marry Jillian and follow her to the ends of the earth. If I live.*

# CHAPTER TWENTY-EIGHT

"Charlie . . ."

Charlotte was afraid to open her eyes. She still smelled that frightening sour odor, and felt an excruciating pain in her arm. But she also smelled something much more familiar: Edward Vaughan. Edward's presence was all around her, his scent blanketing her skin.

She felt a palm cup her face, and she squeezed her eyes tighter. "Noooo."

"Charlie, it's me. Can you open your eyes? Wake up for me," he said. His touch vanished.

Charlotte heard the sound of fabric tearing, and she opened her eyes to find Edward beside her in the pavilion. He was using a knife to rend a long strip from an inside layer of her petticoat, and he froze when he saw her watching him.

"Charlie, do you know who I am? Do you recognize me? Do you know where you are?"

Dazed, Charlotte struggled to sit up. Edward moved quickly to her side and helped her lean against the base of the pillar, her legs stretched out in front of her. "I'm in the park where we last met." She looked up at him. "I knew you would find me here. I just knew."

Edward lightly caressed her cheek. "I don't understand how, but I sensed you were here. It is as if you and I are bonded somehow."

She felt the same, but it didn't make sense. Not really. Not beyond some romantic daydream. "What do you mean?"

Edward paused and then shook his head. "I don't know. I just feel that I can sense you from afar. That I knew to come here. That you needed me. These things . . . they are because we are somehow joined." He cleared his throat and added in a voice that seemed almost comically businesslike, "It would be best if you don't watch."

Very suddenly, he ripped a strip of fabric fully off her skirt. He brought it up to her arm, and in spite of his admonishment Charlotte followed the action with her eyes, gagging in shock at seeing her blood getting all over his trousers. Edward wrapped the fabric bandage around her before cupping her face in his hands again.

"It's all right, Charlie. I'm going to take care of you."

"I know you will, Edward," she said softly. Then, catching his gaze with hers, she asked, "I don't suppose you have Lord Gilliam's carriage this time, do you? I doubt anyone shall remark upon any scandal *this* time."

He relaxed a little, apparently relieved that she could joke. "At any rate," he muttered, "I think Gilliam has more to answer for now than we ever did. He can't have truly understood what his inventions were capable of doing."

Charlotte leaned against the pavilion column, panting slightly, and Edward wound a second strip of cloth around her arm. His touch seemed to ignite her skin. She thought she could hear the pounding of his heart—or was it her own? Everything was louder, brighter. Everything was so much *more*.

A peculiar sensation swept slowly through her body, as

if it was working its way through her bloodstream. Charlotte stared at Edward's face, at the tear tracks on his cheeks and the vein throbbing in his jaw. "I feel capable of . . . anything," she whispered. "And it frightens me."

Edward looked up, his eyes bright. His hands trembled as he struggled to tie off the end of the last bandage. He touched her cheek, and his fingers slid across her hot, damp skin. "You have a fever."

"I don't feel sick." She watched his face. It seemed so pale. The edge of his lips had turned just very slightly purple. "I think I feel so warm to you because you are so very cold. If something were to happen . . . ," she said, her eyes filling with tears. "I should like to say . . ." She glanced down, too shy to go on. But she had to! "I should like to say . . ." It was all too much. She couldn't bring herself to say what she really felt. "Thank you, Edward."

He looked a little disappointed. "I think so highly of you, Charlie," he mumbled. "I wish I had . . ." He shook his head.

*Had what?* Could they not break the infernal boundaries of etiquette even now? *Had* what, *Edward?*

Wild barking sounded in the nearby streets. Every now and then a scream would ring out, or a very sudden and disturbing flapping of a score of tiny wings. Then silence would return, and the sense of being entirely alone in the presence of something terrible and great.

The ground beneath them trembled slightly. Edward and Charlotte looked at each other as the sensation became more powerful. "Something new is happening," she remarked, looking uneasily into the night.

Edward shrugged. "I must find you a doctor."

She followed his gaze to where he fussed with her bandage. "So much blood," she murmured, her voice oddly detached. Floating. "It looks worse than it is, I should think. I feel fine. . . ."

He nodded. "Put your arm around my neck."

Charlotte reached up with her good arm, pressing her bad one against her body to hold it steady. Edward lifted her off the ground, and she curled into him as he walked.

It was slow going across the park. Bodies lay everywhere, and wolves still roamed, making themselves known in the darkness by their whining and pawing. Halfway to the street, Edward stopped and set her down. They were in a small grove of trees. He made her comfortable, and then sat down beside her.

"I feel very strange, Charlie," he whispered, turning to look at her.

Charlotte stared at him. His skin was pallid in the faint glow of a nearby gas lamp. She saw what she had not noticed before: on his neck above where his cravat had slipped were two puncture wounds caked with dried blood. Her heart sank. "Did the wolves get to you? Have you been hiding—?"

He shook his head. His lips were tinged even bluer, however, and his eyes looked hollow. His cheekbones were dark angles of shadow in the moonlight.

"It wasn't wolves, Charlie," he said. "It wasn't the wolves."

Edward put his arms around Charlotte and pulled her close, but he could not find her warmth. He was so very cold. He hugged her nearer and buried his face in her neck, his lips pressed against her bare skin. He closed his eyes and breathed in her scent. It was strong and beguiling, a perfume he could mistake for no other.

"What is happening to me?" he whispered. Something foreign had settled in his bloodstream, something that was changing him from the inside out.

Wanting to feel more of her, he tugged at her sleeve. Her dress tore, exposing her shoulder and the swell of a breast. Charlotte shuddered, staring up and him, and Edward pulled back, confused and guilty. But when he looked into her eyes, he found that something equally foreign had settled in her—as if the wolf bite had unlocked something and set her free. Something she accepted.

Raw lust filled her eyes, and it poured into Edward's body like liquid. His cock hardened. He should have moved away from her, but he did not want to. He wanted to bury himself inside her, wanted to indulge the passions he'd been denying for months.

Charlotte sucked in a quick breath, and he knew she could feel him throbbing against her thigh. He watched her gaze drop to his mouth. She made a sound—a wild noise of pure animal desire—and stared deep into Edward's eyes. Her hand swept the length of his body. Her fingers found the tender well of his throat, caressed the bare skin there and down across his chest. She did not hesitate, did not pause. The rules and etiquette of London society were dissolving this night in the howls of wolves and the screams of bats. It was as if they both had been tainted, possessed by a beast that compelled them to express or act on their every desire. In this moment, it felt more like a gift than a curse.

Charlotte's hand moved over the buttons of Edward's waistcoat, and her fingers found his waistband. Without hesitation, she moved her hand against his sex, which was jutting hard against the fabric of his breeches. Moaning slightly, Edward put his hand on hers to push it away, to stop her impropriety, but with one more touch he was undone.

His hands found her bodice and tore it, exposing her breasts, which his mouth found and worshipped each in its time. She moved under him, and he slid his hand beneath their bodies to spread her legs. Charlotte gasped as he settled into the apex of her thighs. Her hand still explored his manhood through the fabric of his trousers. He unfastened their front, and Charlotte did not shy away. Pressing her palm firmly against the length of his cock, she pressed him strategically against her and groaned in delight.

His hands found her hips, rocking her against the base of him as he thrust. "I want every part of you," he moaned, a combination of pain and joy edging his voice as he rose up and pushed at her skirts.

She nodded, pulling him back down in a kind of desperate frenzy.

He ripped at her underclothes, ready and wanting, tearing at the fabric and lace and ribbons as she arched up into him, growling and clawing at his back. He pressed into her hot, wet center. Her nails pierced his skin.

Her neck was bared, and he struggled with a dark need to sink his teeth into that pure white expanse, to take her essence into his body so that he might have her forever. But her cry of pain pierced the fog of lust as he broke past her maidenhood, and he forced himself to slow. She took a deep, shaky breath, and after a moment urged him to move again—a slow, sensual rhythm.

"Oh, we are finally joined in every way, you and I," Charlotte gasped, her voice reflecting the wondrous sensations she was feeling.

"We are bound forever," Edward agreed, moving deliciously inside her.

He tried to maintain the slow steady beat, tried to be satisfied with a controlled, easy exploration of her vise-like velvet depths. But though she'd been pure, some wild abandon, something animal now ruled her heart. She wanted more, and he did too. He found himself losing control.

She met his every thrust with one of her own, and their bodies slammed together with increasing ardor. He felt suddenly unfettered by mortal, worldly concerns, by all of the things that should be said and done, and more importantly—always so importantly—the things that should not.

"I love you," Edward cried out, compelled in some strange way to speak the truth. "I've loved you from the first." Pumping himself hard into her, he gave himself over to sensation. He came, spilling his seed in her, feeling a sudden strange certainty that he was trading his life for another.

Charlotte tossed her head back, her loose hair falling against the moss-covered stone upon which they lay. She opened her eyes, and he saw the moon reflected in their blue depths as she cried out in animalistic completion. She seemed to have gained strength. Her color was high, her eyes wide and alert, and she seemed intensely aware of everything around her.

Even as Edward reveled in a divine sense of fulfillment, he knew with a sinking feeling that while his beloved's strength was growing, his own was ebbing. "Charlie," he said with his eyes closed, wishing the moment could last forever. "They have changed us."

"What do you mean?" she asked, stroking his hair. But she surely felt the change as he pulled out of her body and lowered himself beside her. She put her arms around him, and Edward could not think when he had ever felt anything quite so sweet. It almost made up for his next words.

"Those animals have changed us. You—you must ask Lord Gilliam for help. It was his machine that did this, and I fear . . . I fear I am going to leave you. Forever."

# CHAPTER TWENTY-NINE

One afternoon plus a sleepless night trying to figure out her next move was all Jill could manage alone at her apartment. She imagined wiretaps and concealed cameras hidden throughout the rooms, and every time she heard a noise, she was convinced it was from human agents sent for her arrest. She must have looked as bad as she felt, because when she got to the Rogues Club with a toiletries bag, a change of clothes and the gift from hell, Bridget leaned over the security desk with her eyebrow arched and blurted, "You are not okay."

Jill shook her head. "I'm totally freaked out. Are there any rooms left to rent?"

"Just a couple. Everybody's got the same idea. It's way safer here than out on the streets of strata zero. I'll add the charge to next month's bill, since we don't know how many days we're talking about." Bridget checked the computer system, typed a few lines and handed a cardkey over the counter.

Jill nodded. "Thanks," she said, and tried to draw her hand back. She couldn't; Bridget held on fast, curious eyes shifting to the blue paper-wrapped package she clutched against her body.

"It's not your birthday," she pointed out.

*It's not your business*, Jill didn't reply. "Belated." She flashed her friend an amused smile. "Don't start fencing intel on *me* now," she said with a laugh, even as she tightened her grip on the present. The gaudy wrapping and ribbon were more a liability than a cover. Jill had to get rid of the thing, one way or another.

Bridget let go and gave Jill plenty of space. "I've got your back. FYI, Hayden's here."

Jill sighed.

Bridget nodded and whispered, "What's the deal, anyway?"

Jill gave her a blank look. "With what?"

"With Hayden. Crashing Dumont Towers, creeping around Fleur. Is it just the same old same old, or is he planning something extra shitty? Rumor says he's targeting Tatiana." Bridget lowered her voice even further. "I know someone who does security up there and they said Hayden's got his hands *all over her.*"

Jill swallowed her shock. *One worthless, murdering son of a bitch out there who nobody's going to miss . . .*

"Jill? Are you okay? You're totally white. I'm sorry, I guess I thought you already knew about it."

"No, it's just . . . It's just going to be weird seeing him here now," Jill lied, struggling to stay composed. What was Hayden up to with Marius's wife? Revenge against the Dumonts was one thing, but doing something bad to Tatiana for that purpose would be totally beyond the pale.

"Do you want me to try and keep him out of your hair?" Bridget asked, looking confused. "I can probably do it, at least for the day. Or . . . did you want to talk to him? Do you want to get back together with him?"

*Do I want to keep him out of my hair, talk to him, get back together with him . . . or kill him?* "I'm too tired to think about Hayden right now," Jill mumbled. "Gonna grab a catnap." She pocketed the cardkey Bridget had handed over, grabbed up her package and headed for the back.

The rear section of the Rogues Club was a mix of sleeping quarters and the common areas that made up the lion's share of the space. They included a lounge and meeting room backed up alongside a medical wing. The medical wing held an examination room, which included basic medical supplies, a bed/examination table and storage lockers that could contain biologicals. Jill headed toward this, anxious to rid herself of what felt like a time bomb in her hands.

Inside, Jill glanced over her shoulder, closed the door and set a temporary locking code on the room. Then she turned. A row of small lockers lined the wall above a set of larger vertical lockers, each with its own temperature control. Jill picked one and tried to slide her box inside, but it proved too wide to fit.

Swearing, she set the package on the counter, untied the ribbon and pulled off the lid. Inside were four thin palm-sized metal kits and a miniature datareader. She stuck them all in the locker except for one. This kit opened without resistance. Inside, nestled in black shock-absorbent material was a pair of combo syringes—glass tubes with syringe attachments, one with a red fluid, one with blue. Both tubes were insulated and sealed, and both had biomedical hazard symbols etched into the glass.

With shaking hands, Jill clicked on the datareader and scrolled through the instructions. That the directives were so simple made the purpose that much more frightening. She was to use the blue serum and disregard the red unless otherwise notified. *My god.* This was the stuff that killed Gregory Bell. This was the stuff that was going to kill Marius.

Jill pulled a blue liquid cartridge from its nest and slowly adjusted the seals and locks until the needle slowly emerged. The road to damnation was seductively easy.

Behind her, the pressurized door to the room flew

open, and the sudden rush of air blew Jill's hair up around her face. She slammed the locker shut on the extra kits and quickly hid the loaded syringe behind her back, turned and sucked in a quick breath before blurting, "Dammit, Hayden!" Her ex stood in the doorway, his hands spread wide and braced against the doorframe.

"I've missed you, too."

Jill walked quickly to the main table and sat down, transferring her syringe to her lap as she made a clumsy disaster of slamming the lid back on her package and covering it with her arms.

"It's not your birthday," Hayden said cheerfully, eyeing the box.

Jill pressed her hand to her chest. "You scared me. What the hell? I coded the door."

"I saw you come into the lobby." He shrugged and moved toward her with a too-innocent grin. "You didn't automatically switch your usual password after we broke up?" He pressed his hand to his heart. "I'm touched. Really. Even if it is another man's name."

Jill rolled her eyes, instinctively leaning backward to put more space between them as her ex sat down in a chair opposite. "We just broke up. It hasn't been that long. Besides, you just hack in wherever you want to go. You always have."

She accidentally let go, and the syringe nearly rolled off her lap, so she pressed her legs together hard at the knees to keep it from falling to the floor. A sheen of sweat was forming over her skin, tickling her upper lip, but Hayden was staring at her so intently she didn't dare wipe at it. His gaze dropped to the mess of gift wrap and ribbon she clutched.

"So, how you been?" he asked, craning his neck a bit to get a better view.

Jill swallowed hard, slipping her hand under the table

and wiping her damp palm on the thigh of her jeans. Her thumb touched the syringe and she took the instrument delicately in her fingers. "Okay. You?"

He reached out and pulled a long red ribbon toward him, began winding it around his hand. "Great."

She eyed him. "It seems like you've decided we can be friends now . . . ?"

Hayden nodded. "Sure." He paused and then gestured with his chin to the locker she'd closed so hastily upon his arrival. "Got a new gig?"

"Storing some stuff is all," she replied, rolling the syringe between her fingers. Her voice was hoarse. She wasn't sure what she was contemplating or even capable of.

"In a biomedical locker?" He craned his neck to look behind him, and then turned back to her. "You're not going to tell me." With a short laugh he added, "I guess we're not on the same side anymore."

"I don't . . . I don't take sides the way you do. Or at least I don't see sides as clearly. And we're not together anymore," Jill reminded him. "This is private stuff. I won't be asking you about *your* business. Not even what you've been scheming at Dumont Towers."

Something flashed in Hayden's eyes, something like a karmic wince. Jill only recognized it because they'd once been intimate.

"But we are friends," he said.

"Friends." After a pause, Jill asked, "If I asked you to, would you leave the Dumonts alone?"

Hayden recoiled, his eyes narrow. "No. Nothing's changed there. You know better than anybody how I feel, and . . ." He crossed his legs at the ankles and cocked his head. "The fact that I'd like to see Marius Dumont burn has never come between us before. What gives? You dump me and then expect favors you couldn't get when we were fucking? Keep dreaming." His laugh was brittle.

A dull roar built in Jill's ears. Why did Hayden have to make it so easy for people to hate him? "You want to be friends? I'm asking you to leave them alone." She kept rolling the syringe between her fingers.

Hayden growled bitterly, smashing his fist down on the table. "They deserve to die. All of them."

Jill clutched the syringe so hard she thought it might burst. Again she thought, *One worthless, murdering son of a bitch* . . . Somebody who only thought of himself, who had no sympathy for the pain of others. Somebody who would do terrible things to anyone, and do them without regret. Someone who was the opposite of Marius.

"Don't kid yourself," Hayden continued. "Marius isn't the white knight you think he is. He gets off on keeping you chained up. He jerks the chain whenever he wants your attention, and then he leaves you sprawled in the dirt. How is that love? Talk about blind devotion—"

"Do you have to be so damn cruel?" Jill interrupted. She didn't believe his words—not anymore—but she'd always been amazed by Hayden's ability to go for the throat.

"I'm cruel? *I'm* cruel? I'm just lying in the dirt next to you. I'm here, while Marius and Fleur Dumont . . . Fleur—life just goes on for her, I guess. For all of them. They use us and say it means something and then leave us." He stared at Jill. "If I could . . ." He shook his head, unable to form the words to complete the thought, but the red-hot look of hate in his eyes said everything.

His hate was infectious. It would be so easy to justify, so easy to do what she had to, right here, right now, for Marius. All she needed was *one* death. And wasn't Hayden already always one step away from an ignoble end?

She clenched the needle under the table and leaned forward, her free hand grasping Hayden's leather jacket and pulling him close. She shook as she positioned death above his thigh. "You could be so much better than you are, Hay. If you could let the past go, you might actually have a future to look forward to. I know there's *someone* out there who could love you the way you've always wanted, if you just gave them a chance. If you just stopped looking back."

Hayden flushed and looked down. Jill prepared to inject him.

She hadn't noticed her fingernails were digging into the sleeve of his leather jacket, but a moment later his hand pressed down on her fingers. He laughed, his voice distant. "I'm not sure I remember how to be a good person. Sometimes I think I'd be better off dead."

Jill nodded. Her needle touched the fabric of his jeans.

Hayden shook his head and smiled. "You know, Jill, for a moment there we really were on the same side. It wasn't meant to last, but I won't forget you're one of the only people who has ever defended me. I owe you. I'm sorry that . . . well, I'm just sorry I'm not who you want me to be. That I'm not who *everyone* wants me to be. I am who I am, and it's too late to start being somebody else."

He was right. It was too late to start being somebody else. Jill swallowed the hysterical laughter welling up inside her and stared at him helplessly. She looked down at the table, slowly triggering her needle's release. It collapsed harmlessly into itself, and then she slipped it into the thigh pocket of her cargo pants. When she brought her hand up into sight, the two of them stared at her shaking fingers.

"I think you've picked me out of the dirt a time or two," she offered with a halting laugh.

The corner of Hayden's mouth quirked up. "I have. A time or two."

Jill clasped her empty hands on the tabletop, released a deep breath and finally said, "I'm in trouble. I'm in big trouble."

Hayden raised an eyebrow. "Anything to do with Total Recall?"

"Promise me you'll never tell another soul what I'm about to reveal," she demanded, probing Hayden's eyes for signs of a double cross. Generally he maintained his own code of ethics, even if that code was twisted. "*No one. You say you owe me? Well, time to pay up.*"

"I said I did and I meant it. For all the times you stood up for me," he explained, adding with a grin, "and for some great sex, I promise that I'll never tell another soul what you are about to tell me." He extended his hand, and Jill gripped it with the hand that had held the syringe. They shook.

Holding Hayden's hand like a lifeline, Jill told him what the humans had given her. She told him what had come in the box and what it could do to vampires and werewolves—that it was a possible reversion to human form but more likely a death sentence. That Marius was infected, she kept to herself.

"They said they'd infect someone I care about if I don't do what they ask . . . if I don't infect someone else." Once that was out of Jill's mouth, a feeling of intense relief swept her, but Hayden sat across from her in silence. "What should I do?"

"It's pretty cut and dried," he replied. "I mean, as someone on the outside looking in. Someone I care about versus someone I don't, with your own death likely the fabulous prize if you do neither? Get it done." He shrugged. "Pick someone you don't care about."

Jill fought back a wave of nausea.

A funny look came over Hayden's face, and he quipped, "I'm suddenly really glad we made peace. I'd guess most people think of *me* as the somebody they don't care about." Rising to leave, he leaned in one last time. "Here's another option, since I see you're squeamish: get someone else to do your dirty work. Might cost a bit, but there are plenty of options at Bosco's. Just tell them what to do."

"Pay someone else? There's hardly a difference," Jill said coldly.

"Hardly," Hayden agreed, standing up. "But there is one. And it might make your choice a little easier to live with. Whatever you do, I'll never tell."

He leaned over and pressed a kiss to her cheek. Jill had never felt so cold in all her life.

"Hayden," she called.

He turned.

"Think about what I said about moving on. About opening yourself up to real love again. You never know how long you have left. None of us does."

Hayden managed a nod, and then closed the door behind him. The lock beeped and clicked.

Jill slowly stood up. She slid her hand into her cargo-pants pocket and pulled out the syringe, cradled it in her palm and watched the blue fluid swirl in its thin glass ampule. What had she really expected Hayden to tell her, and what had she really been asking him? She retrieved the syringe's protective case from the locker and put it back alongside its red sibling. Then she slid the entire palm-sized kit into her pocket and coded herself out of the room.

# CHAPTER THIRTY

Tatiana Asprey Dumont walked slowly down the corridor of the Rogues Club, fuming over the fact that no matter where she went, she could never completely escape the smell of her husband's mistress. Bumping into the woman herself hardly lessened her ire.

Jill's jaw dropped. "You should have bodyguards with you," she blurted. "What are you doing out of Dumont Towers?"

Tatiana hissed, twitching her nose. Her enemy's scent held traces of both Marius's and Hayden's unmistakable musks. "What, are you the only female with free range over Crimson City? You do have a way of spreading your scent across every man in town," she added, noting that Jill's hands were visibly shaking. It both surprised and pleased her. "I've come to pay a call on Mr. Wilks. Will you direct me to the commons?"

"Down and to the left. But . . . listen. Be careful."

"Civility will do, Miss Cooper. Any pretense at concern is unnecessary and, frankly, offensive," Tatiana replied.

She found Hayden devouring an apple in a back room, lolling with his dirty boots propped up on the arm of a rather nice sofa. She'd caught him by surprise, and he tried to regain the upper hand by side-arming the apple core past her into a trash can.

"What are you doing here?" he asked, frowning when that failed to get a reaction.

Tatiana chose a heavy leather club chair with gilded arms that had clearly been "repurposed" from another club entirely, casually removed her gloves and sat gingerly on its edge. "Paying calls. I thought it was time I got out."

Hayden studied her for a moment then grinned. "This your first rebellion?"

She was a little shocked at the coupling of her name and the idea of misbehavior, but an odd sense of new-found power swept her, and she smiled slyly in return. "I suppose it might be. But I don't think that paying calls on friends is particularly rebellious. Where I come from, we refer to it as simple good manners."

Hayden laughed. "Can't say I know much about those."

Tatiana held his gaze for a moment and then glanced down at her gloves. "I behaved badly," she remarked, and looked back up at him. "I believe you know something about *that*."

Hayden inclined his head. "Badly, eh? Did you enjoy it?"

His eyes transfixed her. Obsidian ink. Tatiana pressed a fingertip into the dust on the side table and traced a simple drawing of a flower, reveling in the idea of being a petulant child. It was nothing she'd ever before indulged. She admitted, "Marius came home. It felt good to say what I really thought. Out loud." She pressed her dusty fingers to her lips and smiled behind her hand. "It was very shocking, I think. All the Dumonts must be rather put off. But this is what my life has left to offer—being *beastly*," she explained. "A monster. Sometimes I think death would be better than living this way."

Hayden gave an arrogant shrug. "Well, sorry to hear some tough shit went down, but just so there's no mistake:

I don't take Marius Dumont's sloppy seconds. Even if he would take mine."

Tatiana's head snapped up. She stared at him, and then it seemed to dawn on her what Hayden was talking about. "How dare you say such a thing?"

"Easy. Aren't you official yet?" Hayden asked, amused. He looked her over then said, "Maybe for you I could make an exception." A lusty look filled his face.

Tatiana blinked in confusion, blushing hot all over. She lifted her chin, trying to recover the moment. "I didn't let him touch me. I won't. I'm going to ask for an annulment," she added as haughtily as she could.

Hayden's eyebrow arched. He stood up and walked to her chair, leaning over with one arm on either side of her. His face moved close. "Why did you come here, Princess? Did you want someone else to make you official?"

She scooted back, pressing herself into the back of her chair. Adopting a withering look, she reminded him, "You invited me on a tour of the city. I thought I might see it before I leave."

He moved his mouth close to her ear, shifting her hair aside with his lips. His breath was moist and ticklish. "You're a liar. I'm not going to give you a tour tonight, am I? At least, not of the city. You've come for something else. Something . . . more dangerous."

She pushed at him and squeezed out of the chair. "I was wrong to come here."

Hayden looked tired. "Why *did* you come here?" he asked. This time, his expression was open, all the usual guile gone.

She swallowed hard, clenching and unclenching her fist around the handle of her purse. "A number of reasons. I hate being a beast. I hate losing control and being forced to be something I never wanted to be. I tell my sister that one day we won't be slaves to the Change, but the truth is, I don't feel as though we will ever be able to rid ourselves of the monster within. I would give anything to be free. I just want to be *free* of it all. Oh, it is so hard to find the courage." She looked him square in the face. "I believed you to be one of very few people who understand that. You would give anything to be free of your vampire nature. I would give anything to be free of my werewolf self. That, and . . ."

"And what?" Hayden said gently when her voice trailed off.

Tatiana ducked her head. "And I also came here because I'm angry with Marius and you are the only one who seems to care."

"You think I have it in me to care? Haven't you read *any* of the newspaper articles about me?"

"Don't fish for compliments, Mr. Wilks. It's not becoming."

Hayden laughed. "What *is* becoming?"

"When you're not busy posturing," she replied simply. "Then I think you say what you mean, which is more than I can say for most others here in this godforsaken city. And I . . ." She blushed suddenly and looked at her feet. "I feel a connection with you that I don't have with anybody else. What am I here for, Mr. Wilks? I'm looking for friendship."

Hayden didn't speak for a long time, and then suddenly he stood up and handed Tatiana her gloves. "Let's go on that tour of the city."

# CHAPTER THIRTY-ONE

The sounds of fear and destruction that Charlotte had heard earlier were now manifesting before her eyes. London was in chaos. The attacks had spread from Hyde Park; it seemed the number of animals had somehow multiplied far beyond those escaped from the Crystal Palace.

Bodies littered the streets she ran through. Charlotte did not pause in her flight to see what had caused these deaths, but some of the people looked as though they had inflicted mortal wounds upon themselves. Madness was clearly everywhere: a dazed woman backed into a corner by a wolf was screaming at it as if he were her husband.

Charlotte pumped her legs faster, passing a man with skin white as snow tearing violently into the neck of a woman. A winged bat lay motionless by his feet. She did not stop, however—the blood from her wound would only incite greater danger. If there was one life she could save tonight, it would be Edward's.

At last she reached the door of the Inventors Club, and she pounded on it as hard as she could. "Please let me in! Please, in the name of god!"

There came a noise behind the oak. They knew she

was there. She could see light flickering through the crack under the door, and the drapes shifted as people stepped close to the windows. She could hear murmurs and frantic footsteps, and a bit of acrid smoke wafted out between the door and the frame. Aware that she looked rather wild, Charlotte took a step back and forced herself to calm down. She collected her loose hair and with shaking hands repinned it back into a semblance of appropriate fashion. Lifting fabric from her top skirt and wiping her face, Charlotte then adjusted her shawl to better conceal her injury.

Satisfied that she looked as good as she could under the circumstances, she took a deep breath and rallied herself. "Edward Vaughan sent me," she cried. "He is one of yours, and he is dying! I must see Lord Gilliam!"

The shouted names set off a flutter of activity behind the door. All suddenly went quiet, and her way was unbarred. A hand reached out and Charlotte was yanked over the doorstep and inside. The door slammed behind her.

A small group of men stood huddled together in the foyer, each holding a hand torch. Their sweating, fearful features were recognizable in the firelight. The troupe was composed of blue bloods from Edward's set, and they stood back from her.

"Have you been bitten?" one of them asked.

"No," she lied, trying not to pull at her shawl and draw attention to the blood on her sleeve.

"We have seen evil things this night," the man continued hoarsely. "We have seen men and women turn into animals before our eyes. We have seen such a wild loss of control . . . Have you been bitten?"

Charlotte dodged his outreaching hand. "No, sir! This is Edward Vaughan's blood."

"Edward has been attacked?" one of the others spoke up, wearing a pained expression.

"Yes, and he is dying," Charlotte answered, her voice catching. "He needs Lord Gilliam's help. Is he here?"

The men looked at each other. "It is for Edward's sake," one of them said. "Let her at least talk to Alastair. Let *him* throw her out if he wants."

No one argued with the man who had spoken. He nodded and gestured for her to retrieve a torch from a sconce on the wall. "The last door," he pointed out.

The group dispersed, each holding a torch spitting gentle sparks that vanished down separate dark corridors. Charlotte could not have said whether they were more afraid of being contaminated by her social status or by Edward's blood.

She followed the main passage toward the back of the building and found Lord Gilliam in a large room he had obviously transformed into a workshop. A fine layer of perspiration gleamed upon his skin, and he worked furiously in the light of three hanging gas lamps. All about him lay scattered metal parts and tools. Vials of fluids and a basket of some kind of exotic berry cluttered his workbench. Specks of iridescent down from a hummingbird glittered in the provided illumination.

Charlotte's heart leapt at the sight. Perhaps he was assembling some type of cure!

From where he sat, Alastair Gilliam looked over his shoulder at Charlotte. For a moment she thought she saw fear in his eyes, and she wondered if he'd been outside to witness any of what was occurring.

"Lord Gilliam, I—"

"You are the draper's daughter," he said woodenly, turning back to his work. "The gardener's cousin. You have no business here."

Charlotte steeled herself. "I have, sir. It is Edward Vaughan, your friend. He has been bitten by a winged creature. Your invention . . ." She fell silent, unsure what to say.

Lord Gilliam remained mute, tinkering.

"You make things. You fix things. It was your invention that made the animals sick, and surely—"

The duke's heir turned. "My invention that made them sick? How do you know this?" he demanded.

"I . . . The hummingbirds stored here at the Inventors Club died. Were they here in your workroom, sir? They were, were they not?" Charlotte gestured to the feathers and the nearby chemicals, struggling to maintain her composure. Why was he denying culpability? "Also, the exhaust from your machine filled the air the bats and the wolves breathed at the exhibition. These are the animals that went wild and escaped. It seems only logical to—"

"You presume too much." Lord Gilliam resumed his previous labors. "Your impertinence is shocking, but I will forgive it, seeing as you are Edward's friend. Still, I must ask you to leave at once. I have important work that—"

"You fool!" Charlotte cried.

Lord Gilliam leapt from his chair. "How dare you!" he growled, facing her. "How dare you come in here and—"

"How dare *you*!" Charlotte interrupted. "Have you seen what is happening outside in the streets? The world may be coming to an end before our very eyes! Your social rank may give you license to hide in your private rooms while your friends face death, but what does honor demand? My *Lord*."

Lord Gilliam stood very still. Charlotte knew he listened, however, and it spurred her on. "If you have seen anything of what is happening outside, you know that your title and breeding mean nothing anymore. Neither does mine. This horror shall affect us all, and it already has. I have come for Edward's sake. For his life, I dare all!"

Lord Gilliam's face was as pale as any she'd ever witnessed, but he remained silent.

"I think you begin to see," Charlotte prompted.

"You know nothing about which you speak." His words were a gravelly whisper.

"I know that if rich and poor alike are to become animals and kill each other, society will cease to exist. You should want to stop this! Find me the antidote. I am not afraid to go outside. I will administer it. You need not—"

"You do not understand," Lord Gilliam interrupted. "There is nothing I can do."

A rage began to develop inside of Charlotte, something foreign and frightening. She had never before experienced anything like it, never imagined such could exist inside of her. Edward was dying. This man was the cause. There was nothing left to lose, and wrath exploded through her. As if it were a drug in her bloodstream, all of the anger and hurt this man engendered besieged her body. Charlotte gave in to the feeling.

As she did, her body began to change. It arched, her hands and fingers curling into themselves. A look of fear came into Lord Gilliam's eyes, but that gave Charlotte a sense of power she had never before felt. Every bone in her body seemed to be shifting, realigning, morphing. But she reveled in the pain, for she saw what her change would mean: revenge.

She twisted her head side to side, her body sinewy and almost liquid. A battle cry emerged from her mouth, surprising her by how similar it was to a feral snarl. But this roar caused a surprising result. Something in Lord Gilliam's demeanor changed. He seemed to recover his wits, to remember his own strength and vitality. He faced her with purpose.

Eyes blank, Gilliam ripped off his gloves and pushed up his sleeves. His arms were a patchwork of metal combined with flesh. He'd clearly turned himself into one of his own inventions, had literally armed himself for a fight.

Charlotte no longer thought in terms of human logic. She had finished taking the shape of a wolf, and she was all instinct. As the man attacked, flicking out his wrist, she threw herself forward. A bullet pinged off the wall behind her, a bullet that would have taken her life.

Charlotte felt a flash of instinctive fear. Wolf against man was one thing; this was wolf against machine. Her canine teeth and claws were made to rip and kill, but they could find no purchase in his chest, and her body bounced away as she collided with solid metal. But adrenaline and instinct drove Charlotte forward again. Her claws and teeth raging, she lunged again and again, searching for gaps in the armor of his strange metal body.

They were there, for Lord Gilliam could not entirely protect himself and still remain human. Charlotte shredded his clothes, drew blood from all unprotected flesh, and he finally dropped to the floor.

"I have no cure!" Lord Gilliam shrieked as her teeth found his throat. "But maybe I can find one!"

Waves of adrenaline coursed through her lupine body, and the desire to maul this man beyond recognition was powerful. But somewhere inside, Charlotte retained her humanity. And as she remembered who she was and where she'd come from, the characteristics of her wolfish self fell away, returning her to human form.

Wild-eyed and panting, clothes in rags, Charlotte climbed off Lord Gilliam's body. She retreated clumsily to the far end of the room. "Please," she said, slumping exhausted against the wall. "Please make him better."

"I have no cure," he repeated weakly. "None of this was on purpose. I did not know my creation was capable of such a thing, of contaminating the animals in such a way. I thought . . . it was just *fog*." He raised a trembling hand and touched metal fingers to the small bloody patch of exposed skin on his throat. He stared at the red for a moment and seemed to forget she was in the room, and for the first time since she arrived, Charlotte understood that it wasn't her inferior social standing or Lord Gilliam's shame that prevented him from helping her.

The duke's heir stared at her. "I did not plan this. I don't even know how it happened. Sometimes with experiments it is possible to achieve a result and not know how one achieved it." He dropped his head back against the wall. "There is no antidote. I cannot save Edward if his mortal flesh has already been poisoned. I might have protected him before, made him something else . . . but it is too late."

Charlotte took in all the details that were Lord Alastair Gilliam, the trappings of his station: waistcoat, trousers, cravat, shirtsleeves. All were reduced to bloody strips, and revealed was a strange creation, part man and part machine. She wondered what he'd intended. His eyes gleamed feverishly as he again began to speak.

"But we are not doomed, Charlotte Paxton. This blood-taint . . . Those of us who live through this night will be stronger. Mark my words, my dear. My machines will allow us to survive. The flesh is too weak by half, and bit by bit we shall overcome. For Edward, I am sorry. For the future, I rejoice. Even you are stronger than you were."

Charlotte growled. Rising to her feet, she stepped over the metal machine parts and tools, bullets and blades, scattered across the floor. Lord Gilliam's chest heaved as she neared, but he did not flee.

He watched warily as she raised her palm and touched her fingertips to his shredded waistcoat. She pressed gently, releasing a soft breath as she felt tissue and bone beneath her touch: his rib cage. Her fingers flexed, and she felt a furious pounding through her bloodstream.

"Lord Gilliam, you have not yet figured out how to replace the human heart. A puff of steam, a cog and a bolt or two? I do wonder how you will manage."

The aristocrat winced, awaiting death. Instead, Charlotte pulled away and wiped at the tears dampening her cheeks. Her spared victim placed his hand where hers had been, frozen in place as if he were taking a pledge.

Charlotte did not stay to hear it.

# CHAPTER THIRTY-TWO

*"Marius!"*

Startled from a too-familiar nightmare in which Jillian desperately screamed his name to no avail, Marius lunged up from where he'd crashed on his bed, and nearly ripped his brother's head off. Warrick didn't speak for a moment, and the two just looked at each other. Marius caught his breath. "What time is it? My god, I didn't intend to sleep. . . . I just lay down for a second." He leapt from the bed and pulled on the boots he'd dumped on the floor.

Warrick didn't address the odd welcome. His focus was on something else. "Listen, Jillian Cooper's been recalled and we think she's up to something. She left Bosco's with a package earlier, and she's apparently gone back."

"She picked something up at Bosco's?" There was no possibility of her taking a random freelance job right now. It had to be something from the human government. Cursing under his breath for sleeping at such a critical time, Marius grabbed a lightweight trench coat from the closet.

"Right. It looks . . . suspicious. But then, we weren't sure if you and she had something in play . . ." He trailed off. "Do you want me to—?"

Marius interrupted his brother with a muttered "No, thanks," grabbed his gun holster from the floor and slung it on. Heading out into the hall, he patted Warrick on the back and then waited a moment before heading to the elevator bay. He didn't want his brother to see him too weak to fly.

*Jillian, can you hear me?* he thought. *What are you up to? Just wait for me.* But he knew it was futile. The virus had killed their connection. And he was a fool for thinking she might give him time to accomplish his plan with the mechs. For good and for bad, Jillian would never change.

Outside Dumont Towers, human passersby were dressed for a chill night. Marius's body was not maintaining normal temperature, however, and a thin trickle of sweat seeped between his shoulder blades as he moved briskly through the street-level crowd.

He hardly looked the picture of Dumont decadence that fed the stereotypes and the tabloids, what with his tousled hair and plain T-shirt, but once he reached Bosco's there might be a few people who might still recognize him out of context, so he flipped up the collar on his trench coat and hunched down his body.

In the back of the bar he found Jill, a flat beer on the small table in front of her, her hand awkwardly pressed against her coat pocket. Her chest heaved noticeably. Marius approached, and she registered his presence. Her cheeks flamed red and she swallowed, tears glinting in her eyes. He pulled out a chair then took her free hand in both of his.

"What are you doing here, Jillian?"

"I can't do it," she mumbled. "I said I would do it. I *want* to do it. I want to . . . want to . . ."

Marius pulled on her hand. "Let's leave this place."

Jill shook her head.

"Yes," he pressed. "This is not for you. Come with me outside, just for a moment. Let's talk."

Jill stood up and let him lead her out of the bar by the hand. She looked like a frightened child as he maneuvered her down a side street and into a small alcove. The fresh air seemed to do her some good.

Marius searched her terrified features, trying to get his mind around the full situation. "You said you would do what?"

She wouldn't look at him, so he pressed his fingertips to her chin, turning her face to his. Looking into his eyes, she broke. She told him about her meeting with a female I-Ops agent, about the human government's kits and what they contained. About a possible antidote. All they'd imagined was true, and Marius sat there, heavy with the horror of what she'd been asked to contemplate in order to save him, the crime she'd almost committed.

She pulled away and removed a small metal box from her pocket. Opening it, she revealed two syringes. "You were right. Gregory Bell was infected because he crossed the human government. This is what they're doing. This is what they want me to do. I get to choose four victims. Four. They figure with my contacts at Bosco's and the Rogues Club, I should know plenty of higher-ups. Of course, they also implied they'd accept jerks and criminals who won't be missed. I suppose I could choose someone like that. . . ."

"You've never killed anyone, Jillian," Marius said. "You're going to start now?"

She shrugged. Biting her lip she said, "If it was someone really bad . . ."

Marius shook his head. "The abstract is one thing. Reality is another. You'll have to live with what you do. We'll come up with a workaround."

She gave him a look. "A workaround? There is no workaround. Not one that will come in time, unless you've just come from the Librarian with one." When he didn't answer, she added, "Then this is the only way to save you."

Marius grabbed her hands. "No," he said. "I won't have you become a murderer for me."

"It would be for the greater good," she replied. "Isn't that what you always fight for? Saving you would be for the greater good. You've done more for every species than anybody. Without you, Crimson City will suffer. If we choose criminals or—"

"*No*. I know you want to justify this, but there's no good to come from knowingly conducting evil. It's that simple. There is no honor in this choice, and you will regret it for the rest of your life. I won't let you do it."

A sudden change came over her, a hardening of emotions. Jillian looked him square in the eye. "I'm the only chance you've got."

Marius put his hand over hers. "I would rather die."

Bitterly, she laughed. "That's always been the difference between us. You're always so ready to die, as long as it's with honor. I'd rather you live."

"Without honor?" he asked.

Jill looked away.

"How can you claim to love me without *knowing* me?" Marius sighed and ran his hand over his face. "I will never let my life or death be something that weighs on your conscience. If anyone dies so that I may live, it will be by my hand. Not yours. Never yours."

"You don't understand," Jill said in a faltering voice.

Marius pressed his mouth to her open palm. "For the first time, I do."

Jill stared at him in confusion.

He nodded, his eyes searching hers. "I understand everything now. You have always stood beside me, despite how I've disappointed you."

"No. I didn't. I turned to Hayden for a while. I'm not going to pretend I didn't do that." She looked up at Marius with tears in her eyes. "I knew how that would hurt you. I'm sorry."

"For god's sake, don't apologize! Not for any of your choices. I never made things easy. I have always played a part. I was both strong *and* weak, and . . ." He straightened his posture and grasped her hand, pulled her farther into the alley. In the shadows, he took her in his arms. She clung to him, and he wanted to tell her to hold on tighter. She was like time itself slipping through his fingers, and he could not find the strength to hold on. He was going to die.

"Jillian, I beg of you. Don't ruin yourself trying to save me."

"Without you, I'll have nothing worth living for," Jill said, tears spilling down her cheeks. "Not even one night. Not even a memory."

"Yes, you will," Marius whispered. "You'll have that."

Jill could barely let go of Marius long enough to swipe the cardkey on her rented room at the Rogues Club. They stumbled across the threshold, the door slamming shut behind them. Marius lifted Jillian in his arms and carried her to the bed, laying her gently on the blankets. He settled beside her and brushed hair from her face.

"I want to see you," he said. "I want to see what I have sacrificed for so long."

As he slipped her shirt buttons free, slowly undressing her, he pressed a line of kisses to the skin revealed. She trembled as he stripped her bare, his movements rough and greedy from long-thwarted passion.

He eased the last of her clothing away, and Jill laughed. She lay naked before him. "I've loved you so long, and yet you've never seen me like this," she whispered, her cheeks coloring.

He pressed his mouth against her body again and again with lips that felt like flame. "Perhaps I have never before been with you. But I have seen you like this, many, many times in my mind." He smiled sadly, clearly thinking of missed opportunities, and stood upright before her to remove his clothes. He did not take his gaze from her body.

She drank in the sight of him with the same brazen desire. Marius's beauty was otherworldly. His skin bore the scars of combat, but neither those nor the darkness lurking in his bloodstream could dim her love for him. Theirs was a bond for eternity.

She smiled shyly, receiving him with open arms as he returned to the bed. She gasped in heady delight as the length of him settled against her. He rested his weight on his forearms, sweeping his fingers over her hair and lips and cheeks, pressing slow, sensual kisses across the contours of her face. Then he kissed her, and his tongue swept into Jill's mouth. Her moan was lost as he moved his sex against her. The scent of his skin and the way he captured her under his body, possessing her, finally *owning* her, was everything she'd ever desired.

She felt his mouth curve into a smile against her neck as she arched her body closer, and then he used his weight to press her down to the bed. "I want to savor every second," he murmured, kissing her so tenderly that it brought tears to Jill's eyes. She had always imagined that the physicality of their union would be something almost divine, but she could never have imagined that even the smallest touch, the gentlest kiss, the slightest movement his body made against hers could make her tremble so much.

She ran her hands over the lean curves of Marius's back, thrilling as his muscles rippled with power. He took one of her nipples into his mouth, running his tongue in a circle over the taut peak as she writhed beneath him, and for a moment Jill felt a slight glow in her mind, a frag-

ment of the bond that had drawn them so close in the beginning but which had failed them both so terribly. A
moment later it was again gone.

His hands and mouth swept slowly across her delicate
skin as if he was committing every image and sensation to
memory. The years of wanting and waiting made Jill im-
patient to experience everything she had been so long de-
nied, and she was tempted to push him, to force Marius
onward so that they might lose control together, but this
one night might have to last forever. She refrained.

Yet when Marius's eyelashes swept down and he closed
his eyes, it was too much. She could wait no longer. "Marius," Jill pleaded.

The raw sexuality in her voice did him in. He opened
his eyes. Desire warred with deliberation, but the battle
was swift. A rough growl escaped his lips. Never breaking
their locked gazes, Marius gripped Jill's hips and positioned himself between her thighs. Then he entered her,
slowly, thickly, both of them groaning with pleasure as
he drove deep inside. Firmly rooted, he held himself still.

Jill moaned as Marius's cock throbbed inside her, and
he used his tongue to demonstrate what was to come. In a
sweeping rhythm he plundered her mouth. Yet while the
blood clearly pounded in his veins and raw need threatened to capsize his reason, still Marius would not give in.
He moved only enough to cause the smallest amount of
friction.

Arching forward, Jill tried to draw Marius into her
more, but he pulled back with a smile. He lifted her hand
to his lips and kissed her trembling fingers.

"We've waited this long . . . ," he whispered.

"Don't hold back," Jill begged.

"Not yet," Marius replied.

Ecstasy gathered between Jill's legs, coiled for release.
She pressed her naked body against Marius, wanting to

feel every part of him. He looked deep into her eyes and began to rock, moving himself in and out with slow, deliberate strokes. She lifted her legs to improve his angle. With a groan, he began to move faster. Jill inhaled sharply as he thrust into her, harder now, again and again. Relentless.

"Yes," he whispered, his movements becoming wilder.

Oh, yes. Jill, too, gave over to pure sensation. "Make me yours," she said. "It's what we both want. I'm not afraid of being like you."

Marius brought his face down close, his jaw clenched, his eyes gazing into hers a whisper's-breadth away. "I don't dare," he gasped, even so biting against her neck hard enough to leave marks on the surface of her skin.

He moved inside her with a violent passion, drawing them both to the edge.

Jill cried out. In her mind's eye, in that wondrous space of connection that had once been a fiery light but was now nearly extinguished, where she and Marius had once been so brightly bonded, Jill envisioned a thousand white flower petals raining down upon them. Exquisite pleasure washed over her. Marius cried out as well, his face a mix of joy and pain as he spilled his seed deep within her.

Their bodies trembled as they held tightly to one another. Marius pressed his mouth against her neck, his long-held desire to bury fangs into her flesh and make her truly his still strong, though his form had so weakened. He could not have done it anyway, for fear of transferring his death sentence along with his genetic markers. And they were so blunt, now, and would hurt her all the more. Oh, but still. To taste of her blood would be the ultimate privilege.

"Jillian," he murmured after their breathing evened and their bodies sank heavily once more into the bedsheets. "Nothing will ever separate us now. Not any choices made in this physical world, not the loss of my vampire nature, and not even death. We are joined forever."

"Death? No, don't ever leave me," she said in a voice choked with tears. "Not now, when we've finally gotten everything we ever wanted."

"Jillian," he replied, his voice cracking. "Would that I could promise you that."

As she lay there in his arms, his life force glowing deep within her, she knew that they would be soul mates for eternity, whatever earthly difficulties were yet to come. It was a thought that caused her to smile through the tears streaking down the side of her face and soaking her tousled hair. Arms and legs intertwined, they held each other close.

She could not have said how long they dozed in the small, quiet room, but all peace was shattered in an instant as a cry of agony burst from Marius's lips. She felt his entire body spasm. He pressed his palms to his temples, his face twisted in pain.

"Tell me how to make it better," Jill begged.

"It comes and goes," he replied. "It . . . will pass." He peered up at her, and his eyes held a strange blankness. When he blinked rapidly, Jill realized that he could scarcely see.

He grimaced against another bolt of pain, and Jill gasped as she saw the edges of his fangs had morphed down to blunt ridges. *I'm losing him*, she realized. *He's losing himself.*

She ran to the bathroom and brought back a cold, wet towel, which she pressed against his feverish skin. He took her hand, squeezing it as if he would try to comfort her even in the throes of his own misery. Suddenly, Marius went still. His eyes fluttered closed and he took a deep breath, then went frighteningly quiet. This was what it would be like to walk in and find him dead, Jill realized, staring down at his drawn face.

"Marius?" she whispered, a numb, black feeling taking root in the pit of her stomach. "Marius, can you hear me?"

He lunged suddenly up from the bed, his heart pounding so hard that Jill could feel it just by holding his arm. "What is it?" she asked.

He looked around, sucking in huge gulps of oxygen, and then stared at her as if he were only now really seeing her. He reached out and touched her cheek, brushing his fingertips against her skin as if he'd never felt the like. She sensed a change in him. It was as if he was consumed by hyperawareness. Everything had been fading on him. Now his senses, his energy and his entire system seemed to reach for new life.

"Talk to me," Jill begged. "What just happened? Are you better? Do you feel better? This is a good sign, right? Marius, what is it?"

He regarded her. Fresh color bloomed too bright across his cheeks, and utter anguish reflected in his eyes. "Some say there is a euphoria that comes just before death."

# CHAPTER THIRTY-THREE

Edward lay where Charlotte had left him, curled in the pavilion, his arms wrapped around himself. Charlotte cried out to see him looking so vulnerable, so pallid, and quickly sat down, pulling his body into hers and cradling him in her arms.

"You're so still," she whispered. "Too still. Edward, don't leave me now. Not like this."

He opened his eyes and took a labored breath. "Gilliam?"

She shook her head.

Edward looked as though he couldn't quite believe. He winced in pain, and a small trickle of blood dotted his bottom lip. He seemed to have bitten through—his top incisors were sharp and protruded. Charlotte swooned a little from bloodlust, which repulsed her. She thought again about Gilliam's claim that she was stronger than ever.

Edward clutched her hand. "Pocket," he whispered. "Waistcoat pocket."

Charlotte quickly patted his waistcoat until she found a lump. She reached into a pocket and pulled out a ring. It was an acrostic, spelling her name out in different gemstones. "Always meant this for you . . . but never had the courage to . . . God, I love you, Charlie. Say you'll marry me."

"Yes, I'll marry you," she swore, hot tears sliding down her cheeks and falling onto Edward's cold white skin. "I've loved you for such a long time."

He smiled, but the expression could not erase the pain etched on his face. "The knife."

"What?"

"My knife," he whispered hoarsely. "A ring . . . for me."

Charlotte slid her hand into his pocket and found the blade. She unfolded it, trembling all the while. Edward then turned his head to the side, and she understood what he wanted. With a full heart she brought the blade to the side of his face . . . and cut away a lock of his hair. The shearing sound was almost as thunderous in Charlotte's ears as the thump of her own heart.

Her hand came away with the shorn lock. Charlotte swallowed hard but could not speak; she was too overcome.

"Now yours," Edward whispered, never glancing away.

Charlotte raised the blade to the tresses falling disheveled across her shoulders and made the cut. She took the two locks of hair and twisted them, twining them into a loop that she placed over Edward's finger. His mouth eased into a slow smile.

"I will love you forever," he said. He tried to reach up to touch her face, but had not the strength. His fingers instead swept down Charlotte's hair, and his arm fell listlessly back to the stone beneath him.

In that mysterious place where their bond still glowed warm and strong, she knew that he was telling the truth: he would love her forever, and she would feel his love until the end of her days. But some mortal bodies obviously could not withstand the intensity of the initial shock of such foreign poison, and Edward's body lost all warmth.

Charlotte pressed her beloved's pale face gently to her breast, rocking him in her arms, and wept his name.

# CHAPTER THIRTY-FOUR

Flushed and tousled from her time out in the city with Hayden, Tatiana gulped at her cold champagne and absently watched the anchorwoman on the television mounted above Bosco's bar. Camera flashes flared beside her, but this didn't bother her in the least. She'd had less problem with the paparazzi here than in New York. But the establishment's patrons stared at her and at Hayden, especially as the daily report looped once more.

*They're wondering what we're up to, why I'm with him. Well, they'd never guess, and I'm not sorry.* It had been a glorious day. The remnants of Venice Beach, a Hollywood film set, and best of all, the Exposition Park Rose Garden. Not even the botanical gardens of New York were so grand!

She shot her observers a look of disdain and gestured for a refill of her champagne glass, which had never been less than half-full. Hayden remained silent. She stared at his profile, regarding him with open curiosity.

They were creating a stir by being here, she and Hayden, but she didn't care. Tatiana had half-expected one of Marius's brothers to storm in and grab her at any moment . . . but no one at Dumont Towers seemed to have even noticed she was gone. The reason for that was being reported as breaking news above her head. Fleur Dumont was of slightly greater gossip value.

"An explosion at Dumont Towers threatened to claim the life of Fleur Dumont early today. We are only now just hearing the details of what has turned out to be a very close call for the former vampire house and Assembly leader. . . ."

Tatiana watched uneasily as Hayden's expression turned dark.

"Miscarriage was a concern, but Ian Dumont has released a statement that twins—one boy and one girl—were delivered safely and the mother is resting comfortably in spite of the scare."

"Twins," Hayden spat. "One boy and one girl. How fucking perfect. How goddamn fucking perfect. What good fortune those Dumonts have. A bomb goes off while she's giving birth, and she's just fine. She should have died, but the dynasty goes on."

Tatiana recoiled, nearly falling off her stool. Hayden stared at the monitor, and she was surprised to see that his eyes were watery. He called for a double shot of whiskey and downed it, shattered the shot glass in his grip. Tatiana gave a strangled cry as shards tinkled to the ground.

Hayden shook his head, then pressed the back of his trembling hand to his mouth. He stood and left her at the bar, snaking through the milling crowd to a hooded character reading a book by the wall. There, as she watched, Hayden had an extended conversation. At last he gave the man some money, took what looked like a small piece of plastic and unceremoniously slammed it into his bare arm.

*Oh, my god. He did it. He tried to kill Fleur Dumont and her babies.* Nearly paralyzed with fear at her sudden realization, Tatiana understood that she had to get away. Ashamed and somewhat overcome by the alcohol, she weighed her options. The crowd went suddenly silent. For a moment Tatiana assumed they were similarly horrified by Hayden's action, but she was quickly proven wrong.

"Tati?" came a tremulous voice.

Tatiana wheeled around on her bar stool and found her sister behind her, wide-eyed and trembling.

She leapt to her feet, unexpectedly wobbly from too much champagne. "This is no place for you, Folie!"

Her sister leaned close and whispered, "This is no place for *you*. I would have come sooner, but nobody knew you'd gone missing until they looked for you in the garden. Tati, there's been such a scare at the Towers over Fleur. We think Hayden Wilks tried to hurt her, and I've been so scared for you!"

Tatiana felt faint. "Marius will never forgive me for being seen with his enemy," she murmured. "He'll never let me back into the Towers!"

Hayden returned, slipping a proprietary arm around Tatiana's shoulder. When he saw Tatiana's sister, he managed an unsteady bow. "Folie. As lovely as always. What brings you here?"

Showing no sign of her previous interest in Hayden, Folie gave him a frightened glance and brought her lips directly to her sister's ear. "Do not worry about Marius. He would want you to be safe. Come away from this place. You *must* come back to Dumont Towers. Remember everything you said on your wedding day? It's not too late. You are being led astray by a very bad man! Please, Tati—"

"Don't say anything more. I'm so ashamed." Tatiana's chin trembled. "I want to go home." She steadied herself and turned to Hayden, afraid to say anything about Fleur. "I'm going home now, Mr. Wilks. To Marius."

Hayden looked stunned. "Do you even know where he is?"

"I need to go home," she repeated, trying to pull away.

"Leaving, just like that? What happened to our special connection, Tatiana?" Hayden growled. "What about that friendship you were seeking? Didn't you still want to be friends? Or was that just a lie, a way to get what you want?"

She tried to steel herself, wobbling a bit as she put her body between Hayden and her sister. She didn't want Folie to accidentally get harmed. "Yes, it was just some lie I made up. I'm sorry, Mr. Wilks, but I'm leaving now. I shan't be seeing you again."

Hayden swayed, his irises huge, clearly under the influence of whatever drug he'd bought and injected. "Women," he said. "You always leave. You leave and move on as if other people are nothing. Fleur, Jill . . . *you*."

Tatiana felt a flush of shame wash over her. "I must go to Marius. I must—"

"Marius is with Jill!" Hayden yelled. "Will you get that through your thick skull? Nothing has changed. He loves somebody else. He's sleeping with somebody else. He's in a room at the Rogues Club with Jill Cooper as you sit here drinking champagne. What do you think they're doing there—playing poker?" Hayden gestured to the man from whom he'd just bought his drugs. "This kind gentleman was good enough to point out their location, but the intel fencers sold it to the tabloids while you and I were busy tooling around Chinatown. Everyone will know soon. He's made a fool out of you, don't you see? It's been bound to happen since the start. You're as much a fool as I am."

"You're lying," Tatiana said imperiously. She turned away. "I want to speak to my husband now."

"You want to see your husband? I'll show you your husband," Hayden roared. He turned to Folie. "Get out of here, kid. Go home!" Then he grabbed Tatiana's elbow and dragged her from the bar, ignoring her pleas for Folie to get Ian and Warrick. "Send the bill to Dumont Towers," he called to the bartender. "They're good for it."

"You're hurting my arm," Tatiana screamed, stumbling outside behind Hayden. "You tried to kill Fleur Dumont and her babies, didn't you? You are everything bad that they say!"

Hayden stopped short. He slowly turned to Tatiana with a magnitude of fury she had never before in her life seen. Still holding on to her, he raised his arms and roared out his anger to the sky.

Tatiana swooned. The alcohol had made everything fuzzy, and she blinked as her delicate shoes slipped against the uneven pavement. His nails dug into her skin, and his palm was cut from breaking the shot glass. She could feel the blood smear thick and warm over her hand, and the smell of it caused an adrenaline surge, the kind of which she'd only felt during her struggles with the Change.

A frightened sob slipped from her throat as Hayden wrenched her into a taxi. They made quick time, it seemed, to Dumont Towers; he must have paid extra for speed. With relief, Tatiana half-fell out of the cab, Hayden helping her upright—at which point she discovered that she was not at Dumont Towers. She was instead at the Rogues Club, being manhandled and dragged and treated most unpleasantly by this man who was suddenly more frightening than anything she could imagine.

"I want to go home," she reiterated, trying to use a royal voice but finding her intentions lodged in her throat. It was as though everything happened in slow motion.

There came shouting in the foyer of the Rogues Club—a *lot* of shouting. Tatiana staggered, heaving as her body was overwhelmed by adrenaline. She tried to wipe away the blood coating her hand and arm, but it wouldn't come off.

Hayden let go of her. He pulled a gun from inside his jacket and brandished it.

Tatiana reeled. Holding her blood-covered hand away from her body, meaning to keep the stench and her anger from triggering a Change, Tatiana clung to Hayden's jacket with her other hand, terrified of him but more terrified at the prospect of losing a protector amidst all the bellowing. Hayden yelled something, causing even more of a commotion.

She tried to focus as people scattered and he dragged her farther into the bowels of the establishment. He seemed to have a destination. Tatiana could not ask. She couldn't even think straight. She'd never felt so animal before, so out of control, and she thought she might be sick. But that was nothing compared to the nausea she felt when Hayden brought her abruptly to a halt and kicked open a door with the heel of his foot. Inside, Marius lay with his shirt off, a sweaty mess on a bed. Jillian Cooper was kissing his face.

"It's . . . it's not what it looks like," Tatiana's nemesis said, standing up, tears streaking her cheeks. "Marius is sick. He has some sort of hypersensitivity, and . . ."

Tatiana stumbled backward from the door and fell awkwardly to the ground. Hard.

Hayden could not seem to take his eyes off Marius. "Nice," he sneered. "You Dumonts. Classy acts, one and all."

He raised his gun, showily switching it to the UV setting. Everyone stared in horror as he walked forward and pointed it at Marius's face. Running the muzzle from his enemy's forehead to his temple, he finally rested the gun barrel against Marius's lips. Eyes closed, his enemy didn't move.

"I could do this. So much pain would finally be over."

"You wouldn't," Jill whispered. "I know you."

Hayden didn't look at her. "You *never* knew me, Jill."

Marius began to convulse, gripping the sides of the bed. Jill took his hand. Tatiana sat slumped on her knees and watched the white knuckles of Marius as he half-consciously squeezed back. *That should have been me holding his hand*, she realized. *I failed in my duties. I should have found a way to make this work.*

Hayden's laugh was almost hysterical. "Oh, that's *rich*," he announced. "He's already dying, isn't he? He was already infected. God, I hate you. I hate all of you!"

In a flash, he pulled away. He grabbed Tatiana's elbow and dragged her out over the threshold. She shrieked, but he ignored her. He hauled her down the corridor, yanking her unceremoniously up every time she fell. Cursing the Dumonts all the way, he bashed his gun against every wall, sending plaster flying.

Tatiana screamed as Hayden's dark purpose revealed itself. A frightening sense of doom swept over her. She could smell his intent, which flowed through his pores like a demon's perfume: *death*.

"Marius!" Tatiana screamed. Her husband seemed her only hope.

But Marius didn't answer, and beyond Hayden's insane anger, all she could hear was Jill yelling Hayden's name. "Wait," Tatiana's enemy cried. "Please, Hayden, wait!"

# CHAPTER THIRTY-FIVE

The sound of Tatiana screaming his name rang in Marius's ears, and he shook his head and wobbled upright on the bed. Jill had gone after her and Hayden. Marius stood up, then crashed to the floor, but this time it wasn't because he was weak. Adrenaline, suppressed as the virus worked its way through his body, now poured through his system all at once. He steadied himself and headed into the hall.

As he regained control he began to run, moving straight for the common rooms. In the close confines of these stone-lined back passageways, all of his senses were raging. He could feel danger. He could smell Hayden's anger and Tatiana's fear. Everything inside of him seemed to roil and burn with a greater intensity than he'd ever felt—it was difficult to control the rage coursing through his bloodstream. Nonetheless, he followed the scent of danger and Tatiana's desperate cries. He'd gone from one extreme to the next, and he had no filter.

Suddenly, warning lights and an evacuation siren switched on. Marius came upon a crowd, a steady stream of Rogues Club members all passing him on the way out. He pushed through, ignoring their protests and warnings.

"You are all hypocrites!" he heard Hayden shout.

"There is nothing in this world worth living for, and you all know it."

He turned a final corner. There, in one of the club's glass-walled medical rooms, Hayden had barricaded himself with Tatiana. Jill and her friend Bridget pounded on the glass, begging him to set her free. Hayden clutched several vials containing red and blue liquid in his fist.

Jill looked over her shoulder in desperation. "He knows what it does, Marius!"

Tatiana pressed her hands against the glass, and though her voice was muffled by the wall and clogged with tears, her cries for help rang loud in Marius's ears. "Please help me, Marius. You're my husband!" she sobbed. "Please help me."

Marius matched his palms to hers on the other side of the wall. "Is there a lock override?" he asked, not looking away from his terrified wife.

Bridget stared at him. "He's got vials full of some fucking mystery substance in there. Do you seriously want me to open that room without getting him calm?"

"We know what it does," Jill said, pounding desperately at the pane. "Hayden, let's calm down and talk about all this! *Please!*"

Hayden paced the chamber in a frenzy, kicking over chairs and cursing, the blue and red fluids shaking violently in their vials. Tatiana screamed Marius's name again, but that only seemed to enrage Hayden further. He stepped over and wrapped his arm around her waist and dragged her from the glass.

"See his eyes? Is he on poppers?" Bridget asked.

Jill nodded. "I don't know what he's going to do."

Tatiana's legs had given out. She hung pathetically in Hayden's grasp, crying. They saw her mouth move: *Let me go. Please, I beg of you.*

Hayden responded, lifting her chin. Neither Marius nor Jill nor Bridget could hear his words until Bridget hit a button for an intercom, then, "—you going to go? Nobody wants you. Nobody cares. Marius was in her *bed*. Get it? He doesn't give a shit about you."

Marius pounded against the glass with all his strength. "That's not true! Tatiana, I will make things right. I promise you this, I will restore all you had. We will find a way to give you back your dignity, even if I must make a public apology before all of the world! My honor means everything, Tatiana, but I could not deny my love. I'm sorry."

Tatiana stared at him, then over and up into Hayden's eyes. Tears were coursing down her cheeks.

Hayden spoke softly, and those collected outside could barely hear him over the intercom. "We'll go together, we beasts." The strange look in his eye turned Marius cold, and the feeling only grew as Tatiana seemed to nod. She turned her head—perhaps looking at the exit? But the rogue vampire met her mouth with his, caressing her cheek as he took the werewolf princess's lips in a gentle kiss. "I didn't try to kill Fleur," Hayden whispered. "It wasn't me. I need that understood." He then smashed his palm into Tatiana's, the vials he held there splintering. He ground their hands together.

"No!" Marius cried. He turned and picked up a chair, flung it at the wall. It dented the glass, making a rough bull's-eye pattern but not breaking through. Tatiana screamed in shock and pain at her bloody hand, and Marius threw the chair again and again and again—

"What have you done? I don't want to *die*!" Tatiana fell to her knees and bent over Hayden's boots. "Please! I beg of you. I don't want to die!"

"Open the door!" Marius screamed. He was punching

at the fractured glass with his fists, Jill at his side with a fire extinguisher she'd wrenched from the wall. Bridget worked furiously to break the code on the electronically locked door.

Looking up from her palm, Tatiana began to choke and tear at herself. Her skin flushed bright red, drained to white and flushed again. She lost her ability to suppress the werewolf in her and began to change form.

Hayden looked down at her in a kind of dawning horror. "What's . . . ? Why is it working so quickly? It's not consistent. I'm supposed to die *with* you," he said, his voice strained. "I'm supposed to die with you!"

Tatiana's hands began to convulse and curl into claws. She clutched at her face, snarling like a wolf, and pressed her back against a wall of lockers. Her body twisted and morphed out of control.

Hayden reached out, then turned to face Jill. "Why am I not going with her?" he cried. "Why not me too?"

Behind him, Tatiana writhed in agony. She took an enormous breath of air and went still, but a moment later she bashed her head backward into the metal lockers. Screaming and crying and begging for help, she twisted as her body reversed course and began to strip itself entirely of everything lupine.

Hayden wrapped his arms around Tatiana and held her close. The intermittent smash of Marius's fists on the glass punctuated the silence, along with the hideous gasps and moans bursting from the dying werewolf's lips. Her skin was slick with sweat as she struggled against the poison's pull.

"Don't let me go. Don't let anyone see me like this," she whimpered, her body taut.

Hayden held on tighter, pressing his mouth to her ear. His tears dampened her hair. "I'm so sorry," he murmured.

"Tatiana! Do *not* give up!" Marius's bloody fist finally cratered the glass, almost enough to break it completely.

"Don't break the glass!" Bridget yelled. "God only knows what's in those vials he smashed."

Jill put her hand on Bridget's arm. "It won't hurt humans. I swear."

Inside the room, Hayden had gone very still. He held the princess, clearly trying to make Tatiana comfortable as she completed her death throes. "I'm sorry. I'm so sorry. I'm sorry," he intoned. "I didn't have the strength to go alone. I thought that maybe together . . . Oh, I'm sorry, Tatiana. Oh, if only demons still haunted this world and could keep your soul alive. . . ."

"Why aren't you dying, you fucking bastard?" Marius yelled as the wall finally gave way. A hail of safety glass showered Hayden and Tatiana. "What have you done?"

He leapt inside, but it was too late. Tatiana convulsed in Hayden's arms. Her hands reached out and grabbed his shirt, werewolf claws appearing one last time, piercing his skin like razors, then retracting for eternity. Just like that she was gone. Dead.

Marius glared at Hayden. "It should have been you," was all he could say. "I made mistakes, but . . ." He reached out and ran his palm down his dead wife's hair.

Hayden loosened his grip, and Tatiana's body slipped away from him. He cradled her gently in his arms and pulled her face from his chest, laid her on the ground in front of Marius.

The werewolf princess's mouth and neck were covered with blood; it also leaked from beneath her fingernails. Marius crouched, frozen, paralyzed with shock, and then he gently touched her neck, praying for signs of life. Why had she died so fast? Why had the virus not affected her as it had him? He removed a handkerchief from his pocket and with shaking hands did his best to clean her face. Then he turned to the rogue vampire who had killed her.

"I thought I would die," Hayden said. "I thought Jill said one was for vampires. I thought I would die with her, but that she and I would have time to . . . I'm . . . I'm sorry."

Out of options, Bridget slumped against the wall, watching in horror. No one stopped Marius as he slowly wrapped his hands around Hayden's neck and began to squeeze. Hayden's arms flailed out, but he simply pressed a hand to the wall for support.

"Beg for your life the way Tatiana did," Marius spat.

"Just kill me. I won't fight back," Hayden gasped. "I'll make it easy."

"You cowardly bastard," Marius swore, his voice brittle. "I've no interest in anything being easy with you." He released Hayden and flung him across the room. The rogue vampire spun to a stop, choking and coughing.

"Get out of here," Marius hissed.

"Marius," Jill whispered. "You're going to let him go?"

He looked at her. "Haven't we spilled enough blood? Hayden will live and think about Tatiana for every second of the rest of his pathetic life. If this virus doesn't kill him, which I assume it will, he'll think about how he destroyed an innocent life for no other reason than his inability to accept himself."

He stood up, walked over and pulled Hayden off the floor. The rogue staggered back against the wall, but Marius yanked him upright and then reached down and took the switchblade from Jill's boot. He cut the initial T into Hayden's unwounded palm. Then Marius pushed him away.

"Get out of here!"

Hayden stumbled, seemingly oblivious to any physical pain. He looked down at Tatiana's lifeless body. "Make sure you use her roses in the funeral. She loved those damn roses," he whispered. Then, staring ahead with dull eyes, the vampire turned and fled.

# CHAPTER THIRTY-SIX

Jill stepped over glass and blood and sat down next to Marius, who was clearly spent, staring hopelessly down at his dead wife's body. She looked up at Bridget, who was already heading for the door. "You planning to clear everybody out?" Jill asked.

"Yeah. This whole place is gonna need to be disinfected." Bridget looked awkwardly at Marius and then back at Jill. "Sorry this had to happen. Hayden . . . he . . ." Unable to find the words, she just shook her head and left.

In the silence, Jill knelt and took the princess's hand, feeling she had to speak. "I know you wouldn't believe this if you were still with us, Tatiana, but I'll say it anyway. I'm so, so sorry."

"She should never have died," Marius muttered. "What was she doing with Hayden Wilks? And for her to die without me even being able to explain . . . Look, she's not wearing her wedding rings. I truly failed her. Just as I failed you for so many years. Always a day late and a dollar short. Maybe a couple hundred dollars, at that." He coughed. Jill nervously took his hand, and he gave hers a squeeze.

Marius shook his head and slowly knelt down next to Tatiana. On one knee, he took her blood-stained hand in his and gently kissed its back. He stood up and murmured, "She'll have her roses. She'll have every rose on the—"

He froze. "Her roses," he muttered. He brushed a messy strand of hair away from Tatiana's cold, dead face and saw the ratty bloom that was in her coat pocket. He pulled it free, and the too-fragile petals fell apart in his palm. "White roses, red stripe . . . We've got to get to the mech lab, Jillian. I must talk to Leyton."

He was too weak to move, though. All his energy had been expended pounding through the glass wall. Jill put her arm around Marius's shoulders and helped him walk.

Slowly, very slowly, he put one foot in front of the other. Jill led him through the deserted club to the exit and brought him up to street level. It was darker than usual for the time of night, and it took an excruciating amount of time to find a cab that wasn't headed hurriedly away from the center of town.

One finally pulled up, and the window rolled down. "The human government is blowing circuits. No meter. No way to dial up or out, so if you want a ride, you gotta pay cash," the cabbie remarked.

Jill shoved the semidelirious Marius into the back and took out his wallet. She raised a handful of cash so that it was visible in the rearview mirror and gave directions to the alley where the mech lab was hidden. Marius lolled against the back seat in a state of half consciousness for the entire drive.

A block from the alley, she told the driver to stop. He clearly thought she was crazy for coming to the middle of nowhere, but the cash she handed over staved off any questions. She helped Marius outside, then waited for the cab to disappear before walking them both to their destination and talking to the mail slot.

"Please recognize me," Jill murmured. "At least recognize that this is Marius hanging half-dead in my arms."

The camera moved out of the mail slot. Jill faced it and said, "Tell Leyton that Mr. Dumont is dying. It's an emergency."

She spent several minutes in silent, heart-pounding worry, but at last two mechs appeared. They ushered Jill and Marius into their lab complex, then lifted Marius out of Jill's arms. Meeting up with Leyton, the quintet all relocated to a sick room, where Marius was eased onto a bed.

He tried to reach out—for what Jill wasn't sure, because his arm fell back limply to the bed. Before Jill had even finished describing Tatiana's death, Leyton called for more lab tests.

She sat by Marius's bedside, holding his hand as he struggled against the pain. He sprawled in semiconsciousness, his body and its virus trying to rid itself of all vampire genetics. Jill wiped sweat from his brow and fought back tears.

At last Leyton returned, throwing the door loudly open. It woke Marius. "I did not think to test for this before," he said, and glanced curiously at his patient. "It did not even occur to me."

Marius shook his head as if to clear it, and gestured for Leyton to continue.

"The speed with which your werewolf bride deteriorated . . . Well, it spurred me to consider factors I might otherwise have ignored. In fact, I *did* ignore these other factors. The common denominator here is werewolf genetics. You, Marius Dumont—along with the entire House of Dumont, I would suspect—have a recessive werewolf gene that does not present outwardly." He placed a lab report in Marius's hand. "But it is unmistakably there. This is not a vampire virus at heart. This is a *werewolf* virus. I wonder if I-Ops entirely knows what it has. I would be very surprised if your Mr. Wilks is even infected, being a 'made' vampire as he is."

Marius gasped and the paper fell from his grasp. "We're supposed to be the purest. Old Lucien . . . If anyone thought we were dirty vampires, mated with werewolves . . . St. Giles—"

Jill stroked his forehead. "Are you insane? Politics aren't important now. We need to get you well."

The blood vessels in Marius's neck visibly throbbed. "It must have been far back in our history. . . . The first Recall destroyed all those records, so who can say. But long ago, maybe even during the time of the Blood-Taint, our genetics altered, and now we Dumonts are not so very pure after all." Suddenly, he shook his head and tried to sit up, a look of hope filling his features.

"Marius?"

"Charlotte Paxton's papers! She was an amateur gardener. Her project was merging two kinds of roses into one, red and white blooms blended together in just such a way that there was only a red stripe running down the center of each white petal. . . ."

"Yeah?"

"She spent a very long time on them. Years, even after the Blood-Taint. I think they became a symbol of something, something she was uncomfortable leaving in her journal. There were passages torn out from the main body of her notes." Marius looked dazedly into Jill's eyes and added, "The mech at the library. When that mech said you smelled the way Asprey roses might smell . . . I think he was imagining Charlotte Paxton's roses from the time of the Blood-Taint, not Tatiana." He felt a ludicrous burst of laughter threaten and shook his head, clutching Jill's wrist. "Don't you see, Jillian? Do you see?"

"You're scaring me," Jill said quietly, pressing the back of her hand to his sweaty forehead. Leyton moved in silently to press a wet cloth against his skin.

Marius tried to push him away, delirious almost as much with enthusiasm as with sickness. "The last page I read, she wrote a letter to her sister Maggie and signed it Lady Charlotte Asprey. She was sending her vampire son away. She was bitten by a wolf—she herself was a werewolf. So her union with Edward Vaughan was a union between a vampire and a werewolf, both infected by the original strain of the Blood-Taint. Her son must have maintained a recessive werewolf gene. That's what her flower represents in the end. And if Leyton's right, that means we, the entire House of Dumont, come from a similar pairing."

"And that means Charlotte Paxton is Charlotte *Asprey* . . . a werewolf ancestor of Tatiana's royal family?" Jill said, shaking her head in disbelief.

"I'm an idiot. It's been right in front of me all along," Marius whispered. He turned his head slightly and tried to focus on Leyton. "You said that if I could find genetic material from the first generation after the Taint, it would be the last thing they needed for a reverse-engineered antidote." He tried to get out of bed but couldn't manage, and his strength was fading quickly. He coughed, and blood dripped from the side of his mouth. His fingers twitched to touch Jillian's face but he could not reach her. She moved closer and he said, "The rings, Jillian. The rings Tatiana wore at our wedding, passed down within her family. Sentimental jewelry from the Victorian age. They were Charlotte Paxton's. Charlotte's and her lover, Edward's. He was turned, and I believe he died, which is why she married someone else. She must have worn their rings as mourning jewelry."

"Victorian mourning jewelry . . . Much of it was made

from hair," Jillian said. "That's DNA, right there! Just what we need! But Tatiana wasn't wearing her rings. They must be at Dumont Towers, in her room."

Marius didn't answer. He just stared straight ahead, and Jill understood that he'd come to the end of his strength. She looked up at the mech. "Is there anything that can ease his pain, Leyton?"

"Nothing but the rings, Miss Cooper."

Jill leaned over and whispered in her beloved's ear. "I'll go get them, Marius."

She caressed his face and said his name, but he did not answer. His breaths were shallow fits and starts, and it obviously took great will for him to force a smile.

Jill took his face in her hands and kissed him over and over. "I'll be back for you. Just wait for me. I need you to live for me. It's the only honorable thing to do now."

# CHAPTER THIRTY-SEVEN

*London, England*
*April, 1854*

Charlotte watched the children playing outside in her rose garden, her dark-haired eldest son and her towheaded girls. The boy turned and waved, smiling wide, two fangs gleaming in the twilight. The girls, the spitting image of their mother, turned and followed his gaze, then likewise gestured. Charlotte waved back.

"Lady Asprey, your clippings have arrived."

Charlotte looked up in delight. She put her pencil down, thanked the maid who'd come to inform her, took up a lantern, and tried not to run as she made her way to the greenhouse.

The gardener stood holding a plant carefully bound with paper to avoid damaging the buds and leaves. He set the plant down on a nearby table, presented her with a card and bowed, then retreated. Charlotte set down the lamp. Then, steeling herself, she bit down on her lower lip and opened the envelope.

*Well done, Charlie. Well done. I shall look into naming*
*privileges on your behalf.*
*Your cousin Joseph.*

Charlotte approached the packaged plant with a fast-beating heart. She slipped on a pair of gloves and picked up her gardening shears, severing the string binding the paper over the top of the plant. The plain wrapper fell to the table, and Charlotte gasped and stepped back. A beautiful rose, white with a single red stripe down the middle of each petal, lifted victoriously toward the sky.

Charlotte started to laugh. She raised her hand and pressed her lips against her rings before rushing off to pen a letter.

*Dear Maggie,*

*I hope this letter finds you well in America. Though we now know the infections effect change at different rates, I think we would know by now if you were destined to be something other than human. I shall assume that your departure from England was in time, and I hope you are safe in New York.*

*I am smiling here in London with such wonderful news! Joseph was kind enough to review my attempts at creating a hybrid rose. He has sent me a most glorious result, and tells me he will inquire about naming it.*

*I will have to call it the Asprey rose, of course. I have no choice, really. But in my heart it will forever be the Vaughan rose. I feel quite proud and accomplished, really, as though I have finally achieved some sort of closure. Enclosed is a dried specimen, but I will have young Edward bring a fresh cutting to you when he makes his voyage next week.*

*He does not leave a moment too soon. Edward is the spitting image of his father. You would never know by looking that he has any werewolf in him at all. Just as well, for in London, to be of mixed blood is worse than anything. I couldn't bear the other children calling him a* "dirty" vampire, now that he is of age to start school. At least everyone believes him to be pure.

I miss you so, Maggie. I miss our talks. I think about you, before all of the strangeness, warning me against Edward's touch. Sometimes I feel Edward is still with me, and that perhaps he didn't die after all. Perhaps it was all just a dream. But, no. Certainly, I cannot talk to my Lord Asprey about such thoughts. He has been the kindest of men, and I am so grateful he was willing to step forward after Edward died to accept my son into his werewolf household . . . though he does not wish to speak of it. A vampire, and a bastard child, at that! He was Edward's godfather, and that he would marry someone like me speaks volumes about his generosity. That must be enough.

I do not know when I will come to New York. Lord Asprey still needs some persuading, in light of the news that as many vampires are emigrating to America as are staying in London. I am trying to explain to him that the vampires are going to the West Coast and that I want to go to the East, but he does not understand how large the continent is. Did I tell you that Jane St. Giles and Lucy Vaughan are headed west? Bitten by vampires, they were. Fitting. I told you how they tortured the bats so at the exhibition.

At any rate, I will try to join you both as soon as possible. In the meantime, I need only look into my garden to see a symbol of my boy. White blossoms for the dominant vampire he is, with a red flourish down the center of each petal for the werewolf deep inside. My lord need never know, and I will plant them everywhere on this estate and think of father and son with the greatest joy.

Perhaps when he is older I will give him my rings, so that he might have a small token of his father. There is the one I had made from Edward's and my hair and

*also the acrostic that spells out my name in gems—
chrysoprase, hematite, aquamarine, ruby, lapis, onyx,
two topazes, and emerald. At any rate, I shall send them
with him to New York for safekeeping until I am there to
reclaim them. It is getting quite dangerous here in London, what with all of the divisiveness between species.*

*Well, you know this, dear Maggs. Between you and
me, I know that Lord Gilliam is working hard on a series
of surgeries and inventions to replace human flesh with
metal in a misguided effort to withstand the ravages of
the Blood-Taint. He calls himself a 'mech,' and it is all
very strange. I said at the beginning of this letter that I
imagined you were still human. If you should receive this
as something else, do not be afraid. I am after all, a werewolf, but the same Charlotte you have always known.*

*Your loving sister,*
*Charlie*
*Lady Charlotte Asprey*

# CHAPTER THIRTY-EIGHT

Jill ran as fast as she could. Her comm device was going nuts, but she had no time to field calls; she was letting voice mail take all messages.

Bridget had also texted her three times about a meeting humans against Total Recall were having at Bosco's to discuss taking up arms, and Jill maintained a desperate hope that a rebellion was rising up against the human government, a coalition of sanity against the madmen who were set upon destroying any hope of citywide peace. But as she passed the bar on her way to Dumont Towers, it was not a sense of controlled rebellion in the air, but rather widespread panic. People were shrieking and running everywhere. The scene was entirely unorganized, and left her little hope. People were scrambling, shouting at one another in confusion.

"Make yourself scarce," a Bosco's regular called out. "It's an I-Ops raid!" The man vanished into the shadows before she could learn anything else.

"Bridget!" Jill called, seeing her friend burst through the back door of the bar.

Bridget stopped short, nearly tripping over herself. "No time to talk now. We've got to get out of sight for a while. The human government has started a crackdown."

"What about the meeting?"

"It's failed. There was a leak or something, and I-Ops

agents were all over this place. There aren't enough of us to fight, and B-Ops is here for the kill!"

"Come to Dumont Towers," Jill yelled over the noise. "That's where I'm heading. They're the only ones who can help us, and they'll get us off this strata. I've gotta get there ASAP." No way was she going to get caught up in this mess with Marius's life on the line. But she was unable to see where they might veer toward the Towers, because of a row of armored vehicles that was driving slowly up the street to cut off all escape. These were followed by several large buses with bars on the windows and were clearly manned by B-Ops troops.

"This was a trap, Jill. They just wanted to round us all—"

The crowd surged, and Jill turned just in time to see Bridget take a brutal blow to the side of the head and go down. There was nothing she could do but watch, and her friend was dragged flailing into one of the buses with bars—a makeshift paddy wagon.

Jill headed for a side street but was intercepted by a familiar face. Emily. The human operative moved toward her, a clipboard in one hand and a military-issue machine gun in the other. The two women made eye contact. The pen slipped from her clipboard as Emily slowly raised her weapon.

"Not now. Not *now*," Jill pleaded. "There's something I've got to do, the most important thing of my life. Give me a half an hour before you take me in. . . ."

Emily stared straight at her and walked forward. She stopped a couple of feet away, swung the muzzle of her machine gun toward the ground and leaned her weight on the weapon as if it were a walking stick. "You obviously didn't like your present. You could have told me. I hate wasting money and time on ingrates," she remarked. Slipping her arm through Jill's, she linked their elbows.

Jill tried to break free. "The thought was lovely, but I haven't gotten around to trying it on." Snorting with disgust, she dropped their ludicrous pretense. "Do you even know what you gave me? That virus only works on vampire genes that have been compromised with those of werewolves—or on werewolves themselves. You know that, right?"

"Dead fang, dead dog—what's the difference?" Emily said. "A little less observation time on the victim, I suppose."

Jill wrenched her arm free. "Well, if it's all the same to you, then Tatiana Asprey's dead. Infected. That's what you wanted. Now do you have a cure for Marius?"

Emily eyed her with distaste. "I don't think I can give you credit for that injection, Jill. Unless you injected Miss Asprey yourself and you have the proof."

"Do you have a cure?" Jill shrieked.

"You didn't provide any data points, so I don't have a cure for you."

"We're done here," Jill said through gritted teeth. "If you won't help me save him, I'm going to find someone who will." She turned to flee.

The agent caught her hand. "Why do you have to make this so hard?" she asked. "This doesn't have to be hard. You said you were going to do something and you didn't. I tell my bosses you're going to play ball and you don't, and guess who looks like an idiot? Me. *I* look like an idiot."

Jill shook her head, staring despondently at the pen dangling from Emily's clipboard by its ball chain. "I just need a little time to sort everything out."

"We're all out of time."

The agent twisted Jill's hand, coiling her arm around and slamming her facefirst against a wall. Jill could hear the music playing inside Bosco's and the sound of a television news report. Her cheek scraped concrete, but the elbow twisted high up against her back was worse.

Jill took her chance when the agent went to cuff her wrists together, utilizing the meager martial-arts training she'd had to enact a seesawing motion and change of weight. She wheeled her body around and delivered the heel of her boot to the side of Emily's face. It would have been a devastating blow to an untrained civilian.

The agent was no untrained civilian. With cold precision, the girl used hands, feet and her clipboard to make short work of Jill, who knew that she must surrender to the inevitable before her brain wound up as pulp on the street. In a daze, with blood streaming down the side of her face, Jill dropped to her knees and cringed as far into the dirty sidewalk as she could. The pressure of Emily's gun muzzle was soon digging into her flesh. She tried to clear her vision by blinking, but her eyes were already swelling. Powerless to fight further, she curled into herself, wincing as the agent landed a final blow with a boot and cuffed her wrists.

Emily trussed her like a chicken while Jillian lay in a gritty, tepid pool of water. She tried to scream, but a rag in her mouth muffled all sound. It was twenty minutes or so before a couple of heavies came by and tossed her into the paddy wagon–bus with Bridget and the rest of the so-called traitors to the human race. She was likely going to die, but Jill could only think one thing.

*There's no one left. Bridget's caught, your brothers don't know what you're up against. . . . I've failed you, Marius.*

# CHAPTER THIRTY-NINE

Jill slumped on the floor of the holding cell for what seemed like hours, her hands wrapped around her head to keep out the screams. It didn't work, and she knew that she had no chance for survival if she didn't give in. She glanced around at her sodden cell mates. Some had already been returned after torture; some, like her, were awaiting future horrors. Saucer eyed and shivering, they all stared at the ground and rocked.

Torture. What would that entail, and what would her captors want to know? She didn't have much information they wouldn't have, so there was no point in refusing to talk. Apart from what she'd learned with Marius . . . *Marius*. She could not even think of him without bursting into tears. He was surely dead by now. If they asked her if they'd loved each other, she would say yes. That was the only thing in life she'd ever cared about, so it seemed fitting those words might be her last. She loved a vampire. She didn't regret anything.

A ruckus at the other end of the room jolted Jill and her cell mates out of their private hells. The sound of shoe soles clicked briskly across hard floor.

"I just want to get this over with," Jill mumbled to herself.

"*I'm* gonna do whatever they want. Whatever they want," the guy next to her muttered in similar desperation.

A face appeared at the bars. Horschaw. Jill moistened her lips as he gave her a pleasant smile.

"You ready?" he asked.

Jill nodded and stood up. Her cramped muscles betrayed her, however, causing her to stumble a bit just when she'd hoped to appear strong. She sighed and took his proffered hand as he opened the cell door, gingerly stepping over the limbs of her frightened peers.

She walked in front of him down a very narrow, undecorated hall toward a black door.

"So, Jill," he said conversationally. "I feel really shitty about all of this, but I guess we're stuck with it now."

The door loomed large as they approached. There was the faint residue of fingerprints lining the corridor's metal walls, and then a more recent smear of red, as if someone had fallen sideways in a moment of weakness—or had been thrown.

They reached the door, and Jill stood there trembling. Horschaw reached around and opened it. They walked into a room with two more doors, and he pointed to the one on the left. "We're going in that one. We could go in the other, but we're going in that one."

Jill's heart pounded with fear as his hand reached out and turned the doorknob. She wished she had a gun.

The door opened into a picturesque sitting room. Tastefully if blandly appointed, the chamber's banality frightened her even more. Horschaw grabbed a folded blanket from the back of the couch and handed it to Jill, who wondered if they had a massive closet full of facsimile blankets for each species traitor they brought here.

She looked around for signs of blood or struggle but saw nothing. Wrapping the blanket around herself, she sat down on the couch as Horschaw pulled up a chair and opened a file on the coffee table. Jill's full name was printed on the tab.

"Emily tells me that you did not provide us with any information for our experiments," Horschaw said briskly, thumbing through the paperwork. He looked up. "She gave you four sets of serum with instructions, and it seems you produced nothing of use—though she claims you had some limited role in the death of Tatiana Asprey. Just to be fair I'm going to give you another chance. I'm going to bring in a fang, and you're going to stick him. That's the only way to save your life."

Jill laughed bitterly. "Save your serum."

Horschaw leaned forward, shaking his head. "Jill, Jill, Jill. If you don't give us anything to work with, we can't help you. You do understand that, yes?"

"I understand," Jill said hoarsely. "But I won't kill anybody. I had nothing to do with Tatiana's death, and if I could bring her back, I would. If this means I have to die, so be it. You're a bunch of sick fuckers, and I hope you all rot in hell."

Horschaw's eyes were cold. "It's exactly that spark which will make you so useful to us. You're not going to die, Jillian Cooper. Not yet."

Jill stared, trying to discern the I-Ops agent's meaning.

He smiled. "The Dumonts trust you, Jill. Marius's unfortunate obsession gives you a free pass into their homes, and we're not going to squander that. How foolish do you really think we are?"

Jill shrugged. "I'm not going to kill for you, and I'm not going to spy."

"You will, my dear, after we repatriate you. You will if we wipe your brain, turn you into an agent and send you like our own little stake right into the heart of Dumont Towers," Horschaw suggested almost cheerfully. "We can probably infect the entire Dumont family through you."

Jill sat frozen in place.

"For god's sake, Cooper, give us something to work with! It doesn't have to be this way. We're just asking for a little loyalty to your own species, and especially to the people on the front lines looking out for your personal interests. Vampires are monsters! So are werewolves. They are creatures made to prey on humans, and it's only a matter of time before they strike. I say, we strike first. Why can't you see it's the only option?" Horschaw demanded, impatiently pushing his files to the side. "Marius Dumont is *dead*. Your lover is dead, so why not start thinking rationally? He's no longer a factor."

Horschaw's words had the opposite of his intended effect. Instead of considering his words, Jill could only think, *Marius Dumont is dead. Marius is dead. These people killed him.*

The I-Ops agent's mouth was moving again. With a smile he was delivering new threats, new impossible choices. He had no idea what it was like, Jill was sure, to feel love so intensely that it defined your soul. He had no idea about true loss. The bastard only knew hate and ignorance.

*Marius is dead.*

Jill stared unseeing at her captor. Instead, she saw her beloved. Marius was gone, and yet she could remember his touch, his scent, the sound of his voice and the flashes of love and lust in his eyes. She remembered their brief time together, the wonder of making love with him. And though sorrow seemed to flow through her bloodstream, it came with a kind of peace, as if he were holding her in his arms.

Marius would always be a factor. Until she took her last breath, he would be in her every thought. His love was a solace stronger than any desolation, and though Jill feared the evils that awaited her in this underground bunker, she would never willingly betray Marius or his sense of honor. He had begged her not to kill others so that he might live, and he was right. By the same token, there was no honor in letting someone else die so that she might live.

"I will not bend to your will," Jill said.

"I see," replied Horschaw. "That's not what most people decide." A strangely unsettled look flickered in his eyes. He paused and then wrote something in her file and closed it before pressing both palms down on the folder. "In that case, you'll want to exit by the door behind you. The one on the right. Please leave the blanket."

Jill stood, her legs shaking so hard they threatened to give way as she crossed the room.

"Good-bye, Jillian," Horschaw said, an edge of regret in his voice.

Jill paused at the door. Looking back, she saw the I-Ops agent gesture her forward, his hand on a holstered pistol. She had no other choice.

The knob turned smoothly, and as the door opened she stepped over a threshold into a room that was empty save for a set of olive green vinyl chairs lined up against a gridded metal wall. A young man sat alone in one of the chairs, shackled to the grid. He gaped at her, knee bouncing a mile a minute. Jill swallowed hard and sat down, and an attendant appeared and shackled her likewise.

Grateful for company, she glanced over at her similarly bound companion. He gave her a faint nod of recognition, and they stared at each other without saying a word.

"Marston!"

The young man gasped. The attendant walked over, unshackled him and dragged him from the room. *It's just me now.* The door behind her slammed shut, and Jill was left alone. She bowed her head in despair.

You could try to prepare yourself for the worst, but

some part of you still hoped for a rescue. *I'll always come after you.* That's what Marius had once promised. *I'll always come after you, for as long as I live.* He would have come if he could. He would have done anything for her, and she knew that now. It didn't matter that he was dead. They'd had their time together and were finally united.

*Marius loved me. He loved me. That is enough.*

Jill smiled and closed her eyes, imagining again their night of lovemaking. It was followed in her mind by a cascade of white blossoms falling from a blue sky.

"Cooper!" a voice snapped. A pair of hands unlocked her chains and roughly boosted her to her feet. She was blindfolded, leashed and pushed from the room by a weapon poking into her back.

*Think about how much he loved you.* She remembered Marius's lips on her skin, the delicious sensation of his body pressing her into the bed. She recalled the way he looked at her then, as if he'd never let her go. She thought about how honorable he was, that he was the one man in this crazy city who was always trying to do right. It had killed him, but he was a hero. He was *her* hero.

Her mind was awash in memories, in sensations, in warmth. Images of their long years together flashed past in quick succession: the day she'd first laid eyes on him, white roses by her door, the sensation of him shielding her from the world with his arms. The pain, the joy. Ultimate fulfillment. And as she relived their moments, she reminded herself that he was hers. His presence, if only in memory, lifted her spirits.

*I was always yours. I always will be. No matter what,* Marius seemed to say.

"I feel you," Jill murmured. "Stay with me until the end."

*I'm not leaving,* his ghost said in her mind. *You were right. We were meant to be.*

Jill smiled.

The temperature in the room suddenly spiked and a blast of hot air hit Jill in the face. Someone screamed. She leapt back in terror but was unable to see, lost her balance in the blackness. Her captor cursed as she stumbled to the ground, and her leash tightened. Tears streaked down Jill's face.

"It won't take long," said her captor.

*I'm here for you*, Marius said.

"I wish you really were," Jill whispered, focusing harder on good memories from their past and on maintaining her composure.

*I'm* here *for you*.

Jill nodded, focusing on the warm glow within her that she could imagine was Marius's soul. God, it was so *real*. It was a blessing, in fact: right up until they fried her brain, she could make herself believe they were together. She could experience again how Marius was part of her, just as he used to be.

He was looking down upon her. She could feel him as if he were in the very same room, as if their bond had never broken. Perhaps she was going to die, not just be repatriated. Perhaps he was waiting, watching, ready to be reunited. She was certain he would be wherever she ended up.

*No more waiting, Jillian.*

An explosion rattled the walls. Jill's captor screamed, and the leash went slack. The sound of crushed metal echoed everywhere. Jill used her shoulder to dislodge her blindfold, but was so taken aback that she was unable to free herself or even scream with joy. Flanked by a small team comprised of his allies from throughout Crimson City, Marius stood in the flesh before her, making a ruin of the room into which they'd just arrived. Jill recognized the top echelon of the vampire leadership beside him.

Marakova, Giannini—even Dominick St. Giles was there taking orders!

"How . . . ?"

Her question went unanswered as enemy soldiers spilled in from the corridor. Mechs, werewolves, vampires and also humans from the Rogues Club worked side by side to fend them off. The vampires were hovering, and the werewolves, mechs and humans formed a phalanx on the ground in front of her. It was a flurry of fangs and bullets, claws and sword blades, but the interspecies alliance fought back their enemies. Then, inch by inch, they fought their way forward to the holding cells, secured the area and pulled out all the prisoners.

Just as the last captive was rescued, a new group of mechs appeared—metal soldiers still under the human government's control. But the interspecies coalition's response was quick. The Librarian stepped forward into the melee and shouted conflicting orders. Within moments, the mechs stepped back and stowed their weapons. In their midst was Horschaw. They threw the I-Ops manager to the floor.

Giving a snarl of fury, Marius sailed down to land on Horschaw, his boot finding the man's chest. The agent swallowed hard and froze, staring at Marius's extended fangs. After a moment, he transferred his gaze to a new target.

Jill's body trembled with adrenaline, but Horschaw's glare was unable to evoke any fear. She was protected by a wall of Dumont brothers, standing with fangs bared, weapons drawn, as willing to fight to protect her as they would one of their own. She'd never felt so safe, and was able to truly savor a sense of relief when she caught a glance of Bridget being helped over a pile of broken concrete toward freedom by a mech.

Marius leaned down and lifted Horschaw off the floor . . . then flung him across the room. .

Horschaw recovered, and scrambled back into a corner as Marius stalked toward him across the room. "If you let me live," he gasped, "I can make sure you exit these premises safely. If you kill me, our fail-safe will detonate the entire building. All I need do is press this button." He held up a small device.

Marius laughed. Striking with such speed that Jill saw only a blur, he knocked the detonator from the human agent's hand. "You humans have such a one-track mind," he grunted, shaking his head. "Always about the killing."

He sighed and looked upward, focusing on the security cameras mounted in the room's corners. "How did you like your taste of all-out multispecies war, friends of Mr. Horschaw? Oh, yes, we know what you've been trying to do here. My brothers have been watching as your plan unfolded. But don't you see that you brought on yourself the very destruction you fear? My wedding was meant to be a new beginning for our peoples. You simply made it a regrettable end.

"Did you think we would hesitate to stand together against you, all of us who seek to be free? It is time for you to take notice—don't try to tip the balance again or you will see worse. It is for *that* reason I'll let you live, Mr. Horschaw, so that you may learn. Let the deaths of Gregory Bell and Tatiana Asprey count for something. Let them count toward building a bridge for peace."

Marius looked up from Horschaw to Jill, and then again at the cameras. "Whatever happens now, I want to make one thing clear: Jillian Cooper is part of the House of Dumont. She is not yours to recall. She is not yours at all." His voice softened as he added, "She is mine. Forever."

He gestured to the Librarian, who gestured to all the

mechs, who raised their weapons and blasted the cameras. Then the coalition returned to fighting formation and made their way out of the human stronghold.

Jill tried to walk, but her legs betrayed her—she couldn't seem to stop them from shaking. Marius gently picked her up and carried her, and she was soothed by the familiar scent of his skin as he cradled her in his arms. Their phalanx soon stepped free and clear, out of the human bunker and into the city streets.

St. Giles gave his hand to Kata Marakova, who stepped daintily behind Rafe Giannini up and over the rubble that was the stronghold's main entrance. St. Giles turned back and looked at Marius. "We've still got business, Dumont. Everything's different now."

Marius nodded, glancing at Jill. "I quite agree, Dominick. Everything's different. Thank you for helping me."

Several Maddox-clan werewolves caught up with Marius before heading back to their underground strata. "We've checked it all out—what you said about that virus," one of them admitted. "And we believe what you vampires are telling us. Part of me wants to pop you in the jaw for Tatiana Asprey, but after what you said in there . . . Well, I know we would have been in epic trouble without you. We'll want to follow up about Folie . . . consider bringing her down to strata -1 if she doesn't go back to New York. Can't imagine she's gonna want to hang around Dumont Towers after this, even if she did support this mission." He glanced at Jill. "We'll talk later, Dumont. Go rest . . . or whatever."

Marius nodded, and the werewolf turned and took his brethren off home with him. Marius smiled at Jillian and pulled her tighter to his body.

"H-how did you survive?" Jill finally managed to ask.

Marius shook his head, his expression one of amused disbelief. "I feel as though I went from zero to sixty, and the last thing I knew, I had a team of volunteers to command and was on the offensive to save you."

Leyton stepped forward from the smoking ruins, where he had been standing with the Librarian. "I am happy you are safe, Miss Cooper."

He turned to Marius. "We mechs don't trust easily. And we don't impress easily. It is in our nature to always expect . . . the other shoe to drop, as it were. But your continued selflessness was something I have never seen before. I could not let it vanish." He sent a wary glance at the defeated humans on their knees in the rubble behind him. "I went to Dumont Towers myself once too much time passed and it became clear that Miss Cooper was stymied in her quest for the rings. The young lady Folie was most gracious, even in her time of distress. She lent them to me, and we were able to collect the original genetic material we were hoping for, both vampire and werewolf DNA from the origins of the Blood-Taint. Everything else was in place, waiting. Your reversion from the strange human-vampire purgatory in which you've been living was swift. In all honesty, I wasn't entirely sure that the cure wouldn't kill you. It is with more than a scientist's pride that I say I am pleased it did not." The mech bowed slightly. "You said that you did not expect my friendship, Marius. Please know that you have it."

Leyton returned to the Librarian's side. The two mechs managed a crisp salute, then turned and signaled to the waiting corps of volunteer mechs who'd joined the fight against the human government. Marius saluted back. And the mechs took off at a synchronized run.

"Bet they're glad to get out of this place," Jill murmured, burying her face in her beloved's shoulder. It seemed everyone was coming up to Marius and acknowledging him, first his brothers and then Rogues Club humans, one after the next. They were talking about the losses incurred during the raid, and about ways of utilizing the data they'd captured. All Jill could think was that she wanted Marius alone.

It was as if he read her mind. Jill squealed in delight as he suddenly waved off all his friends and allies and soared up into the air. His strength was well and truly returned. He carried her effortlessly down several shadowy side streets until he finally landed, breathless and laughing himself, in front of a nondescript door.

"Safe house," he explained, punching in a code. As the door slid open, he pressed a fervent kiss to her mouth and pulled her inside.

"Thank god Leyton found a cure," Jill muttered against his lips. "You can read my mind again."

Marius grinned and pressed a line of kisses slowly down her neck and across the swell of her breasts. "Yes, and I've put business in front of pleasure—in front of *you*—for too long. You've waited long enough, and it's time I straightened up my priorities and showed you what it's like to be the focus of my attention for a few days."

"A few days?" Jill gasped.

"What, that's not enough?" Marius teased.

Jill smiled and snuggled into his chest. "It's a start. And now that your fangs are back . . ." She ran her fingers across her neck.

Marius smiled and pressed a kiss there, gently scraping her with his fangs. "Yes," he murmured. "If you are sure, I am sure, and we will be as one." He paused for moment before adding gravely, "I'm so sorry it took me forever to understand what's important in this life. I'm sorry Tatiana had to die, and I'm sorry that it's never going to be easy maintaining peace between our species. But you and I are bound, Jillian Cooper, and we always were. I can fight it no longer, and I don't want to. I want to marry you, Jillian. I love you, and I don't care if the whole world knows."

He took her mouth with his in a kiss that was everything she had ever dreamed of. Nonetheless, through their kiss Jill managed to say, "I'm guessing it will hit the papers tomorrow."

"Lovers of *Stardust* and *The Princess Bride* rejoice!
A must for every fantasy library."
—Barbara Vey, blogger, *Publishers Weekly*

# THE BATTLE SYLPH

*Welcome to his world.*

"A fantastic debut. I couldn't put it down."
—C. L. Wilson, *New York Times* Bestselling Author

"Refreshingly different, with an almost classic
fantasy flavor . . . an exceptional literary debut."
—John Charles, reviewer,
*The Chicago Tribune* and *Booklist*

"Wonderful, innovative and fresh. Don't miss
this fantastic story."
—Christine Feehan, *New York Times* Bestselling Author

"A remarkable new voice and a stunningly
original world . . . An amazing start to what
promises to be a truly engaging series!"
—Jill M. Smith, *RT Book Reviews*

(CHECK OUT A SAMPLE:
www.ljmcdonald.ca/Battle_preview.html.com)

*New York Times* Bestselling Authors
# Katie MacAlister
# Angie Fox
# Lisa Cach
# Marianne Mancusi

# My Zombie Valentine

**FOUR WOMEN ARE ABOUT TO DIG UP THE TRUTH**

Tired of boyfriends who drain you dry? Sick of guys who stay out all night howling at the moon? You can do better. Some men want you not only for your body, but your brains. Especially your brains.

It's true! There are men out there who care—early-rising, down-to-earth, indefatigable men who'll follow you for miles. They'll take the time to surprise you, over and over. One sniff of that perfume, and you'll have to use a shotgun to fight them off. And then, once you get together, all they want is to share a nice meal. And another. And another.

Romeo and Juliet, eat your hearts out.

ISBN 13: 978-0-8439-6360-1

To order a book or to request a catalog call:
**1-800-481-9191**
Our books are also available at your local bookstore, or you can check out our Web site **www.dorchesterpub.com** where you can look up your favorite authors, read excerpts, glance at our discussion forum, and check out our digital content. Many of our books are now available as e-books!

# INTERACT WITH DORCHESTER ONLINE!

Want to learn more about your favorite books and authors?
Want to talk with other readers that like to read the same books as you?
Want to see up-to-the-minute Dorchester news?

## VISIT DORCHESTER AT:
DorchesterPub.com
Twitter.com/DorchesterPub
Facebook.com (Search Pages)

## DISCUSS DORCHESTER'S NOVELS AT:
Dorchester Forums at DorchesterPub.com
GoodReads.com
LibraryThing.com
Myspace.com/books
Shelfari.com
WeRead.com

*New York Times* Bestselling Author

# ANGIE FOX

"Fabulously fun." —*Chicago Tribune*

# *A Tale of Two Demon Slayers*

Last month, I was a single preschool teacher whose greatest thrill consisted of color-coding my lesson plans. That was before I learned I was a slayer. Now, it's up to me to face curse-hurling imps, vengeful demons, and any other supernatural uglies that crop up. And, to top it off, a hunk of a shape-shifting griffin has invited me to Greece to meet his family.

But it's not all sun, sand, and ouzo. Someone has created a dark-magic version of me with my powers and my knowledge—and it wants to kill me and everyone I know. Of course, this evil twin doesn't have Grandma's gang of biker witches, a talking Jack Russell terrier, or an eccentric necromancer on her side. In the ultimate showdown for survival, may the best demon slayer win.

"This rollicking paranormal comedy will appeal to fans of Dakota Cassidy, MaryJanice Davidson, and Tate Hallaway."
—*Booklist*

ISBN 13: 978-0-505-52827-8

To order a book or to request a catalog call:
**1-800-481-9191**
Our books are also available at your local bookstore, or you can check out our Web site **www.dorchesterpub.com** where you can look up your favorite authors, read excerpts, glance at our discussion forum, and check out our digital content. Many of our books are now available as e-books!

*USA Today* Bestselling Author

# JENNIFER ASHLEY

"Ashley's signature blend of sexy romance and dark-edged
danger is simply irresistible." —*Booklist*

### ~ *Shifters Unbound* ~

To most, they are animals—even when in human form. They
are to be collared and kept on the fringes of society, scorned
because they are feared, hated for their extraordinary powers.
And attorney Kim Fraser has to go right into the heart of
their lair.

It's her job to defend those in need. But there's absolutely
nothing defenseless about Liam Morrissey. His soft Irish lilt
and feline grace can't disguise his sheer strength. Nor can the
silver chain at his throat, designed to control the aggression
of his kind, completely reassure her that this man has been
tamed.

Yet when a feral shifter begins to stalk them both, Liam is the
only one she trusts with her life. She'll let him claim her—
for her protection, for her pride, and for a passion that knows
no bounds.

*Their bond is stronger than any magic . . .*

# PRIDE MATES

ISBN 13: 978-0-8439-6005-1

To order a book or to request a catalog call:
**1–800–481–9191**
Our books are also available at your local bookstore, or you
can check out our Web site **www.dorchesterpub.com**
where you can look up your favorite authors, read excerpts,
glance at our discussion forum, and check out our digital
content. Many of our books are now available as e-books!

New York Times **Bestselling Author**

# C. L. WILSON

Once he had scorched the world. Once he had driven back
overwhelming darkness. Once he had loved with such passion,
his name was legend…

### Lord of the Fading Lands

Now a thousand years later, a new threat calls him from the
Fading Lands, back into the world that had cost him so dearly.
Now an ancient, familiar evil is regaining its strength, and a
new voice beckons him—more compelling, more seductive,
more maddening than any before.

### Lady of Light and Shadows

He had stepped from the sky to claim her like an enchanted
prince from the pages of a fairy tale, but behind his violet
eyes she saw an endless sorrow and the driving hunger of
his beast. Only for him would she embrace her frightening
magic and find the courage to confront the shadows that
haunted her soul.

### King of Sword and Sky

The magical tairen were dying, and none but the Fey King's
bride could save them. Rain had defied the nobles of Celieria
to claim her, battled demons and Elden mages to wed her.
Now, he would risk everything to help his truemate embrace
her magic and forge the unbreakable bond that could save
her soul.

### Queen of Song and Souls

As war rages all around them, and the evil mages of Eld stand
on the brink of triumph, Rain and Ellysetta must learn to
trust in their love and in themselves, and embrace a forbidden
power that will either destroy their world or save it.

To order a book or to request a catalog call: **1–800–481–9191**
or you can check our Web site **www.dorchesterpub.com**.

# ☐ **YES!**

Sign me up for the Love Spell Book Club and send my
FREE BOOKS! If I choose to stay in the club, I will pay
only $8.50* each month, a savings of $6.48!

NAME: _____

ADDRESS: _____

TELEPHONE: _____

EMAIL: _____

☐ I want to pay by credit card.

☐ **VISA**        ☐ **MasterCard.**        ☐ **DISCOVER**

ACCOUNT #: _____

EXPIRATION DATE: _____

SIGNATURE: _____

Mail this page along with $2.00 shipping and handling to:
**Love Spell Book Club**
**PO Box 6640**
**Wayne, PA 19087**
Or fax (must include credit card information) to:
**610-995-9274**
You can also sign up online at **www.dorchesterpub.com**.
*Plus $2.00 for shipping. Offer open to residents of the U.S. and Canada only.
Canadian residents please call 1-800-481-9191 for pricing information.
If under 18, a parent or guardian must sign. Terms, prices and conditions subject to
change. Subscription subject to acceptance. Dorchester Publishing reserves the right
to reject any order or cancel any subscription.

# GET FREE BOOKS!

You can have the best romance delivered to your door for less than what you'd pay in a bookstore or online. Sign up for one of our book clubs today, and we'll send you *FREE\* BOOKS* just for trying it out... **with no obligation to buy, ever!**

Bring a little magic into your life with the romances of Love Spell—fun contemporaries, paranormals, time-travels, futuristics, and more. Your shipments will include authors such as **MARJORIE LIU, JADE LEE, NINA BANGS, GEMMA HALLIDAY**, and many more.

As a book club member you also receive the following special benefits:
- **30% off all orders!**
- **Exclusive access to special discounts!**
- **Convenient home delivery and 10 days to return any books you don't want to keep.**

**Visit www.dorchesterpub.com
or call 1-800-481-9191**

There is no minimum number of books to buy, and you may cancel membership at any time. \*Please include $2.00 for shipping and handling.